ELDERS AND BETTERS

BY THE SAME AUTHOR:

PASTORS AND MASTERS

BROTHERS AND SISTERS

MEN AND WIVES

MORE WOMEN THAN MEN

A HOUSE AND ITS HEAD

DAUGHTERS AND SONS

A FAMILY AND A FORTUNE

PARENTS AND CHILDREN

MANSERVANT AND MAIDSERVANT

TWO WORLDS AND THEIR WAYS

DARKNESS AND DAY

THE PRESENT AND THE PAST

MOTHER AND SON

A FATHER AND HIS FATE

A HERITAGE AND ITS HISTORY

THE MIGHTY AND THEIR FALL

A GOD AND HIS GIFTS

THE LAST AND THE FIRST

ELDERS AND BETTERS

by

I. COMPTON-BURNETT

LONDON
VICTOR GOLLANCZ LIMITED
1977

NOTE

Every character in this book is entirely fictitious and no reference whatever is intended to any living person.

First Published in 1944

First Reissue 1964
Second Reissue 1970

Second Impression April 1964

Third Reissue 1977

ISBN 0 575 02371 6

Printed in Great Britain by
The Camelot Press Ltd, Southampton

CHAPTER I

"Well, so this is the background from which we are to face the world!" said Clara Bell, bending towards her two companions. "I hope it will prove an advantageous setting for us."

"It is quite a good house," said Maria Jennings, the elder of these, standing with her eyes prominent with interest, though her tone matched her words.

"That is not much to say for it," said the youngest of the three, in the tone of the leader of them.

"Well, I mean it is a very good little house indeed," said the second speaker.

"It is not so very little," said Anna Donne, turning and going through the door, as if she were pushing her way. "And it will keep the weather off us. I believe it is wind-proof and watertight."

Miss Jennings followed with an air of adapting herself as a matter of course to Anna's moods, and Miss Bell walked, upright and deliberate, after them, looking about in self-possession and interest.

Anna Donne was a short, high-shouldered woman of thirty, with a large head that seemed to dwarf her height; round, open hazel eyes set under a receding forehead and close to an irregular nose; and an unusual reddish tinge in her hair and brows, that contributed to an odd appearance. Her father's first cousin, Clara Bell, known as Claribel to the family, and to as many people outside it as she could contrive, was a tall, thin, upright woman of fifty-six, with an air of being distinguished and good-looking, that made her small, rough features a surprise; carefully dressed grey hair, that she frequently touched with a view to her re-assurance; and a rather discordant voice, that was generally used, and often raised, to draw attention to herself. Maria Jennings, whose daily name was Jenney, and who was housekeeper in the motherless home, was a woman of similar age but different attributes; having a frame at once spare and sturdy, small and strong; prominent features that seemed to rise from her face with eagerness or interest; large, gentle, happy eyes, an even, almost absent manner, and an air of asking little from life, and being content and almost excited when she got it.

"What made you choose the house?" she said, coming to a sudden pause in the hall, as if she must be satisfied on the preliminary point, before passing on to others.

"Well, we had to live somewhere," said Anna, in her rather rough tones, pursuing her way without turning.

"But there must have been other houses," said Jenney, taking some running steps after her.

"Why must there in a place where the inhabitants are few and far between?"

"Oh, I suppose there were very few," said Jenney, pausing to grasp the circumstance.

"There were three or four others, too large or too small, or too dear or too cheap, or too ugly or too pretty, or something."

"A house could hardly be too pretty," said Jenney, in a tone of speaking to a child.

"There is a certain sort of prettiness that I could not face."

"Indeed no," said Claribel, seeming to shrink into herself.

"But it would be as well to have it cheap," said Jenney, in a more tentative tone.

"A certain sort of cheapness!" said Claribel, bending towards her cousin.

"Well, I think this avoids both," said Anna. "I think we can settle here, without feeling either pretentious or too easily satisfied."

"If we escape the first, it is enough," said Claribel. "I

should be much less troubled by the second. But I think this house will take our stamp; and if it becomes our own, we will ask no more of it."

"We are very fortunate to have it," said Jenney, speaking for Anna's ears. "And there is not much to be done to it, is there?"

"There is nothing now," said Anna. "What was necessary has been done."

"So you had to attend to all that!" said Jenney, in a tone of appreciation.

"And it was a more complex business than might appear."

"We are very grateful to you," said Claribel. "For laying the foundations, and leaving us free to complete the artistic whole."

"We shall all do our share of the last," said Anna. "But the fundamental part had to be done. And Father did not give the right kind of help."

"No, I don't suppose he did," said Jenney, in a tone of suddenly seeing the matter in all its bearings.

"He wanted a bargain, and did not know where to stop. I also inclined to one, but I knew how far we could go. It is no good to think that other people are out to serve our interests."

"Masculine arrogance, masculine simplicity, whatever it is!" said Claribel.

"Oh, I wonder if the boys will like the house," said Jenney, recalled to the male half of the community.

"There is no reason why they should not," said Anna, "if it appeals to other people."

Jenney again took some little, rapid steps to overtake her. Claribel followed with her calmer, longer tread, her small, alert, black eyes darting from point to point.

"The bookcase will stand here," said Jenney, in a final tone, pausing at a bend in the hall.

"Here or there or somewhere," said Anna, hardly glancing back.

"There isn't anywhere else where it could go," said Jenney, in grasp of the accommodation that she was on her way to discover.

"There is Father's upstairs study."

"Is his study to be upstairs?"

"Well, I implied it, didn't I?"

"Will he like that?" said Jenney.

"He prefers to sit upstairs when he can. In the last house he clearly could not."

"No, there wasn't a room for him, was there?" said Jenney, in almost agitated recalling of the situation. "How good he has been about it all these years!"

"Wonderful, not to complain about what could not be helped," said Claribel. "So much more than should be expected by our humble sex."

"Well, now that demand upon him will cease," said Anna. "But others may succeed it, with a family of relations living at a stone's throw."

"What a different life for all of you!" said Jenney, standing with a withdrawn expression to follow the change.

"I am not conscious of so much misgiving," said Claribel "I feel that my personality is wasted, if it is not allowed a certain play on other people's."

"I don't look forward with too much confidence," said Anna. "I have not discovered why there is this advantage in our presence."

"I always feel that my company is a boon to those who have it," said Claribel, bending her head and hardly articulating the guilty words.

"It is Father who is the desired person in this case."

"Oh, I do not withdraw from equal competition with him. I do not believe in these foregone conclusions."

Anna pushed on in the laborious, ungainly manner that seemed to be the outcome of her physique. Her hands and feet were too small for her frame, and her movements were stiff and over-mature, though her face was young for her age. Claribel paid her no attention, and Jenney regarded her with the unthinking acceptance of one who had brought her up from birth, and never paused to consider whether the process was worth while. The feeling was tempered now by a touch of submissiveness, that was hardly enough to disturb her ease.

"I wonder how Reuben will take to the house," she said, with an increase of feeling.

"Why should he be an exception?" said Anna.

"Well, in a sense he can't escape being one, can he?"

"I hope I am to have a room assigned to me, with due thought for my individuality," said Claribel.

"Could he have a room on the ground floor?" said Jenney to Anna, in a manner of proffering a wistful personal request.

"There is a room behind the dining-room, that I had chosen for him. It is underneath yours."

"Oh, then I can hear him at any minute of the day or night!" said Jenney, in a tone of hailing good news.

"Shall we push on and see the rooms designed for ourselves?" said Claribel, who was obviously in suspense.

"I will take you round and show you how I have allotted them," said Anna, in a manner of introducing the final decision. "And we will not waste time on empty questions and comments. The furniture should arrive at any moment."

"Oh, I hope it will come!" said Jenney.

Anna, without allusion to the immediate breach of her condition, walked forward in single purpose. Jenney followed in compliant silence, and Claribel with an air of submitting in patience to an interlude.

"The drawing-room and dining-room are what we should expect," said Anna, throwing open the doors. "The kitchens are below them. The staircase leads to those above."

"A natural use for a staircase," murmured Claribel to Jenney, as she set foot upon it. "I am glad we are to be allowed to put it to its purpose."

"This is the third bedroom," said Anna, casting a half-indulgent look at her cousin, and making no reference to her assignment of the first and second to her father and herself. "I have seen worse rooms."

"Oh, I think I can make this room my own," said Claribel, advancing and looking round with all her interest. "The little balcony makes a distinguishing feature. I don't think I saw one outside the other rooms." She spoke with a hint of anxiety, and bent towards Anna in humorous admission. "Now that I have seen my own room, I will take an interest in other people's."

"No, they haven't a balcony," said Anna, answering her real meaning. "They are much what they would be in this kind of house."

"I think I am satisfied with them for you," said Claribel, turning after a moment of inspection with a touch of relief. "They are light and pleasant, and not so much better than mine, that they put me out of conceit with it. And my little balcony gives me great satisfaction. One can make so much of an individual touch, or I always feel that I can. My flowers will be quite different from those in the garden. I can't help feeling that degree of self-confidence."

"The two little rooms are very nice," said Jenney, referring to her own and Anna's youngest brother's. "Reuben cannot feel alone, with me just above him."

"And you will never have a moment's peace by day or night," said Claribel.

"Well, it is bad for him, when his leg aches, and he is alone in the dark," said Jenney, in a tone that lingered on the scene.

"His leg has not ached for years," said Anna.

Jenney was silent, having yet to disengage her mind from this point of the past.

"And now for our inspection of the upper floor and the boys' quarters," said Claribel. "And then a return to our own rooms to concentrate our attention upon them. That amount of egotism is permissible in us."

Jenney smiled at her in kindness, accustomed to showing

sympathy with everyone in the house, and too engrossed in human affairs to find it difficult.

"Bernard's room, Esmond's room, spare room, Father's study," said Anna, walking about the landing and throwing open doors.

"What about the servants' room?" said Jenney, clasping her hands and then unclasping them, as if fearing disapproval of the action.

"Up there," said Anna, with a gesture towards another staircase. "We need not trail up and inspect it."

"Anyhow we will not," said Claribel.

"I think I will just run up," said Jenney, seeming to be poised between one world and another, and then making a dash towards the second. "Then I can tell them about it."

"I should have thought they could judge of it for themselves," said Anna to Claribel, meeting a smile of fellow-feeling that arose from personal content.

"It is quite a good room," said Jenney, returning and remaining with her eyes on the staircase, as if she must reserve a degree of comment. "And there are two good lumber rooms as well. It is all very nice."

"Well, I am glad you approve of it," said Anna. "It took some seeking and finding."

"It is a beautiful home," said Jenney, overcoming her disinclination to enthusiastic phrase. "We ought to be very happy in it. It was clever of you to find it. Of course this last staircase is rather steep."

"Done to economise space," said Anna, throwing it a glance.

"The servants will be here this afternoon," said Jenney, as though the disadvantage might perhaps be remedied before this stage.

"Well, no doubt they will have to arrive like the rest of us."

"I daresay the resemblance will end there," said Claribel.

"They will expect their room to be ready," said Jenney, in a voice that seemed to have no inflections.

"It will be ready as soon as they make it so," said Anna. "And I shall expect them to do the same with ours."

"I hope they will settle down in the house."

"If they don't, we must find others who will."

"These have got used to our ways," said Jenney.

"We have none that is different from other people's, except that you and Father don't expect enough from them."

Jenney's mind had not been on the demands of herself and Mr. Donne, as her eyes, resting on the two other claimants of attention, betrayed.

"Spoiling people does not make them happier," said Anna, voicing a theory that Jenney always thought a strange one.

"It only exalts them in their own estimation," said Claribel, as if this were indeed a thing not to be done.

"Here are the van and the men!" said Anna. "For a wonder up to time."

"Oh, we are fortunate!" breathed Jenney. "If they had been late, the house would not have been comfortable before to-night."

"Well, there are only three women to be afflicted," said Claribel. "And we do not take such things as hardly as men."

Jenney did not say that she was thinking of a larger number of women.

"It would have been odd if they had dared to be late, after what I said," said Anna, in a grim tone, going out to meet the men.

Jenney looked as if her own methods might not have succeeded here, but followed with an air of deprecating any others.

"Those large things straight into the dining-room," said Anna, with a wave of her hand.

"Wouldn't they like something to drink first?" whispered Jenney.

"Work first, drink afterwards," said Anna, in an audible undertone.

"I hope that my private and personal things have sustained no harm," said Claribel, looking round with a smile for her self-regard. "Our own possessions acquire such an appeal. We feel that they are owed tender treatment."

"I hope the men feel the same," said Anna, hurrying to and from with a preoccupied face. "Everything belongs to somebody."

"But these things belong to *me*," said Claribel, throwing back her head.

Later in the day two figures came up the drive, the taller stooping over the shorter in a manner of sympathetic protection. Jenney ran out to meet them in an eagerness that she checked on her way, as if there were some rashness in betraying it.

"So you are here; I knew you would be," she said, as though some doubt might have been felt on the matter. "You are just in time for tea. Your room is ready. We remembered that you liked one large one better than two small."

"Cook cannot sleep alone," said the taller woman, in a flat, deep voice. "She is of too nervous a type."

"You will like this room," said Jenney, in almost excited assurance. "It is very large and bright. That is the window up there."

The housemaid raised her eyes to the window, putting back her head rather further than was necessary, and then sweeping her eyes from the window to the ground.

"There are only two real storeys to the house; that is, only three floors above the ground floor, if you count the small one you have to yourselves," said Jenney, seeming to resort to complication to cover some truth. "You will like to go up, when you have had your tea." Her tone drew attention to the more immediate prospect.

"There is a basement," said Ethel, in a tone that added no more, as no more was necessary.

"Unusual in the country," said Cook, using her voice for the first time, and then not seeming to do so completely, as it could barely be heard.

Ethel turned eyes of grave concern upon Cook.

"I never know why maids in the country are supposed to require less privacy than those in towns," said Jenney, as if speaking by the way.

"How is our luggage to come from the station?" said Ethel, in an even but somehow ruthless manner.

"It will come to-morrow with the master's and the young gentlemen's. It has all been thought out," said Jenney, with a touch of triumph. "You need not worry about that. Have you things for to-night?"

"I can manage for Cook and myself," said Ethel, glancing at the bag in her hand.

"Well, come in and put that down," said Jenney, as if offering a further benefit. "You need not take it to the kitchen. Put it here in the hall."

Ethel glanced about the hall, as if it might be fraught with some risk, and walked on with her burden.

"It is only one more storey to carry it back," she said, as if this could hardly be taken into account under present conditions.

"How did you come from the station?" said Jenney.

"In the fly," said Ethel, in her deepest tones, glancing down the drive. "We could have driven up to the house, if we had known the path was so wide. Cook need not have taken a step."

Cook was short and thin and pale, with yellowish hair and lashes, no discernible brows, prominent, pale blue eyes, a violently receding mouth and chin, and a large, bare, oval forehead. Ethel was tall and dark and upright, and had an imposing presence in her professional garb. She believed that she bore a likeness to Claribel, and in height and in asymmetry and insignificance of feature she equalled, if she did not resemble her. The two maids often exchanged a glance, a practice that does not encourage an observer, and in this case did so less than in most. It seemed that their feeling had been used up when it passed from each other, and there been a full expenditure of it. If it was hinted that their devotion bordered on excess, Ethel would reply with quiet finality that they were first cousins. When they were asked their ages, she answered for both that they were about the same age. This was not true, as Cook was ten years the elder, and now over fifty; but Ethel resented the circumstance for her, and drew a veil over it. Cook never replied to questions; she merely looked at a questioner with a smile, which the latter could never be sure was not some other expression, as it took place so far behind the rest of her face. No one repeated the questions, and Jenney had no need to put them, as she relied on her instinct in such matters. No one knew Ethel's surname, or knew for certain that Cook had any names. The latter was sensitive on the matter, and flushed when it was broached; and Ethel would interpose with the quiet statement that Cook preferred to be called Cook. She addressed her in this way even in their personal relation, a circumstance which to Jenney was ground for the belief that their cousinship was of recent origin.

"Now you must want your tea at once. It is all ready for you in the new kitchen," said Jenney, using the suggestion as a cover for leading the way to the basement, and putting a festive note into the last words.

"It would help Cook to keep up," said Ethel, stretching a warning hand towards Cook, as they approached the dim staircase.

"We shall get used to the extra stairs," said Cook, in a tone the more courageous for being faint.

"Oh, yes, you will," said Jenney, with a confidence that was perhaps justified by her knowledge of how often they would traverse them. "You will run up and down without noticing them in a day or two." She ran down herself, to show that she had reached this stage.

"We can't get out of the basement without them," said Ethel, putting the same thought in another form.

Cook came in silence to the kitchen table, and gave a smile to Jenney, who was enabled by experience to recognise it as smile. Ethel walked without comment to the kettle, and made and poured the tea, and after carefully supplying Cook, casually supplied herself and sat down at the board.

"Did you enjoy your drive?" said Jenney.

"The fly?" said Ethel, raising her eyes as she stirred her cup. "Well, the air was good, but Cook felt the jolting. She won't be able to go right upstairs just yet."

Cook gave Jenney another smile, which this time no one could have recognised.

"Did you not bring any of your luggage?" said Jenney.

"We thought that, as we could not bring it all, we might as well leave it," said Ethel, with the dependence on others in matters outside her own sphere, that came from her life. Cook looked up at Jenney, as if there might conceivably be a criticism implied in her words.

"It can easily come with the other luggage," said Jenney, hastening to correct such an impression.

"Those that bring it, might as well bring it all," said Ethel.

"It is all one trouble," said Cook.

"There is Miss Anna," said Ethel, without changing her tone, but lifting her cup to her lips to make the most of a fleeting opportunity.

"It is strange how you know a footstep on different stairs," said Cook.

"You would always recognise some," said Ethel.

"Their steps are themselves," said Cook.

Ethel rose and stood with her back to her companions, as if this secured both her and them some privacy, produced a cap and apron from her bag, and without any sign of haste turned to face her employer in conventional garb.

"Well, Cook and Ethel, so you have arrived in time for tea," said Anna, in a brisk tone that seemed to suggest that other objects had been lost sight of.

"Good afternoon, Miss Anna," said Ethel.

Cook framed the words with her lips, as she rose from her seat.

"You look tired, Cook," said Anna, speaking as if fatigue were a light matter.

Cook smiled and almost glanced at her chair.

"Oh, pray sit down, Cook," said Anna, with a touch of impatience. "You won't have much to do to-day. Miss Jennings brought some cold food with her. There will not be any real cooking to-night."

Cook rested her eyes on the stove, as if such process would have to be postponed for investigation and adjustment. Her sparing use of words made less difference than might be thought.

"Well, do you think you will like this house?" said Anna, who did not subdue impulse to diplomacy.

"Well, we did not really want a change," said Ethel.

"You often complained of the other one."

"There are disadvantages everywhere, Miss Anna."

"And they strike you at first," murmured Cook.

"So complaint is inevitable, I suppose," said Anna, taking a seat on the table and swinging her legs.

Cook glanced from Anna to the tea-things, in silent recognition of their juxtaposition.

"I am sitting on your tea-table, am I?" said Anna, getting off and speaking as if this were a new idea.

Ethel quietly placed a chair.

"You have more room both upstairs and downstairs in this house."

"The other was an easy kitchen, Miss Anna," said Ethel, with a note of reproach.

"Homelike," uttered Cook.

"You often said it was crowded and stuffy."

Ethel and Cook sent their eyes round this one, as if they would not call attention to its attributes.

"A place is always ten times as nice as it seems on the first day," said Jenney, allowing for an only partial acceptance of her words. "And now they would like to see their room. People cannot feel at home until they are comfortable upstairs." She made the last two words sound in natural conjunction.

"We shall not be able to unpack," said Ethel, in a tone without feeling.

"Did you not bring your luggage?" said Anna. "Is that all you brought in the cab? You might as well have walked."

"Cook could not have walked, Miss Anna. A quarter of a mile is her limit."

"But the man could have put your luggage on the cab. That would not have imposed much strain upon her."

"The fly could not take our large trunks, Miss Anna. So we thought we might as well bring what we needed for the night." said Ethel, her tone not disguising the ominous touch in her words.

"Well, I would not waste a cab like that."

"Oh, Cook has often hailed a fly to save her a hundred yards, Miss Anna," said Ethel, sufficiently exhilarated by this difference for her face to clear.

"Well, it is your own fault that you can't get properly established."

Jenney's eyes wavered at the light use of such words.

Ethel laid hold of her portmanteau and Cook's handbag, and Cook rose and stood emptyhanded, ready to give all her strength to the coming ordeal.

"I have the valises," said Ethel.

"I will lead the way and show you the lie of the land," said Anna, springing from her seat and running from the room, by way of an object lesson upon the situation.

Cook and Ethel met each other's eyes with a slight, simultaneous smile, and followed without hastening their steps.

Jenney moved about with a dubious air, putting things in place, or rather disposing them so as to give the best impression. In a moment Ethel re-entered, still bearing her bags, and walked up to her.

"I think Cook will be able to stand it, Miss Jennings," she said without a change on her face.

Jenney's features showed no sign of emulating this control, and Ethel gave her a stiff smile and walked from the room. Anna came breathlessly into the kitchen, flung herself into a chair and stretched out her limbs.

"Well, what a lot of effort and contrivance! They force us to do their business as well as our own."

"They are good women at heart," said Jenney. "I like Ethel very much."

"I never get that kind of feeling for them. I always feel a being apart, as if there were a kind of barrier between us."

"We let them do a good many personal things for us, said Jenney.

"I would not say that. Useful, material things, if you will, but I do not use the term, personal, quite so easily. We could never make a friend of one of them, or I never could. Well, I think my little manœuvre had its effect."

"There are a good many stairs. We can't alter that," said Jenney, resting her eyes on Anna's prostrate form, as if unable but to recognise that she had not done so.

"Oh, they are so much stronger than we are. They are brought up to be tough from birth," said Anna, dropping her hands over the sides of her chair in the manner proper to her different training.

"And is that good for them or for us?" said Jenney, in a drier tone.

"It fits in for us both," said Anna, idly.

"We are very dependent on them."

"And they on us. They have to earn their living. And they will not do it by jibbing at a few stairs."

When the footsteps of Cook and Ethel were heard, or rather those of Ethel, as Cook's made no sound, Anna rose and made a parade of rushing from the room.

"I can't face any more fuss and trouble. If you are so fond of them, stay and cope with their moods."

Jenney remained and enjoyed an equal chat with Cook

and Ethel. Her position between the family and them gave her an opportunity for living in two sets of lives, and she could not have lived in too many. She relinquished the easiest chair to Cook, who took it with an air of being helpless in such a matter.

"Here is the cold food," said Jenney. "There are only the vegetables to be done now."

Ethel rose and without discontinuing her talk, turned back her cuffs and moved to the sink. To prepare the vegetables was Cook's work, but Ethel placed no reliance on her strength, even though it had been fostered from birth. Perhaps this was further evidence that their intimacy was not of the earliest.

"It is a comfortable bedroom," said Ethel at length, lifting something out of the water.

"And they are good beds," said Cook, in the voice of one whose thoughts would turn to this item.

"You must go to yours in good time to-night," said Jenney.

Cook sighed at the meaning under the words, and by leaning back with her feet raised, contrived that the prospect should be as little removed as possible.

"I can wash up the dinner things," said Ethel. "The cooking I never could take to."

"I was always inclined to the skilled work," said Cook. "And it is better for Ethel to have the place where her height tells."

"She looks very nice when she is waiting at table," said Jenney.

Ethel's expression did not change, as it might have at a new idea.

"There is Mr. Bernard coming up the drive," she said, in a tone that did not seem to introduce another subject. "I thought the gentlemen were to come to-morrow."

"Mr. Bernard does not follow others," said Cook. "Some can be a law to themselves."

Bernard Donne entered the house, exchanged a word with his sister, and descended to the basement.

"Three stairs at one step," said Ethel, looking at Cook with an approach to a smile.

Cook returned the smile in a manner that did credit to her sympathies, considering the sphere in which they were required to function.

"He is never detained by Miss Anna," she said.

"Well, Jenney," said the eldest son of the family, "I do not feel that this house will ever be a home to me."

"You will have some tea, sir?" said Cook, who had risen and replaced the kettle on the stove.

"I will have any comfort that is available. And I will have it here. It is known that the kitchen is the nicest room in the house."

Cook and Ethel met this remark in a natural silence.

"It is not so far from your dinner time, sir," said Ethel, on a note of warning.

"One meal never spoils me for another. It only prepares me for it. I never know why food is a sort of inoculation against other food. Food is not an illness."

Bernard Donne spoke in an almost serious tone. He was a large, nearly stout young man of thirty-two, with a full, pink face, broad, ordinary features, and bright, unusual, grey eyes. He had indolent, heavy movements, and actually depended on full and frequent meals to avoid fatigue. He had a way of remaining still, while his eyes roved and danced from one thing to another. As Ethel brought his tea, he drew her into a chair by his side.

"It is something that we do not go alone from the cradle to the grave."

Ethel hastily rose, adjusted her cuffs and returned to the sink, as if this position were more secure for her.

"Anna spoke coldly and almost harshly to me, Jenney. She said my room was not ready, and that the dinner would be cold."

"Your room will be comfortable, sir," said Ethel. "And the vegetables will be hot."

"I have never heard of them cold. And the rest of the dinner must be what I have not heard of at all."

"You should have given us notice, sir," said Ethel in grave reproach.

"So my home is not a place where I can walk in at any minute."

"The furniture only arrived to-day," said Jenney.

"Of course you have done wonders in the time," said Bernard. "But those wonders are not as good as other kinds. Cook, will you join me in a muffin?"

"I should not dare, sir."

"Why does it frighten you?"

"Cook means that muffins disagree with her," said Jenney.

"It is an odd idea that muffins don't get on with Cook. It seems to complicate the claims of her calling."

"I don't often take the risk myself," said Ethel, in a dispassionate manner.

"You and I will face it together, Ethel."

"I have had my tea, thank you, sir," said Ethel, her tone indicating that Bernard's view of consecutive meals was by no means her own.

"What have you done with your luggage, Bernard?" said Jenney in sudden thought.

"I added it to a pile that was waiting at the station."

"Ours," said Ethel and Cook, at one moment.

"Mine too now," said Bernard. "We can have a cosy little unpacking together."

"Did you walk from the station?" said Jenney.

"Walk? Me? If I had done that, I would have carried the luggage. I got a lift in a cart."

"A tradesman's cart?" said Ethel, in simple apprehension.

Cook paused in what she was doing, and waited for the answer.

"I think all carts have to do with trade," said Bernard. "This one had. It was full of closed packages, so I could not tell what trade it was."

"The man would have told you," said Jenney, whose interest did not fail in any human matter.

"I don't mean that I was uninterested, or thought it was not my affair. I just did not think to ask, and he did not think to tell me."

"Well, the cart will not come to the house," said Ethel.

"The man said it was going to come every morning," said Bernard.

Cook and Ethel faced this prospect in silence.

"I had better go to Anna, Jenney. She will say that I have hardly spoken to her."

"And you have not done much more, have you?" said Jenney.

Cook and Ethel followed Bernard with their eyes, as he left the room.

"He is always himself," said Ethel.

"The tradesmen's cart!" said Cook, with the ghost of a smile.

"Well, he does not look as if he had to," said Ethel.

"It only wants the dignity to carry it off," said Cook.

"I wish the luggage was here," said Ethel, on a wistful note. "It is inconvenient to be kept in an unsettled state."

"I have sent the master a card," said Jenney, overcoming any obvious haste to reply. "He is sure to think of it to-morrow. It is the last time I shall send anything to that address." She ended on a note of sentiment, forgetting that, as she never left the family, it might be also the first time; and Cook and Ethel also forgot it, and moved their heads in sympathy.

"We come to the end of chapters," said Ethel.

"They go past us," said Cook, sitting down at the table and laying her hand upon it.

Ethel took a seat at her side and closed her fingers over the hand, and Jenney accepted this as a signal for withdrawing. She also accepted it as the signal of a good deal more, and would have been taken aback by the talk that ensued.

"Miss Jennings will have a front place," said Ethel, with a sigh.

"If anyone in the house," said Cook.

"We can't estimate the privilege of living with her," said Ethel, using words that would have given Jenney not so much a sense of compliment as of security.

"Such an example. And before our eyes," said Cook, with less feeling for an example in another place.

"You would think that Miss Anna would be influenced by it."

"A leopard can't change his spots," said Cook, moving to the stove with an air of accepting the law of immutability for herself.

"The bell! Miss Anna's, of course," said Ethel.

"What can she want on the first night?" said Cook, with her own ideas of cause and effect.

Ethel returned with a grim smile on her face.

"The gentlemen's rooms are to be done the first thing to-morrow. As if that couldn't wait for the morning! Bringing a person up for it! She must do it to assert herself."

"Those do that, who need to," said Cook.

"If she thinks I am going to begin them to-night, she makes a mistake," said Ethel, sitting down and locking her hands round her knees, as if to ensure their leisure.

"There are only four of them for dinner," said Cook.

"And I daresay Miss Jennings would as soon be down here with us," said Ethel, as if this partly disposed of Jenney's needs. "To say nothing of Mr. Bernard. I hope the gentlemen will remember the luggage. It was best to bring none of it, as we couldn't bring it all. And these things are nothing to gentlemen, are they?"

CHAPTER II

THESE MEMBERS OF the household arrived on the next afternoon, bringing the luggage that was nothing to them, by means of several cabs. But they appeared less concerned with it, than those who had left it behind.

"Well, my daughter," said Mr. Donne, embracing Anna in a conventional but ironic manner, and introducing these qualities into his speech; "so we are united once again. A family roof will continue to hold us together."

"As the necessary amount of thought and effort has come first," said Anna, with blunt readiness.

Bernard strolled into the hall and confronted rather than met his father.

"Well, Bernard," said the latter, in the same tone.

"Well, Father," said Bernard, as though he found the filial term unsuitable but hard to avoid.

Benjamin Donne was a short, thickly-built man of sixty, with black hair that was not so much varied as confused by streaks of white; round, hazel eyes like his daughter's, but of a darker shade, and set in a network of wrinkles from which hers might always be free; a nose that overshadowed and almost distorted his face; sudden, uncontrolled movements, and an expression rendered enigmatic both by nature and himself. He bent over Anna with his hand on her shoulder, and listened to Jenney with the interest accorded to a guest, the ironic atmosphere pervading all that he did. He was a man at war with himself, and tended to find himself in this relation to other people. His friends took different views of him, some seeing him as harsh and forbidding, and others as a man of natural, if suppressed affections, and both being right. He had been a widower for twelve years, and had not thought of marrying again, having found the conflicting elements of married life too much. He had greatly desired children, but was sufficiently provided with these.

His two younger sons, who had travelled with him, edged past him and disappeared into the house. Esmond, the elder, was four years younger than Anna, and taller and darker than she, with fairly good features, a developed head, unsettled, grey eyes, a drooping carriage, an irritable and often irritated manner, and a certain uncouthness in person and dress, that in her appeared in manner and speech. He gave a limp hand to the women of his family, less by way of greeting than of indicating that he did not intend an embrace, and turned his eyes on the house with an interest limited to its concern for himself.

Reuben, the youngest by a number of years, evinced the ungainly quality in his physique. He was a boy of thirteen, with coltish, uncontrolled movements, a lively, nervous face, defensive, dark eyes that were sadder than his feelings warranted, and a definite lameness resulting from an early accident. He had a straight but unobservant gaze and a confident, carrying voice, and thought less of his handicap than of what other people thought of it.

Jenney's eyes showed that he was her chief concern; Anna gave him a rough caress; and Ethel took his bag before doing anything else. Neither his father nor his brother had thought of helping him, or rather the latter had not thought of it, and the former had been in the grip of his usual inner conflict. It was his habit to address his young son with ironic courtesy as an equal, but he failed to embarrass him by doing so, as Reuben saw him as an insoluble enigma, and simply withheld his thoughts.

The family had a faintly Jewish look, and biblical names had a way of recurring amongst them, but they neither claimed nor admitted any strain of Jewish blood. The truth was that there had been none in the last generations, and that they had no earlier record of their history.

They went into the drawing-room and faced each other

with a sense of actually doing this. Their reunion in new surroundings showed them each other afresh. Anna was concious of her choice of the house, and wore an absent, indifferent air and hummed faintly to herself, while Claribel had almost the manner of a hostess.

The latter greeted Benjamin with bare cordiality and ignored his deliberate survey of herself. He had put her to his purpose of duenna for his family, and she felt that she owed him nothing, and would not suffer at his hands. Her attitude and Reuben's were of the kind reputed to ensure respect, but failed to do so with Benjamin, who had little command of this feeling. He had not even much for himself, which tends to mean a meagre residue for other people.

"Well, we begin our new life," he said, in the harsh, uneven tones that seemed to carry an undercurrent of emotion. "We shall feel that the house is our own, when we have planted memories in it." His eyes rested on his sons, as if he awaited their fulfilment of this duty.

"We shall always remember Bernard's half-shy look of welcome," said Reuben, pulling at Jenney's sleeve and raising his voice. "He may be ashamed of the feeling that brought him, but it makes us like him better."

Esmond pushed through his family and stood in the middle of the room and looked up and down.

"Cannot your feelings find expression?" said Claribel.

"It seems that that is the case," said Bernard.

"It is usual to reply to a question," said Benjamin.

"A reply was not wanted," said his second son.

"Well, that is true," said Anna. "People who withhold their wisdom before the event, need not produce it afterwards."

"It is a smaller house than the other," said Reuben.

"There is plenty for the servants to do in it," said Anna, "though it would not be wise to give them a hint of it."

"They are the last people who should require it," said Bernard.

"You seem to be agreed upon your course," said Esmond.

"Bernard has been spoiling them, as usual," said Anna. "It only makes them harder to manage."

"Since when has he taken your place?" said Benjamin.

"He has not done so, Father, or he would know better."

"They are both of them nicer than most of us," said Bernard.

Reuben gave the laugh that he felt was appropriate, though Ethel and Cook had a larger measure of his affection than anyone but Bernard and Jenney.

"Now keep your tongues off them for the moment," said Anna, in her rough manner. "Here is Ethel with the tea."

"I had muffins for tea yesterday," said Bernard.

"Oh, I forgot to have them toasted," said Jenney, springing to her feet. "I can see about it in a minute."

Ethel produced a covered dish, with a fleeting smile at Bernard.

"Oh, I am glad you remembered, Ethel," said Jenney.

"It was Cook," said Ethel, turning to the door to hide her smile of conscious pride.

"And what more suitable person?" said Anna, keeping her eyes on the door until it closed. "Is nothing further removed from Cook than her natural duties? Ethel should put the tray in front of me. Will she ever learn her business?"

"Oh, I know how you all like it," said Jenney proceeding to pour out the tea.

"Experience does nothing for Anna in that matter," said Esmond.

"I take the precaution of asking you," said his sister.

"It is tiresome to explain the same things day after day."

"That should hardly be too great a drain upon your energy."

"It is upon my patience."

"We may all come to the end of that quality," said Benjamin.

"Well, it is nice to have one's little ways remembered," said Claribel. "After all, they are the outcome of one's personality."

"Pass the muffins to Reuben," said Jenney, as if she were speaking to children who might keep them to themselves.

Her tone irritated Anna and Esmond, who made no movement; Bernard would not leave his easy chair; Claribel assumed that a woman did not wait upon a boy; Benjamin rose and handed the muffins to his son and then to Jenney.

"Considering the standard of your manners, Father, you might have passed them to Jenney first," said Anna, who was more at ease with Benjamin than his other children, partly because she did not follow his mind or try to do so. This effort seemed to involve his sons in his own uneasiness.

"I did as she asked," said Benjamin, returning to his seat.

"Jenney gets much more obedience than I ever get."

"What claim have you to it?" said Esmond.

"I am supposed to be the mistress of the house."

"That position involves certain functions."

"Oh, does it?" said Anna. "Well, who arranged the house, and planned the move, and was here to receive the maids and assign the rooms, and do the hundred and one things that had to be done?"

"Jenney was that person," said Esmond.

"No, she only worked under my direction. And Father and I chose the house by ourselves. Nobody else was with us."

Esmond glanced round the room and subsided almost with a nod to himself, as if he could credit this statement.

"You may leave the house, if you have a better one," said Benjamin.

"All in good time," muttered Esmond.

"Then let your criticism wait for that."

"I suppose we shall see the other household to-morrow," said Claribel. "I wonder which of us is engaging their thoughts."

"Oh, of course you will," said Jenney, in an excited manner. "What a sudden plunge into a new life! I wonder how you will all manage in it." She felt Benjamin's glance and hastened to retrieve any false step. "I expect you will all enjoy being together."

"We must see that we do so," said Benjamin. "Anything else would dispose of the good in our presence."

"Aunt Sukey will impose her demands, if I make no mistake," said Anna.

"I hope you make none," said her father. "We have come here to fulfil them."

"Very morbid," murmured Bernard.

Benjamin had lately retired from a government office, which had required his daily presence, and had moved nearer to his sisters, who desired his support. His sons had adopted the same occupation, a fact which caused Esmond to suffer, and Benjamin to smile to himself, and sometimes to suffer also, as he recalled his sons' earlier hopes. Bernard worked with ambition and success, and Esmond in contempt for a task beneath him, and resentment that a conviction of ability did not command a price. The brothers lived together in rooms in London, always wishing that they were apart, but held from the change by Bernard's lack of initiative, and Esmond's leaning to the cheaper course. They took their holidays in brief and frequent spells, in order not to break their life at home. Esmond's dislike of this life was extreme, and his father's dislike of his part in it appeared to be on the same scale; but he did not dare to break away, and Benjamin contrived without word or look that he should not dare. It seemed that Benjamin must prefer his presence, and he had a feeling, both conventional and natural, for having his family about him.

"It may not be all giving on our side," said Claribel.

"We shall impose our own wills without knowing it. No one with any force of character avoids that."

"It would not do to go through life alone," said Jenney, mentioning the disadvantage that struck her as the worst.

"I suppose we all do that," said Reuben.

"Oh, in that sense," said Esmond, irritably. "That does not need saying."

"But I was proud to say it," said his brother.

"You have a nice room on this floor, Reuben, underneath mine," said Jenney.

A relief spread over Reuben's face.

"Come upstairs and see the house," said Bernard, rising and offering his arm.

The brothers mounted the staircase, Bernard giving his support without seeming to know that he did so. Reuben no longer needed it, but would not repudiate his brother's thought, or the effort of rising from his chair, which he did not underestimate; and found that the longer he followed this line, the more bound he was to it. Jenney welcomed protection for him, feeling simply that he was a creature dependent on it; Benjamin saw the matter as it was; Anna saw its surface; and Esmond was not concerned with it.

"It is a good thing those two are such good friends," said Anna. "It would make a problem, if Bernard were sensitive about Reuben, or anything like that."

Jenney's face showed her view of this idea, and Benjamin's betrayed that his was the same. His reaction and Jenney's often resembled each other.

"I don't think we feel embarrassed by people belonging to ourselves," said Claribel. "Our relations form the natural background for the creatures that we are."

"Are you going to the other house to-morrow, Father?" said Anna, making no pretence of attending.

"To-night, my daughter. Your aunt will be expecting me. She must not do so in vain."

Benjamin's voice accorded with his words. His feeling for his sisters was the strongest in his life, rooted in its background and beginning. Their qualities appeared to him essential and natural; their troubles roused his pity, and helplessness in them found him a protector; their ease with him appealed to him more than any other experience. They did not know the man who was known to his children.

"There will be trouble and expense for us there," said Anna.

"Why should there be expense?" said Benjamin. "Your aunts have their own incomes."

"We can hardly breathe without paying for it," said Esmond. "We cannot so much as eat and drink like the beasts of the field."

"They have few other advantages," said his father. "You need not desire a further affinity with them."

Esmond appeared not to hear the words that he did not dare to answer. The expression that he believed indifferent, was one of aversion. Benjamin's eyes dilated as he looked at him, a change that did not improve them, as they were already prominent. He was exasperated by signs of dislike in his sons, and the feeling led him to give them further cause for it.

"It is a modest but pleasant house," said Reuben's voice, "and a home is where a family is gathered together."

"That is what makes family problems," said Bernard.

"We have none of those," said Benjamin, in a tone that defied contradiction.

"None," muttered Esmond. "Problems imply a solution."

"Jenney is proud of me for being able to talk like other people, though I cannot walk like them," said Reuben, rightly interpreting the expression on Jenney's face.

"Your walking is very much improved," said Anna. "There is not much amiss with it now."

"People would hardly believe the pathetic little figure I used to be."

Jenney's eyes rested on Reuben, as if this still appeared to her the natural view.

"If I had been like other boys, people might not have loved me so well."

"They must have some ground for their regard," said Esmond.

Benjamin looked at his youngest son without expression. He could hardly sneer at his infirmity, and was unversed in any other course. In his heart he thought less of Esmond for his dealings with him, and found that they fixed his position as the least dear of his children.

Ethel came into the room with her usual step, but with her eyes rather wide and fixed.

"Cook's smallest bag has not arrived, Miss Jennings."

"Oh, what a nuisance!" said Jenney, looking about as if half-expecting to see the bag. "Where did she see it last?"

"She packed it with her own hands, Miss Jennings."

"Who usually packs Cook's bags?" said Bernard.

Ethel gave him an enigmatic look, and did not say upon whom such a task of Cook's would normally devolve.

"Well, does it matter so much?" said Anna. "It will follow by itself."

"Cook had it with her in the compartment, Miss Anna."

"You mean it had no address? Why did you not bring it in the cab?"

Jenney's eyes went from Anna to Ethel, as if to measure their mutual effect.

"We only brought what was needed for the night, Miss Anna," said Ethel, throwing some light on this.

"Did you leave the bag to speak for itself at the station?" said Esmond. "A label would have saved it the trouble."

Ethel met his eyes in silence.

"You must know what you did with it," said Anna.

"We thought it would come with the other luggage, Miss Anna."

"It would have been wiser and kinder of it," said Bernard.

Ethel tried not to smile and entirely succeeded.

"Someone must go to the station about it," said Jenney.

"Who can do that?" said Anna. "We have no means of going."

"I am the last person who can offer to walk," said Reuben.

"You must manage for yourself, Ethel," said Anna.

"I might be able to walk one way," said Ethel, in a tone of offering a dubious, but perhaps not impossible solution.

"And would Cook walk the other?" said Bernard.

"Would the bag carry you back?" said Esmond, at the same moment.

Reuben burst into laughter, and Claribel leaned back and tapped the ground with her foot, wearied by the impersonal discussion.

"You may make yourself easy, my good girl," said Benjamin, who took this line with young women of Ethel's class, and believed Ethel to be young because of her calling. "One of the tradesmen will be passing the station, and will bring it in his cart."

"Cook cannot settle down, sir," said Ethel, as if further words were unnecessary; and indeed any would have fallen flat after these.

"It does seem like a bag not to think of that," said Bernard.

Ethel suddenly moved to the door, as if hearing something audible only to her own ears.

"Cook says that that bag was unpacked first of all," she said, turning back and addressing Jenney in an empty tone.

"Do you mean that it has been here from the first?"

"Did it unpack itself and say nothing about it?" said Bernard.

"So Cook has been settled all the time," said Anna.

"She cannot be that in a moment, Miss Anna. And when Cook is exhausted, she hardly knows where she is."

"Cook and the bag sound rather alike," said Bernard. "They say that living together breeds resemblance."

"It is Cook's dove-coloured bag, sir, that is utilised for smaller articles," said Ethel, with a note of reproach.

"And it behaved like a bag of any other kind. It can only be said that it did."

"The trouble is over, isn't it?" said Benjamin.

"It never existed," said his daughter.

"If Cook does not know where she is, she may be thinking that she was left at the station too," said Reuben, in an insistent manner.

"I wonder she was not," said Anna; "the cab seems to have brought so little."

"It was our own cab, Miss Anna," said Ethel.

"Well, we have come to the end," said Benjamin.

"Thank you, sir," said Ethel, in an impersonal tone, and left the room.

"We had better send a message to Cook, that both she and the bag are in the house," said Bernard. "It may be a relief to her mind. Or perhaps Ethel will think to tell her."

"Why is it all so funny?" said Anna.

Claribel shook her head and lifted her eyebrows in hopeless fellow-feeling.

"Did Ethel mean that they paid for the cab themselves?" said Reuben.

"Well, it was an unnecessary expense," said his sister, "as they brought nothing in it."

"They brought themselves," said Bernard, "even if it was a happy accident. And that was our responsibility."

"And now it is that to keep them here," said Jenney, with some dryness. "I had better give them the money."

"It will come out of the housekeeping," said Anna. "I should have been consulted."

"If you had thought to meet them at the station, you would have been," said Esmond.

"They could not walk three miles after their journey," said Jenney.

"Why not?" said Anna. "They had not been using their

legs. I should have thought an hour in the air would do them good."

"Did you adopt that restorative when you arrived?" said Esmond.

Claribel heaved a faint sigh at the persistence of the subject.

"I cannot think why you don't see the difference," said Anna. "We are not all alike."

"Ethel made an offer of walking one way," said Bernard. "And a vain sacrifice is known to be the most tragic."

"Oh, Ethel is too hefty to have any chance of appearing anything else."

"Cook appears to be more fortunate," said Esmond.

Ethel entered the room with the letters.

"How much was your cab?" said Anna.

Ethel looked at her for a moment.

"Four shillings, Miss Anna, the cab itself."

"How do you mean? The cab itself?"

"There was the shilling we gave to the man, Miss Anna."

"There was no need for that. Four shillings was an ample charge."

"It is the accepted thing, Miss Anna. We should only have incurred a glance."

"Well, I am afraid I cannot help that. If you make people presents, it is your own affair. I will give you the four shillings."

"Cook and I would prefer to pay it out of our own pocket Miss Anna."

"What an odd preference! I should not feel it."

Ethel met this statement with silence, which is known sometimes to suggest a further attitude.

"Why do you want to pay it yourselves?"

"It is better to do everything or nothing, Miss Anna. And it is a trifling sum."

"Oh, well, if those are your notions! We cannot do more than have what we would choose."

Ethel left the room, and Anna looked at her family.

"Well, that is a little piece of luck."

"You will have to give them the money," said Esmond.

"Oh, Ethel would be offended to death, if I brought up the subject again."

"Jenney can give it to them," said Reuben. "I expect they would really like to have it."

"Well, it must not come from the mistress of the house. And I think it would be better to leave the matter. It would be wiser, wouldn't it, Father?"

Anna was the only one of Benjamin's children who ever addressed him of her own will, and the only one unable to feel that he valued the habit. Benjamin was a natural victim of the ironies of fate.

"I think as Ethel has made her decision, we need not question it," he said, something in his face and voice showing him and his daughter as father and child.

"If we did not accept things at this stage, there would never be and end to them," said Anna.

"And we still hope that will not be the case with this one," said Esmond.

"I see why they left their luggage," said Bernard. "The cab was their own, and they would put it to what use they chose."

"I don't for a minute think they meant it to be theirs," said Anna.

"Is it all coming up again?" said Claribel. "I would so much rather talk about something more interesting than cabs and bags."

"That was not their reason," said Jenney. "They were bewildered by everything, and they had no room for it all."

"We had to take an extra cab because of it," said Esmond; "so the question of cabs seems really to be cancelled out."

"I will tell them that at some time," said Anna.

"There is no need," said Benjamin, almost with a smile.

"I should rather enjoy it, Father. Ethel's consistent smugness becomes too much."

"So it is fair that she should have a dose of yours," said Esmond.

"Well, why not have things fair? I see no objection to it. We cannot be always treating them with such magnanimity. It only results in a tiresome degree of self-satisfaction."

"We are most of us fairly content with ourselves," said Reuben.

"I don't know that I am," said his sister, with a sudden touch of rueful honesty. "Doubts rise up sometimes. Dear, dear, what clever talk it all is!"

"It sounds so," said Jenney, on a puzzled note. "And yet it is all about nothing, isn't it?"

"Show us how to talk about something, Miss Jennings," said Benjamin.

"Jenney must have enough practice with those two servants," said Anna. "I have no taste for their personal gossip myself."

"I have a passion for it," said Bernard. "And I have an admiration for people who engage in it. It shows a creative mind."

"They make most of it up, if that is what you mean," said his sister.

"I share the gossip, when you are all out, and I have my tea with them," said Reuben.

"Is that your idea or theirs?" said his sister.

"Mine. My mind is also creative. It produced the idea," said Reuben, in an almost shouting tone.

"I suspect that they like to save the trouble of bringing up your tray."

"They have the woman's tenderness for what is weak, especially when it is masculine."

"What a way to talk!" said Jenney.

"Well, one cannot be always turning one's eyes from the truth."

"You might do so sometimes," said Esmond, "even when it is truth as exemplified in yourself."

"Are we to go in a body to visit our relations?" said Anna.

"I will go by myself this evening," said Benjamin, taking the question to himself. "And the rest of you should go to-morrow."

"I hope they will disguise any shrinking they have from what is abnormal," said Reuben.

"Your concern with yourself approaches that," said Esmond, "and they may not have any liking for it."

"Would you have chosen to be quite like other people?" said Anna to Reuben, in an innocently rallying tone.

"Anything to attract attention!" said the latter.

"Well, I will pay my visit," said Benjamin. "It will not be a long one the first time."

"I always feel rather uncomfortable with that family," said Anna, when her father had gone. "But don't tell Father that I said so."

"We will try to break our habit of running to him with everything," said Bernard.

Reuben burst into laughter.

"That sort of thing is not hidden," said Esmond.

"You make me feel that I have awkward manners," said his sister.

"Being ill at ease is known to have that result," said Esmond, leaning back in personal freedom from the handicap.

"I never think of people's opinions, when I am with them," said Claribel. "Perhaps I feel it is their part to be thinking of mine."

"I did not mean that I only felt discomfort for myself," said Anna.

"Anything else would hardly improve your address," said Esmond.

"Well, let us stop talking about our manners. We shall only become acrimonious."

"I must point out that I have not mentioned mine."

"No, not in words," said his sister.

"Anna was dealing with drawbacks in manners," said Bernard. "You did not feel called upon to make a personal contribution."

"Which has the more peculiar face, Cook or Ethel?" said Reuben.

"Oh, which has?" said Jenney, in interest so great that it almost became excitement.

"Is it important to decide?" said Claribel, keeping her features towards the fire, and holding a letter to protect them from the heat, and perhaps from any other assault.

"Esmond has the classic features of our family," said Anna, in a tone that made little of the circumstance.

"Esmond is blushing!" said Reuben, capering from foot to foot.

"A thing you will not do for a similar reason," said Esmond, idly reaching for a book.

Ethel brought in the evening paper, and Reuben caught Bernard's eye and went into mirth.

"He is excited by the move," said Ethel to Jenney, with a kindness that did her credit, considering the effect of the change on herself.

"I wish it would work like that on me," said Anna. "A move to a new home thrusts me down into the depths."

Ethel gave a faint sigh, as if others might have to contend with such a barrier to spirits.

"Cook says she feels that houses have natures like ourselves," she said.

"I hope she finds this one congenial," said Bernard.

"Well, sir, Cook is sensitive to atmosphere."

"So it is antipathetic to her?"

"Well, sir, she does feel it a trifle eerie."

"Do you mean haunted?" said Reuben.

"Well, Master Reuben, we don't know its history," said Ethel, prepared to accept any foundation for Cook's feeling.

"Come, there couldn't be a brighter house," said Jenney.

"There are always the nights, Miss Jennings."

"Those might be brighter of course," said Esmond.
"The moonlight only adds to it," said Ethel.
"Adds to what?" said Anna.
"To what is not of this world, Miss Anna. Cook heard a shriek last night."
"An owl," said Reuben.
"A hunted rabbit," said Esmond.
"Oh, me with a nightmare!" said Jenney, as if it occurred to her by some chance to mention this.
"Cook with a nightmare, I should think," said Anna.
"Cook does not sleep until the small hours, Miss Anna," said Ethel, in definite reproach.
"Then why does she go to bed so early?"
"It rests her limbs, Miss Anna."
"But does the opposite for some other parts of her," said Bernard.
"Cook is inured to it, sir."
"Well, the shriek is explained," said Anna.
"It was on the stroke of midnight," said Ethel, as though Jenney's dream could hardly have been timed to this, going to the door before any explanation could be given.
"Dear, dear, what a night!" said Claribel. "Cook lying awake and Jenney suffering from nightmare! I feel a most insensitive creature, in that I enjoyed normal repose. Perhaps I had already brought my room under my own spells."
"I did not sleep very well," said Anna.
"I trust these effects are not going to be permanent," said Esmond. "The family life would suffer."
"It already has its problems," said his sister.
"What are they, Anna?" said Reuben, pushing up to her.
"Father is the first, I am afraid. He misses his work, and he is too much alone. I have not contrived to be the classic companion-daughter."
"And I am the second," said Reuben. "How I am to be

fitted to take my place in the world. Our relations will make it worse by showing they are thinking about it."

"They may spare a thought to other subjects," said Esmond.

"But I shall not be able to believe that," said Reuben, quickly. "So it will not improve matters for me."

"But it will for them," said Esmond, making a sudden movement with his foot, that resulted in a blow for his brother.

"That is not a suitable thing to do, Esmond," said Anna. "You can hardly need to be told that."

"Then why act on the opposite assumption?"

"This moment will always return to Esmond with a pang of shame," said Reuben. "He has hurt himself more than me."

"Was it your weak leg, Reuben?" said Jenney, in a tone low enough to escape Esmond's ears, or to seem to be designed to do so.

"No, even in his temper Esmond guarded against that."

Benjamin returned to the room, glanced at his seat which Bernard had taken, and remained standing until his son relinquished it.

"How are the aunts, Father?" said Anna.

"Well, I find them further on in their lives."

"Do you find Aunt Sukey worse? You were afraid you would."

"Her trouble progresses, and there seems no chance of cure. It is hard for her to live without hope."

"And she has not found life easy at the best of times."

"I hardly think she has. Her sister has been her help. But she had a welcome for her brother," said Benjamin, whose tone in speaking of his sisters seemed to come from another man.

"Such family devotion as yours is very unusual, Father."

"The relation of brother and sister goes back to the first days. It has its roots in the beginning. There may be stronger feeling, but never the same understanding. It is not your time to know it."

"Is Aunt Jessica just the same?"

"She forgets herself until life itself seems to forget her. But I saw how her family depend on her, and her sister the most of all. And that fulfils her own need."

"It seems a pretty good demand on someone who is not too sound. Isn't she supposed to be a thought weak in the nerves?"

"Your cousin, Terence, has offered to teach you for the time, Reuben," said Benjamin, seeming not to hear his daughter. "And I have accepted his offer."

"Well, that would be a solution," said Anna. "There is no school near. And a tutor is never too easy to arrange in a small household."

"What does Reuben say to that?" said Esmond.

"Of course I thought my education was finished," said his brother.

"Is Terence to do it out of kindness, Father?" said Anna. "Or are you to make it worth his while?"

"The latter, but it will save me some expense."

"I daresay the lad will do his best," said Reuben. "And no doubt he will treat my handicap with delicacy."

"That is more than can be said of boys at school," said his sister. "But Terence has troubles in his own family. He ought not to make so much of it."

"So there will be subjects for us both to avoid."

"I daresay you could both make blunders, if you tried, but there will be no need to do so."

"I think you will not regret giving my suggestion a trial," said Benjamin to Reuben, in his tone of ironic equality. "Terence seems an intelligent young man."

"Reuben will soon find out if he is not," said Anna.

"It is his verdict on Reuben that will be the point," said Bernard.

"When do we pay our respects to the other family, Father?" said Anna.

"I am the bearer of a message asking you all to come to-morrow."

"In a body?" said Esmond, turning his eyes to his sister.

"Your aunt did not separate you in her invitation," said Benjamin.

"At what hour do we storm the premises?" said Bernard, also looking at Anna.

"What time, Father?" said the latter.

"At about an hour before luncheon."

"Happily a time of day when human resistance is still high," said Bernard.

"I admit that I do not look forward to the meeting," said Anna. "They all have a way of making me feel on a lower level than themselves."

"I never put that interpretation on people's ways," said Claribel. "Perhaps I feel that, if there is any looking down to be done, I am the person to do it."

"My sister, Jessica, has never looked down on anyone. She is above it," said Benjamin, implying another standing for those who took this line.

"I know she is a lofty-minded person," said his cousin. "I always used to feel of the world, worldly, beside her. But we were good friends, and I hope shall be so again. A woman with a family needs a friend, who has escaped her own drudgery in life."

"She will look with a certain tenderness on me," said Reuben. "She knows that I cannot remember my mother."

"As that is the case, you feel no disadvantage," said Esmond.

"She will feel that is my tragedy, that I do not know what I have missed."

Esmond was silent over the opposite misfortune.

"Sons lose the most when the mother dies," said Anna. "I may not be as unhappy as might be thought. There is a certain gain to the daughter in being the mistress of the house. What did Mother die of, Father?"

"Have you never asked that before?" said Esmond.

"I may have, but I forget. I was away at school when it happened; and when I came home, it was all wrapped in silence and mystery, and I did not like to ask. Eighteen is a sensitive age."

"Which cannot be said of all ages," muttered her brother.

"There may be evidence that it can't both in you and me. But that is how I felt at the time. I suppose a boy is thicker-skinned."

"I came home when I knew she was ill."

"Then of course you knew it all. I did not return until the end of the term, when I arrived to receive the keys of the house at the age of eighteen."

"Better than giving them up for ever at the age of forty-five," said Esmond, still in a mutter.

"You had Jenney and Claribel to help you," said Bernard to his sister.

"Yes, I remember Claribel's arriving to play duenna. But I have the impression that I steered my own course, and more of less that of us all."

"I was content to observe from a distance," said her cousin. "I saw no reason to interfere without need. That is not my personal inclination. I am afraid I am not one of the Marthas of the world, popular character though it is. We poor Marys get much less esteem."

"Well, what did Mother die of?" said Anna, in her blunt manner. "Does anyone know? Do you know, Father?"

"I could hardly fail to. And you shall know also at some fitting time, if it is still your wish."

Esmond gave his father a glance of sympathy, a rare if not a unique occurrence.

"Oh, don't make me feel as if I were some unfeeling monster, Father. What is there unnatural or unfit in wanting to hear about your own mother's last illness? It was your business to see that I knew. If anyone had asked me about it, we should have looked a strange family. Why can't I be told in a normal way, instead of being made the victim of other people's self-complacence? And of course

I don't want any embarrassing appointments for the future. I can tell you have been with Aunt Jessica. That is just her touch."

"It was a chill that went to the lungs," said Benjamin, and said no more.

"Well, what could be more ordinary than that?" said his daughter, rising and hastening to the door on some other concern. "I was almost wondering if it were something equivocal. Such mystery-mongering does no good. It gives any kind of impression. There is no loyalty or sensitiveness about it."

There followed a long pause.

"So that is the method of dealing with Father," said Esmond under his breath.

"It is a pity we are above it," said Bernard.

"I do not agree with you," said his brother.

"No, I think I am glad to belong to the highly-organised part of the world," said Claribel, bending towards them, "inconvenient though it may be for me and other people."

CHAPTER III

"O GREAT AND good and powerful god, Chung," said Theodora Calderon, on her knees before a rock in the garden, "protect us, we beseech thee, in the new life that is upon us. For strangers threaten our peace, and the hordes of the alien draw nigh. Keep us in thy sight, and save us from the dangers that beset our path. For Sung Li's sake, amen."

"For Sung Li's sake, amen," said her brother.

"Guard us from the boldness of their eyes and the lewdness of their tongues," went on Theodora. "For their strength is great, and the barbarian heart is within them. Their eyes may be cold on the young, and harsh words may issue from their lips. Therefore have us in thy keeping. For Sung Li's sake, amen."

"Sung Li is a good name," said Julius, as they rose from their knees. "Enough like Son and yet not too much like it. It would not do to have them the same."

"Blasphemy is no help in establishing a deity," said his sister, in a tone of supporting him. "And the power of Chung is real, though it is only used for those who believe in him. And he would always help people's unbelief."

"After the age of fourteen his influence fades," said Julius, in a tone of suggestion.

"Then people have to turn to the accepted faith. Their time of choice is past. But the power of the young gods is real for those who are innocent. That would be the test."

"But we are not innocent," said Julius.

"Yes, I think we are. Children's sins are light in the eyes of the gods."

"We steal things that are not ours, Dora."

"Yes, but not jewels or money or anything recognised as theft."

"A sixpence would be thought to be money."

"But it is not gold or notes or anything that counts to a god."

But the steps of the pair faltered, and they turned with one accord back to the rock.

"O great and good and powerful god, Chung," said Dora, as they fell on their knees, "forgive us any sins that go beyond the weakness of youth. Pardon any faults that are grievous in thy sight, for temptation lies in wait. For Sung Li's sake, amen."

"Temptation does beset us," said Julius, gaining his feet.

"It is a pity that so much of the pleasure of life depends on sin," said his sister. "We could not be expected to live quite without joy. No god of childhood would wish it."

"O powerful god, Chung," said Julius, in a rapid gabble, turning and inclining his knee, "be merciful to any weakness that approaches real transgression. For Sung Li's sake, amen."

Dora repeated the last words and made a perfunctory but sincere obeisance, and the pair walked away rather quickly, as if to guard against any impulse to return.

"I wonder what revealed to us that there was a god dwelling in that rock," said Julius.

"Well, a god would have a temple somewhere. And there would be gods dwelling in the wild rocks and in the hidden places."

"Yes, of course there would. I wonder if it was fitting to name our gods out of a book that we . . ."

"Purloined," said Dora, going into laughter; and the pair rolled along in mirth.

"It was only part of a book," she said; "and we did not take the real names, only made up some that were like them. And a name with a Chinese sound is more reverent than an English one."

"We could not call a god John or Thomas," said her brother, seeking further cause for mirth.

"Or Judas," said Dora, supplying it.

Julius was a red-haired, round-faced boy of eleven, with large, honest, greenish eyes and ordinary features grouped into an appealing whole. Dora was as like him as was compatible with a greater share of looks, the opposite sex and a year less in age. They both looked sound in body and mind, but a little aloof and mature for their years, as if they steered their own way through a heedless world. A nurse was regarded as a needless expense in their rather haphazard and straitened home; and the housemaid looked after them, and a daily governess taught them, so that their spare time was uncontrolled. It was held that their amusement was their own affair, and confidence on the point was not misplaced, as their pastimes included not only pleasure, but religion, literature and crime. They wrote moral poems that deeply moved them, pilfered coins for the purchase of forbidden goods, and prayed in good faith to the accepted god and their own, perhaps with a feeling that a double share of absolution would not come amiss. As they staggered along in mirth, they forgot its cause, and maintained it from a sense that mirth was a congenial thing.

Their mother came out of some bushes and approached them. "What is the joke?" she said with a smile.

"We were having a comic dance round our Chinese temple," said Dora, with an instinct to suppress the god.

"I saw you kneeling in front of that rock. That is the temple, is it?"

"Yes, we had to sacrifice to our priest," said Dora, speaking as though the game were real to her.

"He takes his share of burnt offerings," said Julius in the same tone.

"Does he live in the rock?" said Mrs. Calderon.

"Yes, it is his temple," said Dora, with a faint note of impatience, as if at her mother's inattention.

"And what do you sacrifice to him?"

"Flowers and grasses and acorns and things," said Julius.

"I don't see any of them there."

"No, if we put them there, it would not seem that he had taken them."

"Then how do you know what kind of things they are?"

"We have a store of them," said Julius, "and take some out when there is time to clear them up."

"And where is the store?" said his mother.

A communication passed between her children, best described by saying that it stopped short of a glance.

"In the cave of the secret offerings," said Dora, with a touch of solemnity.

"We broach it at the appointed hour," said Julius. "It is too near to lesson time to-day."

"I should think it is," said Mrs. Calderon, something troubled and searching leaving her face. "It is long past ten o'clock. I think you must have known. Now didn't you really guess the time?"

Another interchange of thought occurred and decided the course.

"We . . . I didn't until I heard the clock strike," said Dora, in a suitably discomfited tone, raising her eyes to her mother's.

"Well, but that was fifteen minutes ago," said the latter, with the relieved reproof of one whose view of deceit made other sins virtues beside it. "You know you are wasting your time and keeping Miss Lacy waiting. Didn't you know, Julius?"

"Yes," said the latter, also raising his eyes. "After the clock had struck, I did."

"And didn't either of you say anything about it? Didn't you, Dora?"

"No," murmured Dora, dropping her eyes and stirring the gravel with her shoe. "I thought Julius mightn't have heard."

"And what about you, my boy? Did you think that Dora had not heard?"

"I didn't know she had," said Julius, in an abashed undertone.

"Oh, you guilty pair! I hope I shall not hear such a thing again. And now do you expect me to come and steer you through your interview with Miss Lacy?"

"Yes, please," said Julius and Dora, putting each a hand into hers. "It would be better if you were there."

"Now it must be the last time," said Mrs. Calderon, walking between them to the house. "You make me feel that I am a party to disobedience."

Jessica Calderon was a tall, spare woman of fifty-four; with dark, troubled eyes, thick, black hair so plainly bound that it escaped attention; a pale, even skin that was her only likeness to her brother, Benjamin Donne; and a fine, oval face whose signs of wear were so undisguised, that they became a personal characteristic. She gave the impression of being under some strain, and secretly preoccupied with it, so that those who were with her felt unsure of her full attention. She held the accepted faith and lived according to it, a trait that had possibly descended in another form to her children.

A small, grey-haired lady of sixty was seated in the hall, reading the paper. She glanced up as the group approached, but returned to the page. Her pupils were prepared for attention and reproof, but on relinquishing the paper she removed her glasses and polished them, and greeted them with a smile.

"I am afraid they are late, Miss Lacy," said Jessica.

"I am not; I know they are," said Miss Lacy, laughing and continuing to polish. "I am the better of it by a large part of *The Times*."

"I have told them it must not happen again. I am sure you will not allow it."

"I don't know how I am to prevent it," said Miss Lacy, in a low, sibilant, incisive voice, raising small, bright, blue eyes from a round, sallow, peculiar face. "I am not able to cast my spells upon them from afar. And I am afraid that afar was the word."

"They are generally in the garden," said Jessica.

"But I am not," said Miss Lacy, so much on the instant that the feeling under her words was clear. "I come here to teach, not to find occupation in the garden."

"If I put a bell here, will you ring it?" said Jessica, in a humbler manner.

"By all means, if it is where it will catch my eye. I will impersonate the muffin-man to the utmost of my power."

"Now obey the bell at once, children," said Jessica. "I am quite ashamed that Miss Lacy has waited for you."

"I have not done so; I do not follow that practice; I do not recommend it. I am not sure that I do not regret my half-hours with *The Times*."

"Does this happen often?" said Jessica.

"Often? Does it?" said Miss Lacy, wrinkling her brows in an effort to recall what did not make a deep impression. "No, I don't think so; I must not do people an injustice. But I would not say that it strikes me as quite unfamiliar."

Jessica turned to an elder daughter, who was with her brother in the hall.

"Might you not have fetched the children, Tullia, my dear?"

"I happen to be of Miss Lacy's mind," said the latter, in a slow, clear voice. "And when a young man is present, the errands are his affair."

"What a cruel theory to hold about a class of unconscious creatures!" said the person named, remaining in his seat. "And Miss Lacy gave no sign that anything was amiss. She seemed to have come to read *The Times*, and to be attaining her end."

Miss Lacy's laughter was heard from the stairs, which she was mounting with her pupils.

"Is there any news in *The Times*?" said Tullia, as if giving no further thought to the matter.

"I did not like to take the paper from Miss Lacy. And I did not really want to. I cannot bear news. It is all about foreign countries that are separated by the sea, and that is so cheerless for a lover of an English fireside. And I am always afraid of meeting some sort of heroism; and that seems to consist of finding some dreadful situation and throwing oneself into it, or of finding oneself in it and wilfully remaining there. And then I imagine myself in it, behaving in just the same way, and my emotion is too much for me. And when I think of other people seeing me in it, the thought quite unfits me for real life. So I cannot hunt for two hardy children in the garden. I think I have made it clear."

"And yet you are going to teach Reuben Donne."

"I am trusting to his being a poor, lame boy. I hope he is not a great, hearty creature. If he is, I have been misled. I know he is thirteen, and that is a suffering age. And he won't have the unconsciouus cruelty of real childhood. It is so shocking for cruelty to be unconscious. It makes it seem so deep and ingrained, as if it might lead to anything. And I believe it does. I once read a wicked book, called a school story."

"What made you think of teaching him?" said Jessica. "I do not mean it is not a good idea."

"I think it is a gross and humiliating one. All of you made me think of it, when you kept on saying that I had no regular work. I believe you said I was not earning a penny, though it sounds too crude to be believed. I do like the old-fashioned way of never mentioning money; it was much better not to know when there was not enough. And people really did not know, because they used suddenly to find themselves on the brink of ruin. There is a certain largeness about that. I believe that one of you referred to me as a strong young man, as if I were applying for a situation, and that is quite unjust."

"Indeed it is," said Tullia.

Terence Calderon was an odd-looking youth of twenty-four, who on a second glance presented a normal appearance. He seemed to be elfish and wizened, but had clear features and a supple frame; seemed to be weakly and drooping, but was sound in wind and limb. It seemed that he could resemble nobody, but his bright grey eyes recalled his cousin, Bernard's. In a word the quality of oddness did not lie in his physique. Since leaving Oxford he had lived at home, supposed to be considering professions, and doing so with insuperable distaste. There may have been something in him, that held him from sustaining effort, and the oddness was possibly seated here, though he would not himself have acknowledged that the word was in place. At Oxford he had been accepted as erratic, which goes to disprove the theory that such a place is a mirror of the world. He loved his mother better than anything on earth, except himself, and she did the same by him, without the reservation.

Tullia felt that she was second with both, and moved between them with a rather haughty aloofness, aware of being first in her father's life, and openly shelving other claims. She bore a strong likeness to her mother, and would have borne more, if the latter had softened the marks of time. She had Jessica's height and build and movement, similar but softer features, and the same suggestion of being apart from the ordinary world, which in her case was conscious and almost cultivated. Her eyes were larger and lighter and without the depth and strain. The mother and daughter seemed somehow to dim each other, and this had been suggested as their reason for being often apart; but Tullia did not harbour such ideas about herself, and Jessica could see the beauty of her child only with maternal pride. Terence gave the impression of being between the two in the weight of his personality. He admired them both, measured their difference, and dealt with them accordingly. Standing between the brother and sister, Jessica seemed to complete a family portrait, and to be the natural centre of it. As her eyes rested on Tullia, they lost their harassed look, and became clear and easy, as if meeting no problem here. She laid her hand with a smile on her shoulder.

"Are you looking forward to the family of cousins? Or are they to be faced as a duty?"

"It will depend on whether the hours will stretch, Mother."

"You and I have the day from dawn to dark," said Terence. "Not that that is any more than our due. Our lives are our own."

"Father may spring a demand on me at any moment. I must turn a blind eye to general claims, especially if they are to be doubled."

If Jessica felt her daughter too much inclined for such a course, she gave no sign. She thought too little of her own efforts in life, to judge those of another. Her concern was that she herself should not fail in service. There may have been an element of likeness in the difference.

" I am thankful that Sukey is to have her brother," she said. "I get too absorbed in my own family. I live my own life and forget her need."

"Do you mean that more is due to Aunt Sukey than is given her?" said Terence. "It shows her gift for imposing herself. It is a great power."

"I wish I could be clearer," said Jessica, putting her hand to her head. "I get too many people on my mind, and do justice to none. I am afraid that the little ones need more guidance; there are hours in the day when I scarcely know where they are. And then I feel that your father is missing me, and that his claim is the first. I am not worthy of my place."

"No one could be but a martyr," said Terence. "And martyrs are more pleased with themselves than you could ever be."

"They may have more reason," said Jessica, with a sigh.

"Well, you have the proper sense of unworthiness," said Tullia, "and that is a good foundation."

"No, I do not find it good, my dear," said her mother.

"If Aunt Sukey has not long to live, her claim is so great that it cannot be fulfilled," said Terence. "We can only wish we could bear it for her, and then cower in the background because we are not doing so, or hoping she will think we are."

"I am inclined to salve my conscience with little things, and forget the large ones," said Jessica. "I magnify any little services, instead of seeing them as owed to others. I am not a happy woman for you to have as a mother."

"There is not so much happiness in human life," said Tullia.

"I have taught you to feel that, and it is not a good or a true lesson."

"Don't tell anyone," said Terence, "but I find so much cause for happiness. The ordinary reasons are so great. When I wake in the morning, I am so glad to have another day. I am always afraid I shall betray that I find it enough. What could Father say, if he knew? I believe he does suspect, and that is what puts this distance between us."

"Suppose I had never known you!" said Jessica, looking into his eyes.

"I do feel it would have been a deprivation. There is that little something about me, that no one else can give."

"Why have you so many troubles, Mother?" said Tullia. "I should have thought you had fewer than most women. You have no anxiety apart from Aunt Sukey, and she is not your husband or your child."

"That is what I am afraid of feeling. I tell myself that my family is safe, and that as a woman I can have no more. And then I ask myself if I am failing my sister, if I am becoming reconciled to her falling out of the path that is hers as well as mine."

"You have too many conversations with yourself," said Terence. "You should include other people in them."

"That is what I am doing to-day, and I doubt if it is a just thing. Why should you help and guide your mother? It is for her to do that for you."

"No one can guide anyone else," said Tullia.

"You find yourself your only congenial companion, Mother," said Terence. "You should try to be less exclusive."

"I must remind myself how much cause I have for thankfulness."

"Still clinging to the same company! And it seems to be of a critical kind."

"I have always thought introspection a selfish habit, but telling myself that seems to do no good."

"I think your company is positively offensive," said Terence. "I do not wonder that you are not influenced by it."

"Come with me, both my children," said Jessica, holding out her hands. "I do not ask better company than this."

Terence took her arm, but Tullia lightly shook her head and laid her hand on a book. The mother preferred to be alone with her son, and the daughter would not waste her companionship. Another demand for it came almost at once.

"Well, Tulliola, will you take your father round the garden?"

Tullia accepted her father's arm and went out of the house at his side. She passed the other pair without a glance, though Thomas smiled at his wife, and Jessica kept her eyes on him until she found herself looking back.

Thomas Calderon was a large, solid man of sixty-two; with a broad, lively face, deep, greenish eyes like those of his younger children, rough-hewn features inherited by Julius, and in a better form by Dora; solid, active hands, a deep ringing voice, and an expression that told of joviality and cynicism, sentiment and emotion. He carried his family burdens to the best of his power, never evading or bending beneath them, sustained his wife, sheltered her sister, and did his day's work with little complaint of the demands upon him. It was said that he took things lightly, and it might have been said that he took them well. He had a great love for his daughter, a tried and anxious affection for his wife, and somewhat to his surprise a liking for his son. He was a journalist, critic and writer, which was enough to explain his regret that Terence was nothing, but would have preferred to be only the last. He had suffered the fate of the younger son, and found himself a poor man after a prosperous youth. His earnings were slight in proportion to his effort; his personal means were small; and he was glad of his wife's portion and of her sister's help to his household. Thomas hated shift and straitness, and loved the formal and complete, and betrayed himself more than he knew, when he said, as he often did, that to him his house was home.

"Is your mother well to-day, my dear, and your aunt as usual, and Terence doing what he can?"

Tullia went into her light mirth.

"That is how it all is. It is a fair summing-up of the situation."

"You must throw off the troubles that are not yours, my child. It is not fair that you should carry them. Your own will come in time."

Tullia did not say, perhaps hardly knew, that this was her natural method.

"Such a line is not appreciated in the eldest daughter."

"It is wrong to assign certain burdens to certain places."

"I did not mean that I could not steer my own course. I only meant that it was marked and silently condemned."

"Well, repay silence with silence," said Thomas. "It is a thing that seldom merits anything else. And I hope great things of the coming reunion. The brother and sisters are so bound up in each other, that even their children seem apart. They should have been able to reproduce like some lower forms of life, by means of pieces broken off themselves."

"I am glad I am not made only of Donne material. The best of two people is better than the whole of one, and there is always a chance of it."

"The chance worked out well for me, my Tullia, and in

a life that would have gone ill without it. I am not saying that I would go back and turn its course, but a life sentence is a solemn thing. I talked of the lower forms of life, but I was thinking of the higher. Some of us develop too far, and do not find a place. They turn to others of their kind or back on themselves."

"We are all subject to the failings of over-civilisation," said Tullia, willing to share in these. "Unless the two children are an exception."

"Bless them both," said Thomas, in an emotional tone; "They should not suffer from themselves. A little from others they are already suffering. That is why I let them go their own way. It is not that I feel that children should be left alone, as much as I feel that these should. Supervision would mean too much watching, too much searching, too much love. So far no problems arise."

"And the poor parent is so used to problems, that he can hardly manage without them," said Tullia, with the readiness to leave the depths, that her mother found unsatisfying, and her father a rest and charm. "We must find some for him, and I don't suppose we shall have far to seek. Indeed some seem to be approaching at the moment."

These were doing so in the person of Susan Donne, who was coming from the house with the aid of a stick and the arm of her brother. She was taller and fairer and more statuesque than her sister, and the enforced caution of her movements rendered her easy to observe at a glance. She was the youngest and the comeliest and the most regarded of the Donnes, and her tendency to autocracy and self-esteem had been fostered and responded to the treatment. An affection of the heart that defied cure, increased and excused these qualities, and the life of her sister's house was not easier for her presence. She saw her material help as more important than it was, felt it justified more than it did, and felt that her personal tragedy justified anything. So it came about that she walked alone in the valley of the shadow, as she often described herself as doing, though without knowing that she spoke the truth. This force and feebleness in her personality laid their spell on other people and threw her up on her own plane, and they lifted their eyes to a creature immune and apart. But through it all there ran the current of her human kindness, a force that needed no stimulus and asked no gratitude. Sukey, who placed herself so high, placed nobody low, while her sister, claiming a low place, could see that others held a lower. And some who gave affection and esteem to Jessica, gave Sukey their love.

Tullia spoke in a conscious tone produced by her uncle's presence.

"Well, Aunt Sukey, so you allow Uncle Benjamin out of your personal control."

"He made his own choice of companion," said Sukey, in a musical, suffering voice with its own ring in it.

"So we meet again after many days," said Benjamin, embracing his niece. "I might have found them longer, if I had known what was in store. We need not always regret the hand of time."

"I am glad I am not too much of a shock to you," said Tullia.

Sukey smiled on them both in sympathy, caring too much for beauty in a woman, to have any other feeling for it.

"How do you think your sister is looking?" said Thomas to Benjamin.

"Sukey is always my Sukey, and to me herself and the same."

"This is the sight that moves me," said Thomas, as Jessica and Terence approached, and he disengaged his wife from her son and placed her by her sister. "What a thing to meet in one's daily life! I can only feel myself a blot on the picture."

"I will stand in front of you and hide you from view," said his daughter, doing as she said, and adding to the group a third tall figure and lightly poised head. "I cannot help it, if you obtrude on either side."

"Come and stand by me and see what I see," said Thomas.

"Yes," said Tullia, moving closer to him, as if to suggest another comparison, and allowing her eyes to grow large in admiration. "I wonder which should have the palm. I suppose it is Aunt Sukey."

"That has always been recognised," said Jessica.

"I ought to be grateful, oughtn't I?" said Sukey. "And I should be thinking of some pretty things to say of other people, and I am sure I know a great many."

"All this about such a small matter as looks!" said Jessica.

"Is it so small, Mother?" said Tullia. "People have to look at us. I don't see why they should be put to continual pain."

"It is best to assume that they are looking at something else," said Jessica, who felt there was a snare in any kind of vanity. "And we might be looking at them."

"Of course we might, and often are. That is how we know they are doing the same to us."

"Is my nephew not going to say a word?" said Benjamin.

"I did not like to say that my appearance is better on a second glance," said Terence.

Benjamin gave the glance, saw that this was the case, and bestowed no further time on it.

"Isn't it for you to say a word now?" said Terence.

His uncle gave a laugh, but did no more.

"Here are the children starting for their walk," said Jessica. "Have they done well this morning, Miss Lacy, to make up for their bad beginning?"

"Well, I have not to make a complaint," said Miss Lacy, pausing and resting her eyes on the group. "I should not like to find myself in that position."

"Why are the sun and the moon in the sky at the same time, Mother?" said Dora, not feeling this negative treatment of the matter a safe one.

"I do not know how to put it to you, dear. Miss Lacy will explain."

"No, I have done enough explaining for one morning," said the latter, shaking her head.

"Are you going to find out the Latin names of the plants?" said Jessica to the children, who had once been doing this.

"No, we are going to enjoy our walk," said Miss Lacy, going out into the porch and lifting her face to the sky; "and enjoy the sun, and if we like, the moon. I have left my Latin behind me in the schoolroom. And not much of it there. It won't stretch out over the hedgerows."

"Have you not read much Latin, Miss Lacy?" said Thomas, to maintain the talk.

"No, I am that recognised product of my generation, an old-fashioned governess."

"Do new-fashioned ones know more?" said Dora.

"Yes, they are people of very advanced education. Of making many examinations there is no end, and much study is a weariness to the flesh."

"Why are you a governess, if you don't know much?" said Julius.

"Because there are little people who know much less," said Jessica.

"I shall be grateful if this pair of mine ever know as much as Miss Lacy," said Thomas. "Does she feel there is any hope?"

Miss Lacy rested her eyes in appraisement on her pupils, and appeared hardly to think it worth while to decide the point.

"You are a natural student, are you not?" said Thomas.

"I have some natural interests," said Miss Lacy, simply; "and I have been able to gratify them."

A faint smile went round the family. Miss Lacy's satisfaction in having private means was seen as a ground for amusement, though it would have been odder if she had been without it.

"What are they?" said Dora.

"I will tell you when you are able to share them."

"You really know a good deal, don't you?" said Julius.

"Yes," said Miss Lacy, in a simple, deliberate tone, keeping her eyes on the child, perhaps in compensation for her thoughts being on other people. "On my own rather narrow line, and in my own way, and according to the standard of human knowledge, I know a good deal."

"I shall some day," said Dora.

Miss Lacy again rested her eyes on her, as if in an uncertainty she would not trouble to resolve.

"I don't know if you have met Miss Lacy, Benjamin," said Jessica. "Miss Lacy, may I introduce my brother?"

"I remember Miss Lacy well," said Benjamin. "She was good to my young ones in the old days. I should have known her anywhere."

"I cannot quite say that of you," said Miss Lacy, as she shook hands. "But I think I can claim to know you here. I will hazard the father of the young ones."

Miss Lacy felt this was not an excessive pitch of recognition. She tended to veil her interest in people, lest it might imperil her equality with them, an attitude that came not from unsureness of herself, but from experience of them. That she esteemed her calling and pursued it of her own will, enhanced their opinion of her, but not of the calling; and she identified herself with the latter, and on the first score had never known uneasiness.

"You don't think my young ones can ever equal you, Miss Lacy?" said Thomas, persisting in considering the progress of his children the link between their instructress and himself.

"We will wait until they desire to do so. At present they have no wish to emulate the old."

"They are not as foolish as that," said Jessica.

"They are as natural and ordinary as that," said Miss Lacy. "Yes, I think we must say ordinary."

"You cannot accuse my sisters of a likeness to me, Miss Lacy," said Benjamin.

"No," said Miss Lacy, turning her eyes readily from one to another. "Not that I was going to accuse them of anything."

"I feel that I act as a foil to them."

"Difference does not invite comparison," said Miss Lacy lifting her hand to her hat, and resting her eyes easily on it, as it was blown away. "A different type starts again on its own ground. Difference may give any kind of advantage; I think it always gives its own."

"Run after Miss Lacy's hat, children," said Jessica, as eyes turned to Miss Lacy, perhaps following her own inner eyes. "Don't you see that she has lost it?"

"You see the likeness between my wife and her sister?" said Thomas.

"Now as to that, I feel like the negro who said of his twin friends, 'Caesar and Pompey very much alike, specially Pompey.' I think in this case I must say specially Sukey," said Miss Lacy, taking the hat from Julius without a look or word, and adjusting it on her head with reasoned deliberation. "Now the moon will be risen in earnest, if we linger like this. Thank you, Julius, for restoring my headgear. Come along, Dora, and take my umbrella in your other hand. Thank you very much."

"Why doesn't Julius carry it?"

"Because he is rougher than you, and I have a regard unto it."

Miss Lacy took a hand of each child and swung along in step, causing the hat, now that she could forget what was due to herself, to adhere to her head by means of a distortion of her brow. No one had felt that Julius was old for this treatment, or for an education confined to two hours a day; or no one but Julius himself, who did sometimes fear that the conditions might not prevail until his maturity. Dora was aware that the usual training was different; but assumed that their family was a rule to itself, or perhaps perceived that it was.

"I ought not to stand in the draught like this," said Sukey.

"Then cease to do so," said Thomas.

"I am not going to struggle to the door myself, as if I had no one to take any thought for me. I do not live on a desert island."

"I wonder she does not come to that," said Thomas aside to his daughter, as he went to the door.

Benjamin was before him, and his haste and concern brought a light to his sister's eyes.

"I feel as if my other self had returned," she said, putting out her hand. "I have been like half a person in these last years."

"I should have thought our portion had been a whole one," muttered Thomas.

"And now my nephew will take me to the fire," said Sukey, giving Terence the smile that had won and won back so many hearts. "And I will hold my little court in the hall. I see quite a number of courtiers approaching, and I must work a little improvement before I make my impression. They need not find a slovenly aunt, because they must find a sick one."

Sukey adjusted her hair and her dress before a glass. She did little to disturb either, and the enforced deliberation of her toilet led to a finish in it, that her sister's did not emulate.

"Why should Aunt Sukey be the woman to make an improvement? Why should not Mother do it?" said Tullia to Thomas, making no mention of anyone further.

"Why not?" said Thomas, sighing. "Why not, Tulliola? How shall we answer that question?"

CHAPTER IV

SUKEY TOOK HER seat by the fire, but on second thoughts rose and stood with her arm on the chimney-piece, as if this showed her to advantage. Her niece and nephews came up the drive and entered the hall, that was used as a room by the family. Anna led the way with her quick, short steps, and with her eyes fixed on the remembered faces, as if to appraise any change in them. Jessica stood with a smile that welcomed and exalted the motherless.

"I must be forgiven for ushering in such a horde of brothers," said her niece. "There did not seem to be any way of making their number less."

"It is a good thing our numbers are not reversed," said Esmond to Bernard, keeping his eyes from his relatives as completely as he assumed theirs were on him. "There might be no hope of forgiveness."

"Well, what a dwarf I feel beside you all!" said Anna. "I ought to be related to you, Uncle Thomas, instead of to all these thoroughbreds. We shall keep each other in countenance; that is one thing."

"None of you is changed except this little one," said Jessica. "And I think the difference is that he is not so little. Your leg is stronger, my boy. I see that it is."

"He is taller than I am," said Anna. "It was a humiliating moment when I found myself overtopped for the third time."

"Such moments must come to the only sister in a family."

"Oh, I am much shorter for a woman than the elder boys are for men," said Anna, who could seldom let a statement pass. "And Reuben seems to be following in their wake."

"My daughter and I balance each other," said Benjamin, who was watching his family with emotions that almost escaped him.

"Well, what do you think of all of us?" said Sukey, from her place. "We have passed our verdict on you, and have now to succeed you in the dock."

"Oh, I see little signs of time scattered about," said Anna, casting her eyes from face to face. "That is the only thing, I think."

"I suppose Aunt Sukey cannot have improved," said Bernard. "The advance must be in me."

"She has always been the show piece, hasn't she?" said his sister.

"I must remember that handsome is as handsome does," said Sukey, with a smile.

"And Tullia has made an advance," said Anna, in a casual manner. "She was in a distinctly more coltish stage, if I remember."

"It is natural for the years to pass," said her cousin.

"Can it be?" said Terence. "It seems so wasteful and wicked, when we only have a certain number of them."

"Nature is known to be red in tooth and claw," said Anna. "She snatches things from us all the time. I have found it even at my age."

"I never think of it," said Tullia. "I suppose I am too forgiving."

"I forgive Nature nothing," said Terence. "Least of all our death at last from natural causes."

"You are too young to realise it," said Anna to Tullia. "There must be seven years between us."

"I am twenty-two," said her cousin.

"Oh, eight then," said Anna.

"I feel I shall gain with the years," said Bernard, "but I think that is generally other people's gain."

"I feel I have the gift of perennial youth," said Terence.

"I think Anna has it," said Sukey. "I never saw anyone look so young for her age."

"Oh, I am often accused of that," said her niece. "I

sometimes suspect a suggestion of crudeness and undevelopment."

"There is none from me," said Sukey, smiling. "I should hardly have so much opinion of the effects of time. An invalid of fifty-three has no great welcome for them."

"We people with less to lose have an advantage there," said Anna. "I often feel that I shall be quite a passable person in middle age. It must be hard to feel your superiority slipping away all the time. Not that anyone in our generation will reach your level. It is a case of elders and betters indeed."

"It serves people right for feeling superior," said Jessica.

"Oh, they can't help their personal endowments," said her niece.

"It is a good thing we are not responsible for them," said Sukey, changing her tone as she spoke. "It is strange for me to feel that all that I am, may come to an end on any day. I wonder if all of you know it. Had you heard of it, Anna, my dear?"

"I believe we did hear that something had gone wrong with your heart," muttered Anna, not meeting her eyes. "Father did say something about it."

"Was it not a little more than that?" said Sukey, bending forward.

"Yes, of course it was. It was put in the natural way," said Bernard. "But Anna is quite right not to face it. It is too much for us to believe."

"So I face it alone," said Sukey, as if she were speaking to herself. "I cannot put it from me. I go on with my life, not knowing on what day or at what hour my change will come."

"I don't suppose we can any of us be sure of that," said Anna.

"We simply feel it will not come," said Terence.

"I am glad you can do that," said Sukey, in a tone in which irony and honesty seemed to contend.

"All this nobility and tragedy is rather much for us," muttered Anna. "We were hardly prepared for it."

"Come and sit by me, my little nephew," said Sukey, seeing Reuben's eyes fixed on her face. "You and I know what it is to halt through life behind other people, and it is so good that for you those days are past."

Reuben took the place, and his aunt put her arm about him.

"Quite a touching scene," said Anna. "We shall all wish we were disabled in some way."

"My sister's disability is real enough," said Esmond to Terence. "She deserves some compensation."

"I daresay it is," said Anna, overhearing. "I am downright and outspoken and anything you please, but they may not be such desperate disadvantages compared with other people's. You and I are not a suave and finished pair, and there is an end of it."

"I trust it is not the beginning," said Bernard.

Jessica smiled on her brother's motherless flock, in a simpler kindness than that she felt for her own. It was free from the strain and anxiety of her nearest feeling.

Benjamin rose and walked, as if by chance, by Esmond, and spoke in the husky mutter that had become an omen.

"Perhaps you will try to improve the impression you have made. It is not an advantage to us to be related to a savage."

"I know it is not," said his son, and said no more.

Sukey looked up in surprise at a manifestation new to her, and Benjamin glanced from her to his son with a mingled discomfiture and pride, that could have appeared on no other face.

"Here are Claribel and Jenney coming to swell our ranks," said Anna. "I thought they were full enough for a beginning. And it seems rather the moment for a diversion."

"Well, have the young people made their impression?" said Claribel, advancing with her deliberate stride. "I felt we should not be present at the more intimate reunion.

But perhaps we may now contribute what we have to give. What an elaborate conversation piece! I feel I shall be quite lost in the midst of it." She proceeded to this point of the group.

"Well, you see that the years have gone by," said Thomas.

"It sounds as if Uncle Thomas had been rather struck by the signs of it," said Anna.

"I never think as much of the years as other people," said Claribel. "I seem to be one by myself there. They seem to leave me essentially the same, and so I see other people with the same eyes, and there does not seem to me all that difference. I don't know what havoc you think has been worked in me. Mercifully I am unconscious of it."

"I am sure you may be," said Sukey. "I am the person for whom that is impossible."

"I don't think you have much to complain of," said Claribel, looking into her face. "No more than you ever had, as far as I can see. But that is my characteristic reaction."

"Not on that score perhaps. People seem to be agreed there," said Sukey, choosing to add the general one. "And the real thing is beyond complaint. And so I will not complain."

"And we will not think what we feel cannot be true," said Claribel.

"While there is life there is hope," said Anna.

Sukey turned a smile on her niece, that was almost one of pity.

"What do you think of the march of years, Miss Jennings?" said Thomas.

"Jenney hesitates to say how poorly she thinks of it," said Bernard.

"Well, it would be strange if there were no changes," said Jenney.

"Why are we so cast down by them?" said Thomas.

"Because they show that we are further on in our progress to the grave," said Terence. "It would be odd to be uplifted. But I feel it is all rather ennobling."

"So that is the effect we have on you," said Claribel. "What must you be thinking of us?"

"My son might truthfully say he was thinking of himself," said Thomas.

"You have had a hard time, Anna, my dear," said Jessica. "I have moved a family from house to house, and I know it is not a small thing."

"It was finding the house that was the business, Aunt Jessica. I thought I should never achieve it, but I kept my shoulder to the wheel and brought it off. And Jenney approves of my decision, and that is what matters."

"I also have conceded my approval," said Claribel.

"And I see that the best has been made of our choice," said Benjamin. "And I congratulate and thank my daughter."

"Well, better late than never, Father," the daughter replied.

"You must have a grateful family," said Sukey to her niece.

"Oh, the young males wait for things to be done, and then criticise. I pay no heed to them."

"I always thought that class of person was hardly dealt with," said Terence. "I did not know they deserved it."

"Esmond was the worst," said Bernard. "I should not have said a word, if it had not been for his example. I am the weaker one, and he led me wrong."

"I like the house," said Reuben, looking round. "I never care what other people think, if a thing appeals to me."

"It had been empty for years," said Esmond. "And would be so now, if we were not in it. You should have seen the size of the notice of the sale. The owner could hardly convince himself that he had sold it, and doubted his power to convince anyone else."

"They have no idea how far money goes on that sort of thing," said Anna, looking at her aunts.

"I suffered similar things when I took this house," said Thomas. "Only my Tullia supported me."

"We know better now," said his wife.

"But Tullia did so then, and it shall be said of her," said Thomas, putting his arms round his daughter and his niece. "We three know what it is to be first burdened and then buffeted."

"We are a bad match on either side of you," said Anna. "You and I would make a better pair."

"Tullia was too young to understand. She just took your part," said Jessica. "I had to say what seemed to me to be the truth."

"She supported her father; that is what I remember," said Thomas.

"It is the sort of thing that is remembered," said his wife.

"I came out badly," said Terence. "I thought of what people would think. I did not know that we ought to despise their opinions. After all, they are our fellow-creatures."

"What kind of surroundings did you expect?" said Claribel, looking round. "Most of us have to be content with an inferior setting to this. We are much more dependent upon ourselves."

"I am really happy and contented anywhere," said Bernard. "It sounds as if I did not think much was due to me. And I do not know why so very much is."

"I always said a young man was a pathetic creature," said Terence.

"He arrived without notice, and went down to the kitchen and had tea with the servants," said Anna.

"And which enjoyed it the more?" said Thomas.

"We enjoyed it together," said his nephew. "We have a great deal in common. And there are more things in a kitchen than anywhere else."

"The pair have settled down, I am thankful to say," said Anna, just throwing up her voice and her brows.

"You have a lucky hand with maids, have you?" said

Sukey, feeling that her niece might show a rough kindliness. "It is a thing that means more than it sounds."

"Oh, well," said Anna, lifting her shoulders, "I am often at a loss how to bridge the gulf between us. We have so little idea of the state of things on the other side. I can't just step across it, as Bernard can."

"I have never seen it," said her brother.

"Would they not talk to you, if you helped them?" said Jessica to her niece.

"I daresay they would. They do show the disposition sometimes, but I am inclined to check it. It is no good to get on to their ground. We are not at home on it, and there it is."

"We can learn to be," said Jessica.

"Well, if you think the lesson worth learning. I hardly think it is, myself. I don't see where it leads."

"To a better understanding of other people," said Jessica.

"And of their whims and their fancies and their superstitions. They have already discovered that the stairs are steep, and that the house is haunted. So much has emerged without encouragement. I tremble to think what the output would be, if it was invited."

"Are the stairs a superstition?" said Tullia.

"Yes, they are," said Anna, with some sharpness. "They are no more steep than these."

"Oh, well, yes, they are," said Jenney, as if she could not but bear witness to the truth. "It was natural to notice them at first. They are trying to get used to them."

"I must make the guilty confession that my feelings are with Anna in these matters," said Claribel.

"Anna does not have much to do with the servants," said Esmond. "They are Jenney's province."

"Oh, I have my part to play, if only you knew," said his sister. "I don't take Bernard's line and make friends of them. I prefer my friends in my own sphere."

"A friend in any sphere is a valuable thing," said Jessica.

"Oh, well, Aunt Jessica, when I meet you walking arm-in-arm with the housemaid, I will believe you."

There was a pause.

"A friend in one's own is better," said Sukey. "I agree with Anna there. It is not so natural to be with people from another plane."

"Thank you, Aunt Sukey. You are honest, if nothing else—if no one else is. And you and I are at one. I should have thought that we all should be, but it appears that no one else holds the established and old-fashioned ideas."

"I believe in the equality of all men," said Reuben, glancing at Jessica.

"Need we give so much thought to our own opinions?" said the latter. "It is better to look outside ourselves for our interests."

"But then we could not have any," said her son.

"Oh, most of us cast an eye in our own direction sometimes," said Anna. "And I should not have thought Aunt Jessica was an exception."

"She looks less at herself than inside herself," said Thomas.

A cloud came over his wife's face.

"She is introspective, is she?" said Anna.

"Never become so, my dear," said Jessica. "It is selfish and useless, and becomes a habit. And what is there of importance inside oneself?"

"Not much that would look too well, if it were brought outside," said Esmond.

"You can know no mind but your own," said his father. "So we take your words to apply to that."

"Why think of anyone then?" said Anna. "If no one is important, why not forget the human race? All our thoughts and emotions go on inside ourselves."

"It would be nice to meet people who thought of *things*, for a change," said Claribel.

"We do meet them," said Terence. "They read the

papers and talk as if they had found everything out. It is dreadful to have a masculine mind."

"Claribel was feeling that she had one," said Bernard. "And I think I should like to feel the same."

"Are you so different from such people?" said Anna to Terence.

"Yes, I love personalities and the difficulties of my friends."

"That sounds an amiable characteristic."

"It is a sign of affection," said Terence. "Indeed it is a proof of it. We are quite sorry about the misfortunes of strangers."

"But does it show that you have a feminine mind?"

"Well, I also love scandal. Or I should, if the very word did not suggest that it might not be true. Of course the whole point of people's mistakes is that we should be able to depend on them."

"Mere mistakes do not give much ground for scandal."

"I never use a harder word than mistakes," said Terence.

"That is the charm of women, that they are so good at such things," said Bernard. "I wish I could spend all my time with them. I wish I did not have to work."

"Hush, don't say it out loud," said Terence. "I shall have to too, and I am so afraid people will discover it. They are beginning to suspect."

"Is that an allusion to Cook and Ethel?" said Anna, in a rather loud tone to her brother. "Your giving your time to them is a true enough touch."

"I wish they did not have to work either," said Bernard. "Our difficulties seem so much the same."

"What would they do, if they didn't?" said Anna.

"They would talk and have tea and read books with paper covers. I should do some of those things myself. How I should like it for them! As it is, thinking of Cook makes me want to cry."

"Ethel seems to me the heroic figure, if you must find one."

"Ethel makes me feel inspired."

"Ethel is a thoroughly nice woman," said Jenney.

"We are not the only people who have servants," said Esmond. "We shall not hear as much about Aunt Jessica's half-dozen in a month, as we do about our couple in a day."

"Aunt Jessica's four," said Anna; "and one of those is Aunt Sukey's attendant."

"My wife has the gift of winning their hearts," said Thomas.

"But why does that mean that we do not hear about them?" said Bernard. "You would think we should hear more."

"Of course we should not," said Terence. "You should think before you speak."

"They are always good and kind to me," said Jessica.

"I believe I am Aunt Jessica's true nephew," said Bernard. "I am sure no one else is. I wish she would say that Esmond is not."

"And I am her true son," said Terence. "She has no other true relations."

"Have we produced a pair of kindred spirits?" said Jessica, smiling at her brother and looking at their eldest sons.

Benjamin nodded in understanding, but at once withdrew his glance, lest his children should see it; a needless precaution, as his sons kept their eyes from his face, and his daughter did not think to turn hers towards it.

"Perhaps Esmond has some attention to spare for his other aunt," said Sukey.

"They are all giving you enough," said Claribel. "They have no eyes for anyone else. I should feel most flattered, if Esmond bestowed half the amount on me."

Her nephew gave every sign that he bestowed none on her at all.

Miss Lacy returned to the house with her pupils, and paused by the group in privileged interest.

"What is the matter in hand?" she said.

"That I am Aunt Jessica's especial nephew," said Bernard.

"And I come second," said Reuben, loudly.

"Your aunt loves you all alike, of course," said Miss Lacy.

"Can anyone really love a nephew, when she loves her son as much as Mother does Terence?" said Dora.

"Mother is different from other people," said Thomas.

Jessica's face darkened, as if she could give her own meaning to the words. Her eyes rested on Dora in new and troubled knowledge. The child saw Terence as better loved than herself, and saw it with unconcern. Jessica had thought that feelings that were not revealed, were unbetrayed, and had not reflected that she was unlikely to give voice to them. She often fell into the pitfalls of her path; the very straightforwardness of her nature caused it; the common precautions and contrivances were not for her.

"Perhaps one aunt will have some feeling over for the niece," said Anna.

"Let me be that one," said Sukey, making room at her side. "You and I must support each other. We are not used to being left out in the cold."

"I believe I am pretty well accustomed to it," said Anna, as she took the seat. "I am the person who has to control and contrive. And that does relegate one to a chilly place."

"You are young to be at the head of things," said Sukey.

"I am not young now in any sense, but I was, when I came from school to the place at the helm. And that made me lay an indifferent foundation. And then there was no living it down."

"We must help each other," said Sukey. "I may not have lived too wisely myself. I often see signs of weariness of me and my ways."

Jessica observed the pair, in relief that Sukey should find this companionship. She had not thought of a bond between her sister and her niece, but welcomed it as an advantage and solution. Sukey needed service and support beyond what could be accorded in her sister's home, and Jessica unconsciously assumed that such things would come as a due from Anna's level to Sukey's. That Anna might expect return for what she gave, did not enter her thoughts. Such things did not strike people with regard to Anna.

"Are you having luncheon with us to-day, Miss Lacy?" said Jessica. "Is it a day when you are here in the afternoon?"

"It is such a day, but I am going home," said Miss Lacy, in calm decision of her course. "The children have obtained your leave for a holiday, and I do not superintend their leisure. They do not need to be taught to play."

"I do not remember giving them the holiday," said Jessica, wrinkling her forehead. "They take advantage of my absence of mind, and hold me to what I am betrayed into saying. Now isn't this another case of it, children?"

"Yes," said Julius, with a shamefaced grin.

"Yes," said Dora, pushing a stick about on the floor, and suddenly sending a flash of honest eyes across her mother's face. "We knew you didn't know you said it."

Jessica accepted acknowledgment as an atonement, and also accepted the uncertainty of her brain, an unfair effort, as it had not been at fault.

"Do you notice the difference in the ranks of our young people, Miss Lacy?" said Thomas.

"Is not there an increase in them?" said Miss Lacy, looking round with an air of finding this dawn upon her. "Yes, a perceptible increase."

"You have not forgotten me," said Bernard. "No one has ever done that. I make a simple impression, but it is my own."

"Is it the voice of Bernard?" said Miss Lacy.

"You remember Bernard and Anna, who used to visit your schoolroom when Terence and Tullia were there."

"Then how do you do, Bernard and Anna?" said Miss Lacy, shaking hands and using Christian names as her natural prerogative. "I am glad to see you again, and I hope you will remember my schoolroom with Tullia's successors."

"We can't expect you to remember Reuben and Esmond," said Anna.

"How do you do, Reuben and Esmond?" said Miss Lacy, shaking hands in order of age, but using the names in Anna's order, as if she had no aid from her memory. "What very handsome names! I feel as if a book had come true."

"You knew that Reuben was the youngest," said Dora. "Because you said you were glad his leg was better."

"Am I not doing myself justice?" said Miss Lacy, with some amusement. "And I thought I was making a creditable effort. It was certainly a sincere one. How do you do, Esmond and Reuben? Bernard, Anna, Esmond and Reuben. Or does Anna come first?"

"No, Bernard is the eldest," said Anna. "But people often assume that I am the first, as I take the lead in things. The sister has to do that."

"I should not have assumed it," said Miss Lacy, turning her eyes from face to face. "I should have said that you were the second. But I am inclined to sympathise with people; I was getting unsure of myself. Bernard, Anna, Esmond and Reuben."

"Oh, Bernard and Anna are ordinary names enough. And the others are not as out-of-the-way as all that."

"Anna is a good name, my dear," said Miss Lacy, in a kindly, if absent tone, as she turned to Jessica. "I suppose they do not remember their mother?"

"Good gracious, yes," Anna interposed. "I was eighteen when she died, old enough to be summoned home to steer the family course."

"Poor child!" said Miss Lacy, passing her eyes over Reuben, as if to judge of the result of this guidance, and then dropping her voice to its sibilant note. "Poor children!"

"We have always had Miss Jennings with us," said Bernard.

"Oh, Miss Jennings! I want to see Miss Jennings," said Miss Lacy, her tone somehow implying that she made nothing of any distance between them. "I was great friends with Miss Jennings. And I want to ask her advice on a matter of my own, on a charge that is coming to me."

"Are you expecting some fresh responsibility?" said Thomas.

"Yes, an orphan niece is to make her home with me," said Miss Lacy, in the even tone of one who had found varied experience a part of life. "The daughter of my younger brother, a girl of twenty. Poor child, I hope I shall be able to make my house a home to her. And I am sure Miss Jennings is the person to advise me. How not to ask too much of her; how to ask enough, for that is important too; how to ask enough of myself, without asking too much. Well, it will all have to be decided, or rather it will all decide itself, and we shall be helpless about it."

"Will she like to live just with a much older person?" said Dora.

"That is one of my problems, Dora," said Miss Lacy, in a grave tone. "And you remind me that she may be expecting the older person's welcome. There is no need for me to fail there."

Miss Lacy turned and went with mild haste down the drive, to be overtaken by Bernard and escorted to the gate.

"Miss Lacy has gone to the gate by herself for eighteen years," said Terence, looking after them.

"Then she should be better versed in the problems of the latch than Bernard seems to be," said Benjamin.

"Why do all gates have different fastenings?" said Anna. "A standard one might bring a fortune to somebody."

"I suppose each one was to have been that one," said Thomas.

"And I wonder it was not. Latches are so very clever," said Terence.

"Why does not Miss Lacy help the clumsy boy?" said Benjamin, in open nervous distress. "God knows how long he will be."

"He may know," said Thomas, "but as we cannot, we will not concern ourselves with the matter."

The children broke into the laughter caused by such jests in a household where they were forbidden, and Jessica lost no time in turning the subject.

"Now is everyone clean and tidy for luncheon? The bell will ring at any moment."

"May we just run to our Chinese temple and back?" said Julius.

"Yes, if you do only that."

The children ran out of the house.

"O great and good and powerful god, Chung," prayed Dora, "forgive us, we beseech thee, the lie that has passed our lips. For we have uttered to thy handmaid, our governess, the thing that is false, yea and even to our mother. And this we did to gain respite from our daily task. And most humbly we implore thee not to visit our sin upon us. For Sung Li's sake, amen."

"We couldn't have enjoyed our luncheon with that burden on us," said Julius. "And as the relations are staying, it will be a good one. And Mother does not suspect."

"I should think it is especially wicked to take advantage of her being absent-minded, when it is a sort of illness," said Dora.

The pair met each other's eyes and in a moment were back at the rock.

"O great god, Chung, pardon any wickedness we showed in putting our mother's weakness to our wrongful purposes. For Sung Li's sake, amen."

They walked away, talking of other things, and came straight to the table.

"It is nice to arrive just as we are being helped ourselves," said Julius.

"Oh, is that why you came in late?" said Jessica.

"No, we didn't think of it," said Dora, in the honest tone that served an honest statement as well as another.

"And have you remembered that you have missed grace?"

"Yes, but we didn't know what to do about it."

"Well, say it to yourselves, my dears."

Dora bent her head and murmured under her breath.

"O great god, Chung, remember, we beseech thee, that which we asked of thee. For Sung Li's sake, amen."

Julius muttered the last words after her.

"Do you have your own grace?" said Reuben, in some curiosity.

"Do you, my dears?" said Jessica, who felt that discomfiture in this sphere was not in place.

"Sometimes we say what we like," said Dora.

"Well, I think that is very nice," said her mother.

"It does seem more friendly and informal," said Thomas.

"Some progress ought to be made towards intimacy, as time goes by," said Terence. "That sort of intercourse errs on the side of distance."

There was a pause.

"Terence and I are in disgrace with Mother, my children," said Thomas. "Do you understand why?"

"You talk about God as if you knew Him," said Dora.

"It should be enough that He knows us," said Jessica.

"He knows even the sparrows," said Dora, with innocent voice and eyes.

"That used to seem to cheapen the regard," said Bernard.

"He lets them fall to the ground," said Julius, simply.

"Well everything has to die," said Dora, "or the world would be too full."

"It may be good for us to realise that it will happen to us in the end," said Jessica.

"I expect I am the only person who does so," said Sukey.

"I do not feel that anyone else is with me. I find I cannot often feel that."

"The hairs of our heads are numbered," said Julius, with a touch of solemnity.

"Is it impressive or not, to be included in these wholesale dealings?" said Bernard.

"Impressive," said Thomas. "As it was to find that we lived in the universe. It is awe-inspiring that there is nowhere to live but there."

"I think we are some of us rather too old for this talk," said Jessica.

"It is only grown-up people who can do it," said Dora.

"Just grown-up perhaps," said Esmond.

"I have been said to have an adolescent mind," said Thomas, with a laugh.

"But it should not have been your nephew who said it," said Bernard.

"But Father is pleased about it," said Terence. "Just as young people are pleased to be thought mature. We all like to be what we are not; it shows the disappointment of life. I know I was wiser at fifteen than I am now; and it was not the wisdom of the child; I never had any of that."

"I am sorry to hear of your deterioration, as you are to teach Reuben," said Anna.

"I had forgotten that was before me."

"It does not sound as if you were making much preparation."

"Preparation?" said Terence, raising his eyes.

"I might learn with Miss Lacy," said Reuben, in his louder tone. "A woman would have more tenderness for my infirmity."

"'We won't talk of infirmity, Reuben. There is plenty of the opposite thing behind that head of yours," said Terence, in a mock schoolmaster's manner.

"So the touch can be acquired in a moment," said Anna.

"I have always thought the manner would be the easiest part of a profession," said Terence. "I could belong to any of them, if nothing else was needed. I expect that is how the manners became established. There had to be something that was within people's power."

"Reuben is not the only one who will make progress," said Thomas.

"They must both be kind to each other," said his wife, as if the pair were on a level.

"I will make the humdrum task as easy for my cousin as I can," said Reuben.

"It does not sound as if it matters which is the teacher and which the pupil," said Sukey.

"Oh, don't put that into Reuben's head, Aunt Sukey," said Anna. "He has learned very little of the ordinary things, and we don't want him more unlike other boys than can't be helped."

"So you find it an ingratiating character, the ordinary boy's," said Reuben.

"What do you know about it?" said his sister.

"I have watched the development of Esmond, who is the essence of the typical young male."

"I don't believe I have a single brother who is that."

"You may be right," said Benjamin, in an enigmatic tone.

"You are a fortunate sister," said Thomas.

"Oh, I don't know. I should not have minded a nice, little, ordinary boy like Julius for a brother. It would make fewer problems."

"What do you say to that, Dora?" said Thomas.

"I don't know what it is, not to be ordinary. Most people must be that, or it would be something else."

"Well, a lot of people think they are not," said Julius.

"I plead guilty to the feeling, myself," said Sukey. "No, I do not feel that I am quite an ordinary person, or that I should have been, with another person's chance."

"It is generally recognised, isn't it?" said Anna.

"That is a pleasant thing to hear, my dear. I like to feel I have made some little mark, before I go alone into the darkness."

"Does Aunt Sukey always strike this note of drama?" said Bernard to Terence.

"It was natural to her, even when she was well."

"Fancy maintaining it in sickness and in health!"

"That gives her a better use for it. I can also see the tendency in my mother."

"I think my father is free from it," said Bernard.

"I am not quite sure," said Esmond. "His temper would prevent his showing it. He could not betray concern for the impression he made on other people."

"Aunt Sukey's temper is not her best point," said Terence. "I do not mind speaking evil of a sick woman. I told you I had not a masculine mind."

Julius and Dora turned their eyes on Sukey and withdrew them. Her experience was too far removed, to have any bearing on their lives. They regretted it as they regretted that of the martyrs, but were hardly more nearly affected by it.

"I must take my family away," said Anna. "Seven guests to luncheon is no light matter, when they are related. We don't want to leave you in a state of collapse."

"I will not thank you for coming," said Sukey, keeping her hand. "But it has done me good to see you. Yes, and I think I will say to be seen by you. Those who do not meet us every day, may take a truer view of us. And there may not be many more visits to pay to me, not so very many."

"Must we take this despairing view of things?" said Anna, not meeting her eyes.

"The doctors tell me it is the right one. They do not keep it from me now. The weaker I grow, the more fit I am to bear it. I don't know that it makes anyone feel despair. I don't somehow think that it does."

"I refuse to regard it as possible," said Bernard.

"Yes, that is what people do; that is how they protect themselves. But there is no protection for me."

"I know you felt it was a safeguard for her," said

Terence to his cousin. "I used to think it, myself, and it is a great pity it is not."

"It is not anyone's fault that Aunt Sukey is ill," said Julius.

"Poor little things, it is not yours indeed," said Sukey. "And your life will be the same, when mine is over. So there is nothing for you to be too sorry about."

Dora sank into tears.

"The comforting speech failed of its effect," said Tullia.

"My little niece does not like the thought of life without her aunt," said Sukey, resting her eyes on Dora, so that she seemed not to see that the protest on Thomas's face had almost reached his lips.

"Can't people be cured?" said Julius.

"Not always, my boy," said Benjamin.

"Then what is the use of doctors?"

"I have asked myself that so many times," said Sukey. "And I am sure you have all asked it for me. There is only one answer. They are not much use to me. But now I must not see such sad little faces. I shall have to reproach myself, and that is not good for me; and other people may reproach me too, and that is not very good for them, as I am so much weaker than they are. So let me see the sunshine out again. That one old aunt has to die, does not matter so much, does it?"

"You seem to think it matters," said Julius.

"Well, I am not just an old aunt to myself, you see."

"You are supposed to have a good deal of time left, aren't you?" said Anna, in an uneasy manner.

"Well, we will make the most of it, however much it may be. I am glad to have time to get to know my niece. We have run it close, but I hope we are not too late. Though you must not expect too much of a woman sentenced to death. She cannot give a great deal."

"She affords me the greatest interest," said Bernard to his uncle. "I have never met such a case of concentrated experience. I can hardly believe I am in contact with it."

"You would soon get to realise it, and then to forget it," said Thomas. "We cannot spend out lives on the brink of a grave."

"That is what Aunt Sukey has to do."

"Yes, that is what she would say."

"But isn't it true?" said Bernard.

"It is true, my son," said Benjamin.

"She seems to take her part in everything else," said Thomas. "We do not do much without her."

"No one is improved by the knowledge that her time is running out," said his nephew.

"It should improve other people," said Thomas, with a sigh. "If it does not, it is difficult to manage."

"I think you are a person improved by it," said Terence to Bernard. "And it seemed to be improving your sister. And my mother is so much improved, that she no longer has her feet on the earth. But it has the other effect on my father and me, and I think it has on Aunt Sukey."

"I should have thought the last was inevitable," said Bernard.

"If you become any more improved, things will be impossible. And your sister has been wanting for some time to take you home. I hope the atmosphere is less exalted there. And I should think it is."

"I should like to come and see you as often as I may," said Anna to Sukey, with embarrassed suddenness.

"Then shall we have a time together in the mornings? Before your father comes to see me. But I must make one condition. If you are tired of it, you will tell me."

"Oh, I shall not be tired of it."

"Then we will begin to-morrow, and people will leave us to each other. And that will give them a rest from me, and be a kindness to them as well as to me. So you will be doing more good than you thought, and you meant to do good, I know."

"I meant just to please myself."

"Perhaps Anna's bluntness is the kind that disguises

feeling," said Esmond to Terence. "How are we to tell it from the other kind?"

"We will not try to, but I hope it is the other kind."

"It would be hard to have to be embarrassed by it in more than the usual way."

"Well, we won't keep on promising to depart, and then not doing so," said Anna, not looking again at her aunts. "I will marshal my party to the gate, and no one need come to open it for me, as there are three young men to officiate."

Benjamin rose and gave his arm to Sukey, and led her from the room, as if to protect her from the leave-taking.

"I see how neglected Aunt Sukey has been," said Terence. "It takes two families to look after her."

"Well, it is never too late to mend," said his sister.

"I should think it often is. It probably is this time. Yes, I feel we have let our opportunity pass."

"Those children may be a help to us," said Jessica to her husband. "You married into a difficult family, my dear."

"You are people on too large a scale," said Thomas, "and your problems seem to be on the same measure. And perhaps smaller people are better able for things. They bring less feeling and less resistance to them."

"It sounds an inconvenient type," said Claribel, approaching by herself, as her niece and nephews departed. "And I must plead guilty to belonging to it. It is hard to have a cousin of your own kind, instead of a friend who would bring more convenient and lighter qualities. But I cannot claim to be anything but the typical, strung-up woman of the family. Birds of a feather flock together, and that must be my excuse for bringing more nerves and capacity for various emotions to a place where they exist in plenty."

"There can be no excuse," said Terence, in a voice that could almost be heard.

"Well, Father and I will leave you to make the best of these qualities," said Tullia, taking Thomas's arm. "It seems a wise step, as I am afraid my portion of them is also on the lavish side."

Jessica gave a look from Claribel to her daughter.

"Do you see a likeness?" said Claribel.

"Well, I did for a moment."

"I am always flattered by showing any likeness to the younger generation. It shows that the years have not quite overlaid the thing one was meant to be. One likes to feel that there is a glimpse of it left."

"I think it always gets clearer," said Terence.

"Well, I hope that is meant in a complimentary sense."

"It would hardly have been said, otherwise," said Thomas, his tone conveying a faint warning to his son.

"We are all about the same height," went on Claribel, "Jessica and Sukey and me. I know I ought to say 'I,' but somehow my lips do not take to that little word; I am at one with Cleopatra there. I often discover in myself an affinity with the characters that we know as friends. I wonder if she was as high as we are. We shall make quite an imposing group, if we are seen about together."

"We shall share our interest in the young lives about us," said Jessica, stating another prospect for them.

"And I keep an interest in myself too, and in my own generation. I do not limit my thoughts to the young. I think that experience and knowledge of life often add to people, and bring out what they are. I find myself a more interesting study than when I was a girl. What I see then, is a lighter creature, with less to give. And I find the principle borne out in the young things about me. They have not reached the stage of depths and complexities, and the other things that enhance our value to my mind."

"You must find Miss Jennings a great support," said Jessica.

"Yes, she prevents me from being a creature quite apart. I do not feel that I am the only person with memories of the past, and scepticism of the future. I do not live entirely in an atmosphere of hope, that I fear is too ill-founded. But she does not ask as much for herself as I do; she is content with less. I fear I am a grasping person beside her, a person of deeper needs and more demands. I must deal on a larger scale with life. Well, I will take my unsatisfactory self away, and give you a further dose of it later. I will follow my youthful and unsophisticated flock."

The people thus described were walking in a group towards their home.

"Well, we have had the initiation into our new life," said Anna. "It strikes me that there will be a degree of responsibility involved in it."

"People in Aunt Sukey's situation ought not to be at large," said Esmond. "They can do other people nothing but harm."

"They may limit their concern to themselves in the time they have left," said Bernard.

"Bernard has gone overboard about Aunt Sukey," said Anna. "She will be competing with Cook and Ethel for his esteem."

"I thought I saw signs of your yielding to her spell, yourself," said her brother.

"Yes, I have fallen a victim," said Anna, pursuing her way into the house, "and have let myself in for the consequences. It is not in my line to listen to people's last words and that sort of thing, but I shall have to get up to the level."

"Well, how have you managed with it all?" said Jenney, who had come home early by herself.

"I think we got through with credit," said Anna at once. "Anyhow three of us are to go there every day, Reuben to learn from Terence, and Father and I to attend upon Aunt Sukey, at our different times and in our different ways."

"You are to do that, are you? So you got on well with her. And I hear she is not the easiest person. She is supposed to make trouble."

"She hardly needs to do that, as far as she is concerned, herself," said Bernard.

"No, poor thing, I can see she is very ill. It must be dreadful to live with all those well people, feeling you are in that state yourself."

"You have expressed her exact view," said Esmond.

"Well, anyone would feel the same."

"The words, 'poor thing,' hardly give her," said Bernard.

"Bernard has lost his heart," said Anna. "He had eyes and ears for no one else. And I am somewhat in the same case. She does exert her own spell."

Benjamin's voice came from behind.

"This is a good word to me, my daughter. I hoped you had enough of me in you, to see my sister as I see her, and it seems it is the case. This may be a growing time for all of us."

"Why do people think it is such a good thing for people to take after them, even when they have no particular self-esteem?" murmured Bernard. "I don't think Father has any great opinion of himself."

"But doubtless a better one than he has of his family," said Esmond. "Indeed he implies it."

"We shall have to go forward a bit, if we are to accompany Aunt Sukey to the brink of the grave," said Anna. "We were not expecting any such thrust onwards. But the hopeful point is that with her it is easier than you would think. She seems to carry one with her."

"It seems unfair to take advantage of that, and then to turn back ourselves," said Bernard.

"So much so, my son, that you will understand, if that feeling is at times too much for her," said Benjamin.

"I hardly knew I was Father's son before," murmured Bernard. "I only just knew that Anna was his daughter, though that is not his fault."

"That is what my sisters do for people," said Benjamin, as if he were speaking to himself. "They shed their own light."

"I hardly know what to make of this new chapter of our

family life," muttered Esmond. "I cannot claim to feel at home in it."

"Now what do we all say to Tullia?" said Anna. "I say that the elders put her into the shade, in spite of her youth. I never saw such a case of advantage in older faces."

"It seems rather shallow of her to be settled in this life, when Aunt Sukey is so precariously balanced in it," said Bernard.

"You might say that of us all," said Esmond.

"I do say it," said his brother.

"Aunt Sukey seems so much of this world, in her own way," said Anna, "and yet she has to leave it. And Aunt Jessica is so apart from it, and yet has to stay and struggle on. It seems a pity that they cannot change places, though I cannot imagine their doing so. But don't let it all depress you, Father. We shall do no better in this new life for carrying long faces. There is Reuben at the gate, with those two children. I suppose they have escorted him home. Well, he is not so much older than they are. If he becomes a thought more childish, it won't be a bad thing."

Reuben came into the room, rather conscious over his companions.

"Well, I have not uttered a word that could pollute those tender minds."

"We do not need the assurance," said Esmond. "We do you that justice."

"Oh, but I like to think there is danger."

"Do they love their mother?" said Bernard.

"Yes, I think they do," said Reuben, raising his eyes.

"And their father?"

"Yes, they love him."

"And Aunt Sukey?"

"Well, they don't want her to die, or anything like that."

"And Terence and Tullia?" said Bernard.

"They seem to like Terence. They did not talk about Tullia."

"What a lot of Ts!" said Anna.

"Do they live in a world of their own?" said Bernard.

"They do in a way," said Reuben, looking surprised by this knowledge.

"I never did," said Bernard. "I lived in this world, as I do now. It is the only one I like. Do not try to enter their world, Reuben. You would never get inside."

"I don't think they want me to," said his brother.

"And it would take you out of your own world," said Anna, "and you have enough to do there."

"I hardly think he has one," said Bernard, looking at his brother. "Any more than I had, or not much more."

"I ought to be a boy who lives in the world of books and dreams," said Reuben.

"Oh, a little physical disability does not make all that difference," said Anna. "Not in a bad sense or a good. I hope those children don't make things difficult for you."

"No, they have shown the instinctive delicacy of childhood."

"And I suppose you have done the same," said Bernard. "You have not called attention to their peculiarities."

"They have not any," said Reuben.

"You are mistaken," said Esmond. "Dora is subject to facial contortions, and Julius to bodily ones of a more violent character."

"Oh, the little nervous habits of childhood!" said Anna. "I remember you in that stage."

"I can say the same to you, but that does not alter my opinion that it is a regrettable one. Indeed it supports it."

"The process of getting used to the world seems to be too much for us," said Bernard.

"So it is hard on people like Aunt Sukey, who have to leave it too soon," said Anna. "They seem to serve their apprenticeship without the reward."

"I fear they do so," said Benjamin.

"Well, it is nobody's fault, after all, Father."

"I feel it is mine, when I am with her," said Bernard.

"It seems that some of my strength ought to be taken from me and given to her."

"It would improve you both," said Esmond, resting his eyes on his brother's bulky frame.

"Oh, Bernard has not so much strength to spare," said Anna. "Father and Reuben are really the strongest of us. And thin, wiry people like Claribel and Miss Lacy are the toughest of all. Oh, Miss Lacy wants to have a talk with you, Jenney."

"Does she? Miss Lacy?" said Jenney, in a tone of mild excitement. "To think of her still being there, and still teaching those children! Well how things do go on!"

"No more for her than for any of us," said Anna. "Though I suppose we have now achieved a break in our lives."

"Julius and Dora seem rather to like Miss Lacy," said Reuben. "They do what she says, almost as if she were Aunt Jessica."

"It seems the fashion to treat her with respect," said Anna, as if the case admitted of other dealings. "She wants Jenney's advice about a niece who has come to live with her, and puts her in rather a quandary. Jenney is supposed to be wise about young people and their problems."

Jenney just cast a glance on the members of this class, as if there could be no further light for her.

Claribel came idly and absently into the room.

"I am sorry to be such a laggard, but I was detained by my contemporaries, as you were released by yours."

"It sounds as if you were more of a success than we were," said Bernard.

"Well, it was pleasant to meet a demand for someone of my age and sex. It is not such a frequent occurrence. And to-day that was what was wanted. Your Aunt Jessica asked that and nothing else, and all I had to do was to surrender myself to her need."

"It is odd how that family seems to have a use for this one," said Anna.

CHAPTER V

"WHAT IS IT, Sukey?" said Thomas, breaking into Sukey's room.

"What is it, Aunt Sukey?" said Tullia, a pace behind.

"What is it, my dear?" said Jessica, on a sharper note.

Sukey lay back in her chair and seemed to try to give a smile to her sister.

"I think it has passed," she said, putting her hand to her heart. "There is nothing to trouble you. I have had the fright by myself, and got through it in the same way."

"But what was it?" said Jessica.

"My bell was not answered when I rang. I needed something and could get no answer. And it came over me that I might die here alone, and no one know. And the thought seemed to go through me, and I could not go on without the sight of a human face, the sound of a human voice. So I rang in such a way that someone had to come. If you were frightened, you were not as much frightened as I was."

"We shall be less frightened next time," muttered Thomas. "It will be a case of the boy and the wolf, if she does not take care."

"I am not able to take care," said Sukey, with a faint smile; "I am not equal to that. And I think you forget that my ears are still sharp, though my strength is ebbing. And if you fear what you say, you will be on your guard against it."

"Did you have a heart attack, or just feel that you wanted someone?" said Tullia.

"Just feel it! Just!" said Sukey.

"We must arrange that you are never alone," said Thomas.

"No, I do not want that; I could not even bear it. And I need not make that demand on the house. Things cannot be done in that simple, sweeping way. A little thought and kindness is what I want. If I could feel that I could summon help, I would be content with my solitude."

"We must find out why the bell was not answered," said Jessica. "You sent your own maid out, but the others are within hearing."

"Enquiry might be too late one day," said Sukey.

"The servants thought you rang for your broth, and were bringing it," said Tullia. "I can hear it coming."

"It might not have been an occasion for broth. There must be other needs in the last days of a human life."

"But it was, I suppose," said Thomas. "And it was likely that it should be, as it was the hour. Anyhow here it is, and the situation is met."

"It is not even grasped, I think," said Sukey.

"The bell must be answered, of course," said Jessica. "We must be able to depend on that. Perhaps Tullia could listen for it in the mornings."

"My life hardly allows of my spending hours of each day in a single spot," said Tullia, in a distinct, deliberate tone. "For my time, as you know, involves Father's."

"Did you hear the bell to-day?" said her mother.

"I heard it, and thought it was for the broth, and assumed that the servants were bringing it, and seem to have been right."

Sukey put the tray aside, as if she were past such a need.

"Your attack of nerves should have come at some other moment," said Thomas, in a lighter tone.

"I cannot time them, can I? I would time even the hour of my death for you, if I could. But the suspense and uncertainty are given me to bear, and I must be helped to sustain them. I am doing my very best. I hope you believe me. But different needs may arise, must arise, the doctors tell me. Their words do not make an impression, except on me, but I can hardly forget them."

"Working yourself into a state over nothing can only do you harm," said Tullia.

"It is nothing to be left alone to die," said Sukey, turning a sad smile on Tullia's parents, as if the words would be lost upon her youth. "I see it is to those who are not threatened by it. I should not have thought it would be quite that. I should have thought that some memory of it would follow you through your happy and useful hours. But I must be glad it is not so."

"Sukey, you are doing harm to yourself and to my wife," exclaimed Thomas.

Sukey put out her hand to her sister.

"So there is someone who suffers a little for me, who is not quite reconciled to the thought of my prime and my powers being wasted. A little suffering is inseparable from it, Thomas; we have to pay the price of love. But it shall be as light as I can make it."

Jessica knelt by her sister's chair, and they clasped each other. Thomas looked on with a frown and a restless foot, and Tullia held her head so high that she looked over them. Anna opened the door and came to a standstill.

"They told me to come straight upstairs," she said.

"And the advice strikes you as rash," said Thomas.

"Well, I don't want to rush in where an angel would fear to tread."

"I want you," said Sukey, holding out her hand. "I don't think I realised how great my need would be, of someone not wearied of the sight and sound of me. You may not have come at a happy moment, but you have come at the right one."

"You might all be about to be dead and buried," said Anna, advancing into the room.

"Well, even I am not quite that at the moment. So we will forget the likelihood of my being so soon, and have a happy time together, as if I were an ordinary, tough, old aunt."

"I am glad you are not that," said Anna.

"So there is someone besides my sister, who sees some good in my being what I am; someone who does not think that health and strength to be self-sufficient are quite everything. I know they are a great deal. Who should know it better?"

"Oh, there is plenty of health and strength about," said her niece.

"And yet there is not a little bit over for me, not one little share out of all there is. Well, I must not complain. It is time I learned that."

"I should soon let people hear about it, if I were in your place."

"Yes one does begin in that way. It seems at first that eyes and thoughts would turn to the person whose yoke is heavy. It is rather a hard lesson, to learn that they turn away. There is so much health about, as you say, that there hardly seems to be room for anything else. Sometimes I could almost wish there were a little less, or a little less of the things that go with it. But I should be glad that my dear ones have it, when I would give so much for it myself."

"I should think it might be the most trying thing in the world, to see it all about you."

"I must not agree to that, but I may be grateful for the understanding that lies behind it. For I am tempted to get tired of living apart, to want to go back to the life I shared with other people. You see my time for leaving it has come so soon. But I have to try to wean myself from it; and you may be able to help me; for as I grow weaker, the effort does not get less."

"I will do anything I can," said Anna.

"We have received our dismissal," said Thomas to his wife, "and the aid will be better administered without us. Not that our presence seems to be felt as a check."

"Anna is a change," said Jessica, as they gained the passage. "I forget how much one is needed. I ought to be on the watch. But an attempt to be different might only defeat itself."

"Sukey would be poorly off, if you had any success in such an effort."

"I am so little for her to depend upon. I have come to live for myself. I should not have married, if my being personally satisfied was to seem enough."

"You are not always so conscious of your own good fortune," said Tullia.

"No, I am ill to please even in my sunny place. So what of my sister, living always in the shadow?"

"Well, Anna will give an hour to her, and Benjamin another," said Thomas. "And Tullia will come with her father. She has done her part."

Jessica looked after her husband and daughter, and her pride in Tullia, her jealousy of Thomas's joy in her, her sorrow for the sin in her feeling, followed each other over her face. The cloud in his eyes lifted as he turned to his daughter. Her easy experience and blindness to her mother's soothed him and set things in a clearer light. Her love for him met his need the better, that it was not a weightier thing. Thomas had had his fill of strength and depth of feeling.

Anna came out of her aunt's room, distraught and flushed, as if she had been engaged on something foreign to herself. She caught sight of her father, and paused and drew a deep breath, before she met him.

"Well, Father, I have done my best with this odd new task. And now I leave you to continue it. I think I have scored a mild success. Anyhow I have not been blamed or dismissed, and my good offices are welcome to-morrow. The question is whether I can keep it up. But be that as it may, I can't think that the methods employed with Aunt Sukey in this house are the right or fair ones."

"Ours must be different, and that will be something," said Benjamin. "It cannot be laid to one sister's account, that she is not a change for the other. The more she does for her, the less that can be."

"New brooms sweep clean, of course. But old ones may

be better cast aside, and I maintain that it is the case with these. Meanwhile, let us sweep clean while we can."

Anna left the house, not seeking a word with anyone. She had come for a purpose, fulfilled it, and did not linger. Thomas and his daughter emerged as they heard the gate, and Terence followed their example.

"I cannot bear opening that gate for people," he said. "I hate to hear their perfunctory thanks. Chivalry to women does not come to me naturally. I do not think anything did. I have a sort of innocent selfishness; at least I hope it is regarded as innocent; of course I know its real nature myself."

"Anna will not feel the omission," said Tullia. "Manners are scarce in her family. It did not take long to see it."

"Uncle Benjamin has his own greatness of behaviour. I would emulate it, if I did not suspect that it had its root in unselfishness. If the root were in anything else, I would really try."

"Most things that are good, or called good, are founded on that," said Thomas.

"And those things are very good indeed, too good to be possible. It comes of a foundation that must break down. Most people have tried to build on it. And they remember it, and respect themselves, and are exacting with other people; and I think they are justified. A person who can really be called an unselfish person, has no place in life."

"Some people have a certain conception of themselves, and need to live up to it," said Tullia. "They get their own reward."

"But not a reward that could satisfy anyone. We are talking about Mother, and do not dare to say so."

"When do we think or talk about anything else? It shows what a power her kind of goodness or aspiration is. It does not matter what we call it."

"It is the difference between being dutiful and brutal," said Terence, looking at his sister. "Now I know what it is to feel an unwilling admiration."

"I may as well go the whole length for once. Things are better, brought into the light of day."

"Would you sap the very foundations of civilisation?"

"I would, in so far as they are harmful to myself and other people."

"I know it is dreadful when things are harmful to oneself," said Terence.

"It is the watching and following Mother's feelings that makes the strain. We are never allowed to forget them, or to stop feeling guilty over them. Oh, for easy, ordinary people, who are fair to themselves, and so to others!"

Thomas had heard his children in silence.

"Ought you not to be teaching Reuben, my boy?"

"I am teaching him, Father."

"And how are you contriving that?"

"By my own odd methods, that will have a better result than ordinary ones. Or that is the kind of thing that would happen."

"He is doing something for you, I suppose?"

"He is learning to use his brain for himself, which is the end of all education."

"But is it the beginning?"

"The same thing is always both. The beginning and the end, we say. I never quite understand it."

"I suppose you will go and point out his mistakes?"

"I shall let him see them for himself."

"But if he could do that, he would hardly make them."

"You must know that we learn by our mistakes, Father."

"Has he any need of you?"

"Great need, the poor, untaught lad."

"What does he think of your methods?"

"He does not think; that is not a thing he would do. He is gaining self-respect from them. And he will gain independence; and that is what I want, or I should have to spend my time with him."

"What is his feeling for you?"

"A boyish veneration that will soon approach worship. I shall not feel so free when it reaches that. I shall find it has acquired its own value."

"What would Anna say to your methods?"

"She would think that Uncle Benjamin ought not to pay me."

"And do you think he ought?" said Thomas.

"Well, my service is of a kind that cannot be paid for in money. And that means it is paid for in that way, but not very well."

"Does your uncle want that kind of service?"

"Yes, or he would have to pay better."

"He has a larger income than we have," said Tullia. "And yet they are to spend their lives in that awkward house."

"Cheap things are well enough, when they are a choice," said Thomas.

"Is Miss Lacy paid?" said Dora, at their elbow.

"The labourer is worthy of his hire," said Thomas. "And everyone who works is paid. And it is fortunate for me, and so for you, that that is the case."

"Miss Lacy doesn't need any more money," said Julius. "She inherited enough from her father. I mean she doesn't want a little money, like she earns here. A lot, that would let her have a stable and horses, would be different."

"She ought to have that for teaching you," said Thomas.

"She says she liked teaching Terence the best of us," said Dora, in an unprejudiced tone.

"Where is she now?" said Tullia.

"She is bringing her niece to luncheon, the one who is to be a friend for you and Terence."

"What is she like?" said the latter.

"Oh, grown-up," said Julius, as if this disposed of the matter.

"She calls Miss Lacy, 'Aunt Emma,' " said Dora, with a laugh. "I think we might call her that too."

"On what ground?" said Thomas.

"Well, if it is a wrong thing to do, the niece ought not to do it."

"She does it because Miss Lacy is her aunt," said Tullia. "She in not yours."

"Heaven forbid!" said Dora, swinging her foot.

"I suppose heaven does forbid it," said Thomas, "but I do not know the reason. I am sure it would be pleasant to have Miss Lacy for an aunt."

Dora and Julius broke into mirth, and continued it with their eyes on their father, hopeful of further license. They put no check on their behaviour in his presence, as they did in their mother's.

Miss Lacy approached with her niece at her side, and an air of being conscious of her presence to the natural extent and not beyond. The latter was a girl of twenty, of medium height and build, with a pale, smooth skin, light brown eyes, glossy dark hair, a small, shut mouth, and hands and feet remarkable for smallness rather than proportion. She walked in a drooping manner, with an air of finding whatever was taking place, too much for her; or perhaps of feeling that it would be too much, if she knew what it was. She shook hands in silence and without sign of interest, though her eyes took stock of her hosts from under their lids.

"Only one family to-day," said her aunt, "and I think I am a little glad of it. Now we can do justice to it and to ourselves."

A faintly sighing movement from her companion suggested agreement.

"The other is to join us," said Tullia. "We will not keep you with us on false pretences."

Jessica came into the hall to receive the guests.

"It will be simple enough when it is familiar," she said. "A choice is as good in people as in things. I do not feel it a recommendation to have only ourselves to offer."

"Well, let me introduce Miss Florence Lacy," said Miss Lacy, in a mock-ceremonious tone, "to Mrs. Calderon,

Miss Calderon and Miss Theodora Calderon; and present to her Mr. Terence and Master Julius Calderon."

A faint smile curved the lips of the new-comer, though it seemed that it was not provoked by her aunt's words.

"My little niece, Mr. Calderon," said Miss Lacy, in an easy tone, guiding the girl towards Thomas.

"We are glad to see you, my dear, and you will take the words to mean what they say. My young people have an especial welcome for someone who is not their kith and kin."

"You will not evince the family failings," said Tullia, "though I think that is putting the same thing in another form."

"I thought Florence was a place," said Julius.

"So it is," said the owner of the name, with a resigned lift of her brows, using her rapid, rather blurred tones for the first time.

"It comes of having a travelled father," said Miss Lacy. "His sins are visited upon the child."

"Yes, they are," said her niece.

"It is a pleasant name," said Tullia. "Why are you not grateful for it?"

"It is a pleasant word," said Terence, "and it was a happy idea to use it for a name."

"Is that saying something different?" said Miss Lacy.

Florence swept her eyes over Terence's face, and in a moment let them fall, but a moment was some time for her glance to be arrested.

"Could you be called Paris or London?" said Dora.

"Oh, yes, I expect so," said Florence, with a sigh.

"All things are possible to him that believeth," said Miss Lacy.

"What do you think of our names?" said Tullia. "It is another case of the sins of the father."

Florence contracted her brows as if in sympathy with them.

"What would you all like to be called?" said Jessica.

"Any ordinary names," said Tullia, "that left our personalities free to go their natural way."

"You might be called York or Constantinople," said Julius.

"No, I don't think so, Julius," said Miss Lacy. "Think again."

"Julius has thought enough," said Thomas.

"Dora is an ordinary name," said Julius, in a tone of congratulation to his sister.

"I don't think Theodora is, but I don't mind about my name."

"I think that is wise," said Jessica.

"I feel that Terence is a good name for me," said the bearer of it. "An ordinary name might make me seem unmanly. I could not carry off Thomas."

Florence gave him a faint smile.

"Why not regard a name as something that separates us, for the convenience of other people?" said Jessica.

"That is what we should like to do," said Tullia, "but we were not given the chance. Our names do other things in spite of us."

"You must not reproach your father, Tulliola," said Thomas. "He would have nothing ordinary for you."

Tullia put her arm in his, and Florence's eyes swept over them.

"Are you talking about names?" said another voice. "Then what do you say to going through life under the blight of Susan, and the secondary one of Sukey?"

"The latter is a name that does what may be required of it," said Miss Lacy.

"Well, some people have liked my funny little name for me. I believe a good many people have."

"Anyone would like the name, Sukey," said Florence.

"Do you think so, my dear?" said Sukey, coming to shake hands. "There is a pleasant word for me, for the first one that I hear. It makes me feel that I shall hear some more, and that we may like other things about each other."

Florence looked at the speaker's face, because she had no choice, continued to look in spite of herself, cast a glance at Jessica and dropped her eyes.

"You see the likeness between my sister and me?" said Sukey.

"No, I don't see much. I never think people are really like one another."

"But you notice the family likeness?"

"Oh, family likeness," said Florence, almost to herself.

"It is true that it may not go far down," said Thomas.

"Looks are only skin deep," said his wife.

"It is beauty that is said to be that," said Tullia. "I never know why it is not said of the other thing. It seems rather unfair on either side."

"A pleasant surface makes us think there are pleasant things underneath," said Sukey. "I could never believe that is not the case."

Florence turned to Terence and spoke as if she could not suppress the words.

"What a pity that a name like Sukey belongs to anyone but your mother!"

"Why? Do you like the name very much?"

"It ought to go with a face that has her sort of look in it. It is a look that puts her apart from other people, and yet on a level with them. I have never seen a face like hers."

"My aunt is thought to have more beauty."

"Yes, I daresay she has that."

"It is not such a common thing."

"No, but it might belong to anyone," said Florence, resting her eyes on Tullia. "And here it seems to belong to so many people."

"You know my aunt is a great invalid?"

"Yes, Aunt Emma told me, but that is an accidental thing. We cannot think of people in terms of a chance."

Terence was silent, looking into her face.

"Well, we will not talk of sad things on your friend's first day with us," said Sukey's voice. "And that only means that we must not talk about me. There is nothing else sad in this house. All is happy and careless and free, and only asks for sympathy with joy. It is only if anyone needs a word on any other ground, that I would suggest seeking my room and my companionship. Not that there is only sadness to be met with there. I am a resolute person and keep my own ways, even on the threshold of—well, we need not say of what."

"Aunt Sukey should insult us to our faces, if she does it at all," said Terence.

"She did it in our hearing," said Thomas. "We will not complain."

Florence's lips just parted in a smile, but she did not raise her eyes.

Benjamin came from the back of the hall, having remained in the house since his hour with his sister. Miss Lacy lifted Florence's hand towards him.

"This is my little niece, Mr. Donne," she said, hardly looking at either.

"And this is an elderly man in whom she can take no interest," said Benjamin, shaking hands with the guest and producing no sign of disagreement.

"But here are the man's children, in whom she can," said Sukey.

Florence turned towards the gate with a faintly sighing movement, as it admitted the further addition to her new friends.

Anna led the way with her usual hurrying step, looking neither to one side nor the other. Bernard and Reuben advanced together, with Jenney on Reuben's other side. Esmond and Claribel walked apart, in an aloofness that extended to each other.

"Now I should manage the introductions, as I am responsible for the need of them," said Miss Lacy. "I must present my niece, Florence, to Miss Bell and Miss Jennings; and add that these are Bernard, Anna, Esmond, and Reuben Donne, to the best of my conviction and remembrance."

"I think that a duty to convention is best performed in the ordinary way," said Anna to Sukey. "Miss Lacy seems to manage to make people look a little ridiculous. I should not like to be left to her tender mercies in the larger matters of life."

"You could depend on her in those," said Sukey. "It is on the surface that she presents this front, and we have all got rather fond of it."

"No, I am not quite with you, Aunt Sukey," said Anna, shaking her head. "I don't put her on a level with you and Aunt Jessica."

Sukey did not say that her niece had exaggerated her requirements.

"How many new people has she had to see?" said Dora, with a pointing movement towards Florence.

"Fourteen," said the latter, with unexpected precision, in a tone of polite response to Dora.

"Dora is young to concern herself with another person's point of view," said Bernard.

"I always think of what people are thinking," said Dora. "If they didn't think, they wouldn't be people."

"Now, Miss Jennings, how do you do?" said Miss Lacy, making a deliberate way towards Jenney. "I have promised myself a talk with you. I want to take advantage of your experience of the young, now that I have a young creature of my own to supervise and satisfy."

"How do you do, Miss Lacy?" said Jenney, shaking hands and going no further.

Florence rested her eyes on Jenney's face, transferred them to Jessica's, as if expecting something in common, swept them over the other faces and brought them to rest on Sukey's, surprised to find what she sought.

"Now you two children must run to the nursery," said Jessica. "Your luncheon will be brought up there. There is no room for you at the table."

"Shall we have the same things?" said Julius.

"Yes, I will see to it myself. Father will carve for you

at the same time as the others," said Jessica, who never despoiled the young.

Julius and Dora ran to the door, welcoming the prospect of freedom without a price.

CHAPTER VI

"Now, Miss Lacy, will you lead us in?" said Thomas.

"Well, I feel it does need a certain initiative," said Miss Lacy, laughing and going to the door.

Thomas remained on his feet at the head of the table. Grace at meals was the custom in his home, though he said it without conviction and sometimes with discomfiture. Jessica's word on such matters was law, and he had been surprised to find how many of the kind there were, not having grasped the truth of her assertion that religion entered into the whole of life. The discovery that it was her habit to pray for him, marked a stage in their relation; and it was at this time that Jessica realised that she was second to his daughter in his heart.

"Thirteen at the table!" said Tullia, checking herself as she was about to sit down.

"What does that mean?" said Bernard.

"That the person who sits down first, will be dead within a certain time; I forget how long," said Tullia, in a tone of merely quoting a belief.

"Then I ought to be the one to do so," said Sukey, not seeming to think of suiting her action to her words. "It is so much more likely for me than for anyone else."

"Then do not dream of it, Aunt Sukey," said Bernard. "You would be sustaining too many of the threats of fate."

"Well, I will do as I am told," said Sukey, continuing to stand.

Thomas's eyes had a smile in them, as they went from face to face. He was free from superstition and at ease to observe the scene.

"Men wait until the women are seated," said Terence.

"Perhaps it is true that the real demands of life fall on the latter," said Miss Lacy.

"It is a good thing the children are not here," said Florence in a serious tone.

"It would save the situation," said Bernard. "We should be fifteen."

"We do not remedy it by not sitting down," said Benjamin. "Our anxiety can only be transferred to other people."

"If you do not feel it is improved, you are a person by yourself," said Terence.

"Father does not deny he is that," said Bernard.

Benjamin did not do so, but had his own grounds for the belief.

"I am superstitious, I know," said Anna, standing at a distance from her chair. "I am not going to pretend I am not."

"Aren't you really?" said Terence. "Then you cannot pretend that you do not rank your life above other people's."

"Well, everyone does that."

"No, you do not pretend," said her cousin, "but I think I am still going to."

"Shall I go and fetch the children?" said Reuben, his voice betraying complacence in his separation from these.

"I do not mind being the first to sit down," said Jenney, in a hesitating tone.

"No, don't do it, Jenney," said Reuben at once.

"I wonder how many of us really believe it," said Tullia, tapping her fingers on the table.

"We cannot say that," said Bernard. "We see it is a deep and universal faith."

"No one is sure that there might not be 'something in it,' " said Miss Lacy. "These things may have some reason behind them, some series of links in their history."

"Something more powerful than history is here," said Thomas.

"How dreadful we all think it is to die!" said Jenney, in a deprecating tone.

"Of course we do," said Terence. "Or why should we send for doctors when we are in danger of it, and execute people when they inflict it on us?"

"Perhaps this little difficulty may give you some insight into my life, as I live it day by day," said Sukey.

"I really thought of that at once," said Bernard.

"Yes, I think several of you did," said Sukey.

"It may give us some insight into ourselves," said Anna.

"That is what I was going to say," said Jessica.

"Then we are at one, Aunt Jessica, for once."

"Somehow that does seem odd," murmured Terence.

"Quite true; I quite agree," said his cousin.

"But it is nice of Aunt Sukey," said Terence. "She persists in thinking good of people. If she did not, I don't know what she would think."

"That her position was not too good," said Anna, in a mutter.

"Did we need insight into ourselves?" said Bernard. "It is a matter on which it is hard to be deceived. We can only hope that other people are deceived about us."

"We know they can't be, as they can judge us by themselves," said Terence.

Miss Lacy went into laughter, and gave her chair an audible pull, as if she might sit down on it at any moment.

Florence regarded the action with an enigmatic face.

"It doesn't seem that we ought to feel like this," said Jenney, looking at her chair with an almost wistful expression.

"Well, we never meant people to know we did," said Bernard.

"It is the *last* person who sits down, who takes the risk," said Thomas, with his lips grave.

"Is this pause a real one?" said Terence. "It seems to be full of so much."

"We are living at our highest pitch," said Bernard. "The moment will live in our memory."

"So I always live at a higher pitch than other people,"

said Sukey. "When I see how this touch of imaginary risk affects them, I feel that I may live as much in my short time as they in their long one. It is true that we live in deeds, not years."

The grating of a chair was heard, and Tullia sank into it, as if she lacked the energy to stand for another moment. Sukey did the same, as if it were also for her the only course. A chorus of grating ensued, and as people glanced about to be assured of their personal timeliness, Jessica was seen to be standing by her chair with her usual expression.

"We ought not to let a superstition influence our actions. And I thought Miss Jennings meant to be the last, and we could not let a guest do that for us."

"Surely some confusion of thought," murmured Tullia, stooping forward in an attitude of exhaustion.

"When will Mother sit down?" said Terence. "And who was the last to do so, if she does not?"

Jessica gave him a smile and took her seat.

"Well, as Aunt Jessica has sacrificed herself, there is nothing to do but take advantage of it," said Anna, unfolding her napkin.

Tullia followed the example, seeming hardly to know what she did. Sukey turned to her neighbour and spoke with a faint smile.

"Well, whatever risk my sister has taken, it is not more than I face with every hour of my life."

"Aunt Sukey's reactions are so natural," said Terence. "They are what mine would be in her place. And I find that so surprising."

"Well, now, how do we feel about it?" said Miss Lacy. "Is our uneasiness for ourselves transferred to another? Or did we not really have any uneasiness, or how was it?"

"Of course we had it," said Bernard. "Or we should have got the credit of sitting down first or last, or whatever it was."

"You know it was last," said Anna.

"If anyone had sat down first, in the first place, he would have done well," said Thomas.

"The anxiety was too slight to count much for anyone else," said Terence. "Of course everything counts for ourselves."

"Oh, there was a real hard core of uneasiness," said Anna. "You can't get away from that."

"No, I suppose it is no good to try," said her cousin.

"Oh, I don't think we were really nervous about it," said Jenney, in a tone of compunction, looking at Jessica.

"I daresay you were not," said Bernard. "I think you have almost proved it. You would have faced the danger, if Reuben had permitted it."

"It was clearly not a woman's business," said Reuben, shortly.

"Nor a boy's either, as you saw it," said Esmond.

"Well, perhaps it was not," said Thomas.

"The youngest would have the most life to lose," said Anna. "He would be making the greatest sacrifice."

"It must be recognised that the palm goes to Miss Jennings," said Miss Lacy. "After Mrs. Calderon, of course."

"It is mean of us to pass it off lightly," said Terence. "But I don't see what else to do. I can hardly admit that I valued my life above my mother's."

"Proving it does seem to be enough," said Esmond.

"Suppose something should come of it," said Jenney, half to herself. "Then we should have to reproach ourselves."

"But congratulate ourselves, too, I suppose," said Anna.

"Nothing will *come of it*," said Jessica, in a quiet voice. "If anything does, or seems to, it will be what would have come anyhow."

"Why must we continue in this confusion?" murmured Tullia. "Are we never to emerge from it?"

"It is a pity if none of these things is true," said Terence. "If we cannot protect ourselves by letting other people be the thirteenth, and take the path underneath the ladder, and all of it. It seems to make life not more safe, but less so."

"You have wasted a good deal of contrivance, I suppose," said Anna.

"I don't think it is quite wasted. I think it is just worth while to do it."

"Uncle Thomas was making sport for himself," said Bernard.

"And not without some success," said his uncle.

"Oh, you did not sit down last, any more than anyone else did, Uncle Thomas," said Anna. "Don't think that we did not notice it."

"We can't make out that the matter was not real to us," said Esmond.

"Have we not done a little towards it?" said Terence.

"Aunt Jessica dared what strong men flinched at," said Bernard. "How many of us were strong, flinching men?"

"Four," said Terence.

"Five," said Anna. "Father cannot be excepted."

"I did not mean to except him," said Terence. "I only felt that I was not a strong man myself, though of course a flinching one."

"Then your sacrifice would have been less," said Esmond. "Your chance of life is slighter."

"But life is especially precious when it hangs by a frail thread. And weakly lives have that way of outlasting others."

"Well, the courage of womanhood has come up to the test," said Miss Lacy.

"I was always afraid I was not a womanly person," said Claribel. "And now I know that my level is that of men."

"Oh, courage; what is it?" said Tullia.

"It is the great quality of daring to risk oneself," said Bernard. "Moral courage is supposed to be the best, but that may be because it is impossible to show the other. We must feel that we have some kind."

"Why is it so great?" said Tullia, almost absently.

"Well, we will hope it is not, as we have not shown it, and someone else has. But I fear that it is."

"I have to show it in every hour of each day," said Sukey. "Well, it ought to make me appreciate my sister's showing it on one occasion. And I think I can say that it does. But I did not feel it was for me to make a further call on mine. I am sometimes afraid it may give out one day. And then where shall I be?"

"Having to show it so much must make you think rather little of an isolated instance of it," said Anna.

"No, I must not let it have that effect on me," said Sukey, in a tone so much lighter, that Jessica was startled by her instant response to sympathy. "You will tell me if you think I am letting my own suffering blunt me to that of others. I would not get like that, even for the time I have left. I would not become so unworthy of the self I once was."

"It seems better to have no earlier self," said Bernard.

"It seems easier," said Anna, brusquely.

"If Aunt Sukey had sat down last, she would have lived her last days in a blaze of glory," said Terence, not meaning his words to reach his aunt's ears.

"I should have said that she did enough of deserving glory, as it is," said Anna, with the opposite intention for hers.

"No, I should only have been thought to be making a small sacrifice, as I had not much to lose," said Sukey, with a smile of gratitude for Anna. "It would not be realised that having only a little of something may add to its value, especially when the something is life itself."

"We might all have sat down last," said Thomas, looking with a light in his eyes at the faces round him. "We are fourteen at the table."

His hearers turned from side to side in rapid calculation.

"Oh!" said Claribel, with almost a scream in her voice. "Then there was something in the instinct that prompted me to come to-day! I wondered if I should be *de trop*, and if my young relatives would be better without me, and my elder ones be sufficient to themselves, and all the other things that occur to the worrying and ultra-sensitive. And here I am, justified of myself, and exonerated and even appreciated by other people! I feel in quite a different frame of mind; I am quite uplifted."

"I hope the effect is the same upon us all," said Esmond. "Each one has an equal right to it."

"You have saved us from dark and dreadful things," said Terence to Claribel. "Now no one can know that I did not see we were fourteen at the table, and was not mischievously silent about it. Or anyhow no one can prove it."

"Yes, you owe it to me. I was the only person whose coming was in any doubt. I am the pivot upon which the structure turns."

"No, no, we cannot say it," said Thomas, shaking his head, "though the boldness of the claim almost justifies it."

"We were trembling with love of life and fear of death," said Bernard.

"We were all in whimsical mood," said Miss Lacy.

"But many things take cover behind Miss Lacy's word," said Thomas.

"I think a good many are going to," said Benjamin.

"Why did you not sit down first, Father?" said Anna.

"For the reasons that prevented other people from doing so," said Benjamin, preferring the sacrifice of an honest claim to shyness to facing his daughter's public disbelief.

"Did you know from the first that we were fourteen, Uncle Thomas?" said Anna.

"No, I had just discovered it. I put you out of your misery at once."

"What a good thing there was nothing in it, after all!" said Jenney, in a tone of gratitude.

"You again prove your personal heroism," said Bernard.

"Is there never to be an end of that in people?" said Terence. "I am tired of cringing before their nobility."

"You must not expect to appear a hero," said Claribel. "I cannot manage as much as that for you."

"How do you feel about it, Aunt Jessica?" said Anna. "Have you any sense of relief? Or were you sincere in giving the impression that you thought there was nothing in it?"

"I have a faint feeling of relief," said Jessica, with simple honesty, "but I am not proud of myself for having it."

"So Aunt Jessica is not so far above other people, after all," said Anna, looking round.

"What an odd deduction!" said Esmond.

"I wish it were the right one," said Terence. "I do not like cutting such a sorry figure beside my mother."

"Well, a mother is a person you should be able to look up to, my son," said Thomas.

"But is a son one that she should be obliged to look down on? Of course I am thinking of her and not of myself."

"You are fortunate. Most of us are thinking of her and of ourselves as well," said Benjamin. "A comparison is odious and unavoidable."

"Uncle Thomas was rash in putting his family to the test," said Esmond.

"Well, our family did not come out any better," said Anna.

"No, but he might be less concerned with that."

"I am glad that Bernard and Esmond both put their own lives first," said Terence.

"We all did that," said Anna. "But I suppose women are allowed to do such things."

"Think of the difference between what Aunt Jessica did, and what it was permitted her to do," said Bernard.

"I think it was unmanly of Father to expose her to public trial," said Terence. "Suppose she had not come out so nobly?"

"You see how well I knew her," said Thomas.

"Will you find it possible to settle down amongst such a bevy of strangers?" said Tullia to Florence, as if the other subject were exhausted for her.

"I shall get used to it. I shall have to. I have no home but Aunt Emma's."

"You will show the kind of courage that is the hardest," said Terence. "We have all missed the chance of showing the other kind, and it would have had so many witnesses. The worst of the first is that it never has any."

"Did you find your morning with Reuben what you wanted, Terence?" said Benjamin, going as far as he would go, in enquiring after his son's education.

"Yes, I did, thank you, Uncle."

"You spent most of it out of doors, didn't you?" said Anna.

"Yes, that was what I wanted."

"I hope Reuben passed the time more profitably."

"I hope so. He should be learning independence."

"It strikes me that you assume he has learnt it."

"That is the modern method of training. Trust a boy, and he will be worthy of trust. Whatever attribute you assign to him, turns out to be his. You really assign it."

"It is a pleasant method for the teacher," said Anna.

"Yes, but a teacher should enjoy his work. If he does not, he is not a born teacher."

"Terence's teaching is his own affair, my daughter," said Benjamin.

"Oh, it is mine too, Father. I am not going to be deprived of all part and parcel in Reuben, because he is having his lessons in another house. I have not brought him up from babyhood for that."

"It is Jenney who has performed that office for him," said Esmond.

"Well, she is to be allowed to take a little interest in him too."

"I think there is much in what Anna says," said Sukey. "And I am sure both Terence and Reuben agree."

"Yes, I like as many apron-strings as I can get, Aunt Sukey," said Reuben. "I have not had the chance of being the ordinary embarrassed boy. And I daresay it is not much loss for me or other people."

"We see the result of Terence's method," said Bernard. "Reuben has made a great advance."

"He always talked like a book," said Anna.

"My cousin, Anna, would pin me to a desk," said Terence.

"I only assumed that your choosing to be a tutor had mapped out that course for you."

"Did I really choose to be it? Then what injustice people do me!"

"Teaching by default," said Miss Lacy, with a musing air; "I have never tried that method."

"Well, you could hardly stay at home, by way of undertaking two children's education," said Anna.

"Could I not? I wonder," said Miss Lacy, in independent consideration.

"These new ideas of teaching are an eye-opener to me," said Anna.

"Are you a person who does useful things?" said Tullia to Florence.

"I cannot do much that is any good," said the latter.

"We can't all help the world in a workaday way," said Miss Lacy, acquiescent in owning a relative who did not earn her support. "Some of us must depend on other people. And after all, it shows trust; it shows a belief in other people's powers; it argues a certain generosity. Oh, we can underestimate the qualities of the dependent. We must not sweep people aside, because they toil not, neither do they spin."

"It sounds discreditable to belong to the lilies of the field," said Tullia.

"You are mistaken," said Esmond.

"It is the right company for some of us," said Thomas, looking at his daughter.

"I am worried about our rising from the table," said Terence. "Is it the person who *gets up* last, who dies in a short time? Suppose Mother's sacrifice has been in vain, and we are all once more in danger?"

"I ought to have thought of our being thirteen," said Jessica. "It was foolish to forget the superstition."

"Was it the action of a homicide or suicide?" said Terence. "I think you have no choice but to make it the latter."

"Well, I can do so, my son. I will stay in my seat until you have all left yours."

"One, two, three, go!" said Thomas, rising at the last word and looking round the table.

"Dear me, I wonder we were not all startled into jumping higher than we did," said Miss Lacy, giving the explanation of such action on her part.

"We are *fourteen* at the table," said Tullia, lifting her shoulders and speaking with a sigh.

"I wish I could realise it," said Terence. "It would save me so much."

"It is all right, Florence, my dear," said Jessica, smiling. "We are really fourteen."

"It is all this wretched uncertainty," said her son.

"Can't we any of us count?" said Anna.

"I am glad that Aunt Jessica and Aunt Sukey are not both facing death," said Bernard. "It would be an overwhelming state of affairs in a family."

"Death has a way of running in families," said Thomas.

"If we were immortal, we should begin to complain of that," said Miss Lacy.

"No, I think that is an error, though a usual one," said Benjamin.

"It is odd that it should be so common," said Thomas, "when we conceive the highest beings of our imagination, such as gods and angels, as immortal."

"We say it to comfort ourselves," said Terence. "We condemn everlasting life, to enable us to face a limited one. We must have something to help us to bear it."

Jessica rose to end the talk, not so much because it was

uttered too low for her ears, as because when this was so, she mistrusted its nature.

"I must go upstairs and give an eye to the children."

"I will go too," said Terence. "I shall be in constant attendance on my mother, in atonement for rating my life above hers."

"In public too," said Anna.

"Well, my atonement will also be public. And of course everyone would do it in private. Acts of preferring other people's lives to your own are always done publicly. People don't yield belts and boats to women behind the scenes. Drowned heroes have been seen for the last time in the act of relinquishing them. *Seen* doing it; that is the point. And captains stand in a prominent part of their ships, to go down with them, and sometimes in full uniform. But my public behaviour was on a level with my private, and that is too low a standard. People could only sympathise with it in their hearts, and that means openly condemning it."

"What is that noise?" said Jessica, as they approached the schoolroom.

"The sound of family strife," said Terence.

His mother hastily opened the door.

"You are not fighting, are you?" she said, with a hopefulness in the face of circumstances, that was hardly characteristic.

The combatants fell apart, startled by discovery, but mastered by their passions. Their eyes, uncertain on their mother and smouldering on each other, ranged to and fro.

"What is it all about?" said Jessica.

Her children appeared to be at a loss, a truer impression of their state of mind than she knew.

"We pulled the wish-bone," said Dora.

"We feel we know the whole," said Terence.

"And did you both want the winning side?" said Jessica. "You must have known that only one could have it. That is the point of pulling it."

Julius and Dora exchanged a glance, this time of the fellow-feeling of the misunderstood.

"Julius, you should never fight with a girl, and one younger than yourself. And, Dora, a little sister should set her brother an example. You both understand me, don't you?"

"Yes," said the children, discerning no injustice in the differentiation, and therefore untroubled by it.

"And here is Father, come to see that you have been quarrelling," said Jessica, as if this aggravated the position, as the culprits felt it did.

"Well, what have you to say for yourselves?" said Thomas, in a grave tone.

The children met each other's eyes in sympathy. Julius had unfairly twisted the bone, but confession would have startled and embarrassed his sister, and added to their list of unmentionable memories.

"Well, I am sure you are both sorry now," said Jessica, wiser for occasions when she had tried to exact this statement. So we won't talk any more about it. Indeed, I think the less said about it, the better."

Julius and Dora wondered, not for the first time, what had led to this fortunate method of winding up a painful situation, and also wondered if circumstances ever arose that were entirely unmentionable.

"And why have you not eaten your pudding?" said their mother, believing herself to be broaching a different subject.

"Because the matter no longer under discussion supervened," said Terence.

"Well, you had better have it for tea," said Jessica. "It is as good cold as hot. And just now it would remind you too much of what is better forgotten."

"Mother and the pudding seem to have something in common," said Thomas, causing some mirth.

"And perhaps you will think, when you eat it, of the reason for your having it at such a different time."

"Between the pair of them, there is no escape," said Terence.

"And now you had better run out into the air," said Jessica, putting a hint of reproach into her recommendation of a wholesome atmosphere. "And I hope that cobwebs of all kinds will be blown away."

The children joined hands and ran out of the room, Jessica smiling after them. They walked to the rock with the even steps natural to an errand that went without saying, swinging each other's hands in unspoken amity. It did not occur to them to discuss the ethics of the situation. The guilt was of a kind that might have belonged to either; neither would have felt any shame in incurring it; they had no condemnation of it and little interest in it.

"O great and good and powerful god, Chung," prayed Dora, "we beseech thee to pardon the evil passions that assailed us and overcame our strength."

"Me twisting the bone," said Julius, with a nudge of reminder.

"And to pardon this thy servant, in that he perverted justice and yielded to the lust of desire," continued Dora, in quite unretributive tones, "and to guide us both into the way of righteousness and peace. For Sung Li's sake, amen."

"For Sung Li's sake, amen. We ought to do something for Chung now, so as not to be always asking things and doing nothing," said Julius, looking about him, and suddenly standing transfixed as though by an incredible sight. "There is Reuben watching us! As if he had a part in our mysteries! Our service in our temple is no longer private to ourselves."

Reuben was standing with his eyes upon them, and a face expressive of wonder, interest, and the feelings called for by an occasion of worship.

"What are you doing, intruding upon the hidden and sacred orgies?" said Julius, striking an attitude and employing tones of rhetoric, while Dora accepted the occasion for masculine initiative. "Who are you, that you should break in upon things alien to your common clay? Away, you of the peering eyes and the straying mind. Seek fitter objects for your prying."

"I am not prying. I only came the same way as you did. Aunt Jessica told me to follow you. How could I know there was anything secret going on by this rock?"

"The great voice broods over it, and the mighty whispers surround it," said Dora, in stern rejoinder.

"Are you about to withdraw your steps, or are we to seek strength from the god to assail you?" said Julius, maintaining his threatening posture. "Strength will descend on us in the needed measure."

"I can go, if you want me to; but couldn't I be a humbler kind of worshipper? There are different grades of service."

Julius looked at his sister at this evidence of humility and understanding.

"Only the two chosen of the god minister in the temple of the most high," he said in a wavering tone.

"But couldn't I be a sort of servitor?"

Dora and Julius met each other's eyes, and both fell on their knees.

"Will the god receive the lame and halt attendance of this stray suppliant?" said Dora.

"If so, let him gird his loins and attend humbly in the seat of the lowly," said Julius, turning his head and makng a sign of injunction.

Reuben drew nearer and knelt behind the pair, and the three, as if at a signal, bowed their heads and moved their hands in unison.

"O great and good and powerful god, Chung, graciously accept this our lowly kinsman as a servitor in thy temple. For great is his need of thy guidance and the teaching of thy word. Lighten his affliction, and grant him the heart of the believer. For Sung Li's sake, amen."

"And if you want to make a private intercession, you may

continue on your knees for one swift moment," said Julius, rising and casting a look in his cousin. "But take heed that your words be brief, and that you do not importune the god, or admit any thought or word of the scorner."

"O great and good and powerful god, Chung," muttered Reuben, "grant that I may grow up into an absolutely normal man. And grant me the favour and the friendship of thy servant, Terence. For Sung Li's sake, amen."

He rose and followed his cousins, with the feeling that he had after stirring a wish into the Christmas pudding, that if there were anything in these problematic forces, they could now only operate in his favour.

CHAPTER VII

"WELL, YOU LOOK rather under the weight of things," said Anna, encountering Terence in his hall, on her way to her aunt. "Has anything come upon you?"

"Only the displeasure of Aunt Sukey."

"And is not that enough?"

"Well, it does not seem to count much any longer."

"What is the reason of it?"

"We do not sufficiently attend upon her, or expend enough feeling upon her approaching end."

"Well, I must say I don't think she does get much sympathy on that score. And it does constitute a real claim. It is a lonely business, waiting to be translated to another sphere."

"It is a very long one," said Terence.

"And does that make it better for her?"

"Well, she seems to like her life to be prolonged."

"I don't think I should in her place."

"It shows how much more grasp I have of her mind. Experience has done something for us. But it has destroyed our natural feeling, and now we have to fabricate it, and she is a judge of the real thing."

"Yes, I should say her tastes are for the genuine. And I think she must often wish the end would come. This waiting on the brink of the abyss can't have much to recommend it."

"Well, it is so very like ordinary life," said Terence.

"Oh, make no mistake, it bears very little resemblance to it. How would you like to get up in the morning, without knowing whether you were to go to bed at night? It is a situation that must soon pall."

"It seems to keep its vitality."

"It may be a joke to you. It is not to her."

"It was so little of one to me, that it deadened my sensibilities. I have become a different man."

"It can hardly work in that way with her. She must remain alive to the dangers of her place."

"It is no good to try to work on my feelings. I told you they were dead."

"I am glad I have not become entirely insensitive."

"You have not had time. There would be no excuse for it. I should be very much shocked if it happened so soon."

"Well, you shock me a thought on your own account now and again."

Anna knew no other method of approach, and gave her cousin no idea that she was putting forth her appeal. She thought that holding her own exalted her, and had no suspicion that people might tire of disagreement.

"It is not kind to say such things, when I live in a shadowed home," said Terence.

"That hardly matters, if the shadow has ceased to make an impression."

"But that is a sad thing to happen to a highly evolved creature."

"I am content with my lower state, if it allows of my being of some use to someone in need."

"I should not have thought you were a noble character," said Terence, looking into Anna's face.

"Neither should I; I mean, I do think that being with Aunt Sukey has brought out something in me that I did not know was there. Brought it to the surface, I suppose. Not that you need to be so exalted, to have a little ordinary compassion."

"Mine was not ordinary when I was able to give it."

"And I daresay mine is," said Anna, in resigned acceptance. "But that will not matter, if it can hold to life. Workaday qualities may be the best in the end. Things can be too ethereal to last."

"But it is nice to think that my qualities were of that kind. I should dislike to be a person who would wear well."

"That happens to be my precise ambition," said Anna.

Sukey came slowly across the hall, stooping more than usual over her stick, her face at once flushed and drawn, and her eyes, bent on the floor, very bright.

"Anna, my dear, have you come to be with your cousins, or to spend an hour with me? I don't know which was in your mind, but if it was the latter, you must come to me at once, or my need of you will be past. I have had some work to do this morning; and that is no longer the right thing for me, and my energy is nearly spent."

"I have come to be with you," said Anna, turning and making a scrambling way through the hall. "I was detained by a young man who seems to lie in wait for the unwary, and was involved in an argument before I knew where I was."

"I have never known a boy with so much spare time," said Sukey, as they went upstairs.

"His mornings are supposed to be bestowed on Reuben. I don't pretend to know what his method is. Reuben has lost his heart to him; that is clear, though of course he thinks it is not."

Anna was more fortunate than her brother in that no one suspected her similar case. She had less difficulty in disguising her feelings than revealing them, and her secrets were her own.

"Well, I have had a duty to do to-day," said Sukey, as she came to her chair. "It seems strange that I should be giving my mind to this world's goods, when I shall so soon be unconscious of them. But it seems they are still mine, for me to say how they are to go when I am gone. I still have that little power, and have no choice but to use it. So every stage of life brings its own duties, even the last."

"I don't know why you are always so sure that you are at the end of things," said Anna.

"Something tells me that I am, something that has

spoken to me very plainly in the last days. So I must turn my attention to making things better for others, when I have left them. It sounds a wholesome duty, but it is late for me to discipline myself."

"I should not think it is very good for you either."

"Well, that hardly matters at this stage. Nothing can be good for me in that sense any more. But I have a confession to make, that may strike you as a strange one. You must make it easy for me, as I am not used to playing such a part. It is no such dark and dreadful thing; you need not look frightened, my dear; it is only that I was led by weariness and weakness to make a pretence of doing what it is not in me to do. Many people have done it, in the last days of suffering and sorrow, yes, and disappointment in the poor human nature that they share."

"Is it necessary for you to trouble about it?" said Anna.

"Yes, I owe it to my sister, the last debt of all others to leave unpaid. I had left what I had, to her for her life, and at her death to her children. Your father has more in proportion to his needs, and I have made demands on her family; and those did not count the less, that they had been found too much."

"I suppose they count at once less and more," said her niece.

"That may be so, but they must count to the full. And I could not bring myself to let them. My feet faltered even on that open path. I pretended that I was going to destroy my will, and make one in favour of you. It was a poor reward for your kindness to me, to involve your name in such sorriness. But you see your very kindness gave colour to the scheme. I wanted my revenge for the little neglects, that loom so large to a sick mind. I copied the will and altered the names, and went through the form of signing it and having it witnessed. My sister helped me; she could not think of herself; we neither of us thought of it as possible. And I was to destroy the first will, and leave this one to take effect. But the old one is in the desk, where it has always been.

The key of the drawer is here. And I want you to remember it is there, and that the second is destroyed, if any question should arise, as my sister will only want to follow the truth. You might take this new one and burn it for me; this fire is getting low, and I am tired of my sorry part. I get more tired by my own weakness and littleness than by anything else. You will read me to sleep, and when I wake, we will not talk of it. And some time I will tell my sister the truth."

Anna read aloud, in the voice that had more of the family tones, when she read than when she spoke. The succession of sentences seemed to control it and hold its harshness down. Sukey listened with her eyes closed, and gave no sign of the moment when she slept. Anna read until the sleep was sound, and then closed the book and rose to go, taking the scroll from the table. It seemed as if Sukey knew what she did, for her face settled into youth and calm. Anna looked at her and looked again; stood as if she hardly knew where she was; approached her and touched her hand and her face; made a movement to the desk, and drew back and glanced round the room, as if to make sure she was alone. Then she went to the desk and sat down, with her hands lightly playing on its board; and without breaking the movement, unlocked the drawer and exchanged the scrolls and closed it; and sat with the older scroll in her hands and her eyes gazing before her, as it might be in the vacancy of shock. Then she locked the drawer and left the room, carrying the scroll openly in her hand, and with her rapid, hurrying step sounding as usual. She seemed prepared to encounter anyone and give an account of what she did. She walked to the gate in the same manner, glancing about in readiness to exchange a greeting, but when she was out of sight, quickened her pace and walked swiftly to her home.

The drawing-room at that hour was deserted, and she took the will to the fire and burned it, showing neither furtiveness nor haste. Her aunt had given her directions, and she was fulfilling them. Her word was ready for anyone who asked for it. When it was done, and she found herself still alone, she disposed of the ashes and sat down with a book. She still maintained her natural air; she might have been acting to herself; Anna remembered that walls have ears and eyes.

When her father entered, she looked up in her usual manner.

"So you are at home, my daughter. Did you see your aunt?"

"Yes, she was in a rather disturbed mood. Something had happened to upset her, and I had to read her to sleep. I did not find it a compliment to be used as a soporific; but I was efficacious, and then I could only come away. I don't know what the trouble was."

"Had I better go to her, as usual?"

"It can do no harm, and it might do good. If she is still asleep, you can leave her. We might go together, and go for a walk, if you can do nothing. I should like to know how she is, myself. I confess she is a person who has laid her hold upon me. I should be most uplifted, if we could set her on her feet again. I wish I had known the woman she was, when there was no cloud hanging over her."

"The way she lives under it, shows the woman she is. It is a great thing to show the supreme courage through every hour of each day. We cannot measure it."

"It is certainly not estimated in the household where she lives. Making every allowance for the effect of time, we can only say that."

"It must be easy to forget that time does not blunt it for her," said Benjamin.

"Well, it is certainly forgotten."

"You have risen to this demand, my daughter. She has found you of help in her time of need. I would have asked nothing better than to have a child of mine do that for her."

"You speak as if I were not always equal to the claims of life," said Anna, with a little laugh. "Oh, my life has had its problems. And Aunt Sukey's are not the only ones that people get used to, though mine do not compare with hers. People can see things so often, that they see them no longer."

"The house has rather a strange look," said Benjamin, as they approached it.

"It does look as if it had forgotten the world," said Anna, proceeding at her usual pace. "And it usually looks as if it remembered it in its own way. That is what it does, I think."

"Are not the blinds down?" said her father.

"Some of them are; yes. All of them, I believe. It gives almost a sinister impression. I hope Aunt Sukey has not insisted on a rehearsal of her coming end. She was rather in a mood to give an object lesson to the household. And I don't know that one would come amiss."

Benjamin walked on, as if he had not heard, indeed had hardly done so. Jessica came into the hall to meet him, and took his hands in hers.

"Benjamin, she has left us. It has come at last. It has been coming for so long, that we forgot that each day was bringing it. Our beautiful sister! It is hard to understand why her life should have gone as it did."

"Good heavens! And I was joking about it a moment ago," said Anna, in a smothered tone. "Well, it is true that in the midst of life we are in death. And with Aunt Sukey it seemed to be the other way round. In the face of death she was so full of life. Well, my first real, personal interest is soon over."

"Was it sudden at the end?" said Benjamin.

"As far as we can see, it happened while she slept. We found her lying in her chair, as if she were asleep. They thought that the end might come in a moment, and I often prayed that it would. She has had that piece of good fortune."

"And does not know that she had it," muttered Anna. "That would happen to Aunt Sukey."

"What would she have done without you, Jessica?" said Benjamin.

"Better if she had not had so much of me. It is true that we get used to anything, and it was a sad truth for Sukey. I am thankful that she had you and Anna in her last days, those last days that were with us so long, and were with her always. Anna, how did she seem, when you were with her? You were the last person who saw her alive. Was she as well as usual? Did she seem herself?"

"In the sense that she was in a way especially herself, when she had been disturbed. Something had happened to upset her. And that seemed to bring out the essence of her, if that is clear. In a way I think she throve on it, if you know what I mean, and if it is not callous to speak the truth. I never know how to wrap things up in words. I had never seen her more the especial person that she was." Anna's voice shook and came with a sound of tears. "She seemed to be especially strong and independent, when things had gone against her, or she thought they had. It was hard to distinguish between the truth and her impression of it. It was real to her, and I could only see it through her eyes. If I was ever disloyal to anyone else, I don't think I can be blamed for it. I did not always know what line to take."

"I am thankful that you did just that. I am thankful for any help that you gave her. We shall always be grateful to you," said Jessica. "But what of her bodily state? Did she seem well or ill?"

"Well at first, and almost energetic, as if she were wrought up by something. But that mood passed and she settled down. She had been burning some papers, and that seemed to be a weight off her mind. She asked me to read her to sleep, and I did as she asked, though I never find that a flattering request, and I had come, wanting to talk to her. I read as smoothly as I could, and when she fell asleep, I crept away. I had done it before, though I never thought I should do it in our last hour together. I had no idea that I should never see her again."

"Of course you had not," said Thomas, coming to their side. "It is one of our few protections in life, that we cannot foretell the future."

"From life, I should say," said Anna, seeming to try to speak like herself.

"Anna had no thought that Sukey was more ill than usual," said Benjamin. "She said that something had been amiss, and that her aunt was unsettled by it. But we thought she would wake and welcome my visit, and so came back to the house."

"And had the shock of a lifetime when we saw the blinds drawn," said Anna. "At least Father had. I did not realise what they meant, and even made some jest about them, which was a breach of convention even for me. I find myself going hot and cold when I think of it."

"We could not spare you there," said Thomas. "We did not expect you so soon. A message would soon have gone to you."

"Who had the real shock?" said Benjamin.

"My Tullia," said Thomas. "She took some message to her aunt, and found her, as she thought, asleep; and did not escape without seeing the truth. She will take some time to recover. Her brother is with her."

"Poor children!" said Jessica. "A dark thread has been woven into the pattern of their youth."

"It was right to leave her to sleep, wasn't it?" said Anna, in an almost wistful tone. "Waking a person is never a good thing. I did not think of telling anyone that she was there alone."

"You were right in all that you did," said Thomas. "And you were able to do something. We could find it in our heart to envy you."

"Yes, I am fortunate there," said his niece. "It was a piece of good luck that will last me for my life. And it will have to, as I don't see that I shall ever have any other. I see I have reason to be grateful."

Tullia came into the hall with Terence, walking with her

head high and her expression tense, and taking her stand by a pillar, leaned against it.

"Poor Tullia! Things fell hard on you," said Anna. "And without anything to balance the scale. You did not strike an easy corner."

"I suppose she should not have been left alone," said Jessica. "I mean my Sukey."

"That was accepted at one time," said Thomas. "But the months went by and deadened the sense of risk. An end to daily precautions must always come."

"So I am a sort of culprit after all," said his niece. "I did not think of watching over her sleep. I knew she was left alone at night."

"Her maid slept next door," said Jessica. "She would not have anyone sleeping in the room. If you followed the custom of the house, it was all you could do. It is indeed not for us to ask any more. And perhaps the watching was done for us. She went without pain, and she will never know it again. We cannot say it of ourselves."

"She steered a hard course, and she steered it alone," said Thomas. "We may all come to doing that. But there is no greater good fortune than sudden death."

"Father refuses to feel remorse," said Terence. "And he does not see any direct way of avoiding it. I wonder if a decent family ever had more ground for it."

"Why should Father feel it more than anyone else?" said Tullia, in a faint tone.

"I could not say a harsh thing on this occasion. And I am engaged with my own share of it. I cannot bear not having been a better nephew. Now I have that burden to carry for the rest of my days."

Tullia gave a fleeting smile and moved her hand towards her heart.

"You have not inherited Aunt Sukey's weakness, have you? If you have, I shall fail as a brother. You have an example in my failure of Aunt Sukey. I have not the manliness in me, that is tender to feeble things. I should have been born in a changeling world."

"Well, you were not," said Anna, looking about her, as if surveying a different one. "And this one has very little place for changelings, as far as I can see."

"I don't think you would see any further," said Terence.

"Now what does that mean? Something that I cannot take as a compliment, I make no doubt."

"It is hard on you to be involved in this turmoil of feeling," said Tullia, "when you had only known Aunt Sukey for a few months."

"I had come to appreciate her," said Anna, brusquely. "It was long enough for that, or I found it so."

"Perhaps it was not too long for it."

"Well, have it like that, if you will. Let us say that it was just the right time."

"Anna did well for her," said Thomas. "There is often a place for a stranger in a familiar world. She gave what she had to give, without weariness or strain, and that was what was needed."

"I had got a little beyond the stage of feeling a stranger," said his niece.

"We had ceased to be able to do it," went on Thomas. "We are not blind to the truth."

"It is unusual to face a thing like that," said Terence. "There is something strange about us as a family."

"Anna would have come to feel as we did," said Tullia.

"Well, I had not reached that stage," said her cousin. "And I can't imagine either myself or my father coming near to it. You can't assume that people would always react as you do."

"I have found it a safe assumption," said Tullia, in a languid tone. "Making the necessary allowances, of course."

"Then you must lack perception or comprehension or experience or something."

Tullia laughed, as if she found it odd that Anna should respond in this equal manner.

"What is the joke?" said her cousin.

Tullia gave another little laugh.

"I am glad it is an occasion for amusement," said Anna. "I should not have thought it was, myself."

"My Tullia cannot be herself to-day," said Thomas.

"No, poor thing, she had rough luck," said Anna. "But we have not any of us done too well."

"Her indifference to her aunt did not stand her in much stead," said Thomas, stroking his daughter's hair.

"Well, I am prepared to believe it is assumed," said Anna. "And I shall feel a good deal better towards her, if it is. I know people are supposed to disguise their feelings, but I never know why it is a natural ambition to be without them."

"One is not without them, because they are one's own affair," said Tullia.

"We should not think of them as different from other people's," said Jessica. "They may be our own, but they are not peculiar to ourselves."

"I hope that is true," said Terence. "It seems to give us less reason to be ashamed."

"Well, one life is over," said Thomas. "Our own will come to the same pass. Things go from one generation to another. We cannot expect to check their course."

"We are learning to leave Aunt Sukey's death behind," said Terence. "Or anyhow Father is teaching us."

"The children are coming downstairs," said Anna. "Are they to know or not to know? Is it to be talked about before them, or not? I can hear that Reuben is with them. I will accept any decision."

"Eventually it must strike them that Aunt Sukey is no longer amongst us," said Terence.

Miss Lacy came forward in front of the children, her eyes fixed on Jessica's face in mute question.

"Yes, the simple truth, Miss Lacy," said the latter, in a quiet tone.

Miss Lacy drew back to allow the mother the initiative, and Jessica was not at a loss.

"My little ones," she said, stooping towards the children, "I must tell you something that is both sad and happy. Aunt Sukey has gone away from us, but she is near to us all the while. We grieve for ourselves, but we do not grieve for her."

"Is she dead?" said Dora, at once.

"She is what we call dead, but we know it is not true, while we say it. She is more alive than she has ever been."

"She hasn't been quite as much alive as other people for a long time, has she?" said Julius, speaking to cover a smile that he could not explain or control.

"No, she has been ill and weak. But now she has a fuller life to make up for it."

"Won't she ever be in her room any more?" said Dora, in a slightly unsteady tone.

"Not so that we can see her. But we shall feel that she is there."

"Then will you keep the room for her?"

"She would like us to use it for ourselves, but we shall always think of it as hers."

"Why tell them that anything has happened at all?" said Tullia to her brother.

"I suppose for fear they should notice her absence, and make erroneous deductions."

"Is she buried already?" said Julius.

"No, not yet," said his mother. "But we need not think about that. We must just feel that her spirit is free."

"She was tired of this house, wasn't she?" said Julius. "She said she was tired of everything."

"It is really a merciful release," said Dora.

"Well, we can feel it is best for her," said Jessica, in a slightly different manner.

"Shall we know when she is buried?" said Julius.

"Well, there will be a funeral, of course. You are too young to go to it. But you will be able to put some flowers on her grave. Perhaps you would like to keep some always there."

Dora and Julius looked at each other, foreseeing a tax on their supplies for sacrifice.

"It would be better to grow some roots," said Dora.

"Yes, that would be nicer still," said her mother. "The gardener will give you some, and you can plant them yourselves."

"I daresay we can pick them sometimes," said Julius, in a low tone.

"It would be better to leave them for Aunt Sukey," said Jessica. "You mean them for her, don't you?"

"He meant the dead ones," said Dora, raising her eyes. "Flowers don't grow so well, if those are left. He didn't know if you might pick anything from graves."

"I think you may take care of the plants. Aunt Sukey would like you to do that. That is not the same as picking flowers for yourselves."

"It would be all right to use them for a sacred purpose," said Julius, in a rapid undertone.

"And now you will not go for a walk to-day," said Jessica, speaking as if this daily exercise maintained life on a festive level. "You will just have a quiet hour in the garden. Here is Reuben to go with you. It will be nice for you to be together."

"And now what messages have to be taken?" said Miss Lacy.

"None that we may give to you, Miss Lacy," said Thomas. "We must not burden you with them."

"What messages have to be taken?" said Miss Lacy, in the same manner.

"Miss Lacy can help us, if she will," said Jessica. "There are messages, as she knows. She can be of great use, if she will be so kind."

"And she will be," said Miss Lacy. "Or rather she will be not kind at all, but an ordinary family friend."

Some messages were written and given to Miss Lacy,

and others put aside for Terence; and Miss Lacy quietly gathered them all into her hands and went.

"Why is it nice for us to be together?" said Julius, as they reached the garden. "For some religious reason?"

"So that we can share our feelings," said Dora, in an absent tone. "Why do we nearly laugh, when people tell us that someone has died?"

Her companions could not tell her, though they had found themselves under the same compulsion.

"It is not as if we were amused."

"And that is where it is not fair on us," said Julius. "Our innocent action would be misinterpreted."

"We were not seen so it does not matter," said his sister.

"Do you really mind that Aunt Sukey is dead?" said Julius.

"Not so that it makes any real difference. Of course I should choose for her to be alive. No one would condemn another person to death."

"Terence doesn't believe that people live after they are dead," said Reuben. "I know it from something he said."

"You should not repeat things, that are just let fall by accident," said Dora. "And we never talk about Terence's opinions about those things. We know he is under a sad error, and will one day know it. And it is not fair to tell people the one thing that is sad about him."

"Will it be better or worse for us, now that Aunt Sukey is dead?" said Julius.

"You mean that Mother will have more time for us," said Dora. "But I hardly think she will, because she hasn't had enough for Father, and will have to give it all to him. And I don't think she would ever supervise us much. She would always think of other things."

"I think I would as soon have Jenney as a mother," said Reuben.

"I daresay it would be as good," said Dora. "And there would be less painfulness over things. I should not think that Jenney ever makes that. But there is nothing to complain of about our mother, and it would not do to have no one."

"Perhaps Father and Miss Lacy would be enough," said Julius.

"I am not sure that they would," said his sister. "It wouldn't do for things to be too much without seriousness. We might be ill or in trouble or get imprisoned; and Father and Miss Lacy and even Terence might not even come to see us. It would not do only to be thought about light-heartedly."

"Do you suppose we are more likely to die, because of Aunt Sukey?" said Julius. "Those things do run in families."

"Aunt Sukey died of her illness."

"That is what I meant. We might inherit it."

"I don't think children ever have illnesses like that. I think their hearts are always sound. But we will cast our burden on Chung, and go our way."

Dora sank on her knees before the rock, and Julius knelt by her. Reuben stood aside, waiting for the word to join them.

"O great and good and powerful god, Chung, deliver us from any danger that besets us from the illness of our late kinswoman. For we would walk long upon the paths of this earth. Therefore save us from the threat of the valley of the shadow. For Sung Li's sake, amen."

"A word for Aunt Sukey's soul, so as not to intercede only for ourselves," said Julius.

"And have a care, O god, for the soul of thine erring handmaid. Bear in mind that the trials were great, that beset her, and that though her spirit was willing, the flesh was weak. For Sung Li's sake, amen."

As they rose from their knees, Reuben disappeared into the bushes, feeling he could bear no part in this fellowship. He looked back to see if he was missed, but his cousins were too little concerned with him, to observe his going.

"I don't suppose the cloud will lift until after the funeral," said Julius. "But we need not take much notice of it. We can keep out of doors, and a little preaching and weeping in the house won't make much difference."

Julius was wrong in his forecast, as his mother was even now approaching.

"Where is Reuben?" she said.

Her children could not tell her.

"You have not been unkind to him, have you?"

"No," said the pair, looking surprised.

"We hardly spoke to him," said Julius.

"We did not even see when he went," said Dora, in support of her brother.

"Well, would you like to come and have a little talk about Aunt Sukey? It will be nice to do that, while we still almost feel that she is with us. She has been so much of our life, hasn't she?"

"And after she is buried, we shan't ever be able to speak of her again," said Dora.

"Oh, I always think that is such a sad way of doing things. I shall like to talk about her, just as if she were still one of us. And of course we shall feel that she is."

"But will you be able to do that?" said Julius. "You talk about her now in a different way."

"And people often don't speak of people after they are dead," said Dora. "Miss Lacy had a brother who died, and his name was never mentioned in the house."

"Well, I think that was a great pity," said Jessica. "It would have been better to speak of him whenever he came into their minds. Because they must often have been thinking of him."

"If it is possible to do it," said Julius. "But I don't think it often is. You are not really doing it now. I mean, not like you did, when Aunt Sukey was alive."

Something in his voice recalled that his mother's words had not always been in praise of her sister.

"It might be suitable to make a difference," said Dora, in a mature tone.

"Well, let us just say what we cannot help thinking," said Jessica. "That she was a beautiful and unusual person for us to have in our home, and that we can never replace her."

"People can't ever do that, whatever the dead person is like," said Julius.

"Was she as beautiful as Tullia?" said Dora. "I don't think Father thought she was."

"Well, her face was not young when you knew it. But in a way its experience made it better. We can often read a story in people's faces."

"Was there one in Aunt Sukey's face?"

"Yes, a sad one, I am afraid, the story of wasted gifts and beauty spoiled by suffering," said Jessica, not feeling she was in danger of making too deep an impression. "I don't think anyone could have had a harder thing to bear."

"Did you know about it, when she was alive?" said Dora.

"Yes, but I did not always remember it. But I think she felt that I knew it in my heart."

"If you had said it, other people would have known. It might have been better for her, if they had."

"Well, let that teach you that we should do what we can for each other, while we have the opportunity. When that once goes, we can never recall it."

"But didn't you know that?" said Dora.

"Yes, but I am afraid I was inclined to forget it. You must try to do better than I did."

"Could children do that?" said Julius.

"I hope you will. You have a weak and stumbling person for a mother. You must never think her example is one to follow."

"You are better than anyone else in the house, aren't you?" said Dora.

Jessica was silent, finding that the family standard hardly struck her as a high one.

"I think Uncle Benjamin knew about Aunt Sukey," said Dora. "He didn't mind about her illness making her different. I think he was the only person who didn't. Of course the other people mightn't have known."

"Did Father know?" said Julius.

"Yes, he knew," said Jessica. "He felt it more than he showed."

"It seems really to be better to show things," said Dora. "Even though deep things are supposed to be hidden. They don't seem to be much good, if they are not even seen."

"No real feeling is ever wasted," said her mother.

"But it is wasted for the person it is about," said Julius. "And that is a kind of waste."

"Why isn't it wasted?" said Dora. "It isn't any good to other people."

"Well, I hope you will act on all this wisdom," said Jessica. "I could have left Aunt Sukey to you sometimes, if I had known how much you understood."

"We didn't understand anything until you told us," said Dora.

"I feel I should blame myself for telling you too late."

"Things do seem to be too late, don't they? I think everything does. A person is dead before any of it is any use to her. And it might be a good deal of use in making people different."

"Do you think we were not kind to Aunt Sukey?" said Jessica, unable to repress the question.

"We don't think you weren't," said Julius, "and we know that Anna was kind."

"And Uncle Benjamin seemed to know about her," said Dora; "and the other people couldn't help not knowing. I don't think even Father knew, because he once said it would be a solution, if Aunt Sukey were to go. He said it to Tullia."

"He meant go away on her own life, strong and well again," said Jessica, not feeling it a case for observing the letter of the truth.

"No, he meant if she were to die. You would have known he meant that, if you had been there."

"Well, he said it to Tullia, and not to you or me."

"He did not say it in at all a private way," said Julius. "Not like he sometimes does to Tullia. He knew people would know what he meant."

"That is another thing that shows he didn't know about Aunt Sukey," said Dora. "He would have told Tullia, because he always tells her everything. And I am sure Tullia didn't know."

"No, poor Tullia, I don't think she did," said Jessica. "But it is a good rule never to quote anyone, unless you are sure he would wish it. You may have said things about Aunt Sukey yourselves, that you would not like to hear repeated."

"I think she was a person who did make people do that," said Dora. "But we didn't often talk about her. There wasn't much to say."

"Well, I think you will talk of her now, and think of her, and try to keep your memory of her green."

"Do people like a memory better than a real person?" said Dora.

"I am sure I do not," said her mother. "But when a memory is all we have, we must make the most of it."

"Did Aunt Sukey spend all her money?" said Julius. "Or did she leave any behind?"

"Some of it she spent, of course. And some she gave to me, to help me with the house. I don't know what she has done with the rest."

"I didn't know she was so kind," said Dora.

"So it wasn't really good of you and Father to let her be here," said Julius. "I think he sometimes thought it was. Perhaps he didn't know about that either."

"It certainly was not good of me," said Jessica. "I could not have borne for her to live anywhere else. And I think we see from this talk that it was Aunt Sukey who was good. And that is what I wanted to show you. So you will talk and think of her as the person she really was. And you need not think about other people's ways with her. Just see that your own are the right ones; that will be enough."

"It is not our fault that Aunt Sukey is dead, and that people failed in their duty to her," said Julius, gloomily, as they left their mother. "Children should not be used for the outlet of grown-up people's guilty feelings. What have we to do with their remorse? It is the due reward of their deeds."

Jessica heard the sound of Dora's laugh, and assumed that a childish mood had supervened. She hardly looked as if she had met the relief that her son suggested. Her face was harassed and confused, as if something had complicated her burdens. When Thomas and his elder children approached, she seemed hardly to see them.

"Well, we have a healthy piece of bad news to destroy the sanctity of Aunt Sukey's memory," said Terence. "She will not rule us after death, as she did in life. We shall have our freedom, but we shall pay the price."

"What has happened?" said his mother.

"I feel I cannot tell you."

"Need we talk about it yet?" said Tullia. "Surely we can let an hour pass, before we settle to our material calculations. A person's death should mean something more than an inheritance."

"It should mean as much," said Terence.

"What is the matter?" said Jessica.

"To know all is to forgive all," said her son. "And I do not wish you to forgive Aunt Sukey yet."

"Why must we discuss it?" said Tullia. "It is not a thing that we need put into words."

"That is fortunate," said Thomas, with some grimness, "as we do not seem to be able to."

"I long to thresh it out," said Terence, "but I cannot be the first person to state what it is."

"Has Sukey left her money to Anna?" said Jessica.

There was a pause.

"You know all indeed," said Thomas. "And we shall be grateful to be put in the same position."

"How did you find it out so soon?" said his wife.

"How indeed?" muttered Tullia, raising her shoulders. "Rushing to a dead person's desk and dragging out her personal testament! We do not deserve to find anything to our advantage."

"I am glad of that," said Terence, "because I cannot bear a sense of injustice."

"Did Sukey confide her purpose to you, Jessica?" said Thomas. "And could you not deflect her from it?"

"To tell you the truth, I thought I had done so," said Jessica, almost with a smile. "She was vexed with us on that last day—to-day it is; how strange it seems—and she decided to alter her will, and asked me for my help."

"And you did your best to further her purpose? You are wrong to reproach yourself with lack of attention."

"The old will was made in my favour, and I guessed that the new one was in Anna's. But Sukey had made other wills before, and had always destroyed them. And I felt that she was going to destroy this."

"Mother's thoughts had quite a long run on tangible things," said Terence.

"I even had a feeling," said Jessica, "that if I helped her and recognised her freedom, she would return the sooner to her normal mind. If that was a wrong or unscrupulous course, it seems to have recoiled on us all. But I thought the impulse would die down; I thought it had done so, when I left her. Indeed I thought I could see the reaction taking place. And when Anna spoke of her burning some papers, I assumed it was the new will that she had burned, especially as she had found it a relief. It had happened before, and she had been relieved, poor Sukey!"

"And I suppose it was the other one," said Tullia.

"There was only this one in her desk," said Thomas.

"It seems that she had not worked off her troubles," said

Jessica, in a bewildered manner. "But she was in a natural mood when I left her. I am sure of that."

"The sun went down of her wrath indeed," said Thomas.

A spasm went across his wife's face.

"If she burned the old will," she said in a slow tone, "it was not her own act, not the act of the person she was. She must have done it in delusion or error, or in some weakness that had no meaning."

"Many wills are made in such a way," said Thomas. "It is an evil that has no remedy and no redress."

"It might be said that her feelings took longer to change on that day—to-day," said Jessica, looking more troubled by her sister's experience than by its outcome; "that she might have been slower in altering her mind. But I know that her mood had passed. She did not die in anger with us." She turned away to hide the tears, that seemed to convulse rather than relieve her.

"Aunt Sukey will continue to influence our lives," said Terence.

"Her last mood will do so," said Thomas, putting an arm round his wife. "It was only one hour for her. It is for us that it will alter the future."

"Can anything be done?" said Tullia.

"Nothing, unless Anna recognises the truth of the position, and waives her claim."

"I can make her see how it was," said Jessica, recovering herself, and speaking as if this would be as easy a matter with another, as it would with herself. "The truth of the matter is plain. The mistake can only make her sad for poor Sukey, and anxious to do what she wished."

"It is not quite clear what that was," said Thomas.

"It is to me. I am quite sure of her real mind."

"We will not anticipate trouble," said Tullia. "We seem to have enough without going to meet it."

"So we are people crushed by grief," said Terence. "And people in that state find that they are oddly distracted by trivial things. And the one that is troubling me, is that Anna has earned a little of the money, even if she gives up the whole. And it would be such a pity if she wanted any."

"It will be easy to arrange for her to have some memento of Sukey," said Jessica, in an almost absent tone.

"And I don't think that sort of thing is ever money," said Terence. "People are not provided for as a memento."

"Is the money so much?" said Tullia.

"Enough to make all the difference to a poor man with a family," said Thomas.

"Then it would make a disproportionate difference to Anna."

"Of course it would," said Terence. "Aunt Sukey could not have meant that. No one who was giving up everything herself, could want to give so much to someone else. Divided amongst a family, it would not seem too much to be borne."

"And why did she not leave the money to Uncle Benjamin, if she wished to benefit his family?" said Tullia.

"That is another reason against a decision to leave it to Anna," said her mother.

"Perhaps she burnt the wrong will by mistake."

"I think that is probably the truth," said Jessica. "She had the two wills in her hands together, and got them confused in her weakness. How I wish I could talk to her about it! We have talked of everything for fifty years. I can hardly believe that it is over."

"Perhaps this might be a subject to be avoided," said Terence.

"No, she was always open about things," said Jessica, looking as if she saw her sister. "She had nothing to conceal in her life. Things were so easily put right between us."

"I only trust this will not be an exception," said Thomas.

"Does Anna know that everything is left to her?" said Tullia.

"No, she went before we discovered it," said Thomas. "Her father was told the fact, but did not dwell on it. He was shaken by his sister's death. He is still in the house."

"We must hope that Anna will also pass it over," said his son. "And the truth should be told him with its accompaniments, as it is those that are to neutralise it. It is a risk for it to be considered by itself. For it is likely that it will recur to him."

"Sukey always wanted her sick fancies forgotten," said Jessica.

"Then it was a mistake to act upon them," said Thomas.

"It was a mistake in every sense," said his wife.

"I see that Father has grave fears," said Terence. "But Anna may perhaps feel that Aunt Sukey's real wishes are sacred."

"Well, she has always posed as being of that mind," said Tullia.

"It was not a pose. That is not fair to her, my dear," said Jessica.

"Would you waive your claim in her placc, Tullia?" said Terence.

"Well, naturally," said his sister, as if this went without saying.

CHAPTER VIII

"WELL, I HAVE a shock for you," said Anna, hurrying in to her family. "I daresay it won't be much to anyone but me. But I have had the bad hour of my life."

"What is it?" said more than one voice.

"Aunt Sukey has departed this life," said Anna, as if with an effort to be nonchalant, but moving her eyelids rapidly. "She was at a low ebb this morning; some family scene had upset her. I always thought that these troubles would hasten her end, and this one achieved it. I read her to sleep and left her. And when Father and I went back, the sleep had proved to be her last."

There was a silence.

"How did they find it out?" said Jenney.

"I suppose they pursued their usual round, and gave her a certain amount of attention. I believe Tullia made the actual discovery."

"Poor Tullia! She is not fit for that sort of thing," said Bernard.

"I don't know if Aunt Sukey was fit to die alone and forgotten. Though it seemed to be accepted that she was."

"Did she die without knowing it?" said Jenney. "What a good thing if she did!"

"We hope she went to sleep and did not wake," said Anna. "I seem to have managed my last office for her well. It was the best that could be done."

"Well, it is better for her," said Jenney.

"Why do people say that, when the worst has happened?" said Bernard. "It would have been better for her to recover."

"Well, but there wasn't any hope of that."

"Then it would have been better to go on for a while as she was. The life she lived was better than none, and it was clear that she thought so. I suppose people want to convince themselves that it is no occasion for grief."

"Well, we had not known her long," said Jenney, as if accepting this standpoint. "I suppose your father is still at the other house."

"He will be following me soon," said Anna. "I think he is rather shaken."

"Oh, I expect he was; I expect he is," said Jenney, turning to the window, as if ready with welcome and relief.

"Who told you?" said Esmond to his sister, appearing still to read.

"The house breathed of it. The blinds were down for one thing. That was a shock when we grasped it. I missed it at first, and Father had to tell me. It was Aunt Jessica who said the actual word."

"Oh, where is Reuben?" said Jenney, picturing the boy alone amongst these influences.

"He went into the garden with the children. He seemed quite himself," said Anna. "The loss will not touch him very nearly."

"What a good thing you were not alone!" said Jenney, recalled to Anna's claims. "I am thankful that your father was with you."

"Yes, I was glad of manly support. And Terence and Uncle Thomas were kind. I think they realised that I was rather hit by the business."

"Did you come home alone?" said Claribel.

"Yes, I purposely drew a veil over the moment of my going. They would have had to offer me an escort, and there was enough claim on the house."

"What was the trouble that brought the climax for Aunt Sukey?" said Esmond, putting the marker in his book where it had been on Anna's entrance.

"Oh, just the question of general indifference and lack

of sympathy. I always thought she had reason on her side there. I never pretended I did not."

"I wondered at that," said Bernard. "I saw things with the eyes of the family, when I was with them; and with Aunt Sukey's, when I was with her. It is the first case I have met of anyone's doing anything else."

"Well, it was a dreary business, steering a solitary course towards the grave. It wasn't a case for putting her on a level with everyone else, and strictly keeping her there. Anyhow I didn't see it as such."

"It wasn't, was it?" said Jenney. "Poor woman, I am sure it was not. And she was a person who had been so much."

"How did she seem when you saw her?" said Bernard.

"As usual, except that she was in rather a bitter mood. She had been burning papers and otherwise wearing herself out. She asked me to read her to sleep; and though I never fancy that office, I performed it, as it was required of me; and I am glad now."

"There is your father coming up the drive," said Jenney. "I wonder what he will have to tell us."

"I hope his object will be our information," said Bernard.

"That does not appear to be the case," said Esmond, as Benjamin went into his study and shut the door.

"Oh, I will go and get him something," said Jenney, starting to her feet.

"I had better go and do something of the sort for myself," said Anna, rising rather heavily from her chair.

"Go and lie down, and I will bring it to you," said Jenney. "You cannot expect to be yourself to-day."

"Does it seem odd that Anna should have the same feelings as other people?" said Esmond to his brother.

Claribel sat up and looked with a smile from one to the other.

"Perhaps it does, that she should have deeper ones," said Bernard.

"You began by being drawn to Aunt Sukey yourself."

"Yes, but she did not give me enough ground for continuing. She simply turned to Anna."

"Not a very frequent choice from this family," said Claribel, in a tentative tone.

"I find myself admiring my sister for sorrowing over Aunt Sukey's death," said Bernard. "A feeling heart beats under her rough exterior."

"That sort of surface seems to be used to cover such things," said Esmond, rising and slouching to the door. "And it is hard to see any other purpose for it."

Claribel laughed and looked at Bernard, but as he lay down on the sofa with a book, followed Esmond from the room.

Presently Cook and Ethel entered, having realised in some way not given to others, that Bernard was alone. They carried a table between them, and having set it in place, appeared to be occupied in adjusting it.

"It has been away for repair," said Ethel, seeming to address the world at large.

"Have you heard of our trouble?" said Bernard.

"We knew that Miss Donne had passed away, sir. The news reached us before Miss Anna came home."

"And you did not tell us?"

"There seemed to be no occasion, sir. Bad news travels fast enough."

"It is only fair to it for you to say so," said Bernard.

"She was a great sufferer," said Ethel, after a pause.

"As will be seen now," said Cook.

"I think it always was," said Bernard.

"That was for them that knew, to say," said Ethel.

"And from what we can hear, she did so," said Cook, seeming to rely on her low tones, to go almost beyond the bound.

"Tell me what you have heard," said Bernard.

Cook and Ethel laid hold of the table and slightly altered its place.

"Have you heard disquieting reports?"

"It was definite, sir," said Ethel.

"Well, then you can repeat it word for word. Have you always heard such things? Or only lately?"

"Since the death, sir."

"But that was this morning. And not many people come to this house from theirs."

"Those that have, have spoken," said Cook.

"So I see. And I wish to hear what they said."

"The things that are known too late, cannot be remedied," said Ethel.

"But they can be described. And I make it clear that they must be."

"Things sound worse in the telling, sir."

"Well, that makes it more worth while."

"It is the story of misunderstanding, sir," said Ethel, turning away, as if this should satisfy her questioner.

"I shall not ask many more times."

Cook and Ethel drew nearer at this threat.

"Her warnings were neglected, sir, and her premonitions of her end not heeded," said Ethel, in a deeper tone.

"But she had had the forebodings for years. People could not spend their lives in thinking about them."

"It was the least they could do," said Cook.

"Well, that is always too much for people," said Bernard.

"The poorest in the land would have done it," said Ethel.

"So I have always heard," said Bernard. "Is it really true?" Cook and Ethel glanced at each other.

"We have not had opportunities of judging," said Ethel.

"Not close ones," said Cook.

"I should really like to know," said Bernard.

But his companions could not help him, and a pause ensued.

"And then to die alone!" said Cook. "Without the sound of a voice or a word."

"But it was a great thing to die in her sleep. You would not wish your death to be a social function."

"There are occasions for the touch of the human hand," said Ethel.

"Passing alone!" said Cook.

"We must all do that," said Bernard.

Cook and Ethel looked at him in surprise, this not being their personal intention.

"They may atone at the funeral," said Cook.

"It is not too late," said Ethel.

"It sounds as if you thought it was," said Bernard.

"I have heard that the simplest arrangements are being made," said Ethel, in an empty tone.

"Well, have you nothing definite to tell me?"

"It is no good to dwell on it, sir."

"It really does not seem to be."

"If thoughts and feelings can do anything, the poor lady has them," said Ethel. "We have always said a word of her from time to time."

"It must be a comfort to have done what you can."

"And Miss Anna has nothing to reproach herself with," said Ethel, including another in the category.

"Nor the master, poor gentleman!" said Cook.

"I liked and admired Miss Donne very much, myself," said Bernard.

"I always say there are different ways of doing everything," said Ethel, in a cordial tone.

There was a pause.

"That table will never be the same again," said Ethel, giving the table a push, as if to fulfil some purpose for it.

Cook laid her hand on it and looked underneath, and Bernard resumed his book, as his part in breaking up the scene.

As Cook and Ethel reached the kitchen, Jenney ran up to them and took the door from their hands.

"You have got the table into place then?"

"Yes," said Ethel. "It will never be the same again."

"That is true of many things," said Cook.

"Who is in the drawing-room?" said Jenney.

"Mr. Bernard by himself," said Ethel, with a sigh as for solitude under the circumstances.

"The days get shorter, don't they?" said Jenney.

"And this is a dark room. I always say it has a kind of oppression. I filled the kettle from the hot tap, Cook."

Cook, informed that the water would soon boil, moved to the stove and resumed her hold on life.

"Poor Miss Donne will never take a cup of tea again," said Ethel as she sat down.

"That is what it means; death," said Cook.

"Have you heard anything about it?" said Jenney, as if vaguely struck by this possibility.

"People have spoken," said Ethel, holding some tea in her spoon and resting her eyes on it. "Words pass from mouth to mouth. It is the only way you can become conversant with things."

Jenney was far from disputing this, and Ethel and Cook proceeded to assist her in the matter, so that she left them in half-an-hour with a satisfied, if serious face.

She entered the drawing-room at the same moment as Benjamin, who had come from his study to join his family. He stood in the doorway with his eyes resting on their faces.

"I see that your hour is over. I am glad it has been a short one. Mine must be longer, in payment for the years behind. I do not expect you to share it."

"Come and sit down and forget it for the time, Father," said Anna, pulling out a chair. "I have not found it so much of a day myself. It is something that it is over. We can't live it again."

"There are others to follow," said Benjamin, remaining where he was. "And there is something that I ought to tell you, before we add this one to the past. It may not seem to be much of a thing, but its meaning will grow. You know that your aunt had money of her own, or you would have known, if you had thought about it. It would not normally make any difference to you."

"It would not, I suppose," said Anna. "If it would, we

might think about it soon enough. People do seem to think about those things. I daresay we are happy in having our feelings uncomplicated by them. I wonder if the other family is as fortunate."

"Someone must face the disadvantage of inheritance," said Esmond. "It sounds as if Aunt Sukey had imposed a share of it on us."

"She has left her money to Anna," said Benjamin, and took the chair that his daughter had set for him.

There was a silence.

"Well, what a rich and rare piece of news!" said Claribel, almost with a scream in her voice. "Those seem to be the only words. And will the disposition take effect? Or will it have to be put aside in favour of the other family?"

"She was supposed to have left the money to Jessica," said Benjamin; "partly in recognition of her service to her, and partly in view of her means being smaller than mine. But it seems that she changed her mind."

"Good heavens!" said Anna. "What a thing to have to face! Well, it shows that my efforts gave satisfaction; that is one thing. It is rather a good thing to think. I confess I do rather like it."

"How much is it?" said Esmond, addressing his father before he thought.

"Some hundreds a year," said Benjamin. "It had accumulated with time. Your aunt did not spend her income in her later years. She hardly had the opportunity. But it helped her sister's household to have what she gave."

"You would not have thought that she made any great contribution, from their attitude towards her," said Anna.

"I would hardly say that," said her father. "I can think of no home that would have done better. I cannot feel that she would have been as well off with us."

"She would have died of displeasure at a much earlier date," said Bernard. "That appears to be what she has done."

"I wonder how soon Father will do it," muttered

Esmond. "The disease seems to be mortal and to run in the family."

"Oh, I don't think she would," said Jenney, in a tone of compunction. "We should have done what we could, and I am sure she would have been satisfied."

"And it would have been almost better than nearly dying of it hundreds of times, and then doing so at last," said Anna.

"It seems that we ought to have had the charge of her, if one of us is taking the reward," said Claribel. "It must seem to the Calderons money easily earned."

"It was not earned at all," said Anna. "Nothing was done to earn it. Aunt Sukey can hardly have thought so. She must have done what she did, for other reasons."

"From motives of affection?" said Esmond.

"Something like that, or because of some feeling of her own."

"Well, I never heard anything like it," said Jenney, as if the truth had just come home to her.

"What have you to say, Bernard?" said Benjamin, his tone revealing that other people's words had not escaped him.

"Well, I was feeling that I had been almost as nice to Aunt Sukey as Anna, perhaps quite as nice, considering the standard of a man. I dont think I mean that I ought to have had the money; I am almost sure that I don't. But I find it difficult to rejoice in others' joy; I never quite see the reason for doing it. And I have never seen it done, so that anyone would notice. People could not have been rejoicing very much."

"You know your Aunt Jessica," said Benjamin.

"Well, if she is rejoicing at the moment," said Claribel, "she proves herself indeed."

"Well, I don't feel much joy yet," said Anna. "It seems a feeling rather foreign to the occasion. I have not exactly found it that kind of day."

"A lifetime will make up for it," said Esmond.

"You do not congratulate your sister?" said Benjamin.

"Oh, of course they do," said Jenney.

"Do you—does she so misunderstand us?" said Bernard. "We have done it in our own way."

"Oh, I understand you," said Anna.

"I can see why Aunt Sukey left you her money," said Bernard. "I almost think you ought to have had it, and that is a great deal to say."

"I don't think I ought to have been left anything. Except perhaps some sort of remembrance. But I can't help what has happened. I don't see why I should have any feeling of guilt. I should have more reason, if Aunt Sukey had been dissatisfied with me, instead of showing herself rather too much the other way."

"You feel it to be that?" said Claribel.

"Well, too much for some people's minds," said Anna. "It is a matter of seeing rather than feeling. Now, Father, settle down and rest. You are as white as a ghost, and we don't want to have you following in Aunt Sukey's wake."

As Benjamin obeyed, his face told its own tale, one of almost incredulous gratification that a child of his did not desire his death.

"Will Anna be rich now?" said Reuben, who had not failed in attention. "Shall we stay in this house, or move to a better one?"

"Hush, hush. We shall stay here, of course," said Jenney.

"How did Father know about Aunt Sukey's will?" said Esmond, addressing no one in particular.

"Your uncle told me before I left his house," said Benjamin. "Your aunt's papers were in her desk. She had told him where to find them."

"And he lost no time in acting on the information," said Bernard. "The scene of her death was also another scene for him. And he does not seem to have disguised it."

"His hopes met a speedy fall," said Esmond, laughing in pure amusement. "It is clear what was the main point to him about the event."

"Heavens, is it?" said Anna. "I am afraid that I shall not be a popular character. But I am used to that in that house. I don't think I have made an appeal to anyone but Aunt Sukey. And as she was the one who appealed to me, it is fair enough. Terence and I meet to cross swords, otherwise words, pretty often; but otherwise my comings and goings take place in an atmosphere of indifference. And I suppose if the feeling remains at that, I shall be fortunate."

"If you gave them the money back, they would be pleased with you," said Reuben.

"No, no, they would not; they would be pleased with the money, and regard it as theirs by right. It is precious little that I should get out of it. They would probably despise me for thinking so little was due to myself."

"I don't think you ought to do that," said Jenney. "It would not be what Miss Donne wished. It would be no good to make a will, if people did not abide by it. And people never do give up anything, do they?"

"The will has caused surprise," said Benjamin to his children. "We must recognise that. Your Aunt Jessica knew that her sister had made it, but believed she had destroyed it and kept an old one in her own favour. It seems that she had done such things before, as a means of relieving her feelings. Her last chapter was indeed a hard and sad one."

"And did she destroy the old will in this case?" said Esmond.

"It appears that she must have done so. She had been burning papers, when Anna saw her, and there was no sign of it in her desk. We can only conclude that she did."

"It might have saved trouble to keep a few odd wills by her for regular use," said Bernard.

"Perhaps she burnt the wrong one by mistake." said Claribel.

"That is what I was going to say," said Anna. "But she was too much mistress of herself for that. I only know that she had been burning something; and whatever it was, it was a weight off her mind. And I was glad she had got to the stage of relief, as she had clearly been in a different one. Poor Aunt Sukey, she ought not to have had that kind of end."

"Neither ought the family who had housed her," said Esmond.

"There was a smell of burning in this house, when I came back for some books," said Reuben.

"It could hardly have carried from Aunt Sukey's room," said Esmond.

"There was a live coal on this rug," said Anna. "It spurted out of the fire. It was a good thing I was here to stop it from smouldering. I had just come back from Aunt Sukey, and could have dispensed with being startled at that moment."

"But you didn't know that she was dead," said Reuben.

"No, but I knew she was ill and exhausted. It gave me a sort of nervous feeling to be with her. It seems that I ought to have guessed more than I did. But I went back with Father, full of faith and hope in the result of my soothing and reading and all of it. It makes me feel foolish now. It did, when I met the family and heard the truth."

"The shock makes you exaggerate things," said Jenney. "Dear me, what a day it has been! Well, it is not all bad news; that is one thing."

"Isn't it?" said Anna, looking at her with her brows drawn. "Oh, you mean the bequest or whatever it is. Well I must say I think the bad news preponderates."

"You are right that it is a bequest," said Esmond. "You will have to meet Aunt Jessica and all of them, in the character of usurper of their dues."

"You seem to take a questionable pleasure in the awkward side of my situation."

"Well, a pure pleasure could only come from being in it himself," said Bernard.

"I wonder what Terence will think," said Reuben. "I

don't think that he will mind as much as the others."

"And surely Aunt Jessica will not mind," said Anna. "If she does, her attitude to things is a strange pose enough."

"Terence never feels like anyone else. I think he will just be amused because people mind."

"Why should there be all this minding?" said Anna, looking perplexed. "They are not so fond of money, are they? I should not have supposed that they would give a thought to that aspect of Aunt Sukey's death."

"Then what actuated our uncle in the course he took, on learning of it?" said Esmond.

"Oh, I expect he had to find out about the business side of things. He would feel he must do the part of a man at such a time. You know what you would feel, yourself."

"We do, now you tell us," said Bernard. "And I am better adapted to the part than I thought. But I don't think it often needs to be done."

"Anna has done a woman's part," said Claribel. "And now she has the human part of accepting the reward."

"I wish you would all stop talking about me, as if I were some kind of criminal," said Anna. "Why am I a worse person than any of you? And why is Uncle Thomas a culprit, because he does something that has to be done, without making any bones about it? It had to be done at some time, and it may have been the best opportunity."

"It was," said Esmond; "it was the first."

"You have not come out so well under the test," said his sister, looking at him. "You have shown yourself as jealous and grudging as could well be. You would rather that I had nothing, than something you did not share. And I did not want it to happen as it has. I should have preferred some remembrance of Aunt Sukey, chosen for me by herself. But I was not asked what I would have. No thought was given to my personal feelings. I don't even know what the inheritance is; I suppose investments or something. Even Reuben could only suggest that I should give it up.

I believe no sister ever had such curmudgeonly brothers. Bernard is the best of you."

"Oh, I am," said the latter. "Much the best."

"You may make too much of it, my daughter," said Benjamin. "I looked to hear your brothers congratulate you, but I understood that they had done it in their own way."

"I do it now in the ordinary way," said Bernard.

"If I had been left ten times as much, it would not have been my fault," said Anna. "I have had no more to do with the will than the rest of you. And I suppose that is not much."

"If you had, I wonder if it would have killed Esmond," said Bernard.

"I thought all ordinary congratulations went without saying," said Claribel.

"You must see that you were mistaken," said Benjamin.

"What is the good of belonging to a family, if every formal convention has to be observed?"

"Perhaps Anna has not found it much good."

"We ought to begin to rejoice," said Jenney, in an uncertain manner. "It is right to appreciate what comes to us, even if it does come from people's trouble. Money never comes, except from a death, does it?"

"Perhaps that accounts for the sinister touch about it," said Bernard. "It is really death that is the root of all evil. I have always thought it was."

"If there wasn't any death, we shouldn't ever inherit anything," said Reuben.

"That is what Jenney said," said Bernard. "We see why people are reluctant to make their wills. It is odd that we should be surprised by it. It does not bring death any nearer, but it shows it as a possibility, and that is enough. And of course we talk about generous benefactors by will. Ungenerous people would never imagine their goods going to someone else. It explains why so many people die intestate. Bequeathing is a great test."

"One that Aunt Sukey will hardly be thought to have passed," said Esmond.

"Which would you rather, Anna?" said Reuben. "Have the money, or have Aunt Sukey alive again?"

"The second, of course, if she could be well enough to find her life worth while."

"We should keep two things apart," said Benjamin. "Anna is glad of what has come to her, and grieved for the loss that occasions it."

"Would you rather that the money had come to you, or come to Anna, Father?"

"The first," said Benjamin, in an almost stern tone, that he softened in his pleasure that his son should address him. "It seems that I should have more use for it, and that it would be better in my hands. But I am glad it has come to any one of us, and glad of the reason."

"Poor Father!" said Anna. "You had done more to earn it than I had."

"I think we should say that it was not earned, but given."

"Well, I like it better as a gift."

"Perhaps you might even love it on that ground," said Bernard.

"Perhaps Anna will make it over to Father," said Reuben.

"I was to give it to the Calderons a little while ago," said his sister. "But I daresay Father will have the chief hand in directing it."

"I hope for favours at your hands," said Bernard, "and I have the generosity to say so. I notice that Esmond has not."

"I think it is Anna who will have to show that quality," said Claribel.

"There is no need for it, when the means of giving fall into your lap," said Esmond.

"Don't you really want any favours?" said his brother.

"Shall we be able to live differently?" said Reuben.

"How many more people will find a use for it?" said

Anna. "I begin to see why Aunt Sukey left it to me. To choose one person and abide by the choice may have seemed the only thing."

"But why not choose Father?" said Esmond.

"Oh, we cannot talk as if Aunt Sukey were alive, and we could discuss it with her."

"We shall never know that," said Benjamin. "And we must remember that a will stands by itself, independent of anything that goes before. It is an absolute thing."

"Can it be that Father has a high character?" said Bernard, under his breath. "I think this must be a proof of it."

"Anna ought not to give the money back to the Calderons, ought she, Jenney?" said Reuben.

"It is hardly useful to talk of a thing that is never done," said Benjamin. "Jenney is right that a will would be no good, if we did not follow it. And the phrase, 'give back', is not the right one. The money belonged to no one but your aunt."

"She might have been said to owe it to other people," said Esmond.

"Anything to divert it from your sister!" said Anna.

"Well, it will make a difference to them, as a proportion of the money went to the house."

"Well, money does make a difference, of course," said Anna. "That is the meaning of it."

"What is the first thing you will do with it?" said Reuben.

"I don't know," said Anna, putting back her hair from her brow. "Forget it, I think. I never spent such a day. I would have avoided it, if I could have, money and all."

"It would be natural to wish to avoid much of it," said Esmond.

"Oh, don't pretend to be such a fool. Jealousy may be an excuse for a good deal, but you have gone far enough."

"If Esmond should go too far, would you stint your

bounty to him?" said Bernard. "I almost think he has done so."

"Here are the whole Calderon family coming up the drive!" said Anna. "Uncle Thomas, Aunt Jessica, Tullia and Terence. I wonder they have not brought the children. I had better go and hide my head. I do not want to face any green-eyed looks. I have come to the end of my tether."

"I think we all have," said Esmond.

"I thought you always had," said his brother.

"I would not behave as if you were afraid to meet them," said Jenney to Anna. "You have nothing to be ashamed of. You have not done anything."

"You should be full of pride," said Bernard. "You have ousted them in Aunt Sukey's esteem, and they cannot fail to respect you. And if you give up the money, they may think less of you for not having it."

"But perhaps more of her on other grounds," said Esmond.

"Yes, but that is a lighter kind of esteem."

"It would only be a thought that would occur to them at intervals during their lives," said Anna.

"And the other will become entwined with their every experience," said Bernard.

"Well, if Anna likes to look forward to that!" said Esmond.

"I have done with any thoughts of the future," said Anna, resting her head on her hand. "I can only live in the moment; I am quite tired out. And I foresee that the moment will be enough."

CHAPTER IX

JESSICA'S GREETING OF her brother showed no thought of anything but their common grief, and her manner did not change when she turned to his children. Her trouble about her sister's state of mind overwhelmed all others. Anna, who had risen in vague apprehension, drew back and took no part in the talk. Tullia bore herself as if all eyes were watching the effect of her bereavement, and was fortunate in being in error, as the result was hardly what she thought. She held it beneath her to talk or think of money, and assumed it was always there, which would indeed have disposed of its problems. Thomas showed a simple indulgence in the matter. His daughter asked little for herself, and had a right to spurn what she did not need. Thomas and his son behaved as usual; indeed any change in them appeared in an especial care to be themselves. Claribel stood with her eyes darting from face to face, and her mouth slightly open, as if she would speak when the words came. Jenney and Reuben watched the scene in the spirit of spectators at a play, and indeed wore this expression. Thomas was the first to broach the matter in their minds.

"Well, Anna, my dear, we congratulate you on your aunt's feeling. As for the way she chose of showing it, you are already placed above material troubles."

"Am I?" said Anna, awkwardly. "I don't know if that is the case. With this swarm of developing brothers about me, I should hardly have thought so. You must ask Father. I suppose it was not Aunt Sukey's view. But thank you for what you say about her feeling. I am glad to have deserved that, or somehow to have won it. We can't give an account of these things."

"That is the reason of their value," said Jessica. "I too

congratulate Anna, and almost envy her. I would give much for the certainty and peace of her memory."

"Oh, I don't know if it is as much as that," said Anna, looking away. "I also have my moments of compunction and doubt. I can't stop wondering if I should have left Aunt Sukey on that last morning. But she wanted to be left to sleep, and I knew that Father was coming. I could not foresee what was going to happen; I don't see what else I could have done." She raised her eyes to her uncle in mute appeal.

"You could have done only what you did," he said. "It worked out well for our sister, and we can only thank you. You can have a mind at rest."

"I don't think Aunt Sukey had any feeling that she was worse that morning," said Anna, in a tone that seemed to reassure both herself and other people. "I don't think she had any inkling that things were as they were. I only thought she was suffering from some sort of shock or strain. I had no other idea. And her mind was quite at rest when she went to sleep. I am sure you need not fear that she was keeping anything from you."

Thomas and his wife looked at each other, almost without knowing that they did so. The interplay of thought was hardly conscious, but Jessica's eyes were more direct on her niece.

"You know that my sister had made a fresh will more than once before," she said, in a more natural tone than anyone else could have used on such a subject; "and that each time she destroyed it. It was one of her ways of easing her mind; her life had become too much for her. But she never altered the one that was kept in her desk. She never laid a hand on it, except to use it as a basis for another." Jessica's faint smile was as open as it was pitiful. She was as honest on her feelings for her sister, as she was on anything else; a want of sincerity would have seemed to her wrong. "It seems to me that she must have made a mistake. How does it seem to you?"

"I have not thought anything about it," said Anna, looking into her aunt's eyes for one swift moment. "I knew nothing about her wills; I believe I had never thought about people's making them. I have heard about this one, of course; Father told us when he came home; but I had no idea what Aunt Sukey had to leave, or if she had anything. I believe I had a sort of notion that she lived at the expense of the household; something seemed somehow to suggest it. I don't know much more now. I know no more than he said. How could I?"

"You could not, of course. But now you know what I have told you."

"I don't feel that I know much," said Anna, putting back her hair once again. "It seems to me that no one can know anything. It must be all conjecture and imagination, anything one tries to construct. I think it is better not to build up theories. They only lead one further from the truth."

"But we need not neglect what we know to be the truth," said Thomas.

"We are not neglecting it, are we? But we know so little. Just that Aunt Sukey was burning papers, and only left this will behind. Just that and no more."

"Even if she burnt the old will on purpose," said Jessica, in the same tone, "it seems that it was essentially a mistake. A mistake in the sense that she would have rectified it, when she was herself. Do you not agree with me, my dear?"

"I don't understand all these thoughts and feelings about wills," said Anna, in a bewildered tone. "I had never thought about such things; I don't remember that we ever talked about them. I suppose Mother made a will; indeed I know she did, because she left most of her money to Father, and just a little to each of us. But we never thought of disputing it; we just accepted it as it stood, even though she was ill when she made it, as I believe she was. I suppose people often are ill, when they come to do that particular thing. I thought people simply accepted wills. I thought it was the law, in so far as I thought about it at all."

"For a person who thought so little, you came to sound conclusions," said Thomas. "No one would dispute this will; there is no ground for doing so. We could not say that your aunt was mentally unsound; we do not think so. But we feel that she was not herself, when she made this change. And we want to find out what her real wishes were; and we want you to help us, so that we can carry them out together."

"But, how can I do anything? I know absolutely nothing. Aunt Sukey never spoke to me about such things. I wish I had had her full confidence, but I had not. And I can't make things up; I am not a person who can do it. I only find myself floundering deeper in the mire. And you are sneering at me already. I will not commit myself by another word."

"Making things up would clearly not lead us to the truth," said Jessica.

"Not to the real truth, of course. It depends where people want to be led. As regards the real truth, I can say no more. Aunt Sukey was clear about what she had done. She would not have slept, if she had been in doubt. You know her well enough to realise that."

"We cannot assume anything about her state, an hour before her death," said Thomas. "She could hardly have been in a normal one, and her actions may not have been her own."

"Her feelings may have gone further than usual," said Jessica, in a musing tone. "But they had passed when I left her. I know that I saw them pass. If she did not burn the wrong will by accident, which is the most likely solution, she must have hidden her mind in a way quite foreign to herself. It is another proof that she was in an unnatural state. If I were not sure beyond doubt, I would not say a word of it."

"I know you would not," said Anna; "I don't suppose

anyone would, or anyhow anyone here. No one would build on anything that was not real evidence. There would be no end to the constructions that could be made."

"She would have wished to put right what she had done," said Jessica, half to herself. "And so Anna must wish to do it for her. I cannot see it in any other way, and so I do not suppose she can. She can make over the money by deed of gift; it will be no trouble for her." Jessica did not suggest, or mean to suggest, that generosity would be involved. Her niece might shrink from perplexing formalities, but would do the only thing to be done.

"By deed of gift," said Anna, seeming inclined to laugh. "I never heard that phrase before, but it sounds a very good one. That would be a neat way of dealing with bequests, as they arose; just to render them null and void." She laughed again, as if she could not help it.

"What do your brothers think about it?" said Thomas.

"We did not know Aunt Sukey well enough to have an opinion," said Bernard.

"What do you think, Benjamin?"

"As Bernard does, though it may seem strange for me to say it. I thought I knew my sister, but there may have been things that I did not know. When I came back into her life, I found that there were. I was surprised by the will, but I have been surprised by wills before. Indeed I have never met a will that did not surprise someone. I have no ground on which to advise my daughter. Many people would alter their wills, if they died at some other time."

"What does Mr. Terence think?" said Anna, in an almost rallying tone.

"I knew Aunt Sukey too well, to take any view but my mother's. But I do not feel that adjustment must necessarily follow."

"Did you know her so well?" said Anna, looking at him as if in some curiosity.

"Yes, I went through your stage with her, and remained in it longer. But it came to an end with me, as it would have with you."

"I never felt it was a stage," said Anna, speaking to herself in the manner of Jessica.

"She could not stay the course with anyone," said Terence.

"Ought not that to be put the other way round?"

"I daresay it ought in a sense. She wore us all down, as you say."

"I never knew such a family for giving turns and twists to people's minds and phrases," said Anna, in a bewildered manner. "I said and meant nothing of the sort. She never wore me down. I felt that I should come to see her every day of my life. I had no thought of its all breaking up so soon. And Father felt the same. It is only fair to her to say it."

"It is, my dear," said Jessica. "And it is good for us to know it; good in two senses, you might say. We have dealt with the matter now; and when you have judged it in the light of what you have heard, you will tell me. And if you say nothing, I shall know we are not of one mind."

"What does Tullia think?" said Anna, looking at her cousin.

"I have not followed the matter," said the latter, withdrawing her eyes from the window. "I hardly grasp what it has been about. Wills and bequests and other kindred things. I thought they were managed by lawyers behind the scenes. I did not know they came into the light of day."

"They are the affair of people who have gone," said Bernard. "That puts them out of harmony with those who are left."

"Something does," said his brother.

"Well, are there no other topics of conversation?" said Tullia.

"I was beginning to wonder that," said Anna. "I was going to ask for a photograph of Aunt Sukey. Even Father has not one of her. She was going to give me one, but the subject passed off somehow."

"Was she?" said Jessica, looking at her niece. "She never had her photograph taken. She thought she photographed badly, and she destroyed all those we had in the house. And they did not do her justice. She had not been taken for thirty years. I don't know what she could have meant by that."

"Or have I got it twisted in some way? That would be rather in my character. I asked her if she would have her portrait painted. And she said she would give me a photograph of it, if she ever did. I think that was it. She did not seem so averse from that. It is like me to turn a little matter the wrong way round. Happily, I get a better grasp of big ones."

"That must seem a painfully apposite metaphor," murmured Esmond.

"We shall always regret that that was not done," said Jessica. "I wish we had made a point of it."

"But why didn't you?" said Anna, in an insistent tone. "It would have been a satisfaction to Aunt Sukey to feel there was a record of her. And now it would be an advantage to everyone."

"We had her with us herself then. It is more natural to want the record of her now."

"When it is too late," said her niece.

"We cannot live on the edge of someone's grave," said Terence, "and keep the person herself looking down into it."

"Another distortion of my thoughts and feelings," said his cousin. "I wonder you ever get a right impression of anyone. I don't suppose you ever do."

"It is a time when we are shaken out of ourselves," said Jessica. "We owe so much to each other, and we give so little."

"Another pointed metaphor," said Esmond.

"Will you be able to use the room now?" said Anna,

with awkward suddenness, as if her mind had passed to another subject. "Aunt Sukey's room, I mean. Or will it be established as a sort of shrine? I don't think I could ever go into it again."

"Then it does not matter to you what purpose it is to serve," said Esmond.

"Well, will you make a habit of frequenting it, yourself?"

"I shall make it into a study for your uncle," said Jessica, addressing them both. "He has always wanted a west room, and has never been able to have one. He will not like the room any less for its memories."

"Gracious, that is a quick way of using up what is left," said Anna, dropping her voice and raising her brows towards her brothers. "It is an ill wind that blows nobody any good."

"As you have found, yourself," said Esmond.

"Well, I said it, didn't I?"

"With regard to other people you did."

"Well, I daresay other people are saying it about me. Indeed I know they are. And you were the first. So all is fair between us all."

"I think it is a tribute to us," said Tullia, in her deliberate way, "that Aunt Sukey used our house as her home, and imposed her will upon us, without thinking it necessary to leave us a reward. That would take the meaning out of it, and make it all into a sort of exchange and barter. I am glad we are spared that."

"I suppose you mean that the ban has fallen on me," said Anna. "Well, that is as it may be. Aunt Sukey had to have her way."

"How much that says for her!" said Bernard.

"So do we all," said Terence. "That is why we are in a baffled state. We are not getting it."

"Oh, Father and Aunt Jessica and I are fairly content," said Anna. "Content with the minor circumstances, I mean, apart from the main thing. And if Tullia means what she says, she also is satisfied. And I don't see why she shouldn't mean it. I generally mean what I say myself, simple, unsophisticated habit though it may sound. And Aunt Sukey may have felt as Tullia says. I never saw any sign in her, that she felt she ought to pay in any form for what she had in your house. She never gave the least hint of it, not the slightest." Anna looked round in general assurance. "She felt she was entitled to everything by right of herself and of the advantage she was to you. I am sure you may feel certain that that was her feeling."

"In a word, disinterested affection has to be disinterested," said Thomas.

"Well, why shouldn't it be what it pretends to be? Or what it is, if you like?"

"I would rather reward it than the other kind."

"In other words, it did not exist," said his niece. "Oh, I may have been the new broom, but to my mind a little clean sweeping was not out of place."

"Yes, there were some cobwebs," said Jessica. "They tend to come with time; I daresay they would have done that anywhere."

"Must we go on?" said Tullia. "What do we think is gained by it?"

"I am afraid nothing," said Terence. "We hoped that Aunt Sukey's fortune would be gained."

Anna laughed in spontaneous amusement, her eyes on her cousin's face.

"It was not a question of gain, but of assignment of dues," said Thomas.

"It bore a certain resemblance to gain, on both sides I must say," said Anna. "I don't think I am going to take the line that we are trying to be generous to each other. We are claiming what seems to us to be ours, a just and reasonable thing, but nothing more. And I have had enough of derogatory and belittling hints. If you cannot get on with people, who keep what they legally inherit, you will be able to get on with very few. Father put it to you in some way of his own."

"This is hardly an ordinary case," said Jessica.

"Now, honestly, Aunt Jessica, have you ever given up anything that was left to you in a will? I suppose you inherited your share of your parents' money; indeed I know you did, because Father did the same. And did it occur to you to make it over to anyone else? Or if it did, did you do it? I amit that it occurred to me; I believe I even spoke of it; but these impulses pass away; it is no good to blink at the truth. They did in my case, as I suppose they did in yours. And we are left with a feeling that, if we do not consider our dues, no one else will do it for us. The more we listen to other people, the more we see our dependence on ourselves. When you think you are entitled to money, that is left to someone else, you must see it is natural to think so, when it is left to you. I do think that my position is better than yours."

Tullia gave a sigh and threw up her brows in silent despair.

"In a sense I have no position," said Jessica, quietly. "But my own money was left to me on natural grounds. It was not a case of an accident or a sick impulse."

"And how do we know that this was? How can we know anything? I begin to think that anything to do with money, be it wills or anything else, is so considered and dwelt upon and turned this way and that in people's thoughts, that no word like rashness or impulse is ever in place. It may be accepted as the definite outcome of the person's mind. I have come to that conclusion."

"What do you think about it, Claribel?" said Thomas.

"Oh, I feel I am simply removed from it, just floating about above it in some sphere of my own, too ethereally constructed to be welcome or useful to anyone involved. It is just left out of me, the quality that deals with the assignment of human goods. I am above it, below it, whatever it is."

"What would have happened, if the quality had been left out of Aunt Jessica and Anna?" said Esmond.

"What has happened now?" said Tullia. "Aunt Sukey decided the matter. But it is a pity it was not left out. We should have escaped this scene."

"Well, there is no help for us," said Thomas.

"No, there is not, Uncle Thomas," said Anna, turning to face him. "And there would be none for me, if things were reversed, and the money left to you instead of to me. And I should not expect there to be; that seems to be the difference between us. Otherwise, there is not a pin to choose between your construction and mine. Even Aunt Jessica seems to be on the line with us. I want nothing that does not come to me fair and square; but if it does so come——" Anna snapped her fingers and turned to the table, on which Ethel had placed a tray. "Now come and slake your thirst and forget the bone of contention. I don't want to have Tullia fainting away before my eyes."

"We ought to have known better than to embark on such an altercation," said Esmond.

"Perhaps we have learned better," said Thomas.

"Altercation, was it?" said Anna, with her eyes on the tray. "I should have thought it was a pretty reasoned discussion. Nothing runs quite on the smooth, when people are looking at things from different angles." Her tone was preoccupied and she seemed to be taking some care in dispensing the tea. "I don't suppose we any of us harbour any personal feelings on the matter."

"I am clear that the money should be my wife's," said Thomas.

"And is that harbouring them or not?" said Terence.

"Oh, are we starting again?" said Tullia in an incredulous tone.

"No, we have finished," said her father. "Yes, I will have some sugar, Anna, my dear."

"I was wondering how long I should have to stand and face you all as a sort of prisoner in the dock," said Anna, carrying round the cups with care not to spill them. "I couldn't help imagining what Aunt Sukey would think of the scene. I don't suppose she meant to expose me to it. I wonder if I shall ever cure myself of filling cups too full. It comes of an instinct of hospitality, and then I don't check myself in time. No, sit down, you young men; this seems to me a woman's business. I may be clumsy for my sex, but I daresay I am less so than you are. I quite began to know how a criminal must feel. Not that I had an uneasy conscience, but being arraigned by your relations in a body produces a feeling of having somehow caused the situation."

"We are answerable to nothing but our consciences," said Jessica.

"I quite agree with you, Aunt Jessica," said Anna, standing with her hands at her sides and her eyes on her aunt. "But other people did not seem to be of that mind. They appeared to think I was answerable to each and all of them. And I thought that you rather gave them the lead. And there did not seem to be so much conscience involved in any of it. You were all occupied with other things."

"I feel I am a wiser person for the last hour," said Bernard. "I think I have gone forward."

"I am sure I have ," said his sister. "I thought people's wills and testaments were accepted as part of the natural order of things. I did not know that we pulled them out, and tore them in shreds, and scrambled for the pieces."

"That is a most unfair description," said Terence. "My family has behaved with kindness and decorum."

"I was not given much chance to do the same. Perhaps that is what is rankling. I daresay it is."

"I believe you are a person who says disarming things," said Terence.

"Am I?" said Anna, in a tone at once casual and conscious.

"Not that you do not say many of the opposite kind. Some of your speeches would arm me to the teeth, if I were as other men."

"And are you not as they are?"

"Of course I am not. You must have seen it."

"Yes, well, I suppose I have that amount of observation."

"Well, is the main part of the matter over?" said Benjamin.

"Poor innocent that I was, I thought Aunt Sukey's death was that," said Anna. "Now I realise what is, I doubt if we shall ever be able to say so. It will crop up at intervals to the end of time."

"Well, throw it off for the moment, my daughter, and think of your guests."

"Thank you, Father. I take that as a sort of permission. It is an odd situation to be sitting in the stocks and dispensing hospitality at the same time."

"You talk as if we had never had people to the house before," said Esmond.

"Well, I think we generally find ourselves in a body at the other board. But I hope there will be more of an interchange in future."

"Why should it be different?" said her brother.

"Oh, shall I ever say a thing that will satisfy my kindred? I shall be afraid to open my mouth. I suppose Aunt Sukey could not often be left could she? And I suppose she had to have a little change and social intercourse like anyone else. Or has it escaped your memory, that such a person existed?"

"We may not be able to keep such an open house in future," said Jessica, in her quiet tones. "We shall be glad of the change and pleasure of this one. And, as Anna says, there will be less to keep us at home."

"Thank you, Aunt Jessica. I keep having to be extricated from some awkward predicament. I am sure I am very grateful. And I hope indeed that we shall often see you all here, so that what you lose on the swings, you will gain on the roundabouts. I mean, it seemed right that we should go to you, when we were fledglings under your wing. But now we are on our feet, we must make our return. And as for going to your house, I do not feel that I could ever enter its doors without a shiver."

"I hope that will not always be your feeling."

"I feel as if it would. And as for entering the room where I always saw Aunt Sukey, and saw her for the last time, well, it would be beyond me. I am sorry, but so it is; we can't alter ourselves. I am quite glad that Uncle Thomas is going to establish himself in it, so that no one will be supposed to open its doors. I shall not have to seem to make a parade of my feelings, which would be the account given of the matter. And it is no wonder that people are annoyed, when they see it like that."

"We have not seemed either kind or sympathetic today," said Jessica. "But when you look back, you will see that we have done our best with a difficulty quite unforeseen. And as regards the trouble that we share, we shall find that we share it."

"Oh, I find no fault with the way you have behaved," said Anna, turning away her head. "I don't see why you should have been any different. Indeed I think you elders set us an example of manners and restraint and everything. But, as you say, things were sprung upon us; we did not see eye to eye, and there it was. Any amount of preparation would hardly have altered it. The difference would have been there. We could not expect to shine."

"I think my mother feels that she has done so," said Terence. "And I am inclined to agree with her."

"We have not been so fortunate in our representative," said Bernard. "But she had a task beyond her."

"It would have been too much for anyone," said Terence. "Wanting to keep something for yourself puts you at such a disadvantage; people disapprove of it so deeply. But it is worse when the effort is not crowned with success. I was once or twice very much ashamed of Father."

"I daresay we should all keep the money in my sister's place."

"I have no doubt that we should," said Terence. "My

mother is the only one who would not. And she would suffer more from the doubt of her right to it, than from the wrench of parting with it. Her pang would be less."

"My own pang is great," said Bernard.

"It must be. Mine would overpower me, if Tullia had inherited so much."

"Well, Anna will not dissipate the money; that is one thing."

"Or does that make it worse?" said Terence. "If it were squandered, there would be an end of it. And now it may increase and aggravate the position. Suppose she put it out at usury?"

"She has not enough knowledge for that."

"But your father may advise her. He has been very successful in such things. And I feel she would take advice. Can it be that father and daughter both like money? She will use it to the greatest advantage. There is no comfort at all."

"Well, I don't feel that she has had very much in her life."

"Well, perhaps there is a little comfort."

"Tullia does not mind her having the money," said Bernard.

"Tullia has no grasp of such things. Father is the one who minds. And I cannot bear the spectacle of a strong man's suffering."

"You seem to be having some good jokes there, you two," said Anna.

"Cannot we have some fresh tea?" said Esmond.

"Ethel ought to bring it," said his sister. "If we ring, she will think she must always be reminded."

"Why cannot we have trained servants?"

"I daresay we can now. That is to say, it is time they were reaching that stage, after all my endeavours. And they are trained enough for our purposes. We could have a third, if it were not for the problem of two being company and three none."

"Anna shows some skill in glossing over her allusions to her wealth," said Terence. "But it would save trouble not to bring up the matter."

Ethel walked smoothly into the room and replaced the teapot by a full one. Jessica gave her a smile; Terence moved something out of her way; Anna behaved as if she did not see her; and Jenney followed her out of the room as though to give some direction, but really seizing the pretext to leave the family alone.

Ethel carried her tray to the kitchen, as if Jenney's company had escaped her notice, and spoke as she set it on the table.

"It is strange that people should keep what is grudged to them."

"So she held to it," said Cook.

"Instead of standing apart, with her head above it," said Ethel.

"There would be no good in wills, if people did not carry them out," said Jenney.

"Well, little good comes of them," said Ethel.

Jenney could not feel that this was so in Anna's case.

"But people must say what is to become of their money, when they die. Or how would people know what to do with it?"

"There ought to be cases where compulsion is brought to bear. That poor Mrs. Calderon! And always with a word for everyone."

"And that sweet smile," said Cook.

"You would think that quiet dignity was sometimes the only course," said Ethel. "And would make people think more of you. And respect is everything."

"Many people respect money," said Jenney.

"Well money is power," said Ethel, sighing.

"But only on a scale," said Cook. "Petty sums can't sway destinies."

"You can do a certain amount on what Miss Anna has inherited," said Jenney.

"But if you forfeit what is more valuable, you are the poorer," said Ethel.

But Jenney could not see the word as applicable.

"They are taking their leave," said Ethel, throwing up her eyes to the ceiling. "I suppose Miss Anna does not want them shown out, as she is there herself."

"It seems needless," said Cook, "where there are only two."

"And now this talk of three," said Ethel. "Well, it has happened before."

"And will happen again," said Cook. "Words mean nothing on the lips of some. But if a third should come, she would find it her own affair."

"I would not guarantee her not feeling out of it," said Ethel. "Nor guarantee anything in the face of change."

"I must go upstairs," said Jenney. "They may want me, now that the guests have gone."

"I would not leave Miss Jennings to the mercy of Miss Anna," said Ethel, as the door closed. "Not made overbearing by this uplift. It will put her on a level with the master. And that will not conduce to her improvement."

"Well, after all, she is his flesh and blood," said Cook.

When Jenney reached the drawing-room, the family had returned.

"Well, Jenney, we got through the ordeal without yielding an inch," said Bernard; "that is to say, without yielding Anna's income."

"You did, didn't you?" said Jenney, in incredulous appreciation. "I kept wondering if you would have to give in. It was not made easy for you. And yet one is sorry in a way for your aunt."

"We have to rejoice in Anna's good fortune as it were behind the scenes," said Claribel.

"Oh, I don't expect unmixed feelings of pleasure on my behalf," said Anna. "I have realised that that is too much to ask. Not that I am not grateful for everyone's support. I half thought you were going to throw me to the wolves.

How they howled round us, waiting for what we should throw them!"

"The simile hardly suggests Aunt Jessica," said Esmond.

"I found her the most formidable. Her weapons were the deadliest; sweetness, righteousness and so forth; it was all I could do to withstand them. But I knew we should regret it, if I didn't, and so I held to my guns. After all, you don't give up an inheritance for being asked. They thought they had only to speak, to get it. You would think they would have more knowledge of life."

"Well, they have it now," said Esmond.

"I am grieved that my sister and I are at a difference," said Benjamin, who indeed had trouble in his face. "I see how it comes, and that it must remain. But I cannot give advice that would be given by no other father. And we cannot know that your aunt did not wish the will to stand. Why should she have made it? The obvious question is the just one."

"And somehow we feel she did wish it," said Claribel, glancing at Anna and clasping her hands in fellow-feeling.

"The Calderons were in effect promised the money, and saw it as theirs," said Esmond.

"I don't think Aunt Sukey felt she had promised it," said Anna, quietly.

"You might have said that you would share the money with them," said Reuben.

"Oh, you have been present at an eye-opening scene," said his sister, turning towards him. "I did not realise that you were here. You have enlarged your knowledge of life."

"That would not have done," said Benjamin. "They have a right to all the money or to none. That would be their view."

"I have a feeling that Uncle Thomas would have taken half," said Bernard.

"I daresay he would have taken half or a quarter or a tenth," said Anna. "But it would have been unworthy of Aunt Jessica. It could not have been suggested."

"I should have thought that dividing the money, when there was a question of its ownership, was a good solution, said Esmond.

"Oh, anything would do for you, that took some of the money from me," said his sister. "Your words mean nothing."

"And perhaps yours mean one thing."

"Aunt Jessica's trouble is Aunt Sukey's frame of mind," said Bernard. "Her life must take on the colour of a course of criticism, thanklessness and almost deception."

"Then she ought to know her better," said Anna, with a touch of heat. "Aunt Sukey was the most open person, and always dealt above-board with everyone. She made no secret of thinking that they failed in sympathy. It was her open feeling about it, that caused that last trouble. And I suspect it had occurred many times. They could have put things right, if they had tried. They had fair warning."

"It is a good thing that you were wiser," said Esmond.

"These things are unconscious, of course. But they may count the more for that. And to Aunt Sukey's mind it seems they did."

"It is a solemn thing to have performed services that were valued at that figure," said Bernard.

"And I was prepared to continue them, and that was the point, I suppose. No doubt Aunt Sukey knew that I was. One can trust people to know that."

"It is a good thing when trust is not misplaced," said Claribel, in a mischievous aside to Esmond.

"Ought we to try to be kind to people, so that they may leave us their money?" said Reuben. "Is it a thing we always ought to think about?"

"Now it is time you were bundled out of the room," said Anna, turning on him as if to perform this office, but desisting and allowing him to remain. "You will get a nice view of things, from listening to talk you half understand. Who would be the person responsible for you?"

"Do you still feel that you would rather have had some personal memento of Aunt Sukey?" said Esmond.

"Oh, what is the good of thinking about what has not come my way? I have not received one, and there is an end of it. Would you have me deal with it, as our relatives dealt with their baffled desires? When you have not been given a thing, you stop thinking about it. You almost get a sense of shame that it ever came into your head. And there is the touch of ill-nature creeping in again! I am getting tired of it."

"What difference will the money make to us?" said Reuben.

"Well, we shall be able to do some things that have not hitherto been possible," said Anna. "And any sort of education for you, or opportunity for the others, may be considered. That is about what it will be. And we shall be able to run the house with ease and hospitality. That will be about the length of the rope, I should think."

"You are wise, my daughter," said Benjamin. "Any change in the scale of life would take your money, and leave you as you were before. You are right to get your advantage out of it. And it will be free to be diverted to your own purposes, in the event of a change in your own life."

"You make the future sound an uncertain quantity. I was thinking that things would go on for ever, only easier and smoother for ourselves and other people."

"Changes must come," said Benjamin. "Death is not the only one."

"It is the one we have had," said Anna. "Mother's death and Aunt Sukey's seem to be the events of my life. I never thought that any money would come my way."

"To make a third event," said Esmond.

"Oh, yes, yes, indeed. I make no secret of feeling it. But I have not had time to savour it yet. As I say, the very idea was strange."

"Perhaps that is why Aunt Sukey left the money to you," said Reuben. "She might not have liked people to think about it. It would have seemed like wanting her to die."

"There may be something in that," said Anna. "Indeed I don't suppose there is quite nothing. Out of the mouth of babes!"

"Will you be able to go to Uncle Thomas's house, as you did before? Or won't he want to see you?"

"I suppose I shall; I had not thought about it. He won't like to show any feeling. If he does, I must just stay away; it won't break my heart. There is no one there whom I especially want to see, now that Aunt Sukey is gone."

"You must get to know your Aunt Jessica," said Benjamin. "That would be a great thing in your life."

"I don't somehow think there is anything much to come to me there, Father. I don't disupte that she may have a great deal to give to many people; perhaps to most; but not to me."

"It is a mistake to be too sure of it."

"It is a pity to have to be."

"Well Terence go on teaching me?" said Reuben.

"Yes, if he will," said Anna. "We can't make a better arrangement. And there is no need to spend money for the sake of spending."

"Well, all the trouble is over," said Jenney. "It wasn't pleasant for you, was it? People ought to be allowed to enjoy what comes to them. It spoils it, when there is all this question about it. No one could make a will, that would please everybody."

"I don't suppose anyone is ever gratified but the legatee and family," said Claribel.

"And in this case even that did not come quite true," said Anna, sighing. "Everyone seemed to be trying to get in some little poisoned shaft. I was quite tired of being the target for them. And my opinion of my family and friends did not go up, and that is not a heartening thing. But it is all wearing off now, the main shock and the minor shocks and everything, if minor is the right word for things in that sphere. I think that Father and Bernard came through the ordeal; and I began to see that someone else's inheriting money constitutes an ordeal indeed. I had not realised it before; I don't think I should have found it so, myself." She ended on a quiet note.

"Doesn't Jenney come through it?" said Reuben.

"Oh, Jenney goes without saying," said Anna, bringing a look of reward to Jenney's face.

"You must remember that it makes other people poorer by comparison," said Bernard, "when they have done nothing to deserve it. And it makes them imagine how things would have been, if the money had been theirs. And then the legatee never seems any richer than before, and that makes them feel that they are poor indeed."

"Oh, those are the reasons," said Anna. "Not very real ones, are they?"

"Aunt Jessica had a better one," said Esmond. "She believed that Aunt Sukey wished her to have the money."

"Are we to start it all again?" said his sister. "Well it should present no difficulty. I know it all by heart."

"I think the ground has been covered," said Benjamin.

"Would Esmond rather that Aunt Jessica had the money, than Anna?" said Reuben.

"He would rather that anyone else had it," said Benjamin, in a tone whose expression was undefined.

"Anna rendered Aunt Sukey real service," said Bernard, quickly; "and it is good when virtue does not have to be its own reward. It is too like having no reward at all."

"You are really quite a tolerable brother," said Anna.

"I am trying to be different. And I have a sincere respect for you for being so well-off."

"Money is power," said Reuben.

"I cannot bear it then," said Bernard. "But Anna's money is in the stage when it means comfort and ease and kindness, just the one in which I should choose it."

"Well, I will try to make it mean those things," said his sister, keeping her eyes from his face.

CHAPTER X

"WELL, I APPROACH my relatives' house in some trepidation," said Anna, as she hastened in this direction. "It is an odd experience to be received as a guest, by a family you are held to have robbed. I hope it will overcome that of facing the house without Aunt Sukey. There is no more potent force than embarrassment pure and simple. I am not proud of being subdued by it, but it may have its use on this occasion. And it is no good to have a higher standard for yourself than you can manage."

"I believe you maintain a generally higher one than you used," said Esmond.

"Well, that is better than letting oneself go headlong downhill. And people tend to go one way or another."

"The feeling of having riches disposes us to be worthy of them," said Bernard. "It is the instinct to do something in return, so as to check any tendency of fate to redress the balance."

"I am glad to be told so much about myself."

"The instinct to be worthy of good may be a sound one," said Benjamin. "We should contribute as well as take."

"Yes it is as well to play fair," said his daughter. "But I hardly think that is the light in which I am about to be seen."

Jessica came to meet them, and greeted them in turn without distinction.

"We are more glad to see you than we have ever been. As we get to be fewer, each fills a larger place. We are trying not to be a sadder family, but we must feel a smaller one."

"An odd effort under the circumstances," muttered Anna to her brothers. "It would be strange if it were crowned by success."

"Aunt Sukey will always be in this hall, for the people who saw her here," said Bernard.

"Not for me," said his sister, shaking her head. "I don't get off so easily. Only the reality does for me. I am sorry to be such a material person, but so it is. It seems to me that the essence of the household is gone."

"I want you to come and talk to me about her," said Jessica, laying her hand on her niece's shoulder. "Her last hour was spent with you, and I want to know how she lived it. Those minutes are always in my mind."

"I will do what I can," said Anna, turning to follow. "But it seems to me that I have done it several times. I can't make the hour different from what it was, you know. I am not good at tinkering with the truth. If it tumbles out, whole and plain, I cannot be taken to account."

"The truth is what I want," said Jessica. "It is what I feel I must have."

She guided her niece up the stairs and was entering her sister's room, when Anna drew back and put both her hands before her face.

"Oh, no, no, I can't, please; I can't quite manage this. I am not such a tough person as you seem to think. You are a deal in advance of me, if this is your standard. I can't quite meet you on this ground."

Jessica drew her into the room, as if she had not heard. It was necessary to do as she did, and words were wasted. Her face had something aloof and almost empty about it, as if she were not so much indifferent to daily things, as apart from them.

"You quite bring my heart into my mouth," said Anna, forcing an easier tone. "To make such a parade of a thing like this is ghoulish, and has something ominous about it. I don't know what your purpose is, but does it really need this kind of foundation?"

"I want you to tell me just what happened in that last hour," said Jessica.

"I have told you. I have given an account of it more

than once. And I am all against going over the same ground again and again. It leads to unconscious fabrication. I have given you the truth and you must be content. Asking for elaboration of it is really asking for the other thing."

"Have I had the truth?" said Jessica, in a tone that was as impersonal as if she were thinking aloud.

Anna threw up her brows and made a hopeless gesture.

"What you have told me, is not the truth to me."

"I daresay it is not," said Anna, with a touch of sympathy. "Not the truth as you would like to have it. But I warned you that I could not adapt it. It would never do to begin."

"I knew my sister to the bottom of her heart. Our minds were open to each other. And she did not destroy her old will, if she was herself; and to my mind she was. Tell me what happened, Anna?"

"I do not know. How can I? It had happened before I saw her. Only the reaction remained, and I will not be led into basing imaginary scenes on that. I am going to be firm there. You show me the danger."

"What did she say about it all? What were her exact words? I must know for my own ease of mind. I do not want anything to come of it."

"Good heavens, what strange, suggestive speeches!" said Anna, raising her eyes full to her aunt's. "I shall hardly know what to think. And naturally I will not respond to your questioning, if it is to lead to this. I should have thought that Aunt Sukey's death was enough in itself, without our trying to get more out of it. I don't feel I can dramatise the situation, Aunt Jessica. Aunt Sukey did not say that you had been the one figure in her life, or that her main feeling was gratitude to you, or anything of that kind. If that is what you want to hear, I cannot help you. You know that she was vexed and upset on that day, indeed was bitter against all of you. If I told you she was not, you would know it was a falsehood. You must not lay this stress on the truth, and then expect me to stretch it. And I am without the power of doing so; it is simply left out of me. I told you that, if you asked for the truth, you would get it. I gave you fair warning."

"She would not have done that to me and mine," said Jessica, looking past her niece. "It was not in her. That is how she came to make the pretence of doing it. If it had been her purpose, she would not have spoken of it."

"Oh, I don't understand your tortuous minds! You mean something and say nothing, or you mean one thing and say another. That is why you expect me to do it. And expect Aunt Sukey to do it too; expect that she did it, I mean, which seems to be worse. And I don't think it was in her, to use your own phrase. And anyhow it is not in me, and you had better realise it, or we shall go on for ever. If you mean a thing, you would not speak of it! What a key to the difference between us!"

"Shall I ever know what she felt and what she suffered?"

"Well, I have done my best for you, and can do no more. I told you she felt you had failed her, or rather that your family had. Not that she ever said a word against you, yourself, Aunt Jessica. And if she meant the opposite of what she said, you ought to take comfort."

"You are harsh to me," said Jessica, turning her eyes on her niece with sudden sight in them.

"And what are you to me? A pattern of flattering kindness?"

"I want the truth," said Jessica, almost with a moan in her voice. "I feel I must have it."

"Well you have it. You can take heart," said Anna, with a touch of rough kindliness. "And surely things are not so bad, that they might not be worse. In a family of this kind, and with Aunt Sukey as she was, I wonder they were not worse. You have nothing on your mind, that would not be the lot of nine people out of ten. And why should anyone expect to be the tenth?"

Jessica shook her head, in rejection of the words or the essence of them, and stood as though her eyes were on something that Anna did not see.

"Well can we adjourn the meeting?" said Anna. "Or rather dissolve it, as I cannot live under the threat of its being called again."

"Did she tell you she had burned a will?" said Jessica. "One of your brothers said something about it, but you did not mention it to me."

"She said she had burned some papers," said Anna, in a faintly impatient but natural tone. "And I think it was to you that I spoke of it first. It would naturally have been. I did not know what they were. How could I, as she did not say? It seemed to be a weight off her mind, as I have said. I am not going to keep saying it again. That is how distortion begins."

"You did not see the two wills together?"

"I did not see any will, or know that there was one. How could I, as I was not told? Aunt Sukey did not take me into her confidence. I suppose I had not got as far as that with her. I wish I could feel that I had; I should like to think I knew the whole of her mind. And I might have given her better companionship in that last hour. I see she steered her way alone. But I suppose she always did, as I suppose we all do really. I daresay it isn't anything to have on one's mind."

"She must have had the two wills in her hands at the same moment."

"I should have thought it would be more natural to keep them apart, especially as she is so methodical and definite. Was, I should say; I shall never get into the way of speaking of her in the past."

"There is no need to think of her like that," said Jessica, in an automatic tone, her eyes looking beyond her niece.

"Well, have I done all I can? Is the matter at an end? I think I must feel that it is, before we leave it. I can't feel that I am liable to be called up here, and worked upon at any moment. I should not dare to come to the house. It is almost too much for me, this having things probed and raked in the room where Aunt Sukey lived and died. And are not these matters personal to herself? Must we pry into them? It seems like taking advantage of her death. Or it does for me, as I was excluded from them. She had a right to keep things to herself as far as she wished; and there I would choose to leave it."

"She must have put the wrong will back into the desk," said Jessica, as if she had not heard the words, or had passed them over.

"Then she kept the wrong one in her hands, and put the same wrong one on the fire. Well, it was not like Aunt Sukey. That is all that can be said."

"She might not have acted according to herself. She would hardly have been herself an hour before her death. The forces of her system would have been running down."

"Oh, don't," said Anna, putting up her hands, as if to ward off a blow. "You are a strong, unshrinking person, and no mistake. I feel a kind of admiration for you. But I am not equal to it. It is beyond my limit, this probing into what we dare not think of. What I dare not think of, I suppose I should say; I must not ascribe the same weakness to you. Who would have thought that you would be the tough subject, and I the squeamish one? I should have been the last person to classify us like that."

"It would have been an easy thing to do," went on Jessica, still with the air of passing over Anna's words. "And she might have put the other will on the fire without looking at it."

"No, no, not Aunt Sukey," said Anna, shaking her head. "She would look to see she had the right one, a dozen times. Any failure in nervous balance would come out like that. That would have been the line of her weakness."

"In her last hours we cannot know."

"Oh, may we not leave those last hours? She was herself when I saw her, and I have a right to that memory. There is nothing gained by tampering with it."

"It is easy to imagine the scene," said Jessica.

"Why should she have taken the old will out of the desk at all?"

"She took it out to copy it," said Jessica, her eyes seeming to be fixed on the scene. "And she meant to put it back; I could tell by her voice and her eyes. She meant to destroy the other. But if only I could be quite sure!"

"That new one she had just made? What an odd purpose for it! Well, that is not what she did, as seems to me natural enough. The other thing is done, and there is no help for it. We cannot know that she was the victim of error or delusion or whatever you assume. I cannot think how you can think so, when you knew her. But don't let us have the last hours again, if you don't mind. I have had enough of it." As Anna became inured to the scene, her manner was more what it was in her home.

"That is how she came to have the two wills in her hands," said Jessica.

"She had nothing in them, when I was there. Her hands were folded in her lap. Something was on the fire, or had been on it, and the will was in the desk. Or so I was told later."

"Sukey never folded her hands," said Jessica, with no touch of pouncing on a weak point; simply in expression of her thought.

"Oh, well, idle in her lap. No, I don't think she did fold them. Actually they were working on her lap, but there did not seem to be any need to press that home. They were closing and unclosing, if you must have the scene as it was. You make it quite impossible to save you anything. And how can you say so positively what she did? You did not watch her quite so faithfully, or that was not her impression. Indeed that was the root of the trouble. And if her system was running down—isn't that what you said?"—Anna drew in her brows with a look of pain—"surely to sit without occupation was natural. And she was never a busy person."

"I can imagine her hands working," said Jessica, once again speaking to herself.

"Oh, she had been through the worst stage," said Anna, with a note of encouragement. "When I reached her, it was the calm after the storm, or anyhow the stage of the last echoes of it. She was at peace at the last. You may be quite easy about that. I left her without any sort of misgiving. She had fallen asleep, as I have said. I told you that was the result of my attentions."

"Anna," said Jessica, in a tone that held no sudden difference, but seemed to come from gathering purpose, "if you ever wanted to tell me anything, you would not be afraid? I would not say a word, if you would rather I did not. And there need be no change in the disposal of the money; that would not be mentioned between us. I only feel that you have no mother, and that your life has had many temptations and little guidance. You would let me help you, as someone who knows that? You would impose your conditions, and trust me to keep them. You would not hesitate?"

There was a just perceptible pause.

"Indeed I should," said Anna, almost with a laugh. "You are the last person I would face in such a situation, if I can imagine myself in one, which I cannot, as complexities and soul-subtleties are not within my range. And I believe you would almost create such a crisis. I can hardly be in your presence without feeling all kinds of uncertainties and possibilities welling up within me." Anna stood with her eyes on her aunt's face and a look of helpless bewilderment. "I should not know myself, if I spent much time with you. You would make anyone feel a criminal, indeed might make anyone be one. I begin to feel my mind reflecting your own. It must be ghastly to have such seething depths within one."

Jessica looked into her niece's face.

"I wonder if other people see me like that."

"Well, it is not your fault, if they don't," said Anna, giving rein to her tongue. "You do your best to cast a cloud of gloom and guilt over everyone in your path. No one can be with you, without being the victim of it, this instinct to drag from their minds anything and everything that it is their right and their duty to keep to themselves. People's little natural weaknesses are their own affair. Are you so free from them, yourself, that you must constitute yourself everyone else's critic and judge? It would hardly do to probe the depths of your mind. Even if I did feel some uncertainty about Aunt Sukey's wishes, there would be no great harm in giving myself the benefit of the doubt. Everyone would do it, as you have done it yourself. Indeed you give yourself the benefit of a doubt that does not exist. I am not going to yield to your peculiar method of coercion. It is unnatural and uncanny, and gives your opponent no chance. Anyone could use it, who would stoop so low. And to think that you are Aunt Sukey's sister, and held in equal esteem!"

"I see few people but my own family. Do I affect them in this way?"

"Well, I have noticed a reluctance in them to be alone with you. Of course I don't know how far they are aware of it. Terence is not a woman or a child, and gives less stimulus to the strange instincts. Oh, I know it is all unconscious, Aunt Jessica; I give you your due; though I can't imagine your doing the same by me, if I were subject to your odd temptations."

"What about the children?" said Jessica.

"They are too young to give a name to your influence. They just feel it, and avoid it when they can. I have noticed their instinct to elude you, and your sad, questioning eyes. They would make any child feel uneasy and guilty and oppressed. It is a shame to cloud their helpless childhood, and drag all the sweetness out of it; and a childhood too, that has no great happiness or advantage to balance the scale. Reuben may not have much of a life, but it is better than theirs. I know he has no mother, but there may not be only a dark side to that."

"Would they be happier without me?"

"Of course they would, in so far as you exercise this influence on them. It hardly seems to be quite human. I daresay it has its origin in the past, and you cannot separate yourself from it, any more than we can from any other primitive survival in us. It is said that savages have strange powers, that survive in certain people; and I suppose this is a case of it. They are the more dangerous for being so deep-rooted."

Jessica loked at Anna almost in wonderment, seeming to return from the world of her own thoughts.

"You said you were simple and unsophisticated," she said.

"Oh, there it is again, your instinct to wound and pierce and condemn. The most I have said, is that I am plain and downright. People do not say those things about themselves; they hardly like to think them. I may have said that I was regarded in that way. I can't help that, can I? I daresay any sister with three brothers hears such things. And I am more innocent than you are. I have never done harm to the helpless, and your life is spent in that miserable course."

"A cloud would be lifted from the household, if I were gone," said Jessica, using a tone between statement and question. "Does my husband feel that I cast this baleful influence?"

"How should I know?" said Anna, with a touch of embarrassment, as her mood filtered. "I have not constituted myself general observer and overseer of your household. And what a word; baleful! It shows that you know the exact essence of your spell. Why don't you stop working it, Aunt Jessica, and try to be a natural, wholesome woman?"

Jessica stood with her eyes on her niece.

"You are my brother's child. You and I are closely bound by blood. Perhaps these things are in us."

"Oh, they are not in me," said Anna throwing up her head. "You cannot turn the tables in that way. I do not possess your qualities, because I see them in you. They are laid bare before my eyes. I cannot help seeing them any more than your family can help it. They may not put the truth into words. It may be wiser not to do so. They may not even see it clearly enough for that. But they suffer from it—don't make any mistake—this sinister, creeping force that poisons their lives."

"They have not inherited these things?" said Jessica, again in the tone that was partly a question. "I have not done that to them."

"No, they are like open, crystal streams, compared with you. That is why your muddy eddy fails to mingle with them, and there is this odd divergence between you. But I daresay you do them less harm for that. And I see you have many fine qualities, Aunt Jessica, and of a kind to strike people more readily than those I have seen. It is not my fault that you have exposed them to me; they are generally much more veiled. But you gave me such an exhibition of them, that I saw you for the moment as a monument of all that was dark and evil. And when it came to attributing them to Aunt Sukey—well, it was too much, and took the leash off my tongue. If I am to see you differently, you must give me the chance. I am quite willing to take it."

"Have you always felt these things in me?"

"Faintly from the first. But I did not put names to them. I just felt as if some hostile emanation from you discharged itself over any innocence or happiness about you. I was first conscious of it in the form of a pity for those who lived with you and under you. But they may feel it less than I imagine. Things are more insistent, when you come from outside, and have not spent your life involved in them. And this last glimpse may have added itself to my earlier impression. It would be difficult to prevent it. Well, to think that you and Father and Aunt Sukey make up a family!"

Jessica rested her eyes on her niece.

"Now you need not look at me, as if we were bound

together by some deep and hidden bond. There is no truth there, and you know it. If there were, there would be some sympathy between us, which it is needless to say there is not. Your feeling to me has been unnatural and hostile from the first. Only Aunt Sukey seemed to see me as her brother's child. And now you want to transfer to me the worst things in yourself. Well, I do not accept them, and that is my last word."

"We will leave the matter of the wills," said Jessica, as if her thoughts had been elsewhere. "I do not wish to speak of it again. The money is yours, and no one will question it. But I ask you to help me to understand the harm I am doing my family. I ask it as a favour, Anna. Because I must cease to do it. I must free them by any means in my power. I must make any sacrifice, even that of sin. I will not flinch from anything that gives them freedom."

"When you talk like that, you take all the wind out of my sails," said Anna, looking aside. "What a sudden and utter change! It is like seeing someone alter her form before one's eyes. It recalls those scenes in books, that we believed and disbelieved in childhood. Have you been a creature in disguise, or is this the disguise? How am I to know? How did I know what was clear to me before? How do we recognise anything? And yet we cannot ignore our own impressions."

"Your impression was what you said it was?" said Jessica.

"I suppose so, or I should not have said it," said Anna, with her normal awkwardness. "No doubt it just came out, as it stood in my mind. That is my accepted way, and I must be taken as I am. I can't make selections from my thoughts. It is all or nothing with me."

"We none of us show the whole of our minds," said Jessica, in a quiet tone. "And there are depths in all of us, that are better left undisturbed. We avoid a wrong both to other people and ourselves."

"There you are again, with your piercing and wounding

and suggesting. Do let us stop preaching at each other. We have made known our mutual opinion, and that is surely enough. Indeed I think it should be. And are we to remain cooped up for ever in this harrowing place? It hardly seems a fit purpose for it, to be used as the background of this base and unseemly struggle. What made you choose it? I suppose some odd impulse of your own." Anna rested her eyes in a new wonderment on her aunt. "I daresay you hardly explained it to yourself. I believe you are helpless, Aunt Jessica. You are like some dark angel, honestly and unselfishly serving the cause of evil."

"You cannot tell me your meaning plainly?" said Jessica.

"No, I cannot. It is all vague and nameless to me. So, if you like, say I have imagined it. I am prepared to leave it like that. And I am not going to waste any more words. I see they are utterly wasted. And who am I, that I should judge another woman? If I had not been made the victim of your dark imaginings, actually dragged into this room, that had been sacrosanct to me, and used as a deliberate sacrifice, I should not have uttered a word. But the combination of horrors was too much. It broke down my defences, which are never too strong. I am not such a rocklike person at heart."

Jessica turned to the door and spoke in her ordinary tones.

"Shall we go down to the others? They will be wondering what has kept us?"

"They will, and we shall be hard put to it to tell them. Are we to make the attempt? I am prepared to fall in with your decision. Do we take the line of complete revelation? Or are we to observe any reticence? I can accept either view."

"Say what you will," said Jessica. "There are things that should be kept for another time, but you can judge of them for yourself. You may tell anything to your father and brothers at home."

"What a generous permission!" said Anna, hurrying

after her. "That would indeed be an advantage to them. Do you really think they could go on meeting you, if I actually revealed the whole?"

"It would not be difficult for us to keep apart. For a short time," said Jessica.

Anna edged forward and led the way into the room, where the families were together, and spoke without any sign of being embarrassed or oppressed.

"Aunt Jessica and I have been indulging in mutual recriminations in Aunt Sukey's room. The setting of the scene was not my choice; I had not the advantage there. Aunt Jessica might have been in a room that she had never seen before, a startling view, even if she had not been there as often as she might. She seemed unconscious that the place had any memories. She was quite above any such weakness." Anna hardly lowered her voice, as Jessica followed her.

"We thought you were never coming down," said Bernard.

"Indeed I thought the same," said his sister, sinking into a chair. "It is with a sense of surprise, that I find myself amongst you. I believe I have been standing all the time, though I did not realise it. Indeed I had other things to fill my mind. I am forbidden to reveal the matter of our discourse, but am sanctioned to do so at home. I have not made up my mind if it would be suitable hearing for you."

"We will suffer any violence it may do us," said Bernard.

"Well, do not preapre yourselves for anything interesting or uplifting. It is a sordid and degrading recital; at least I felt degraded by the business. Aunt Jessica held her head high above it all, but then she inaugurated it and carried it though, so I suppose she was equal to it. I did not find myself on her level."

"My mother looks very tired," said Terence.

"You need not worry about that," said Anna, in a light tone. "Anyone else would be in a state of collapse. Her condition is a definite tribute to her vital powers."

"You look very flushed," said Terence.

"Have you any more personal observations to make?" said his cousin, putting her hands to her face. "It was a scene that would mantle anyone's cheek, or so it struck me in my inexperience. But I am warned against describing it here; it is to be reserved for my own fireside. You will not have the advantage of my account, but no doubt you incline to the other."

"I think the decision to postpone it was a good one," said Jessica.

"Let us change the subject by all means. But you cannot expect me to do it. My head is too full of what you put into it. I don't feel that I shall ever get free. It will pursue and haunt me all my days."

"Your aunt meant what she said, my daughter," said Benjamin.

Anna gave a laugh.

"You make me wonder what you would say to my late experience, when you speak to me as if I were a child. And talk as if Aunt Jessica's words must point the way to the light."

Jessica sat down and drew the two children to her side. Their surprise made them unresponsive, and her face contracted in shock and fear. Anna kept her eyes from her, and joined in the talk.

"You have been troubled, my daughter," said Benjamin, in a low tone.

"Well, I should be an odd person if I had not," said Anna, at her ordinary pitch. "I think I stood up to it fairly well. I congratulate myself on a reserve of strength that I did not know I possessed. I was not equal to what confronted me, but no normal woman would have been. I almost returned to the beliefs of infancy, and credited the tales of Satanic power. So Aunt Jessica has been the means of restoring my childhood's faith, a suitable office for her, and a suitable part of the faith, if truth were known."

Jessica rose and led the children from the room.

"You have driven Aunt Jessica away," said Esmond. "That is an odd thing to happen in her house."

"Not compared to the other things that happen there. They set a standard that makes the house a harbour for anything. I should feel I was talking in a strange way enough, if I were doing it anywhere else."

"What in the world has passed between you?"

"This house is not the place to reveal it. Aunt Jessica was firm there, though she did not scruple to stage the scene in its inner shrine. But she has the right to say, and so we will leave the matter."

"That is a relief," said Tullia. "I was beginning to fear all sorts of revelations. If you choose to have private and unbelievable scenes, you owe it to other people to keep them to yourselves."

"I cannot take that view of Anna's debt to us," said Bernard.

"It takes two to make a scene," said Terence.

"You are mistaken. It does not. It took one," said Anna. "You are thinking of a quarrel. This was not that."

"Aunt Jessica thought it would pollute the ears of her children," said Esmond.

"And she is right," said his sister. "It would."

"I cannot think why you revealed that you had a dispute at all," said Tullia.

"We should have given ourselves away," said Anna, in a resigned tone, relaxing in her chair. "Our flustered condition would have betrayed us. It was better to get in first and intercept the flood of questions. And now the matter may rest."

"That is not the word for its working in our minds," said Bernard.

"Aunt Jessica did not look flustered," said Esmond.

"She looked other things," said Anna. "I don't think that can have escaped you."

"They say that anticipation is the best part of anything," said Bernard. "I find I cannot agree."

"It may well be that in this case," said his sister, grimly.

"Why must you give the account?" said Tullia. "I hope I may be spared it."

"I cannot think you are sincere," said Bernard.

"I don't know," said Anna, in a tone of some sympathy, resting her eyes on Tullia. "I do not see why Aunt Jessica's children should be troubled by the matter."

"A conclusion that you come to rather late," said Esmond.

"Now that we have heard so much, we will hear it from my mother's own lips," said Terence.

"Well, no doubt you will do that," said Anna, in a mild tone.

"I suggest that you leave the matter, my daughter," said Benjamin. "Indeed I direct you to do so."

"I am more than willing, if I am allowed to, Father. I keep on being dragged back to it. I should be glad enough of release."

"You may consider yourself free," said Esmond.

"Then pray let us talk about the weather."

"It is worthy of comment," said Benjamin, looking at the window. "Indeed we are bound by it for the time."

"Oh, don't say that," said his daughter, sitting up with an expression of consternation. "And Aunt Jessica may return at any moment. My escape was becoming the first object in my mind."

"You can achieve it by walking through the rain," said Esmond.

His sister seemed to give the matter her thought.

"That would attract too much notice. I think I must grin and bear the position. Aunt Jessica will be better able to pass me over, than if I made myself conspicuous by my absence."

"You seem to have an instinct of protection towards my mother," said Terence.

"I believe I did have it for a moment," said Anna, with an air of being half-startled by herself. "It was an instinct or an impulse or something; there was nothing quixotic about it. I was taken by it unawares."

"I will take you home, if you want to go."

"Will you?" said Anna, starting to her feet. "Then let us set off before either of your parents appears. You set an example to my unchivalrous brothers."

"Why is your departure less conspicuous for involving that of Terence?" said Esmond.

"The absence of two makes a smaller party. That of one could yawn as an abyss," said his sister, edging through the door, as if it were a case for furtiveness.

"Did my mother seem very unlike herself?" said Terence, as they went into the rain.

"Yes and no," said Anna, almost pausing for consideration, in the face of the weather. "Not so unlike herself, as I know her. Very unlike, as you do, I should say."

"Why should there be that difference? You have hardly seen her alone."

"That was true until to-day. It is not true now. I saw her alone with a vengeance, and I somehow got the impression that she was acting according to herself."

"You cannot mean that you know her better than I do."

"No, I don't suppose I mean that," said Anna, in a manner of uncertainty. "But I rather think I do, odd thing though it seems to say."

"You must have had a strange discourse," said Terence.

"I am not going to give you a summary of it," said Anna, hastening along with a spring in her step, that came from a sense of his proximity.

"Do you mind if she repeats it?"

"Of course not. Why should I?" said Anna, turning to look at him in some surprise.

"Then I am free to ask her any question?"

"I suppose so. What have I to do with it? I would hardly recommend your probing into the matter, but it is not my affair."

"Do I run the risk of any startling revelation?"

"No, I don't think so," said Anna, slowly; "I can only suppose not."

"Do you mean that my mother might not give me a true account?"

"Well, I would not in her place," said Anna, "Not using the words, 'in her place,' in a full sense."

"I have never known her say an untrue word."

"No," said Anna, in a still slower tone. 'But it is easy to leave words unsaid. That would not give her the feeling of using deceit."

"Indeed it would, if it gave a wrong impression. She would not be bound by the letter. She is not a simple person."

"No, no, she is not," said Anna.

"Do you mean that she might play a double part?"

"She might do anything, according to my conception of her," said Anna, in a tone so quick and light that it almost seemed meant to elude his ears.

"My mother cannot stand scenes and arguments," said Terence, in a sharper tone. "She is not fit for them."

"I can hardly see her except as rather well endowed for the purpose."

"You know she is almost a nervous invalid?"

"No, no, that is not so," said Anna, shaking her head. "She is a person of considerable nervous reserve and power."

"It must seem to me that I know her better than you do."

"Yes," said Anna, slackening her pace and looking into his face; "I suppose it must."

"You mean that I am mistaken?"

"Well, I feel that no one can know her but me, that she has not given anyone else the opportunity."

"She cannot have sides that she has hidden from me all my life."

"Does not that sort of thing always happen in families?"

"At what a rate you travel!" said Terence, catching her up. "The rain is much less. Why do you use such a pace?"

"I have received a goad, and I suppose still feel its impetus."

"You talk unlike yourself. I thought you were a person who said what came into her mind."

"I am not the woman I was yesterday," said Anna, between jest and earnest. "I feel like the people in history, who never smiled again."

"So I am to regard you as a stranger?"

"Well, you had not so much of an opinion of me, had you? I suppose you liked me as your blunt, straightforward cousin."

"I wish I could continue to like you as that."

"No," said Anna, shaking her head, "I am not going to be drawn. I hold to my resolve. I will not be led into disclosures."

"My mother would not mind your saying anything that was true."

Anna looked at her cousin with an equivocal expression.

"Well, I should not say anything that wasn't. But I have not her sanction to reveal anything at all."

"So she was in a position to impose conditions. That throws another light on the matter."

"She does seem to have indicated the course to be pursued," said Anna, as if slowly coming to this realisation. "I suppose I let her do so. She must appeal to some sort of chivalrous instinct. I believe I felt that she must be saved from herself."

"I wish that could be done for her indeed."

"Most of us are our own worst enemies, I suppose."

"No, we are our own best friends. Even our criticism of ourselves is confined to the night. And fancy criticism not being more public than that! There is no reason to save people from themselves, only from other people. My mother is an exception."

"I don't think I have these remorseful night-time moments. And any daylight soul-searching does not show me so much to be ashamed of. Not much to be proud of either;

merely a plain, cleanish, dull sheet. I don't mean that I do not welcome any good that comes my way."

"That shows what a friend you are to yourself. Other people hardly do that for us."

"No, they want it all for themselves," said Anna, in a resigned tone.

"You mean that my mother feels that she should inherit her sister's money. But as it is her real opinion, it throws no light on her."

"It is the opinion that throws the light, I suppose," said Anna, seeming not to give much attention to her words.

"She is not so much concerned with the money, as with Aunt Sukey's state of mind."

"Yes, that must be a weight on her," said Anna, in the same manner.

"Was Aunt Sukey in such a depressed mood?"

"Well, not so much depressed, as angry and hard and bitter. She seemed in a state of final disillusionment somehow. And that is sad in the last hours of a person's life. It struck me as sad, though I did not suspect that the end was so near."

"Well, if it was a final condition, any extra time could not have remedied it."

"Not in any way that would have resulted in benefit to your family."

"You know I did not mean that."

"Then what did you mean?" said Anna, in a downright tone. "You were thinking of the will, as you know. Well, your mother claims the money, because Aunt Sukey might have left it to her; and I claim it because she did leave it to me. There is not a hair's breadth between us, or we will say there is not, though some people would not agree. I should not have thought of the money, if it had not fallen to me. Indeed I did not think of it."

"You hardly had any reason."

"People find reasons, if their minds have that particular trend."

"You cannot say that my mother's has it."

"Well, I don't see how I am to say anything else, after my particular experience. But let us say that I know nothing about your mother. That is the best way to leave it. Now with Aunt Sukey, miles though she was above me in looks and manners and mind, I had that sense of affinity, that makes us at our best with our flesh and blood. It is a satisfying feeling; I don't know how I shall get on without it."

"You have plenty of people related to you. But they are not supposed to render us that kind of service."

"Well, I am not much of a one for outsiders. I am happy enough with my outspoken, unadmiring family. If I do not appear to advantage amongst them—and I daresay I don't; indeed I don't think I do—I don't break my heart over it. Father and I are good enough friends, and it was satisfying to meet his sister, and find the same sort of bond. It was a great addition to my lot. It is difficult to give it up, just as I had come to depend on it."

Anna controlled her words and her tone, but once again quickened her pace.

"You do not feel the same with my mother?"

"I feel what she has made me feel. I am not going to expand on it. You will hear her side of the matter, and it is the one you had better hear. There could never be a stronger case of the difference between two points of view. And you must choose one and abide by it. That is what people do."

"But I am not the same as other people. It is absurd to have to tell you quite so often."

Anna gave a laugh as she reached her door.

"Well, thank you for coming home with me. I have no doubt that it went against the grain. It could hardly do otherwise, when I was escaping from your family. So I will not make you the poor return of asking you in."

"It was clearly my business to give you any help I could," said Terence.

As Anna watched him go down the drive, her eyes lighted and deepened her face, so that it almost bore a look of Jessica. Her resolve to hold to her money had its root, had her cousin known it, in her feeling to himself. The woman who relinquished it, would be less acceptable in the end than the woman who held it. Anna could look beyond the hour; no credit or success of the moment weighed with her; a sacrifice easy to accept was easy to forget, and she would have been readier to make it, if it had had less reason.

Her father and brothers returned from the Calderons' house. They could hardly sympathise both with Anna and their aunt, and hesitated to remain under the latter's roof. Anna looked up and spoke in an ironic manner.

"Well, did you bring me any messages from my relatives?"

"One from your aunt," said her father. "She hopes you will go to see them as usual, and they will like to come here."

"Well, that is heaping coals of fire upon my head! But it is a course in which I never place much faith. It either means that people feel they owe it, or that they want to put the other person into their debt. I can always dispense with an obvious rendering of good for evil."

"I think it sits rather naturally on Aunt Jessica," said Bernard.

"I object to afterthoughts," said his sister. "It is the feeling of the moment that counts. We can all do pretty well with enough reflection. Second thoughts are only best in that sense. Did you meet Terence on your way?"

"He came to his gates, as we went out of them," said Benjamin.

"Well, let us forget the other family, Father. The mere fact of being under their roof is too much."

"Your experience went beyond that," said Esmond. "Now we can hear your account of what took place."

"Oh, it was only words, words, words, if you mean what passed between Aunt Jessica and me. There was her opinion that Aunt Sukey's will should be ignored, and another imagined, against mine that it should be accepted as it was made," said Anna, in a swift, almost careless tone, that seemed to put the matter quickly behind. "This creating of wills to meet a situation does not hold water. I could not support it. It had to end in nothing."

"As it had done before," said Esmond.

"The matter should have been allowed to rest," said Benjamin. "I do not say a word about your aunt; she is not to be judged as other people. But your uncle should have ensured it."

"Oh, I agree with you, Father. I had the most terrible hour. It was not a fair way to treat a person under their roof. And to choose Aunt Sukey's room, by way of refining the torment! But it roused the devil within me, and defeated its purpose. I became as different a person as Aunt Jessica. I do not blame her, and did not at the moment. I even felt inclined to yield to her in a sense. But I did not submit to the method she chose. That was not the way to my compassion."

"It was fortunate for you that she chose it," said Esmond.

"Your words have ceased to have any meaning," said Benjamin to his son. "You would do as well not to waste them."

"I cannot picture Aunt Jessica taking such a course," said Bernard.

"I feel now that I could always have imagined it," said his sister. "But I did not have to do so. I was confronted by the stark reality. And my imagination could achieve anything with regard to her now. She stimulates that faculty to uncanny feats."

"Forget it, my daughter," said Benjamin. "It was a difficult passage for both of you, and it is behind."

"No, no, Father," said Anna, shaking her head. "The scene is indelibly engraved on my memory. That room as the background, and Aunt Jessica and I grouped in the foreground, looking each other in the eyes! Or rather I doing that, and Aunt Jessica's eyes going anywhere and everywhere but to my face. Strange, elusive eyes they are; they don't seem to focus anywhere. I thought I should be afraid to meet them, that they would probe into my inmost soul, a thing that no one quite likes to face; but I found myself pursuing them, so that they should have to meet mine. The setting of the scene was supposed to bring me to my knees. But it had the opposite effect. It was such an obvious misuse of poor Aunt Sukey's corner. And I don't like clever and mean ideas. And now I can never enter the room again, and not only for the natural reasons, but for these contrived and nameless ones."

"As it is to be Uncle Thomas's study, you may not incur much pressure to do so," said Esmond.

"I disliked that use for it at first. I thought it was a rather cold and callous way of turning Aunt Sukey's death to account. But it has come to seem a sort of protection. It will save both it and me from worse."

"It is but a room," said Bernard. "Let us hear more of the human scene enacted in it."

"I wonder if Anna knows how little she has told us," said Esmond.

"I should have thought I had told you all kinds of things that I hardly knew, myself," said his sister, putting her hands to her cheeks. "Anyhow I have said all I can bring myself to utter of the sorry scene. The mere discomfort of it was enough. I have never felt such a weight of anything so vague. And Aunt Jessica gave me the strangest sense of guilt, and traded on the feeling until I quite admired her ingenuity and resource. She might have been a member of the Inquisition, and I her victim. And she is such an actress, whether she knows it or not, that I found myself overcome by her pathos, and undertaking not to betray her to her family."

"A promise that you broke on the first opportunity," said Esmond.

"Not at all. She was not referring to her claim on the

money; everyone knew about that. It was the interchange of thoughts and opinions, that she did not want revealed."

"You do not share the feeling," said Esmond.

"Don't I? You told me just now how little I had told you. It would be a certain relief to put it all off my mind. It is a good deal to keep bottled up within me. But she is Aunt Sukey's sister, after all, and I am her niece, and that can be the end of the matter."

"It was strange to exact such a promise after such a scene," said Benjamin.

"Yes," said Anna, nodding towards him, as if she shared the view, "it was the most contradictory state of affairs. We might have been inmates of a madhouse. I hardly knew where I was."

"Then it hardly mattered your being in Aunt Sukey's room," said Esmond.

"But she managed to suggest her wishes, and I found I had fallen in with them," went on his sister, as if she had not heard. "It seems a weak thing to do. I am not proud of it. It was more suggestibility and reluctance to struggle with a virtual invalid, than anything better."

"I daresay Aunt Jessica is not seeking to impute any higher motives."

"Oh, no," said Anna, lightly. "Even if I relinquished the money, she would not do that. She would accept it as her due, as she accepts all else that she is given."

"She would not claim it, if she did not see it as that," said Benjamin. "We do her that justice. She is not a stranger to us."

"Mere justice is not at all to her mind, Father," said Anna, shaking her head. "She is used to so much more. All her family give it to her, some of them reluctantly, I admit, and perhaps Uncle Thomas as a way of avoiding trouble. Even Aunt Sukey showed her magnanimity. She had a much scantier measure herself."

"Except from her sister," said Benjamin.

"Yes, Aunt Jessica came out above herself there," said

Anna in full concession. "Aunt Sukey brought out her higher side. I am the first to recognise it."

"And did you bring out her lower?" said Esmond.

"Well, something did," said his sister, sighing. "And as no one else was there, I suppose it was me. There is a pleasant reflection. Of course it was the money really."

"Well, you have kept your hold of it," said Bernard. "Through fire and water you have come, with it in your hands. And to lose it without the honour of freely relinquishing it would be too much. And that does emerge as the alternative."

"It will be a long time before I can treat it as my own, with Aunt Jessica's eyes fixed upon me. I can hardly imagine myself using it with a free hand. And of course we shall not have it yet. There will be death duties and other things."

"Those are generally paid out of capital," said Bernard.

"I think I should like to meet them out of income," said his sister, in a considered manner. "I don't want to reduce the legacy at the outset. I would rather keep what is virtually a gift from Aunt Sukey, whole and intact, as she left it, so that I can see it as she saw it herself, all my life."

"It might certainly meet a different fate in the hands of Aunt Jessica," said Esmond. "Perhaps Aunt Sukey left it to you, to save it from being dispersed. People like to feel that their hoard will survive them, as a monument of themselves. They do not want their last traces to be obliterated."

"Well, why should they?" said Anna. "And how like you to use the word, 'hoard'! I can understand their point of view. It is said that money is left to people who do not need it, and there may be something underlying it. I do not say there is not. 'Money to money' is a phrase, isn't it? That rather bears out the view, and may throw light on Aunt Sukey's decision."

"Your Aunt Jessica was speaking of the funeral," said Benjamin, his voice recalling that there was another side to the matter. "It is to be on Friday. No doubt some of us should go."

"I suppose all of us," said his daughter. "There does not seem to be any reason for avoiding it, though I should rather like to find one. I do not look forward to the ceremony. It seems to set the final and irrevocable seal on everything."

"Are the rest of us supposed to anticipate it?" said Claribel, glancing at Anna's brothers.

"Do we not realise that this particular lane has no turning?" said Esmond.

"Oh, nothing is the same to any two people," said Anna.

"Aunt Jessica is not going," said Reuben. "She is going to stay at home with Julius and Dora."

"Then I think that releases me," said Anna, looking round. "I do not see why I should face what she will not. I will remain behind with Reuben. I don't much care for the experience for him. And I never think a funeral is in a woman's line."

"My first will certainly be my own," said Claribel, "and I would stay away from that, if I could."

"Well, that is a natural point of view," said Bernard.

"I think it would be better for me to go," said Reuben. "I have never seen a funeral, and if Bernard and Esmond are going, it would attract attention if the third brother stayed away."

Anna looked from him to the others with grim humour.

"Well, my sons and I will go," said Benjamin, his voice betraying his view of his command of this escort.

"And Jenney will go, won't she?" said Reuben, feeling he had made a rash undertaking.

"Yes, I will go with you," said Jenney, in a tone of giving a promise.

"And your daughter will be here to welcome you back, Father," said Anna. "You will be glad of someone who has kept aloof, by the time you reach the climax."

"I suppose Tullia is going," said Bernard. "I did not hear that she was not."

"Oh, Tullia can cast things off," said Anna. "And she may prefer a funeral to an hour with Aunt Jessica."

"She does not feel to her mother in that way," said Benjamin. "You must know that she does not."

"Oh, well, I may read into her mind what would be in my own. It is inevitable that I should do so. Aunt Jessica has made an end of things between her family and me. But I should have thought her way of making people feel at a disadvantage would hardly be in Tullia's line."

"It would not be in mine," said Bernard, "but I cannot say I have felt it."

"No," said Anna, looking at him in unprejudiced consideration, "I don't suppose you have. I should say it would be like that; a man would escape. Now Terence would rather be with his mother than face the funeral."

"Is Aunt Jessica not a nice person?" said Reuben.

"She has different sides, like most of us," said his sister.

"You do not seem to like her."

"Well, I hardly could, considering the aspect she has shown to me. But there is no reason why you should not, if she shows you a different one. And she has been very kind to you, hasn't she?"

"Do you think it is so very wrong to think she ought to have Aunt Sukey's money?"

"No, I think it is quite natural. I should have thought she ought myself, if Aunt Sukey had died without a will. But there are different methods of trying to put right what you feel is wrong, and she did not choose a good or kind one. You have heard so much, that you must hear just a little more. And we should always accept wills without any question, because they are a kind of message from someone who is dead. We all want Aunt Sukey's wishes to be carried out, don't we?"

"Doesn't Aunt Jessica want them to be?"

"Oh, I don't know, I am sure," said Anna, turning away and speaking in a voice with a sigh in it.

CHAPTER XI

"CAN I SPEAK to you, Miss Jennings?" said Ethel.

"Yes, if you have anything to say, and have really thought about it," said Jenney, implying that she must withhold her ear from rash decisions.

"I hardly know how to break it to you, Miss Jennings."

"You make me feel quite nervous," said Jenney, pleasantly and with truth, giving a shake to her needlework.

"It is the worst," said Ethel, in a warning manner.

Jenney felt that Ethel's estimate of her own value was more true than becoming, perhaps could hardly be both.

"There has not been an accident?" she said, as if this was the natural interpretation of the words.

"No one in this house, Miss Jennings."

"What is the trouble?" said Bernard from the sofa.

"It is Mrs. Calderon," said Ethel.

"Who has had an accident?"

"It may have been that, sir."

"Oh, what has happened?" said Jenney.

"The worst, Miss Jennings. I can say no more."

"Do you mean that she is dead?"

"You had the preparation," said Ethel, with a note of reproach.

"Oh!" said Jenney, folding her work in a form suitable for resumption, as she would not have done, if the trouble had been in the house. "Oh, what has happened? Anything is better than suspense."

"I hardly liked to say that," said Bernard. "I always wonder that people admit it."

"She was found," said Ethel, in a deeper tone, urged to

the point, as Bernard had intended, by the threat of digression from it.

"By whom?" said Jenney. "What had happened?"

"Poor Miss Tullia!" said Ethel.

"Do you mean that she found her?"

"It seems to be fated, when it was she who came on Miss Donne."

There was a silence.

"It may be her father next, if these things go in threes," said Ethel. "It was doing something for him, that took her to the room. They were making it into his study."

There was a pause.

"You would think they would relinquish that project now," said Ethel.

"And how did she find Mrs. Calderon?" said Bernard.

"It confronted her, sir, as she crossed the threshold."

"Was she lying on the ground?"

"It was the selfsame chair, sir, where Miss Donne breathed her last."

There was another silence.

"You would hardly think they would use that chair now," said Ethel. "Or use the room at all. You would think they would shut it away from approach."

"Have they any idea of the cause of death?" said Bernard.

"Suppose one of the children had gone in," said Ethel. "Poor little Miss Dora!"

"It might have meant being transfixed," said Cook.

"Come in, Cook," said Bernard.

Cook came forward with a movement that would hardly have been detectable, if it had not resulted in an advance.

"These are times," she said, in the tones that gave people a sense of surprise that they had heard them. "Death upon death."

"And there may be the third," said Ethel.

"But what was the cause of this?" said Bernard. "Is it known or not?"

"We do not speak evil of the dead," said Ethel. "Not a word will pass my lips."

Cook supported the silence.

"But it will have to be known," said Jenney. "And someone must have told you."

"We are never spared bad news," said Ethel.

"We cannot say the same," said Bernard, "and so must ask your help."

"If it is that," said Ethel.

"A strange word," murmured Cook.

"There may have been every excuse," said Ethel. "I am the last to deny it."

"We might all fall," said Cook.

"We will make all the excuses we can, when we are in a position to do so," said Bernard. "You are preventing them from being made. That hardly seems a proper thing."

"Miss Donne was never driven to it," said Ethel. "Not with all she faced."

"So that was it!" said Jenney.

There was a pause.

"How did she do it?" said Bernard.

"She took her own way," said Ethel.

"But she must have followed some method."

"It is not often that a sister's need is made the instrument of such a thing."

"Miss Donne's medicines!" said Jenney. "Were they still in the room?"

"But they were harmless," said Bernard.

"You can attain the amount," said Ethel.

"There was something for preventing pain," said Jenney. "I don't think Miss Donne ever needed it. They knew too much of that would be dangerous."

"To think that with escape at hand, she never availed herself of it!" said Ethel, whose mind was becoming inured to the step.

"Never fell from her height," said Cook. "And with that lovely face!"

"Was it all over when Mrs. Calderon was found?" said Bernard.

"Beyond recall," said Ethel. "If she would have thought better of it, it was too late."

"Is the truth officially known?"

Ethel looked at Bernard.

"Has any definite message come?" said Jenney.

"Things travel in their own way," said Cook.

"We see that they do," said Bernard, "but has this come in any accepted way?"

"We had no choice but to accept it," said Ethel.

Benjamin entered the room with a letter in his hand, followed by Esmond, looking as usual, and by Anna, pale and shaken. Claribel followed with her head thrown backwards, as if in resigned acceptance of the truth. None of them noticed Cook and Ethel, or had the opportunity to do so, as they made an imperceptible retreat.

"That is sad news, Mr. Donne," said Jenney, in a conventional and therefore unnatural manner.

"How did you know it?" said Esmond. "Of course it is the kind of thing that must be known."

"I suppose it must be true," said Benjamin. "The letter is from my brother-in-law. There can be no doubt."

"It is an appalling position for me," said Anna. "Aunt Jessica to do this, just as I had been quarrelling with her! Or so it will be said. Of course she was really making an attack on me, but sight will be lost of that."

"There are other aspects of the situation," said Esmond.

"And other times for sneering," said his sister.

"I wonder if we shall ever know what her real reasons were," said Jenney.

"As she is not alive to tell the tale, I don't see how we can," said Anna. "It seems that she was moody and absent for some hours, and then crept away by herself and did this. Aunt Sukey's room too! There seems to be no end to the pollution of it. No wonder she said such strange things. She must have been in an abnormal state."

"Forget that last hour with her," said Benjamin, "and remember those that went before."

"No, that is the one that must stand out in my memory, Father. I suppose it was the culmination of all that was going wrong. I did not have much luck in being the victim of it."

"Aunt Jessica seems to have had less," said Esmond.

"Her life was too heavy on her," said Benjamin. "It seems that we ought to have known."

"Now why was it?" said Anna. "She had a good husband and a good home and good children, and money enough for her needs. How many people have to manage with less!"

"It often seems that they manage better," said Claribel. "I wonder it is not accepted."

"Happiness does not depend on what we have," said Benjamin.

"She seems to think it does," said Anna. "Seemed to think it did, I mean. How muddled one gets, with one's relations following each other off the earth at such a pace! It seemed that all her peace depended on what she was to possess. It was a strange and tragic thing."

"It was, when the peace was not thought to be worth the price," said Esmond.

"Oh, we all know that yours was disturbed, and the reason of it."

"Aunt Jessica had other things in her life," said Bernard. "We may give the will too large a place."

"No, no," said Anna, sighing, "there is not that loophole. There was nothing else in her mind. Nothing else existed for her. You were not present."

"We shall begin to think we were," said Claribel.

"I shall not," said Esmond.

"I am sure I welcome any sense of fellowship as regards the scene," said Anna. "I have no feeling of proprietorship in it."

"That sense is satisfied in other ways," said Esmond.

"And how yours would be satisfied in the same way!" said his sister, resting her eyes on him. "How one sees that now!"

"There will have to be another funeral," said Jenney. "Well, everything is ready, isn't it?"

"The routine is established," said Esmond. "Anna and Claribel remain at home, and the rest of us are present in person."

"I feel rather one by myself," said Bernard. "I am sorrowing for Aunt Jessica."

"And not alone, my son," said Benjamin.

"I am not," said Anna, shaking her head. "No, not now. I could have been, but the capacity was crushed in me. For Aunt Sukey, yes; I sorrowed for her, if you will. I see the difference too well, to be in any doubt."

"I think I am sorrowing more for Aunt Jessica," said Bernard.

"She seemed to me the better of the two," said Esmond. "I never understood why Aunt Sukey was Anna's choice."

"Perhaps because I was hers," said his sister. "That does give the best foundation."

"Aunt Jessica looked on us all with affection, a rare thing in a woman with a family," said Bernard. "And now that has gone out of our lives."

"It is indeed a loss in them," said Benjamin.

"It was never in mine," said Anna. "And you must remember that Bernard is a man, Father. It was a thing Aunt Jessica never forgot."

"It meant nothing to her," said Esmond.

"Well, what a thing to happen in the family!" said Jenney.

"I was wondering who would say it," said Bernard. "I would not be the first, for fear I had thought it too soon."

"Oh, I can keep my tongue still about that," said Anna. "I do not cast that up against Aunt Jessica's memory."

"We resent nothing that is helpless," said Benjamin.

"Well, that is putting it better, Father."

"We take the matter rather lightly," said Esmond.

"I was wondering why," said his brother.

"I can tell you," said Anna. "Aunt Jessica cast a cloud over people, and it is something to be free from it. I think even Father will understand."

"I wish I had been of more help to her," said Benjamin.

The door opened and Reuben came into the room with a jumping step.

"So Aunt Jessica is dead now," he said, speaking just before he paused.

"Yes, she died this morning," said Jenney, in a repressive manner. "She has gone to be with your Aunt Sukey."

"She killed herself, didn't she?" said Reuben. "Isn't that supposed to be a wicked thing to do?"

"For some people. There are different cases."

"You can be punished for it by the law. I know you can, because Terence told me. Of course he didn't know that his mother was going to do it."

"Hush. You cannot punish someone who is dead."

"It was a case of attempted suicide. That is a crime."

"It went further than that," said Esmond. "It is an instance of success in the enterprise."

Reuben went into discordant mirth.

"You have been talking to the servants," said Anna.

"Of course he has. What else was he to do?" said Bernard.

"Does Father mind very much?" said Reuben, glancing at Benjamin and hardly lowering his voice.

"Very much. You know that he must," said Jenney.

"You mind, yourself, don't you?" said Anna. "You were very fond of Aunt Jessica."

Reuben held himself in a position for further jumping, a sign of indifference that was needed, as his eyes had filled. Benjamin took no notice of him, understanding the manifestation, but knowing it arose from feeling nothing to his own, and rather repelled than otherwise by the twofold difference.

"Will any of us have to go to the house?" said Anna. "I shall not be the first to volunteer."

"Perhaps that would hardly be expected," said Esmond.

"Oh, one never knows," said Anna.

"I shall be going almost at once," said Benjamin. "My place is with my sister's family. And some of you should come with me."

"Well, I will face the music," said his daughter. "I shall not be seeing Aunt Jessica, and can never be called upon to do that again. And I suppose nothing has come between me and the rest."

"Aunt Jessica can't be buried in consecrated ground," said Reuben, in a clear tone.

"Hush. Of course she can," said Jenney.

"But suicides can't."

"Hush. Don't use such a word. This was a sort of accident. It happened because she was not well."

"There will be a verdict of unsound mind," said Benjamin.

"And I believe a true one," said Anna, "seldom though I daresay that is the case."

"Then it sweeps away any reason for resentment."

"Indeed it does, Father. There I quite agree. I begin to understand that feeling of protection I had towards her."

"Poor Tullia!" said Bernard.

"Why, I think she will stand up to it better than most people," said his sister. "I should rather say, 'Poor Terence.'"

"Doesn't Tullia mind things so very much?" said Reuben.

"Well, not as much as some of us perhaps. Or it always seems to me that she does not."

"Perhaps she would say the same of you," said Bernard.

"Oh, I daresay she would. People have often said it of me," said Anna, with a resigned sigh. "Not that it seems to me that I am the right target for that particular shaft. But I don't look for much from that family, or from the women of it."

"Why didn't Aunt Sukey live with us?" said Reuben.

"Well, I was too young for the charge, when the arrangement was made."

"I daresay she would not have left you the money, if she had lived in our house. I expect people get tired of the people they live with."

"There is something in that," said Anna, in a sincere tone. "It is quite possible that she would not."

"So the people who take care of other people, have all the trouble, and don't have so much money."

"They had the advantage of having Aunt Sukey for all those years. I wish we had seen more of her."

"Even though you might not have had the money?"

"We never think about wills, while people are alive," said Jenney.

"Aunt Jessica must have thought about Aunt Sukey's. Or she wouldn't have minded when she found that it left things to Anna."

"Well, we know she did think about it," said Anna; "I am afraid too much. But that is a point where we need not copy her. So we will leave it now."

"You can't help knowing that an invalid might die. And that means there will have to be a will. So you have to think about it."

"We have thought enough about this one," said Benjamin.

"Have you thought how you will miss Aunt Jessica?" said Anna to Reuben, in a tone of some reproach. "You know how you missed Aunt Sukey; and although this cannot be the same, it will make a great difference."

"I think I am more sorry that we have lost Aunt Jessica."

"I am sure you are sad about them both. It does seem a change in our life after a few short months. What an end to Father's plan of giving his time to his sisters!"

"I suppose we shouldn't have come here, if we had known they were going to die?"

"We should have done so all the more," said Benjamin.

"And yet Father's being here did not make Aunt Jessica not do what she did," said Reuben, casting his eyes about, as if undecided about their direction.

"Perhaps nothing would have done that, except not losing her sister," said Jenney. "You must not tell Julius and Dora how it happened. They are to think their mother died in the same way as their aunt. Mind you remember, Reuben."

"I don't expect they will talk about her. They have not said anything about Aunt Sukey since she died. Some people don't talk about people who are dead, and I don't think it is only children."

"I could not follow that line," said Anna. "I could never sweep someone I had cared for, off my lips and out of my mind like that."

"It is your own idea that the one thing follows from the other," said Esmond.

"It may be, but I hold to it none the less. I never think it is a sign of deep feeling to be able always to suppress it. A stronger thing would get out of hand sometimes."

"Do people go to the funeral of a second aunt, when they have been to the first?" said Reuben.

"There is no need for you to go to this one," said Jenney.

"Well, I know what a funeral is like now," said Reuben, looking back at the heel of his boot.

"Reuben is open about the motives that govern his attendance," said Esmond.

Benjamin looked at his youngest son, and knew that this was not the case.

"Why is it a sign of respect to display oneself at a person's obsequies?" said Anna.

"That need not take you to them," said Esmond. "Your feeling stops short of that."

"It both stops short and goes beyond," said his sister.

"Have you done your lessons, Reuben?" said Jenney.

"No; I am not going to Terence to-morrow. I shall not see him until after the funeral."

"Has he sent a message?" said Anna.

"No, but you don't go to people when they have lost somebody, anyhow when it is a mother."

"Reuben has chosen his method of proving his feeling," said Esmond.

"The boy is right to stay away," said Benjamin. "But I must go to my sister's house. And my daughter and my eldest son will bear me company."

He left the room with these members of his family, and Claribel strolled out after them with an expression of troubled aloofness.

Reuben leaned back in his chair.

"Aunt Jessica's being dead won't make so very much difference to us, will it, Jenney?" he said in an almost appealing tone, ignoring Esmond, to whom he had no regard.

"Well, of course you will miss her."

"Well, when I was at home, I never saw her. And when I was at her house, I usually saw only Terence. So my life will be very much the same."

"Well, I daresay you will get used to it."

"It is really best not to think about it. Because it can't do any good. And there is no point in doing harm to yourself, when it doesn't do any good to anyone else."

"You will always like to think of your aunts. They would not wish you to forget them."

"I don't think we ever really forget people. I don't see how we could. So I think that is all right."

CHAPTER XII

BENJAMIN AND HIS elder children went to the Calderons' house, Anna walking behind the men, instead of following her custom of leading the way. Thomas came into the hall, as if he were expecting them.

"I am having as much help as my friends can give me, and you have come to add to it."

"We have come also to seek it," said Benjamin. "It is a dark hour in both our homes."

"It is that one room that stands out as the scene of dark things," said Anna, speaking in embarrassed haste. "I think I should close it, Uncle Thomas. There is no point in leading people's thoughts to dubious scenes."

"I was going to use it myself. My wife had gone there to prepare it for me."

"Well, as the breadwinner, I should avoid it," said his niece.

"I shall indeed have to fulfil that character now," said Thomas, turning his eyes to Benjamin. "With no wife to manage for me, and fewer sources of supply, I shall find my work enough. And I am in no great heart for it."

"Jessica's money is yours, of course?" said Benjamin. "I mean, it does not go to the children?"

"Don't say there is another will, that does not give satisfaction," said Anna, under her breath.

"No, this one should be as we expect," said Thomas.

"I think I had better keep my tongue still," muttered his niece.

"No further light has come on what happened?" said Benjamin.

"None could come," said Thomas. "Full light came at once."

"So Jessica could not face life without Sukey."

"She never more than just faced it," said Thomas in a steady tone. "And the extra demand was too much."

"Don't say that Aunt Sukey's will put any weight on the wrong side," murmured Anna.

"It gave her an insight into the mind of her sister, that troubled her," said Thomas.

"But she did not accept the will."

"She believed her sister meant to destroy it. But the fact of her making it was enough."

"Nothing alters the years of care that she gave her."

"No, but there was the question of her sister's view of them."

"I suppose I ought to feel that I should have given up the money."

"We all keep what is ours," said Thomas, with a note of weariness. "The question of what we should do, does not arise."

"Aunt Jessica thought it did."

"It would have in her case. She was not as other people are."

"I suppose you think I can't hold a candle to her?"

"No one comes up to her in goodness, to my mind," said Thomas, with a note of surprise.

"I am sure I quite agree," said Anna, rapidly. "I am only led to this survey of myself, by the common view of my part in the tragedy."

"It is not the last straw that breaks the camel's back," said Thomas. "It is all the others."

"It can hardly matter which straw one is," said Bernard.

Anna gave a laugh, and Thomas threw a glance at her.

"Oh, I had better go to the younger members of the family. I am not giving satisfaction here."

"No one is more upset than she is," said Benjamin, looking after his daughter. "I admit she has not the usual ways of showing it. But she would give up the money, to bring her aunt back."

"I should expect it, if it would do that," said Thomas. "But I cannot suggest that it would, though I should choose to have a claim on it. My being alone does not lighten my ordinary burdens."

Anna went into the library, where Terence was by himself.

"So you are all alone," she said.

"I am more solitary than I have ever been."

"You still have an appreciable family."

"It is the worst kind of loneliness to be alone among many."

"Well, a straw cannot make much difference, one way or the other," said Anna, sitting down.

"What did you say?" said Terence.

"I am held to be the last straw that broke your mother's back."

Terence broke into laughter.

"Father is in a cruel mood. He has said a dreadful thing to me. He is taking advantage of this moment when we have to forgive him everything."

"Oh, I forgive him," said Anna, in a tone of nonchalant sincerity.

"I do not. I find I cannot."

"What has he said to you?"

"That I must earn my living."

"Is that so very bad?"

"It is most ungenerous, when he has the power to do it, and I have not. He does not seem to wish to share everything with his son. He even said that he did not want to support my wife and family, which is more and more ungenerous. Fancy not wanting to support a helpless woman and children!"

"Well, what we give you for teaching Reuben won't go as far as that. But cannot you really do something more for yourself?"

"A breadwinner is born, not made. My mother quite understood it."

"Then that is what she meant by what she said to me," said Anna, as if to herself.

"What did she say?"

"Oh, nothing; just a word about wanting to feel that your future was safe, or something. I don't remember the exact words."

"If she had had her sister's noney as well as her own, she might have done something for me as the elder son. She was secretly inclined to favour me; it was a thing I respected so much in her. Surreptitious favouritism is so considerate to everyone; she would have scorned to be open about it. And now you have that money, and Father has hers, and you both say that I ought to earn some. I wonder your lips can frame the words."

"No, she did not take that view," said Anna, again as if to herself.

"What did she say about me?"

"Only something that made me feel that I should never get away from that will. It does not matter what it was."

"She did not ask you to give me any money?"

"No, no, not give it to you."

"Well, what was it that she said?"

"Nothing that I could put into words; something that makes me smile when I think of it," said Anna, suiting her action to her words. "And as it is not a occasion for smiling, I will put it out of my mind."

"But put it into mine first," said Terence.

"It was only a sort of instinctive suggestion. It would be meaningless, if it were permissible to say such a thing of Aunt Jessica," said Anna, her face relaxing again, as if she could not help it. "I will not repeat it; there would be nothing gained."

"You should not keep my mother's last words from me."

"It is true that they concerned you," said his cousin.

"I am glad that I was the last person in her thoughts. That is a thing for me to remember."

"Yes, remember that," said Anna, as if welcoming this end of the matter.

"Did she ask you to adopt me?"

Anna glanced at him for a moment.

"You are pretty warm," she said, the words seeming to come in spite of herself.

"In what way were you to do it?"

"Oh, in the way that a woman can adopt a man," said Anna, in a light, incidental tone.

"I am touched that my mother was matchmaking for me in her last hours."

"Yes, it is touching, isn't it?" said Anna, in a serious manner. "I think we can hardly estimate what it meant at such a time."

"You gave the impression that she had not been kind to you. But it was surely kind to want you for a daughter-in-law?"

"Oh, I don't think that I was in her thoughts. I was just the instrument to save you from poverty, or whatever she feared for you."

"It is my father's duty to care for me. But he is like an animal, and takes no thought for me, now I am mature."

"Well, no one but me heard your mother. These things arise from having people about, who are not held to count. No doubt she felt it and took advantage of it. But I find myself speculating how those who incurred her other words would take them; Florence and your father and all of them."

"Why, what did she say about Florence? I do not mind her words about Father. He deserves them."

"Oh, just the obvious things about her not being suitable for you, for material and other reasons."

"That was not the tone of my mother's speech," said Terence.

"Oh, no, no, it is mine," said Anna. "I am not quoting your mother. I should not dream of it. And I seldom make an attempt to give people's tone. It results in a much more erroneous impression, than just giving a natural account."

"I thought she and Florence had a liking for each other."

"They could hardly help it, could they, as everyone had one for them both? You should have seen Esmond's gaze on Florence the other day. My heart quite misgave me for my brother. I don't know what his luck may be."

"Are you attached to Florence yourself?"

"Well, yes, I suppose so. She is a pretty thing to follow with one's eyes. I don't know that I have got much further. And I have seen no sign that she wishes me to make any advance."

"Are you very fond of anyone?"

"Oh, well, yes, of two or three people, the inevitable two or three of a person who does not disperse her affections. I am not one for scattering mine; perhaps I have not enough to spare. My father, Aunt Sukey, Bernard, Reuben. In a secondary way, Jenney. Those are the objects of my attachment, or its victims."

"You are more my mother's niece than you know," said Terence.

"Yes, I know what you mean," said Anna, meeting his eyes for a moment. "I often felt a current of fellow-feeling running between us. I felt it even at that last meeting, when it was the last thing to be thought. That is how my accounts of it came to seem discrepant. I was the victim of a sort of dual feeling. I did not know how to cope with the channel of sympathy, that would flow out of me towards her, when my reason told me that I ought to be angry and insulted. And indeed I was both."

"It is a pity that you did not know each other better."

"Well, I never expect much precipitance in people's approach to me. There is not much about my outer self to help them forward."

"Aunt Sukey seems to have managed better," said Terence.

"There are always some of us who pierce the shells of certain others. I suppose it was an instance of that. I am fortunate that it was so, and do not feel entitled to expect another case of it."

"It is unfortuante that my mother's nerves were worked off on you."

"Oh, I understand it more and more. I may have been dense about it at the time. But she missed the essence of me, and that never helps a person to grasp the inner truth of another. And I may not be alive to the complexities of the subtle type, being built on plain and obvious lines myself."

"You certainly do not seem to have done each other justice."

"And that was harder on her than on me," said Anna, at once. "Because I am used to being missed, and taken for a rougher, cruder creature than I am. And she was more fortunate in her outer aspect and suggestions."

There was a pause.

"I suppose we should go to the others," said Terence. "I must not forget you are a guest."

"I suppose I may be a cousin," said Anna, following him with the hurrying step, that took her so little faster than other people's. "I have done nothing to forfeit that bond, as far as I can see. But you are more versed in the etiquette of a house of mourning than I am."

"You have not seen Tullia, have you?"

"I caught a glimpse of her, and was just vouchsafed a glance."

"I expect she was not thinking of what she was doing."

"I am sure she was not," said Anna, cordially. "How should she be at this time? And why should I expect to arrest her attention at any time?"

"You did not come in here to find her?"

"No, I thought the children were here. I fancied I heard their voices. They must have come from somewhere else."

"I don't think they are heard at all at this juncture," said Terence.

They went to the drawing-room to find their fathers talking by the fire, and the children sitting silent. Tullia was standing upright and aloof, as a person called to a different and tragic place, and Bernard was standing near, with a suggestion of attendance.

"Well, we are quite a party," said Anna.

"That is hardly the accepted aspect of the gathering," said Esmond.

"Now why call attention to someone's little false step?" said Anna, in a rather low but exasperated tone. "You should try to gloss it over, instead of making it as conspicuous as possible. The most elementary social sense should show you that. What do you gain by making someone else feel uncomfortable?"

"Esmond can hardly reply that he gains a mean, personal gratification," said Bernard.

Terence looked at Anna in sympathy, interpreting her outbreak in the light of his changing conception of her.

"Oh, well, I daresay these things slip out," she said, subsiding into a seat.

"It sometimes seems that people are not fair on Anna," said Terence to Bernard.

"She has that odd attribute, carelessness of the impression she makes."

"It would be a great thing to be free of the effort of making a good one. But what would happen to most of us without it?"

"Worse than to Anna," said Bernard, believing what he said. "But as you see, bad things happen to her."

"I believe my ears ought to be tingling," said Anna, glancing at the pair.

"It is good of you all to come and start us on our new life," said Thomas. "It prevents the gaps from yawning too wide before our eyes. To have them filled on the surface is something."

"I suppose the new life will not really seem to begin until after the funeral," said Anna.

"Anna may be an enemy to herself," said Esmond, "but other people do not escape."

"You seem to speak from personal knowledge," said Terence to Anna.

"Well, my life had in effect to start again after Aunt Sukey's death. Yes, I know what I am talking about. I wish I did not."

"It is a pity that we have to know so much," said Terence. "I often feel that I cannot sustain the weight of my knowledge. And with every day it gets worse."

"I feel rather an empty, ignorant person on the whole. Apart from one's own individual depths, of course. I suppose everyone has those."

"I wish I did not know that they had. I am really not equal to it. I wish I could know so much, that I knew that I knew nothing."

"Your young brother and sister must find you a perplexing elder," said Anna.

"I never talk to them," said Terence. "I have only just realised that. I wonder what they would think, if I did?"

"You can easily try," said Anna.

"I should have to break through that intense family shyness. And of course I should find that especially hard. But I must not let it conquer me. Julius, may I suggest that we hold some intercourse?"

"What?" said Julius.

"Because Mother is dead?" said Dora.

"There, you see what sort of reason strikes them as adequate. They may even think that I am trying to take their mother's place."

"Well, it wouldn't be a bad attempt to make," said Anna, resting her eyes on the children, as if in compassion.

"I should not be a success in the character. I have too gentle a nature. I could not manage that wise firmness."

"Well, it does not do to weigh children down, of course."

Terence's face darkened, and he turned to listen to Bernard.

"We are wondering which of my father's sisters was the more beautiful. We are all saying what we think."

"Aunt Sukey," said Anna.

"Mother," said Dora, looking surprised at there being any question.

"Uncle Benjamin doesn't seem like their brother," said Julius. "I think Mother looked the best."

"That is what I should say, my boy," said Thomas. "I should use those very words."

"Aunt Sukey had the advantage in a conventional sense," said Tullia.

"Then Aunt Sukey had it for you," said Terence. "That is the sense that counts. Beauty in any other sense means a lack of it. A face that is beautiful for what is in it, is a plain face to the person speaking of it. I would not give a fig for praise of looks in an unconventional sense."

"Then I think you may keep your figs, my son," said Thomas.

Julius and Dora broke into laughter, continued it with more abandonment for their repression, looked for their mother's reproof and fell into silence, realising that she was gone from their lives, as their deportment was uncontrolled on the occasion of her death.

"We must think of Aunt Sukey in the days when she was well," said Bernard.

"Even when she was ill, she was the best-looking person I have known," said Anna.

"I think I am with you, my daughter," said Benjamin.

"It was as a pair, that they made their impression," said Tullia.

"I thought they were better apart," said Terence. "To my mind they showed up each other in the wrong way."

"It is a pity that no one has inherited their looks," said

Anna. "It seems hard, when there were two of them to hand them down."

"What about my Tullia?" said Thomas.

"Oh, I did not mean to say the wrong thing. I never seem to go long without some blunder. I see my life before me as a succession of traps."

"You are not yet extricated from this one," said Esmond.

"Well, then, I will leave myself in it. There is no point in struggling out of it, to get involved in another. It would be no good to contradict myself now. Nothing I said, would mean anything."

There was some laughter, in which Tullia joined.

"I don't see anything so funny in thinking that our elders attained a higher standard of looks than we do."

"It is the most natural thing," said Tullia, in a light tone, glancing at the window.

"Esmond is our own show specimen, and he does not hold a candle to them."

"I still await a word about my Jessica's daughter," said Thomas, putting his arm round the latter.

"No, I am not taking any risks on that subject," said his niece, shaking her head. "It is better to be silent than to fall short, or damn with faint praise, or anything."

Tullia's laughter led the rest.

"I am glad I am so humorous," said Anna.

"What a lot we laugh, even though Mother is dead!" said Dora.

"Mother liked us to laugh, my little one," said Thomas.

"That isn't why you were laughing, is it," said Julius.

"She didn't seem much to like us to, when Aunt Sukey died," said Dora.

"She didn't laugh then, herself," said Julius.

"I think she would have liked to laugh more than she always could," said Thomas. "She would be glad for anyone else to do it."

"Perhaps she would be glad, now that she knows more

than she used to," said Dora, seeking to reconcile the view with facts as she remembered them.

"Yes, you must always think of Mother as she is now."

"But then we shall think of her as somebody different. Perhaps she would mind that."

"I shall think of her as the same," said Julius. "It seems to be better not to think about dead people too much. But I shouldn't ever think about them as different. It would not be thinking about them at all."

"Have you been out into the air to-day?" said Thomas, as if there must be something wanting in the influences on his son.

"No, we didn't know we might," said Dora. "Not when the blinds were down."

"You may go into the garden," said Tullia. "But you need not go too near the gate."

"Isn't it right for us to be out of doors?"

"Yes, of course it is, or Father and I would not allow it."

The children ran to the door, subduing a tendency to betray signs of relief.

"Poor little things!" said Anna.

"We have no idea what impression this tragedy is making on them," said Terence. "We must wait for the time when they write their lives."

"Why should they do that?"

"People don't seem to need any reason. Unless one of them writes the life of the other, when they may need a little more."

"I should never see any ground for writing mine. I shouldn't have the presumption to expect anyone to read it."

"I think mine would be of the greatest interest. It would reveal the twisted experience of a human soul."

"My experience is straight enough," said Anna. "Too straight to have any appeal, I suspect."

"Then haven't you a vague, yearning sense of unfulfilment?"

"Well, yes, I daresay I have. Yes, I suppose so sometimes."

"I could not bear to have that," said Terence. "I would rather suffer. I am glad that my mother suffered."

"You mean that you can't get her suffering out of your head," said Anna, nodding with an air of grave shrewdness.

"No, I do not. That is the truth. I mean that it was a good thing for her to suffer. It is too much for me to think anything else."

"The feelings will pass in time."

"They have begun to do so, but they will recur all my life. And I almost hope they will. I could not bear to be a shallow person."

"I should say you are not," said Anna, just throwing her eyes over his face. "The children do not know the truth of the matter, I suppose?"

"I do not know," said Terence. "It has been kept from them; and it ought to have been kept from me, when I have all the sensitiveness of a child."

"That is not always so great as is thought. I do not remember the struggles and misunderstandings that are said to be the lot of childhood."

"I still have them," said Terence. "I wonder if it is the gift of perennial youth. I don't think people have that in any other form."

"I wonder how many of us escape a guilty feeling, that our maturity ought to mean some secrets or mysteries or something."

"The feeling is not guilty," said Terence. "You will know that, when you have one that is. My life contains a fair proportion of secrets. I told you how like I was to a child. I do not often allow myself to think of them. Perhaps that is what is meant by putting away childish things."

"I suppose we assume or pretend that we have put them away," said Anna.

"Other people do it for us. They like us to carry burdens. You would not believe the duties that my father has put on me to-day. He simply assigns to me the part of a man. Is not that Miss Lacy in the hall?"

"Do you know her step?" said Anna.

"Yes, for years I listened for it. How like me to listen for it still!"

"Were you so anxious for her to come?"

"No, I used to go and hide. Somehow that strikes me as an amusing and charming thing."

"How did it strike her?" said Anna.

"I never knew. She remains a mystery to her pupils. It is when children don't know people, that they show the helplessness of their age; otherwise they show something different. No doubt she knew that."

"Do you want to hide to-day?"

"Yes, I dread her behaving as if nothing extraordinary had happened."

"Well, I suppose death is ordinary enough."

"Not this kind of death. I do not wish people to go as far as that. Acting should only be carried to the proper point."

Miss Lacy's voice was heard in an effort that did perhaps pass this stage.

"Well, my niece and I have come to spend an hour with you. We are getting tired of each other's company, and are glad of friends at so easy a distance."

Anna looked from Florence to Terence, and in a moment rose and, as if by a carefully unconsidered movement, cleared the way between them.

"It is good of you to come to this shadowed house," said Terence, to the guest. "I hope it will not cast its darkness over you. I am persuading myself that life is so bad, that it is reasonable to want to be rid of it."

"I suppose it often is," said Florence.

"I want you to say that it always is. My mother's life must not have been worse than the average."

"I do not see why it should have been."

"I think it was rather worse. But I think mine is too; so she only had to bear what I do. And I want to keep mine until the last possible moment. I would much rather have labour and sorrow than nothing."

"That is a strange view."

"But almost an universal one."

"And you don't take very kindly to labour, do you?" said Anna, from her distance, where she sat with her eyes on the pair.

"Well, a breadwinner is in such an ungraceful position, always trying to gain something. It is quite dreadful actually to be named after it."

"Women like men to do some work," said Florence.

"I have heard of the hardness of women, but does it really go so far?"

"Just as men like women to do the work that is their own."

"It must be the weakness of human nature," said Terence. "I have heard of that too. But I don't think we need dwell on it. It is better to forget those depressing things that cannot be helped."

"Some women will not marry a man who has no profession."

"Surely they could face poverty together. That is another thing I have heard of."

"That falls too hard on the woman," said Florence.

"But what about the self-sacrifice of women? I seem to have heard of so many things."

"No one should ask sacrifice of anyone else."

"You know that my family asked it of Anna," said Terence. "Even my mother did."

"Oh, that was because she really saw things in that way," called Anna from her place.

The words produced a silence, that was broken by Miss Lacy.

"So Reuben has not gone into the garden with the younger ones. Are they then so much younger?"

"I am not here for lessons to-day," said Reuben. "I just came with Father and Anna. I never go out with the children unless Aunt Jessica tells me to."

"Then are you never to do so again?" said Terence. "I think you have no choice but to take matters into your own hands."

"Poor child!" said Tullia. "Sitting here amongst these melancholy men and women! Pray let him go out and cast off the impression. I hope it is not an ineradicable one."

"Would you like me to be with them, my dear?" said Miss Lacy, half-rising from her seat.

"Well, I expect they would be better for comfort and guidance and everything. I don't know why we should look for such things from our friends, but at these times people feel entitled to them."

Miss Lacy went with a quiet step from the room.

"Now what can I do for all of you?" she said, as she caught up Reuben. "Now don't tell me there is nothing. I am a person who has her purposes."

"Where are the others?" said Reuben.

"I should guess they have gone to their temple," said Miss Lacy, turning her steps in this direction. "If they have not, some part of the garden will discover them."

Reuben hesitated to approach the rock, feeling that the help of religion would naturally be sought under the circumstances.

Julius and Dora were already soliciting it.

"O great and good and powerful god, Chung, grant that our life may not remain clouded, as it is at this present. And grant that someone may guide us in the manner of our mother, so that we may not wander without direction in the maze of life. For although we would have freedom, if it be thy will, yet would we be worthy of being our mother's children. And if there is danger of our inheriting the weaknesses of our mother and our aunt, thy late handmaids, guard us from them, O god, and grant that we may live to a ripe old age. For it would not be worth while to suffer the trials of childhood, if they were not to lead to fullness of days. And we pray thee to comfort our father and our brother and sister; and if they are in less need of comfort than beseems them, pardon them, O god, and lead them to know the elevation of true grief."

Dora's voice trembled for the first time, and her brother took his hands from his face and gave her a look of approval.

"And grant that our father may not form the habit of talking of our mother, and thus cast a cloud upon us; but rather may lock up all such things in his heart, and commune solely with himself upon them, so that his heart may know its own bitterness. Nevertheless not as we will, but as thou wilt. For Si Lung's sake, amen."

"We are more likely to have our prayers granted, for not insisting upon it," said Julius.

"And weaknesses is a good word for the causes of Aunt Sukey's dying and Mother's. It takes in everything, and does not call attention to things we should not know. It would not do to obtrude our knowledge, as if we were proud of it."

"It is really better if Mother did not die of natural causes," said Julius, "because those are the ones you can inherit."

"It is strange how, as we get older, our requests take on a touch of maturity," said Dora, investing her tone with the same touch.

"It is passing strange," said Julius. "Verily we are having a unique childhood."

"Do you suppose that two sisters have ever died in one house in such a short time before?"

"I expect there have been cases of it, but it would be rare."

"Except in the time of the Plague," said Dora. "Then bodies were carried out to carts, and men called out, 'Bring out your dead.' "

"There are Miss Lacy and Reuben," said her brother. "It is a good thing they did not come on us at the rock. It is an escape indeed."

"They would have been particularly bad petitions to be overheard," said Dora, on a reminiscent note.

"We should never have lived them down," said Julius, implying no modification of his own feelings towards them.

"Well, we join forces," said Miss Lacy. "I have never heard that two is company and four is none."

"Did Father tell you to come to us?" said Dora.

"He would not tell her to," said Julius, in a whisper.

"He was glad for me to come, my dear," said Miss Lacy, simply; "and that was to me the equivalent of a command."

"Have we to go for a walk?" said Julius.

"No condition of any kind has been imposed upon us."

"We could not be seen outside the gates to-day," said Dora.

"I don't think there is any ban on it," said Miss Lacy, "but I daresay you prefer the garden."

"We were talking about the Plague," said Julius; "and about the dead bodies being carried out to carts."

"Well, you might have found a more cheerful subject."

"Things are not cheerful now," said Dora.

"Do all dead people become bodies?" said Julius, dragging his foot and looking back at it.

"We need not trouble about what we become after we are dead," said Miss Lacy. "Think of yourself before you were born. That is the way to think about people we have lost."

"Apart from their spirits," said Dora.

"And nothing would have less to do with what is dead, than those," said Miss Lacy, not committing herself to any definite belief.

Julius began to advance by a series of leaps, and Miss Lacy did not reprove him for conduct unsuited to the occasion, as she knew it had arisen from it.

"Can we stay in the garden as long as we like?" said Dora.

"I should think until you are tired of it. No doubt you will get to the stage of wanting an armchair and a fire."

"We don't have those in the drawing-room; the grown-up people take them."

"Well, I should think you may return to your own quarters."

"There is nobody there," said Julius, in a voice that was oddly desolate, considering that they always had the schoolroom to themselves.

"I will ask Terence to come and sit with you," said Miss Lacy.

Her pupils quickened their steps, and their voices were freer and more fluent.

"Once Terence poured out the tea, when he was reading," said Dora, "and he poured and poured until the whole table was flooded."

"And did not either of you notice?"

"We saw and didn't say anything, and hoped he would pour the whole pot away, and he nearly did,"

"And what drew his attention to it in the end?"

"The tea began to drip over the table on to his knees," said Dora, bending forward in the emotion caused by this climax.

"I call it a most discreditable story."

Dora and Julius broke into laughter and proceeded with an airy gait.

As dusk began to fall, Miss Lacy directed her steps towards the house, and Dora glanced about and drew nearer to her.

"Well, this is not the best time of day for anyone to have to be floating about in the air outside a house," she said in a jaunty manner.

"No one does have to," said Miss Lacy. "People go into their houses, and spirits have their own safe home."

"Do they really have it?" said Dora, pressing up to her, and using a tone she could not check. "Don't they really have to be about without friends or ease or comfort?"

"No, of course they do not. Things would not be like that. We have our homes, and there would not be less refuge for those who have passed beyond."

"No, there wouldn't," said Dora, relaxing her limbs, but walking as if her strength were gone.

"Suppose none of it is true," said Julius. "There are people who think that we don't live after we are dead."

"Well, that would not matter," said Miss Lacy. "I told you to think of yourself before you were born. That is how it would be, if that is the case."

"Then it is certain that they don't have any suffering or misery?" said Dora.

"Absolutely certain. There can be no doubt."

Julius and Dora sprang up the steps of the house, without giving a word or look to Miss Lacy, who had given them this release of spirit, and who was left to depend on Reuben for the civility due to a guest. Reuben had hardly been addressed by his cousins, but had acquiesced in having no claim on them at such a time.

Thomas came into the hall as they bounded through it.

"Don't you know better than to let a lady who has been giving you her time, go to the gate by herself without any thanks for her kindness? You have been taught as much as that. What is the explanation of such manners?"

The children could hardly give him the true one, of embarrassment over the betrayal of their hearts, especially as their spirits had evidently struck him as out of season. They stood silent and ill at ease, Julius looking also a little angry.

"In future remember what your mother has taught you," said Thomas. "It grieves me to think of poor Miss Lacy, left to go off alone in the dark, when we owe so much to her."

The children felt some surprise at this estimate of their debt. It was their first experience of the exaggerated gratitude that arises in bereavement. Dora looked back and saw the small, bent figure, pushing its way unsupported through the wind and dusk. Her heart was rent, and she was about to run back through the open door, but Thomas shut it with an emphasis that revealed the passing of his thought to another neglected duty.

"You would think he might keep the house quiet at such a time," said Julius. "Who should set such an example, but the master of it?"

The schoolroom was firelit and inviting, and Terence was seated at the table in response to a message from Miss Lacy. The contrast between its comfort and the outer bleakness held Dora petrified.

"What a peaked and staring face!" said Terence. "Was it very chilly in the garden?"

"It is cold and dark and windy now. Miss Lacy can hardly get along by herself," said Dora, with a hope that succour might be forthcoming.

"It is too late to go after her. She must be almost at home. And no one lives in more comfort," said Terence, with some perception of his sister's mind. "She has larger fires and better things to eat then anyone. No wonder she enjoys a battle with the wind. That always means a life of ease."

"I hope Father is not going to play the pedagogue every time we see him," said Julius. "That is no tribute to anyone's memory, though he may think it is."

"He would hardly be in form at the moment," said Terence.

This allusion to the circumstances struck Dora as so boldly humorous, that she fell almost into hysterics.

"Take care. Shrieks of mirth are not the sounds expected at this juncture," said Terence, forgetting how easily they occurred at such a point.

His sister's sense of the ludicrous received a further spur.

"I hope we shall be able to maintain the required deportment," said Terence. "I cannot say that I detect any signs of promise."

Dora shook in silent helplessness.

"What is so funny?" said Julius.

His sister experienced the sharp irritation of a check at such a moment.

"You would not see it. Terence was only talking to me."

"That is a lie!" said Julius.

"He knows you don't understand so much of what he says."

Julius, confronted not only by a lie, but by the form of it known as the blackest, turned and deliberately struck his sister. She rose and fell upon him, and they gave themselves to combat. It raged for some minutes, illustrating the failings of human nature, as Julius proved that chivalry is not innate in man, and Dora resorted to instinctive feminine methods with tooth and nail. Terence watched with indolent interest, at one time dropping his eyes to his book, and at another stretching out a hand to check excessive violence or his brother's misuse of superior strength. As the contest died down, a system of mere retaliation ensued, and the give-and-take of blows became almost mechanical. Then the combatants fell apart and Julius spoke.

"Where is the book?" he said.

Dora fetched a notebook and accepted a pencil from his hand, and added an entry to a page, of which the items had been crossed out, as they were dealt with.

"Yielding to evil passions," she wrote, and added after a glance at her brother, "and at a time of bereavement."

Julius nodded and framed some words with his lips, and Dora wrote again.

"Neglect of Miss Lacy after kindness. Wrong attitude to father's just reproof."

After completing the last entry she restored the pencil to her brother, and returned with him to the tea-table.

"Your ribbon is on the floor, and there is some torn out hair on your dress," he said, in a tone that might have mentioned that his sister's shoe was loose.

Dora remedied these conditions, Julius giving her rather anxious aid, and not desisting until his hands had rectified the damage they had wrought. She dropped the hair on the fire from between her finger and thumb.

"Say an incantation over the witches' cauldron," she said.

"We ought to have the finger of a dead child, not the hair of a live one," said Julius, watching the consumption of the part of his sister that was available.

"I am glad your violence did not lead as far as that," said Terence.

The children broke into laughter and settled down at the table. They had hardly done so when Thomas and Tullia appeared.

"What was all the noise?" said Thomas.

"What it sounded to be," said his elder son.

"We did not know you were here," said Tullia. "We thought the children were alone, and were flying at each other's throats."

"You were right in the second particular," said Terence. "Why did you not come up at once? They might have attained their object. At one stage it did not seem impossible."

A fainter sound of laughter came from the children.

Thomas walked to the fire, sat down rather heavily in an armchair, and beckoned them to his side.

"Mother has left us, but we do not want her influence to leave us too. What would she think of a brother and sister's fighting on this day of all days?"

The children could hardly explain, perhaps hardly understood, that the converse of the impression received by their father was true.

"It wouldn't be this kind of day, if she was here," said Julius.

"What did she say to you, when this sort of thing happened?"

"I don't think she minded as much as you do."

"She did mind, of course," said Dora, "but she thought that being fond of each other in our hearts was the chief thing."

"But why not have better ways of showing it?"

"Our other ways are quite good," said Julius.

"But isn't it more of a pity, when people who are great friends try to hurt each other?"

"Our passions waxed strong within us," said Dora, unconsciously falling into the idiom of another sphere of her life.

Julius gave her a nudge of warning.

"You did not hit your sister, did you, my boy?" said Thomas, struck by something battered in his daughter's aspect, but assuming that his son would not transgress a certain limit.

"No," said Julius, in a honest tone, producing no change on Dora's face, and only a momentary one on Terence's.

"Well, will you promise me never to fight each other again?"

"Yes," said the children, concerned simply with ending the interview.

"Are you thinking what you are saying?"

"Yes."

"Well, we will hope for the best," said Thomas, rising with a smile and a sigh.

"Are you dull downstairs by yourself?" said Dora.

"Not more than I must be. Tullia is very good to me," said Thomas, stroking her hair with the vaguely double purpose of caressing and smoothing it.

Dora flung herself into his arms.

"We do think about Mother; we think about her all the time."

"I am sure you do," said Thomas, reversing his opinions with what seemed to his children a commendable generosity. "And as you get older, you will think about her more and more."

"And now sit down and get on with your tea," said Tullia. "It will be bedtime before you have begun."

The children laughed, and Thomas gave them a smile and followed his daughter.

Julius and Dora set to their meal in a rather formal manner, that arose from their sense of the latter's outbreak and the impossibility of referring to it. Terence laid down his book and joined in the talk, and afterwards resumed it and remained at the table, feeling his presence a safeguard.

Julius fetched the notebook and laid it on the table before his sister.

"What is that for?" she said.

"The other entry," said Julius, proffering a pencil.

"What about?"

"Hypocrisy."

"What hypocrisy?"

"About Mother. Always thinking about her," said Julius, on a patient note.

"Oh," said Dora, after a slight pause, looking at her brother with widening eyes, "I can't be held responsible for being caught up in a scene that had to be got through somehow. You didn't help, did you? We could not worry the god with things like that. Everyone can't simply stand apart and think they are superior because of it; we might make an entry about that. I don't take you to task for doing nothing, and then being proud of it, and want us to take the matter to the god."

Julius carried the notebook to the shelf and returned to the table.

"Shall we have a game?" he said.

Dora produced some boards and boxes from a drawer, and they settled to a game compounded of several, according to the proportion of pieces that survived. Presently Dora spoke in a preoccupied tone.

"I suppose our new life is fairly under way now?"

"There will be some more fits and starts," said Julius. "We shall be supposed to be settled in a routine, and then condemned for being in it. Or we shall be supposed to be thinking about Mother, and then reproached for not putting our minds into our lessons. Oh, I know how it will be."

"Perhaps Father will begin never to talk about Mother," said Dora, holding a piece over the board.

"Well, I must say one sees the reason of it. If people can't talk about their dead in a natural way, they had better be silent. It is an insult to their memories to indulge in the sort of talk that took place just now."

Dora lifted her eyes.

"I mean that we heard from Father," said Julius at once. "It is pure self-indulgence; that is what it is."

"Of course we did fight," said Dora.

"Well, and why not?" said her brother, with increasing violence. "Are we children or are we not? Are we likely to have the ways of a man and woman, or are we not? Had we been through an impossible day through no fault of our own, or had we not? Is it our fault that Mother is dead? I should like to hear Father answer those questions."

"You did not ask them," said Dora.

"The time was not ripe. The moment is not yet. But I hold them in store. And then let Father rue the day."

"I don't suppose you would dare to ask them. And it wouldn't be any good to make him hate you."

"There is such a thing as wholesome respect," said Julius.

"We are in his power," said Dora. "I suppose he could starve us if he liked."

"Whatever base and dastardly thing he contemplates," said Julius, striking an attitude, and losing sight as readily as his sister of Thomas's having no inhuman tendencies, "whatever dark meditations have a place in his heart, there is no easy way for him towards them; there is no royal road. So let him keep the truth in his heart and ponder it."

"He gives us food and clothes and has us taught," said Dora, in a dubious tone, uncertain if mere fulfilment of duty should operate in her father's favour.

"The minimum that a man could do," said Julius. "The least amount of expense and thought, that would save him from the contempt of all mankind. Would you have him turn us out into the waste to starve? Would you have him cast us forth, as if no tie bound us?"

"As if we were not his kith and kin," said Dora, falling into her brother's tone. "As if we were penniless orphans, driven to seek a moment's shelter within his doors. As if no sacred tie of blood bound us, hand and heart to heart."

"Let him take thought for the dark retribution that is gathering," said Julius, with a deep frown. "Let him take counsel with himself. That is all I have to say."

"The bread he has cast upon the waters, will return after many days," said Dora. "Then will he repent the grudging spirit that stayed his hand."

Terence rose and left the room, disturbed by the activities of his brother and sister, whom he believed to be acting some kind of play, a view in which he was right.

CHAPTER XIII

"WELL, I HAVE a piece of news to break to you," said Anna, entering the drawing-room with her usual haste, but avoiding the eyes of her family. "Say what you will, it is going to come true, so you had better make up your minds to it."

"Is it such unlikely news?" said Bernard.

"Well, it is of the kind that one's own family may tend to find surprising. I don't know that it is so in itself."

"It concerns yourself, does it?" said Esmond.

"So the incredulity is starting from the bottom. I will wait for it to run its course."

"It sounds as if you were going to be married," said Jenney with a laugh, as if this were not a possible explanation.

"That is what I was going to say," said Claribel.

"Right the first time," said Anna, in a laconic manner.

"What?" said her brothers.

"I said you would think it improbable."

"What are you saying, my daughter?" said Benjamin.

"So it is as unlikely as all that, Father?"

"Who is the fortunate man?" said Esmond.

"So family irony is about to begin," said his sister, settling herself in a chair, as though to await it. "It will have to wear itself out. So I will let it go ahead."

"We are entitled to know as much as that," said Benjamin. "Indeed it can hardly be kept from us."

"Do you need telling?" said Anna, looking her father in the eyes, as if the subject held no reserves for her. "How many men have I been thrown with lately? How many have I known since we have been here?"

"I can only think of your cousin."

"Right again," said Anna.

"Terence!" said several voices.

"Well, there is no objection to the marriage of cousins, is there?"

"There is from our point of view," said Claribel. "The first marriage of the family spoilt by its not bringing any change! Cannot you wait until you can offer us a proper stranger?"

"Well, I did not have to help you so much, did I?"

"Does Terence want to marry you?" said Reuben.

"Well, I have his word for it."

"You have that, clear and certain?" said Benjamin.

His daughter laughed.

"Would you say that I am the sort of woman to think that every man who shows me a normal friendship, wants to make me the offer of his hand and heart? Do I strike you in that way, Father? People may not take much interest in their families, but they can hardly be quite so blind."

"Well, what a piece of news!" said Jenney, in an excited tone. "The first we have had for a long time. The first of a happy kind, I mean."

"One of the sort was due," said Bernard. "We are grateful to Anna for breaking the trend of events. It was time that it was checked."

"The first reasonably pleasant words I have heard," said his sister.

"When was the fateful question put?" said Esmond.

"I gave the fateful answer yesterday. The question had run the course of all such questions, or many of them, I suppose."

"You kept Terence in suspense? Did that add to your value?"

"Well, you sounded as if you thought that was desirable."

"You did decide to give the affirmative answer?" said Claribel, as if she would hardly have expected this.

"Anna has done nothing, if she has not made that clear," said Bernard.

"I did not expect this particular line of incredulity," said his sister.

"Oh, I only wanted a little feminine gossip," said Claribel.

"It is not quite the kind of thing one gossips about. Well, how do you all like the thought of your life without me?"

Reuben looked at his sister in a startled manner.

"I must hear more of it, my daughter," said Benjamin.

"You have heard all I have to tell. It is not such a strange piece of news. I suppose nothing is more common than two young people's marrying, though one is inclined to get wrought-up over it, when it involves oneself. I suppose it is the commonest thing after birth and death."

"But, like them, it is not usually passed over," said Bernard.

"Oh, I do not believe in having one's little material for excitement wrested away from one," said Claribel. "It may be trivial and commonplace and anything you please, but it is the interest we have at the moment, and I am going to make the most of it. I cannot only give my attention to the important things of life. I have my own sympathy with all the little human chances and changes."

"This is an important thing to me," said Benjamin, looking at his daughter. "What are Terence's prospects of supporting a wife?"

"I should not think he has any," said Anna as if the thought occurred to her for the first time. "Such things are not much in his line, are they? But I think we ought not to be short of money. I had not given much thought to that side of things."

"And has Terence given none at all?"

"I don't know," said Anna, lightly shaking her head. "I daresay."

"I should think that can hardly be said," said Esmond.

"Well, I hope it can't," said his sister. "It will be a great help if he has a turn for such matters. I can do with a little support in them. I don't want to be always turning to

Father, and I don't suppose Terence would want it for me either."

"Did Terence go on his knees?" said Reuben.

Claribel laughed and awaited Anna's answer with raised brows.

"He did what corresponded to it for him, I suppose," said Anna, reaching towards a book. "That moment must bring out a man in a new light. Terence did things in his own way, as you would expect. But he made his meaning clear and served his purpose."

"He is some years younger than you," said Benjamin.

"Oh, yes, yes," said Anna with easy impatience. "He is marrying me for my money, and I am old enough to be his aunt, and he is not prepared to work for me, and all the rest. But there is something about him that I happen to want; and no doubt he would say the same of me. You do not suppose that we have not considered our own future."

"You said you had not," said Esmond.

"People may accept certain things and regret them afterwards," said Benjamin.

"Then they must be silly people," said his daughter. "We regret them now. Terence wishes from his heart that he had more to offer me; that he was the right age, and had normal prospects, and all of it. But such things can't be altered, and he does not want to miss the main thing, because he cannot have the secondary ones."

"So you have made up your mind?" said Benjamin.

"Well, at the age you think so advanced, I ought to be capable of it. And I suppose you were in the same mind as Terence in your time?"

"My position was different."

"Yes, of course, Mother was younger than you, and you had a profession and private means, and everything in your favour. But you were not Terence, and so I hardly think I should have wanted you so much. And Mother was not me, and so I daresay Terence would have been of similar mind. And we may have our own share of good fortune.

Indeed my having money of my own does strike me like that." Anna spoke as if the thought had just occurred to her.

"Well, from my heart I wish for your happiness, my daughter."

"But you are afraid that you hope for the impossible. Well, time will show."

"It is time that holds the threat, when the woman is older than the man," said Esmond.

"Oh, I am not quite a hundred. And Terence is an ageless sort of person. I declare I wish I had brought him to this interview, and had not tried to steer the course by myself."

"Women are expected to face the disagreeables of life," said Claribel, not specifying who held the view in this case.

"Well, I have hopes that I shall be an exception. Terence is a person to take that sort of thing off me. He was coming to-day, but family duties intervened. And the ordeal is not as much as all that. You are not such awe-inspiring people. You are just simple and callow and critical, as people in your stage must be. I may be an aged crone, but to every state its advantages."

"Father can hardly be described in the terms you use," said Esmond.

"Well, men never grow up," said Anna. "I am glad that Terence was in a sense born old."

"I suppose he shares your taste for maturity?"

"Yes, I think he does. He says he never felt a boy, even when he was one."

"What is he now?" said Claribel, opening her eyes.

"A boy to you, of course," said Anna, in full cordiality.

A faint sound of laughter came from Benjamin.

"Will he go on teaching me?" said Reuben.

"I should think he will," said Anna, "if we can find a house in the neighbourhood. He will be glad to turn a penny of his own."

"But he will have all your money to live on."

"That will be little enough for a separate household."

"What of your schemes for benefiting your family?" said Esmond.

"They must fade away," said Anna with rueful frankness. "My plans for being the godmother-sister were short-lived. I make no claim to put them before my own life. They came up against it and went by the board. That is the truth."

"I do hope you will find a house quite near," said Jenney.

"Terence would like to keep in touch with his family. And I have similar leanings with regard to mine," said Anna, turning her eyes to her brothers with rough affection. "We have no idea of starting life in the classic self-centredness of the newly wed."

"Starting a new life," said Esmond.

"Well, it seems to me that my life has hardly begun until now. I daresay people do have that feeling, when their affairs take this particular turn. No disrespect meant to the old tasks and the familiar round, but one must feel that one's life emerges from twilight into daylight sometimes."

"I wish I could know that the new life will be as safe as the old one," said Benjamin.

"I don't think it will be fraught with any particular danger, Father. I don't somehow see Terence letting it take that line for me. As for his lack of worldly goods, you will find that he regrets it as much as you do. About a thousand times more would be a truer estimate, I expect."

"He has arranged to suffer from it as little as possible," said Esmond.

"Well, I do not want him to suffer," said Anna, allowing a note of feeling to escape into her tone. "And I am not a person used to so much affluence, after all."

"There is Terence coming up the drive," said Reuben. "And Uncle Thomas and Tullia are with him."

"Oh, I do think he might have come alone, and done his first duty towards me in the accepted way," said Anna, with open ruefulness. "I call it a most unromantic way of presenting himself in his new character. No one is at his best with his relations, and I think it applies to him more than to most people. No one knows him, who has only seen him with his family."

"How did you manage to see him without them?" said Esmond.

"Terence contrived it. It was not left to me."

"And does the same rule apply to you?"

"Well, yes, I expect it does, in the measure that it must to everyone. There is something in us all, that does not come out in family life, or is suppressed by it, or rejected by it, or something. But I daresay it keeps the better and fresher for its own purposes."

"We deplore our relationship to you," said Claribel, "and regret that we can do nothing about it."

"Oh, I don't suppose my own best qualities have exactly blossomed and flourished in their native soil."

"You may exaggerate the place of mating in the scheme of things," said Esmond.

"Well, it is natural to do that at this juncture. And after all, a good deal does depend on it. The course of life would soon be held up without it."

"Of course one owes one's existence to a mating," said Claribel, as if struck by this for the first time. "And one sees it as such a primitive and common thing. We are very ungrateful to it."

"Things are none the less deep for being primitive," said Anna.

The Calderons were shown into the room by Ethel, whose manner accepted Terence as a member of the family. She had known of Anna's hopes before Anna herself, and known of their fulfilment but little later.

"Well, this is storming the citadel with a strong force," said Anna to Terence, in the conscious tone of private intimacy. "I rather expected you to appear alone."

"I did not dare to do that. I brought everyone I had

left to bring. I hope Uncle Benjamin will not take advantage of my being motherless. A father is not his son's natural protector."

"Have you come to see me?" said Benjamin.

"Well, a man does come to see his future father-in-law at these times, or is it an honourable man? He has to tell him what he can do for his daughter."

"And what can you do for mine?"

"I can go at her side on the pilgrimage to the grave."

"And you are satisfied with that?"

"Well, it is a great deal. It almost sounds as if we could face death together. And I suppose I have your consent to the marriage, as you talk like such a near relation."

"I meant to speak merely as an uncle. Do you intend to live on my daughter's income?"

"I did not mean to call you Father," said Terence, "but if you go on like this, I shall have to. Anything else would be absurd."

"Can you not contribute your own expenses?"

"Thank you for saying the words for me. They are not easy to say."

"Do you feel that you are giving enough?"

"Well, I am giving myself. So that is hardly for me to say."

"My daughter is also doing that. I was talking of material things."

"We ought not to dwell on those too much, Uncle."

"Do you feel that you can live under these conditions, and keep your self-respect?"

"I am sure I can. I could not ever lose it. I should not have thought anyone could. I never know what people mean when they talk about people's doing so. I think they must mean that they have lost *their* respect."

"Well, could you live without the respect of your fellows?"

"Yes, I am sure I could. I don't think people's respect is as nice as they think. And they so often have to do without mine."

"Terence, I hope my daughter will be safe with you. You do not feel that you are making a provision for yourself?"

"I think it is you who feel that. I feel that Anna is a person from whom I can take anything. I seem to be a person of nicer feeling than you are."

"Perhaps I am one of the people who do without your respect," said Benjamin, allowing himself to smile. "Are there many of them?"

"Yes, a great many; I do think so little of people."

"And what do they think of you?"

"Better than I deserve, Uncle Benjamin."

"And you cannot return the compliment?"

"No, they deserve too much. They are so industrious and persevering and easily satisfied. And those are qualities that I cannot help despising."

"What do they think of your lack of them?"

"Did they say that I lacked them? Then I despise them also for carping criticism and speaking against people behind their backs. I thought they would know that I breathed a rarer air than they did."

"But you did not feel grateful to them?"

"It is foolish to talk about feeling gratitude to such people."

"I don't want to interrupt the catechism, Father," said Anna, "but have you not got off the point?"

"I have said all the same things," said Thomas.

"It is true," said Terence, looking round and nodding. "And they are only brothers by marriage."

"What do you think of the adjustment of relationships?" said Bernard to Tullia.

"Well, I don't know why they require so much attention. They seemed to be enough in themselves. I should not have thought of tampering with them, though people do say that Father and I might be husband and wife."

"But the marriage of cousins is lawful," said Reuben. "A man can't put away his wife, because she is his cousin."

"No, the marriage is for better, for worse, like any other," said his sister.

"And yet it seems to be so different," said Tullia.

"Yes, I feel we are being cheated," said Claribel. "A marriage in both our families, and no fresh member for either!"

"When did you have the news broken to you, Tullia?" said Anna.

"Well, I suppose Terence must have said things about it. But I don't think I took it in until to-day. Not to be clear about it anyhow."

"No one knew about it until to-day."

"Oh, well, then I did not fall short in any way."

"It is good of you to yield him up without a protest."

"You are not going to leave the place, are you?" said Tullia, with a note of surprise.

"No, but Terence will be in a home of his own."

"Well, so shall I. Father's house must be that for me indeed. So I have no reason to find fault with him."

"And it will not put land and water between you," said Benjamin.

"No, but it must put other things," said Anna.

"What things?" said Tullia, in light wonder.

"Oh, all the intangible things that rise up between a married man and his superseded relations," said Anna, in a tone of being driven further than she had meant to go.

"Well, it would be sad to belong to those," said Tullia, with a little laugh.

"If it is a laughing matter, it is all right."

"Well, you make it seem one," said Tullia, laughing again.

"We shall have to set about looking for a house," said Anna, putting the final seal upon the coming change.

"Well, what is there wrong in that? You talk as if all your intentions were in some way unjustifiable. And they sound innocent enough."

"I am glad there is to be none of the disapproval, that I somehow feared was in store."

"But I have been thinking, Terence," said Tullia, in a tone of turning to the serious aspect of the matter, "that I really must leave you to manage your house-hunting for yourself. I have not time to put my heart into it, and it is useless to do it in any other spirit. Father must have the lion's share of me just now. Of course, if I can be of any help at the final stage, it is another thing."

"We don't want any help," said Anna, with a look of surprise. "Choosing a home is a personal thing, and I am not quite without experience. I chose this house, and it has done for us very well. I have no qualms about leaving my men behind in it."

"I wish I could say that sort of thing. But I can hardly leave my father for an hour, and must just submit to fate. Terence must understand or not, according as it is in him. But he has always been a good and comprehending person."

Anna looked at her cousin with a grim half-smile.

"I don't know why I should be talked to, as if I were not capable of taking my own place. I can get some kind of a home for Terence. You need not be afraid."

"That is rather what I meant, Anna," said Tullia, with open gravity. "A house has to have a soul that suits its owner, and if it isn't easy for you to judge of it, I am at your service. That is all I meant."

"I believe you meant a good deal more, but we will leave it like that at the moment. I am to seek your advice, if I am perplexed about the soul of our house. But it is not likely that I shall trouble you. I don't much care for ready-made souls, and Terence and I will soon put our own life into it."

Tullia glanced about the room, as if it threw some light for her on Anna's words, and turned to talk to her father in a manner that implied that little was of moment to them outside themselves.

Thomas put his arm about her, and drew Anna to his other side.

"So I am to have two daughters instead of one, and at a time in my life when I am doubly grateful for what comes to me."

"Are we supposed to comport ourselves as if people were seeing us for the first time?" said Tullia, putting her face on a line with her cousin's.

"I wish we were doing that," said Terence to Bernard. "We should get such a bad impression of them. And I only like people for their faults. That is why women are superior to men, that they are so full of petty failings. And I don't think it is always fair to call them petty. It really places them above the beasts."

"Oh, I can do my duty as a foil in a moment," said Anna, throwing herself into place by Tullia.

"We ought to be alike, now that we are to be so much related," said the latter. "Are you my cousin or my sister-in-law?"

"The first at the moment. Presently I shall be both."

"No, it is too difficult," said Tullia, shaking her head.

"Concentrate on the second relationship. The greater supersedes the less."

"No, no, I don't want to get as far as concentration. That is quite an uphill path."

"Well, leave it to the future. That takes care of itself."

"No, I will have you for a cousin, as I always have," said Tullia, with an air of emerging from a dilemma. "I shall just refuse to admit any change."

"How I do admire them!" said Terence.

"Show the whole of yourself, Tulliola," said Thomas.

"Poor dear, was he jealous then?" said Tullia, putting her hand on his shoulder. "Was I thinking of cousins and sisters and not of him? But it really was a good deal to grasp, and my mind hadn't room for any more."

"I can see a look of Tullia in Anna, though you would

not expect it," said Terence. "It is not enough to be called a likeness."

"I have seen two people more unlike," said Bernard.

"I have not," said Esmond.

"No, I don't think I discern this new-found resemblance," said Claribel.

"Your brothers are behaving with exemplary self-suppression," said Tullia to Anna. "If Terence had been required to make this sacrifice, there would have been—well, lamentation and great weeping."

"But you are not indulging in such an outbreak at the prospect of losing him," said Bernard.

"Oh, you do not lose a brother," said Tullia, as if in surprise at the misapprehension. "It is the woman who is submerged, never to rise again. It is rather a relief to cast off the problem of dividing myself between father and son. If I made a scene about losing Terence, well, there would be another one."

"She is making the scene in her own way," said Anna, in a low tone.

"You are being forbearing over it," said Terence. "It is something that it is veiled."

"I think I prefer the open method. It may be because I am not versed in any other. I have not a chance in these subtle contests, that are conducted under a disguise. My obvious shafts would not find a point open enough for them."

"What is to be the date of the event that is casting its shadow?" said Esmond.

"I have not approached the matter yet," said Terence.

"Oh, is Anna to name the day?" said Tullia, in a rather shrill tone. "I always think that is so courageous. Changing hands in public, as if one had been bartered and disposed of! It is a prospect to chill the stoutest heart."

"I believe the day is my business," said Terence; "and I shall prove myself able, when the time comes."

"When the time comes!" said his sister, her laughter going on to a higher note. "What a phrase for the person who takes the initiative! We shall have to help you to the point, and that will bring shame on you and all of us."

"If Terence is not proof against such things by now, he is in a sorry way," said Esmond.

"I think his position is a proud one," said Bernard. "If I were as honestly regretted, I should not be put out."

"I deplore these exposures of the soul in public."

"I thought they were skilfully disguised."

"What is the good of transparent coverings?"

"They soften the outline," said Bernard.

"Are you bickering about Tullia and me?" said Anna. "We can safely be left to cross swords with each other."

"Cross swords," said Tullia, in an idle tone. "That sounds a picturesque occupation. But I did not know that I was engaged in it. It is too energetic and exacting for me at the moment."

"Oh, yours came out of its sheath. You cannot think we did not see it," said Anna.

Tullia gave an easy laugh and let her eyes drift towards Thomas, as if he were seldom out of her mind.

"I am glad to have occasioned any interest," she said on an absent note. "I cannot claim that my attention was equally held. You see there have been demands in my own life of late."

"Your father should not monopolise your interest," said Bernard. "You should recognise the claims of other people."

"Oh, all of them seem to be tumbling helter-skelter along the road of the life-force. It seems odd to make an open parade of it. You would think it would be a matter for the individual soul. Or the individual something; I don't know that the soul has much to do with it. It all seems rather unreticent and primitive somehow. I suppose I am over-civilised or something."

"I am sure I am," said Bernard. "It is a thing we have in common."

"It is not an advantage. You spend your life on a

quest for people with whom communication is possible. Sometimes Father and I feel that we can only talk to each other."

"I am sure this is communication."

"I suppose you think I ought to want Anna to marry my brother, though there can be no companionship between them. Of course Anna is your sister, but you know what I mean the better for that."

"This is real communication. I will not say a word to check it."

"I have never done much for Terence, or even thought a great deal about him," said Tullia. "And yet I feel that he ought to find me enough."

"So he ought," said Bernard, "but I am glad he does not. Between him and your father there would be no access to you."

"I daresay that would be to Father's mind. I believe he regrets the days of the veiled woman."

"I do not," said Bernard, looking into her face.

"It seems fairer to allow a straight inspection. Oh, why has marrying and giving in marriage something so crude about it?"

"It only has for outsiders," said Terence, overhearing. "The people involved feel at their best. They always have someone taking an optimistic view of them."

"That explains their complacence, and I suppose excuses it," said Tullia.

"The complacence may always be there, and the circumstances discover it," said Bernard. "It certainly goes rather far. They even talk about their own unworthiness, as if there were no chance of people's having observed it."

"I have not done so," said Terence. "I have made the best of myself, as is sensible, and I should think usual."

"I have just done nothing," said Anna. "I have shown my ordinary self, and faced people's efforts to show us in a sorry light."

"Have they done that?" said Terence. "There is no end

to their secondrateness. What kind of thing have they said?"

"That I am too old and you are too poor, and the rest of it."

"Well, so are they; everyone always is. Not that I should have said a word about it, if they had not. I am glad that I pass over people's weaker side. If I did not, I should get tired out."

Tullia gave her brother a sudden glance, as if something were explained for her.

"And that would not suit you," said Thomas.

"There is a touch of meanness even in the best of us," said Terence, resting his eyes on his father. "And how could I put it more nicely than that?"

"You know how I wish for your happiness, my son. I cannot give your mother back to you."

"I can forgive that," said Terence. "I think there is every excuse for it."

"If you knew how glad I am, that you are to remain near at hand!"

"It is a good thing you have told me. It might have been one of those things that you always wished you had said."

"You need not talk as if you were about to sink into the grave," said Anna.

"Well, you never know what may happen to me."

"You might say that of everyone."

"That seems so odd," said Terence. "I always think there may come a time when I am no longer amongst you. But other people will surely be here, or who will feel the miss?"

"Do other people strike you as being immortal?"

"Yes, they do seem so equal to things. I don't see how they could ever be glad to rest. So where would be the reason for them to die? And I notice that they think they never will. I seem to be the only person who faces death."

"Well, that is supposed to take all terror away from it," said Anna.

"It is an odd supposition. You would think it would be the way to see it most fully, and I have found that it is. But people must feel that there is some way of disposing of it. They could not be brave enough to feel it is there. I know how brave you have to be. And to think that with all the strain upon me, a harsh word has scarcely passed my lips. Think of what you will say when I am gone."

"What is that?" said Anna.

"Follow in his steps," said Terence.

"It will be hard not to do that, as they move towards the grave," said Benjamin.

"We all have to rise to these demands," said Esmond.

"Well, I do not think anything could hurt you," said Terence.

"I feel that I suffer from them in some special way of my own," said Claribel, making a gesture. "One cannot help a guilty feeling that no one breathes quite the same air as oneself."

"I wish you would not echo my thoughts," said Terence.

"Well, what is the good of being cousins, if we may not be just a little alike?"

"Would anything produce a feeling of guilt in you?" said Thomas, to his son.

"So many things do," said Terence. "Not doing any work. Not having an income. Being too young for Anna, being too old to have done nothing, being the right age to take up something. Being reconciled to being supported by my wife; and there I am worse than is thought, because I am glad about it. Being the man I am, really hardly being a man. If I had not this feeling of superiority, I do not know what I should do. And I have a right to it, because I could never think so many unkind things about anyone. I feel that to know all is to forgive all, and other people seem to forgive nothing. And no one can say they don't know all. I have never thought of any way of keeping it from them."

Thomas turned to Anna.

"My dear, I wish my wife were here to give you her welcome. I feel that I am a poor substitute for her."

"Did you have parents, Miss Jennings?" said Terence.

"Yes," said Jenney, looking surprised.

"I am sorry I am such a poor substitute for them."

"People will accuse you of harping on one string," said Anna.

"I daresay they will," said Terence. "It would be like them. I think I can see accusation in my father's eye. I have learned to recognise it."

"Don't be too hard on parents. You may find yourself in their place."

"I could not think more of parents than I do. No one has given more honour to his father and his mother. My days will be very long. It is a pity that I have this habit of facing death, when in my case it is hardly necessary."

"In other words you do not face it," said Claribel, who had maintained an air of taking her part in the talk.

"Father and I have done pretty well together," said Anna. "Perhaps the better, that he has had no other woman to depend on. I daresay our relation is the ordinary thing, that my affairs tend to be, but it may wear the better for that. I can leave him without feeling that he will eat out his heart. We can meet at reasonable intervals and be satisfied."

"It does not sound as if your days will be as long as mine," said Terence.

"But what a good description of an ideal state of affairs!" said Tullia. "I can do nothing but envy it."

"It sounds as if it all might prevent your marrying," said Anna, in the serious manner of one who had light upon this subject. "Not that Uncle Thomas would assert his claims in such a case. But you may be doing each other less than justice, in trying to do too much."

Tullia laughed, as if more at Anna's effort at expression than at what she said.

"What did I say that was amusing?" said her cousin.

"Perhaps it was amusing that you should say it," said Esmond.

Tullia went into her light laughter, as if she could not but find this the case.

"Oh," said Anna, in a casual tone.

"So the occasion of our engagement has come and gone," said Terence. "Are we disappointed or relieved or grateful?"

"I do not know why you should be grateful," said Benjamin.

"Neither do I," said Terence. "I think I am a little hurt and baffled. But of course I shall always remember your welcome of me."

"Perhaps our future meetings will drive it out of your mind."

"I should think they will recall it. None of them will find me with any means of my own."

"Surely some work will turn up for you."

"Then why did you cause me so much discomfort on the ground that it would not?"

"I thought that you did not seem anxious for it."

"I scorned to deceive you," said Terence. "I hope I shall always be able to dare the right. But are we having another meeting already?"

CHAPTER XIV

"Are you two going to pace that path for ever?" said Tullia, to her father and Florence, who were walking outside the house. "Are you impervious to rain and blast? You look a most bedraggled and dreary pair."

"That is what we are going to do, my Tullia," said Thomas, coming to meet her with Florence's arm through his. "Pace our path together for ever, with the wind and rain doing us no harm. You have put it into words for us."

"Well, put off talking in riddles until we have got into the house," said his daughter, taking his other arm and going at an even pace in this direction, as if she were giving him time to reconsider his words. "We can guess them better in shelter. And perhaps we may be spared them. They tend to be the prelude to something better not said."

Florence looked across Thomas at Tullia, rested her eyes on her face, and drew back into safety and silence.

"You said it for us, Tulliola," said Thomas, keeping his eyes on his feet, as he wiped them, glad of the cover for his words. "You have done much for me, and now you do this last thing. I would have heard it from no lips but yours."

"Your sound as if you had caught the infection in the air, and emulated Terence and Anna," said Tullia, laughing as if at an impossible idea. "Take your time in disburdening your soul. Remember that follies are harder to live down than sins."

"We do not want to live it down; we are going to live it out," said Thomas. "I owe you so many things, my Tullia. I may owe you this one thing more?"

There was a pause.

"Poor thing, he is not serious then?" said Tullia.

"I have never been more so, my dear."

Tullia threw back her head, glanced down at her shoe as she loosened it, as though it were an equal preoccupation and then gave herself to her mirth.

"What a picture!" she said, as if she could just utter the words. "I don't know which of you to love and pity the more. I think I shall choose you, because you are older and more pathetic. I don't think it is because you are a conventional object of compassion just now. Old men and maidens, young men and children! You none of you seem to be exempt. So that is the meaning of the gathering at luncheon. He wanted to be seen as the successful suitor."

"That is how I shall think of myself," said Thomas.

"And couldn't you save him from it?" said Tullia, turning to Florence, and using a different and more serious tone. "You could have managed without letting him get as far as this. It will be the most difficult thing to live down, or at the least the most awkward. I don't want to make too much of it, but it must stand like that. Of course he has been in an emotional state since my mother died. But you could have kept things within bounds, and spared this exposure for yourself and him. That is the woman's business, or I have found it is. And how are you going to get out of it? Because it is not such an impossible thing. Not in a legal sense."

"We want to keep to it," said Florence, and looked at Thomas for support.

"Can you never do yourself justice at a crucial moment, Tullia? Never show the whole of yourself at a time of test?"

"I don't know what you would say to the whole of myself at this moment. I am keeping back a good deal. Oh, I know you would pay me with flattery, if I encouraged you in a mistake that would break both your lives. I do not find the reward worth while. I have seen Terence do it, and now I am to see you. And this will go further than mere dreariness and disillusionment. It will not stop short of the ridiculous. The sublime comes near to it. Perhaps you do not know how near. And you who were married to Mother, and linked with a unique and experienced spirit! To lose hold of yourself like this!"

"Perhaps I found it too much for me, Tullia. Even a sacred burden may be a heavy one. Do you grudge me the relief and lightness that have come my way?"

"It was hard on us all, of course. But we have not seen it a reason for this sort of collapse. At least I suppose everyone has, with the exception of me." Tullia ended on a retrospective note, and seemed to leave the matter.

"You grudge it to me, Tullia?" said Thomas.

"Well, let him have his rest and play then," said Tullia, after a pause. "Let him gambol a little in private, before he settles down to his ordinary life. But let him beware how he exhibits the antics in public. Friends and family will not put on rose-coloured spectacles to witness them. As he saw those of Anna and Terence, so they will see these of even more discrepant years. It is wise to remember it."

She went into the drawing-room, and her father would have followed, but a look from Florence sent him into the library, and Tullia heard the door close.

The families assembled at luncheon, supplemented by Claribel, Jenney, Miss Lacy and Florence. The last named sat in silence at the side of the table, and did not look towards the head. Tullia sat at the bottom, as she had done since her mother's death, and things were as usual except for the tension in the air. Miss Lacy knew of the impending revelation, and maintained an effort to be normal, with almost too much success. She had broken the news to her pupils, feeling it a wise precaution, and they sat with their eyes on Florence, while they followed the enjoinder of silence. Tullia was lively and loquacious, but seemed hardly to follow her own words. Anna and Terence were preoccupied in different ways with each other. Thomas did his duties with a face that was at once inscrutable, emotional and resolute. When he had finished there came a pause, and as he took his seat, it grew to something else.

"What is coming?" said Bernard.

"Something enlivening, I hope!" said Claribel.

"Don't be too sure," said Tullia in an amused, untroubled tone. "That is not the word I should give to it."

"You know what it is, then?" said Claribel.

"Well, naturally my father's secrets find their home in my ear. But this is not one that would command the sympathy of anyone who did not know him. We must not expect too much of you. It needed experience of him, to anticipate and follow it."

Florence turned her eyes on Tullia.

"We are all keyed-up and waiting," said Claribel.

"You have been my friends in more than one trouble," said Thomas. "And now I ask you to show yourselves so in my joy." He rose and came round the table to Florence, and placing his hands on her shoulders, moved them down her arms until they reached her hands and held them. "I hope you see what is coming to me. My home is not to continue without a mistress."

There was a pause.

"Well, that is not a very nice way to allude to it during my management," said Tullia, looking round with a smile. "Or of betraying any complaints that I found the task uncongenial. I am inclined to take it ill."

"Do you mean that you are going to be married?" said Claribel, in a shrill tone to Thomas.

"I mean it," said Thomas.

"Then of course we congratulate you," said Claribel, letting her voice fall, and looking round with a bewildered air.

"I thank you," said Thomas, "and I am sure I may thank you all."

"I am sure you may," said his daughter. "They are all metaphorically falling over each other in their eagerness to overwhelm you with felicitations. Especially as they seem so necessary to your content."

"Have you been a party to the plan?" said Claribel,

turning to Tullia with her eyebrows raised, as if at an unexpected circumstance.

"Well, in so far as it was entrusted to me. I had no hand in making and furthering it. I am glad the seal is lifted, and that I may relax the watch upon my tongue. Secrets always seem to be guilty somehow, though I have persuaded my poor father that it is not the case with his."

"Did you know before we told you?" said Florence, from her place.

"Well, I have eyes that see, and a father accustomed to being understood. I do not force him to put things into words. I never have."

"And you will be glad to be relieved of the responsibility of the house?" said Claribel, her mouth still slightly open.

"Well, apart from my sense of being deposed, and made use of as a temporary deputy, and other such feelings," said Tullia, seeming to speak simply without reserves, "I shall resume my old place with the relief of a return to my own. It seems to have become sacred to me somehow. I am always sorry for anyone transplanted to a new one. I could never feel that any other quite came up to it."

"One's own place, one's own room, one's own desk," said Miss Lacy, in a comprehending whisper. "They are all so superior to other people's."

"You are behaving very well for all that," said Anna to her cousin. "I would not answer for my own behaviour, if Father had planted such a thing on me, while I was still settled in his house."

"How will you like managing the house and having two growing stepchildren?" said Claribel to Florence, still with her air of being stunned by the shock.

"The children will be Father's and mine," said Tullia, in a manner so incidental that it hardly required her to move her eyes. "I know what my mother wished for them. There will be no change there."

"Well, that is the right and natural prospect for them," said Miss Lacy, in a considering, unprejudiced tone.

"Will Tullia be Florence's stepchild? Or is it only us?" said Julius.

"All of us, from Terence to you," said Tullia. "But it will not make any difference to her. She need not trouble about it."

"I suppose she will owe us a certain duty," said Dora.

"I don't know why you should assume that. She owes nothing to anyone in this house."

"Will she sleep in Father's room, as Mother used to?"

Tullia looked at her father and slightly raised her shoulders, as if not responsible for these results of his course.

"Yes, she will," said Thomas.

"Would Mother like her to do that?"

"She would see it was the right place for her."

"She might have the dressing-room instead of Father," said Julius. "That would prevent things from being quite the same."

"Of course Mother can look down and see," said Dora. "It almost seems a pity that people can do that. It might prevent them from having perfect bliss."

Tullia looked down and seemed to be trying not to laugh; Miss Lacy gave herself to free and natural amusement; and Florence looked up with a smile.

"In heaven there is no marrying or giving in marriage," said Julius.

"Then in one particular it is different from earth," said Tullia.

The children broke into mirth.

"Some of us observe the celestial standard," said Miss Lacy to Claribel.

"We are not of the earth, earthy," said the latter, slightly contracting her brows at the condition she named.

"Why doesn't Uncle Benjamin marry another wife?" said Julius.

"Perhaps because he feels he is already in heaven," muttered Esmond.

"Everyone doesn't do it," said Dora.

"I suppose most widowers," said Anna, tersely, suggesting that her own situation did not blind her to general truth.

"I suppose it has been an experience to live with one who is an exception," said Claribel, her voice not implying that it had been an especially absorbing one.

"I suppose Uncle Benjamin could marry you, if he liked," said Julius.

"If Father had married Miss Lacy," said Dora, "there would not have had to be so much change."

"Now you two have talked enough," said Tullia.

"What do you feel about the marriage of your niece to a widower so much older?" said Claribel to Miss Lacy, keeping her eyes on the latter's face after her speech.

"I do not blame him for being a widower. I do not blame him for his age. I would not accept blame on similar grounds. As for the approach of soul to soul, it is a matter for the souls themselves, and I say nothing."

"They will make an odd pair enough," said Anna.

"No, I do not think odd," said Miss Lacy; "I do not think that is the word."

"I meant oddly matched," said Anna. "I hope you don't mind our voicing our thoughts, but there really is rather a discrepancy."

"What we call one," said Miss Lacy.

"How did you feel, when someone said you were behaving well?" said Bernard to Tullia.

"It was only Anna, wasn't it?" said Tullia, in so light a voice that it hardly uttered the words.

"Well, if someone responsible for her words had said it, how would you have felt?"

"I think I should have agreed. Indeed I do agree. I am conscious of a definite feeling of self-complacence."

"I am glad you are in such a hard and unhappy, not to say humiliating position."

"Why?"

"Because you need to be rescued from it."

"I am content to return to my old habits, those I formed for myself."

"People will be sorry for you, and no one is satisfied with that. They will say that your father has filled your place."

"They will be wrong," said Tullia, seeming to speak to herself.

Bernard looked at his uncle and saw that his eyes were upon them.

"He could not grudge you to me, now that he has supplanted you. I don't mean in his heart; I mean in ways that count. And are you really not jealous of Florence? I cannot help asking. You know I am Anna's brother."

"I might be, if I had any reason."

"Then your situation is impossible. People will think you have reason, when you have none. What could be worse than that?"

"Having reason," said Tullia.

"But your father is going to be married. I don't see how you can pass that over. Other people will not. We can see that they don't."

"Well, he could not marry his daughter," said Tullia, "any more than Terence could marry his sister."

"I am fortunate in your admirers. If they had not been related, you might have married so many. When shall we announce our engagement?"

"What makes you think we have made one?"

"Well, you would have married all your relatives, if they had not been too near. I am the only one who is not. That does seem to settle it."

"I ought to feel complacent," said Tullia. "They say that the best women appeal to their families."

"Shall we announce it at the table? Or shall I ask for an interview with Uncle Thomas? Which would be more painful to him? I feel that he deserves to suffer."

Tullia laughed.

"I think we will announce it now," said Bernard. "Then his suffering will be as public as he allowed yours to be."

"I had none, except what came from other people's opinions."

"That is the last kind to be made public. He ought to have known that. His mind must have been full of someone else. It is a horrid thing to have to say of him, and we must hope that a lesson will do him good. Uncle Thomas, may I follow your example, and use this occasion for an announcement of my own?"

"What is in your mind, my boy?" said Thomas.

"I am glad that you call me that, as it is what I am going to be. You are to have another son."

"What is this?" said Thomas.

"I see you understand the language used between men."

"What is this, Tullia?" said Thomas.

"I have told you what it is," said Bernard. "It was for me to take everything upon myself."

"Tullia, is there any truth in what he says?"

"Why should you be incredulous?" said Bernard. "She is doing a thing that you like to do, yourself."

"Tullia has always looked to me for everything. Tullia, are you doing this, because I am going to be married?"

"Why should it not be because she is inclined to be married herself? She may be your true daughter. I expect you think she is."

Thomas did not turn his eyes to his nephew.

"Tullia, my dear, you do not think I would ever fail you?"

"Well, filling my mother's place, without consulting me, was coming rather near to it."

"I thought you would wish for my happiness."

"I am crediting you with a like regard for mine."

"Florence would do her best for you."

"That must seem to me an odd way to talk to me of a girl younger than myself."

Thomas was silent for a moment.

"Would you be marrying your cousin, if I had not done as I have?"

"I think we are entertaining the table too much at our expense. I am glad to be a success as a hostess, but we must know where to draw the line."

"We are having a most exciting luncheon!" said Claribel. "We are very grateful to all four of you."

"Three marriages and two deaths!" said Anna. "I hope it is not true that all things come in threes."

"Marriages and deaths come in larger numbers," said Miss Lacy.

"Wouldn't Tullia like to be here with Florence?" said Dora.

"No, Tullia would not," said Miss Lacy. "And Florence will like better to be here without Tullia. And Tullia and Florence will be the best of friends."

"Won't anyone be here but Florence and Father?" said Dora, in a rather forlorn tone.

"I shall come very often to see you," said Tullia. "We shall be living very near. And Bernard will be your brother, like Terence."

"Do brothers always live in a different house?"

"We are neither of us held to be human," said Thomas, smiling at Florence.

"No, as regards the children I do not think you are human," said Miss Lacy, in her sibilant tone. "They do not seem to feel it, and it is probable that they know."

"What a mix-up of family relationships!" said Anna. "Can't anyone cast his net further afield?"

"Anna does not seem surprised by the news," said Miss Lacy. "Did she have an inkling of what was coming? I think that must be such a satisfying position to hold."

"I saw the direction Bernard was taking, some time ago."

"And are you not going to give me your congratulations?" said her brother.

"I don't remember that you overwhelmed me with them, or with what corresponds to them in the case of a woman."

"I give you my blessing, my son," said Benjamin. "I

ask nothing better than to have my sister's daughter for my own."

"I wonder which daughter will be the favourite," said Claribel.

"Oh, thirty years give one a start," said Anna. "We can hardly talk as if they could be swept aside. I might as well suggest that I could supersede Tullia in Uncle Thomas's affections."

"That is quite true," said Benjamin.

"I wonder if I should have been different, if I had had another father," said Terence. "Of course, now I am to have one."

"I think we are overdoing this intermarrying," said Anna, as if a serious protest might have its effect. "I know I set the example, but I did not mean to start a fashion. We shall be simmering in a family cauldron indeed."

"Are you really going to support a wife?" said Terence to Bernard. "And in the manner to which she is accustomed? It is impressive to meet a normal man, and see what is expected of him."

"I am going to give Uncle Thomas an account of my position. It is just what might be thought. I am proud of being so like other men."

"It is cowardly of you to insult me."

"Why are so many things cowardly?" said Bernard. "Why is it cowardly to hit a person when he is down, or to strike a woman? Unkind and violent and quite inexcusable, but why cowardly? And why are bullies always cowards?"

"They cannot be," said Terence. "Bullying is very brave. That is why they bully people weaker than themselves. They know how brave it is."

"Which will have the odder husband, Tullia or I?" said Anna.

"You will," said Bernard. "I just escape the term."

"Yes," said Miss Lacy, looking from one to the other. "Yes, I think we may say so."

"I really do not understand the ordinary man," said Terence. "I once heard a friend say that he was glad he had had a hard bringing up, or he might not have been the worker he was. What astonishing things to be glad about! And he was quite ordinary."

"Then perhaps I am not," said Bernard. "I think I should be ashamed to have suffered early hardship. I never know why such a point is made of it in writing people's lives. I would rather be able to respect them."

"Your training was not particularly luxurious," said Anna. "And we are most of us ordinary to other people. I expect I am still the blundering innocent that I always was."

"Now why should innocent people be said to blunder?" said Miss Lacy. "Especially as criminals are the people noted for it."

"We are very unfair to criminals," said Terence. "They only make one blunder out of so many. They ought nearly always to have the credit of the crime. What right have we to be so exacting, when we are only criminals at heart?"

"What kind of things do we hide within us?" said Anna, in an idle tone.

"Bad things, but not those that the world calls wrong."

"Hasty judgements, self-satisfaction," said Miss Lacy. "Too little understanding."

"Those are not bad," said Terence. "They are the stuff of life itself. Which no doubt means that they are very bad indeed."

"You are being clever," said Anna.

"But I am not trying to be. You found that I was."

"Why should we not try to be clever?" said Miss Lacy. "It seems to be a natural ambition for ourselves, and to take account of other people."

"It savours of self-consciousness," said Anna. "And that might lead into dangerous ways."

"Oh, must we be quite so honest with ourselves, my dear?"

"We do not know how to avoid it," said Terence. "That

is why there is horror in every heart, and a resolve never to be honest with anyone else."

"I suppose I am too honest," said Anna. "I ought to edit myself more."

"I expect you mean that you ought to edit yourself differently," said Terence. "You would think that we could choose our wrong impression, but I beleve that a certain false exterior goes with every type. If we could learn how they correspond, nothing would be hidden from us."

"And if we all belonged to a type," said Anna, with cursory interest. "But we have bits of so many different people in us."

"That piece of learning might be a dangerous thing," said Miss Lacy. "Not that I would always say it of a little learning."

"Think of being with people and knowing their hearts," said Terence. "When they show that they know more of ours than we thought, what discomfort it gives us! And how much it ought to give us!"

"Oh, we are not such sinks of iniquity," said Anna. "We are most of us well-intentioned, every-day sort of creatures. Miss Lacy is looking as if she found us an oddly-matched pair."

"You do not strike me as matched at all," said Miss Lacy, laughing. "But you may be a satisfactory pair."

"I hope we shall attain a decent average," said Anna. "There is something in the attraction of opposites."

"We all have a shocking deal in common," said Terence.

"Why shocking?" said Anna.

"Well, the part of us that we have in common, would shock anyone."

"You sound as if you would make resolutions on New Year's Day," said Bernard.

"I did, and I am not ashamed of it. I think it was the only occasion in the year when I was not ashamed. And it was on New Year's Eve."

"Does that make such a difference?" said Anna.

"Well, New Year's Day was the day when I carried them out."

"Don't you make them any longer?" said Bernard.

"No. I have ceased to think as a child. It was too much of a strain upon me."

"I never support this tragic view of childhood," said Anna. "It is the reaction from the theory that it is the happiest time of life."

"It is a great excuse for people, that they thought that," said Terence.

"Would you like to be grown-up, Dora?" said Bernard.

"Yes, I should."

"Would you, Julius?"

"Yes."

"Why would you like it?"

"It is better," said Julius.

"We should do what we wanted to," said Dora.

"We should not work without earning money," said Julius. "Lessons only cost money, and don't produce anything."

Miss Lacy went into mirth.

"We should do things for other people," said Dora. "I should give money to beggars, and I should give them enough. People give them too little to be any good."

"They have to give them little enough, to do themselves no harm," said Terence.

"You should never give away what you would not like to have yourself," said Dora.

"Where would you get the money?" said Thomas.

"Julius would earn it. He is going to earn a great deal."

"But the money would be his."

"He would always give me half," said Dora, in a slightly shocked tone.

"Wouldn't you like to earn, yourself?" said Terence. "I have no doubt that you would. Everything combines to make my position look worse."

"Well, woman don't earn enough to be much use, unless they are scholars or authors or some real thing; and not many can be those."

"There is something in that," said Miss Lacy, looking round.

"Can we go into the garden?" said Julius.

"How about it, Tullia, my dear?" said Miss Lacy.

"Will people have to ask Florence things, when she is married to Father?" said Dora.

"It will do, if you ask Miss Lacy or me," said her sister. "Yes, you may run out now."

Julius and Dora walked to the rock in silence, as if weighed down by the burden to be cast off.

"O great and good and powerful god, Chung, we beseech thee to come to our aid at this crisis in our lives. For our mother's place is filled, and the hand of the step-mother will be over us. Let it not be a harsh sway, O god, and do not turn away our father's heart from us. And if he has erred in thus taking his thoughts from his lawful wife, pardon him, O god, and do not visit thy wrath upon him; for he is but a weak and sinful man, and lacks the wisdom that is in the heart of childhood. And grant that our new path in life may be a smooth one, for we are young and weak and have few to protect us. Our brother and sister go into the homes of the stranger, and our governess, thy handmaid, does not see us with a mother's eyes. But put kindness for us into her heart, and grant that our father may look in gentleness upon us. For though he may be sinful in thy sight, there is no one who can take a parent's place. For Sung Li's sake, amen."

Dora hurried the last words and got to her feet, looking at her brother as a sound struck her ear.

"It is Father and Tullia," said Julius. "Be quiet and let them pass without seeing us. They will not look through the bushes."

Thomas and his daughter went by without doing this, but the younger pair did not emulate them.

"You would hardly think they would behave in just the same way, now that Father is going to marry Florence," said Dora.

"Father's ways are inscrutable," said Julius. "They are not worthy of our thought."

CHAPTER XV

"TULLIA, MY BEING engaged to Florence is not a trouble to you?"

"Well, it was not exactly arranged for my benefit, was it?"

"I did not see that it would alter your life."

"It does not say much for your vision. You were the only person who was blind to it. And I am not very used to pitying eyes."

"No one could have turned them on you, who knew my heart."

"Your heart is a matter for yourself, Father. No one else would claim to have any insight into it."

Tullia's terseness came in contrast to her usual deliberate speech.

"You had not been long in your mother's place."

"I have never seen myself as in it. The place was hers, not mine. And no one is accusing you of delay in filling it. But I have been for some time in my own."

"Tullia, since you were twelve years old, you have been the first person in my life. Your mother never grudged you the place."

"Well, I cannot emulate her. I do not understand this easy adjustment of places."

"Yours must always be the same."

"What does Florence say to that?"

"She knows that she takes the empty place, not the full one."

"She assumes that she takes the only one. She would not have accepted any other."

"She will understand," said Thomas.

"No doubt she will in time, but will that make it any better?"

"If it is a question of you or anyone else, it must always be you."

"You have room for more than one person in your heart," said Tullia, in a mocking tone.

"Only for one first person."

"Did you make your offer to Florence on those terms?"

"I offered her the place of my wife, not the first place in my heart. She knew I had not that to give."

"How could she know? I am not sure that you knew, yourself, and I hardly think Mother did. You have analysed this heart of yours in the last few minutes."

"I had not put things into words to myself. Events crowded thick and fast, and I was lifted off my feet. It gave me a shock to think that you were leaving my home."

"But none to think it was to be a different home to me," said Tullia, with the first break in her voice.

"I did not know that it was. I did not, my dear. And it need not have been. If you decide to remain in it, it shall not be."

"Someone was more definite about his feelings than you were. I am committed to leaving it."

"Tullia, would you be marrying, if this had not happened?"

"I daresay not so soon, but it would have been hard to avoid it."

"Of course I have never expected or wanted you not to marry."

"You have rather an odd way of showing it."

"And I could accept your cousin as a husband for you."

"Well, anything else would lead to trouble now."

"You did not consult me, Tullia."

"I do not remember that you paid me that compliment either."

"Tullia, I am your natural protector. You can hardly say the same to me."

"I am sure I wish someone could. You were sorely in need of one."

"Tulliola, may I feel that you will never change to me? May I take that feeling with me into the downhill path that lies ahead?"

Florence, crossing the hall with the group from the dining-room, looked about for Thomas and his daughter, who had left the table by themselves. She caught sight of them, standing just within the hall, protected by the shadow of the door, locked in each other's arms. She paused and rested her eyes on them, and then went on with the others. When they came into the drawing-room, she took no notice, but presently moved towards Thomas and paused, as if by chance, before him.

"We don't want to marry each other," she said, in her low, even tones, as he met her eyes.

"Don't we, my dear?" he said, his eyes looking as if he were living in another scene, and his voice sounding of it.

"You are too old for me. You have had too many people in your life. You have gone too far in it, to turn back again with me. And I do not want to give so much more than I am given. I am not a self-sacrificing person, and I should not like to be. I would rather have what is natural for my youth."

"You are not jealous of the dead?" said Thomas.

"No," said Florence, in a slow tone, that told him openly that her jealousy would not lie here.

She took his ring off her hand and put it into his, keeping her eyes on it, in order not to lift them to his face. He watched her as she did it, and then rose and took her hand, and putting the ring on another finger, seemed to hold the hand for all to see.

"Wear it in memory of me," he said; "and as the memory dies, it will become your own."

"Give it to Tullia," said Florence, still looking at the ring. "It is more in her taste than mine. I believe you thought of her, when you were choosing it."

"I should always think of Tullia," said Thomas, turning the ring in his hand and saying no more.

"Give it to her as a wedding present," said Florence,

looking up at last and smiling from father to daughter.

"Well, if he thought of me when he was choosing it, it is fair that it should find its proper home," said Tullia. "It will make a companion for Bernard's, which does look rather lonely by itself."

"There are your mother's rings," said Thomas. "I must give you those. She did not wear them often, but she wore nothing else. Some we will put aside for Dora, and the rest are yours." He spoke as if the other matter had left his mind.

"It never rains but it pours," said Tullia. "But Mother would like Terence to choose one for his wife."

"Oh, I should like that," said Anna. "One good ring would be just to my mind. I don't care for a lot of nondescript things, but a single good one that is known as one's own, is a different thing. I think everyone can do with it."

"Would Florence have had the rings, if this marriage had come about?" said Terence to Bernard. "Now somehow I want to know that more than anything in the world, and my curiosity may never be satisfied."

"It would not, if I were in Uncle Thomas's place," said Anna.

"I suppose only Father will ever know, and I believe I shall never forget it."

Terence forgot it, but only Thomas ever knew.

"Mother thought I was too young for rings," said Tullia, lifting her hand to the light. "And perhaps they do give a suggestion of staidness and maturity."

"Well, that comes anyhow," said Anna. "I don't think that rings have much to do with it."

Thomas looked at the last ring he had chosen, on the only living hand that he knew, and hid his pleasure at seeing it there, and his pain that it was not alone.

"And one day, when you give me a wedding present, give me something that you chose without thinking of anyone else," said Florence, speaking with an ease that told of the end of the tale for herself, and in bringing no change to Thomas's face, told also of its end for him.

"You must be relieved," said Esmond, in a quiet tone to Miss Lacy.

"No, I do not think that is my feeling. I watched what happened, as a person apart. As a person apart, I saw it fade away. I had no other connection with it."

"You must have wished that you could prevent the whole thing."

"No, I do not choose to play such a part in people's lives. I do not interfere with their course. I do not feel able for that," said Miss Lacy, with a slight stress on the last word, as if her inability did not extend beyond a point.

"I suppose I have your permission to step into my uncle's shoes?"

Miss Lacy looked into Esmond's face.

"I do not give my permission. I do not refuse it," she said, moving her lips very definitely. "I do not say anything. I have nothing to say. I feel I know nothing. Mine is not that particular knowledge."

"But you will help me, if you can?"

"I would refuse my help to no one who needed it. I hope I have never done that."

"Then ask Florence to come here," said Esmond, in a driven tone. "I can't wait for things to come about in their own way. There would never come an end."

Miss Lacy simply signed to her niece.

"I have been asked to summon you. And I have done as I was asked. There seemed no reason to refuse. And I refuse no request without reason. But I am qualified to do no more."

"I will do the rest," said Esmond, his tone betraying that he was forcing himself to a point all but impossible. "I want to take my uncle's place, and to say that I have always wanted it. He took it before I saw a chance for myself. It seems there must be some hope for me, if there was for him."

Miss Lacy laughed, and continued the laughter to herself as if she could not help it, and Florence also gave a little sound of mirth.

"It is the fashion to make and break engagements in public here," said Esmond.

"And you must be in the fashion," said Miss Lacy, again moving her lips more than usual. "Yes, you must be that. What is the good of belonging to your generation, if your place is not in the van?"

"Shall I follow it to the end, and offer the whole thing to the general ear?"

"Well, fashion does not admit half-and-half dealings," said Miss Lacy, whose powers of assistance in these matters went further than she had claimed.

"I must not be asked to do or say anything," said Florence. "I have said and done enough."

"Fashion does not require it of you," said her aunt. "She makes her demand of the male. She is one of those rare females who consider their own sex. If that be rare; I have not found it so."

Esmond put his arm about Florence and turned to face the room.

"One announcement more or less cannot make much difference," he said, in an almost cold tone. "You must be too used to them, to think much of another. So we will make it and do no more." He hurried his words and turned to a seat, and drew Florence down by his side.

There was the natural pause.

"Another engagement!" said Claribel. "I don't feel that I can keep count of them. I shall soon have married three of my flock. I think I manage most successfully."

"We have so many, that the same people have to be used over again," said Tullia. "I have played a poor part, in that I have been only once at disposal. But I am glad to have come in at all."

"Yes, you and I accept the one man and are done with it," said Anna. "We do not pretend to be involved in a wider choice. But we shall flood the neighbourhood with our intermarryings. It does not seem that it could have been a very full one, as the engagements are between two households, and related ones into the bargain."

"Three households," said Esmond's voice, "and one of them not related."

"Yes, you are in a proud position. You have not had to fall back upon a cousin. But Miss Lacy had a sort of connection with the house. It comes to much the same thing."

"No, I do not agree there," said Miss Lacy, shaking her head. "I admit Esmond's distinction."

"So this household will consist solely of Thomas and the two children," said Claribel.

"Yes, that will be my family," said Thomas, "and I hope I shall be able to do well by it. The motherless children must not also be without a father. I hope there would have been no danger of it."

There was no danger now.

Thomas rose and beckoned to the children, as they ran past the window, and going into the hall, waited for their approach.

"My little ones!" he said, sitting down and drawing them to his sides, in the assumption that his rush of feeling had its counterpart in them. "My little son and daughter! We shall be so much to each other, we three. We have no one else."

The children were silent over this assurance of affection and the ground for it.

"Haven't you got Florence?" said Dora, drawing herself away to look into his face.

"I have given Florence to Esmond," said Thomas, with no thought that he was not speaking the truth. "She is young, and he is young, and they will be better for each other."

There was a pause.

"There is even more difference between you and us," said Julius.

"I am your father, my little son."

"Does having no one else make people fonder of those who are left?" said Dora.

"Well, it concentrates their feeling on them," said Thomas. "It means there is no one to share it."

"But it isn't like the real feeling of choosing someone?"

"There are deeper things than choice, my little girl," said Thomas, forgetting that he had not given his preference to these.

"I don't think Dora and I have ever had much besides ourselves," said Julius. "Not as our chief thing."

"You shall have it now," said Thomas, his tone solemn under the stress of giving what was now at his disposal. "My poor little boy and girl, I shall have to be father and mother to you. I see that is to be my part."

"You didn't really want it, did you?" said Dora, with a certain sympathy in her tone.

"If he is a father, it will be enough," said Terence to Bernard at the fireside. "Do people think that no one can be a loss, as long as they are alive? Why does he not say that he will be brother and sister to them?"

"You must look on me as your elder brother," continued Thomas.

"Oh, he is saying it," said Terence.

"He can be a cousin to them too," said Bernard. "I am going to be sunk in my own life."

"You must look upon me as father and mother, brother and sister and friend," said Thomas, feeling a warmth of giving proportionate to what he offered. "We will remember Mother together. We will go hand-in-hand along the paths of life."

"Of course, we are really used to going alone," said Julius.

"You will soon forget those days," said Thomas, feeling it would be well simply to obliterate what was to be regretted.

"We are not young enough for that," said his son.

"If you had married Florence, would you have forgotten the days with Mother?" said Dora, in some trouble over the workings of the human mind.

"I suppose you would have had to forget them, before you did it," said Julius.

"Mother would have understood," said Thomas, with the common assumption that understanding in the dead would involve sympathy and approval. "But that is over and can be forgotten."

"I don't think people forget so many things," said Julius. "I don't see how they can."

"It was a mistake, and mistakes have no meaning," said his father. "That is all we need say about it."

"The less said about it, the better," said Dora.

Thomas looked at her and put back her hair from her face.

"We must bring your childhood back, my little one."

"She has never lost her childhood," said Julius. "She couldn't if she wanted to. People can't do these things."

"And it wouldn't be such a very good thing to bring back, if I had lost it," said Dora.

"The outward signs of it are good to other people," said Thomas. "We must remember that. But I am sure the real thing is underneath."

"Yes, people do like it," said Julius. "I daresay it makes things easier for them."

"I must put some joy and sunshine into these early days,' said Thomas, still seeking to amend the conditions that now had his attention. "You must have some such things to remember."

"We have chiefly had experience of the seamy side of life, haven't we?" said Dora.

"Well, you have had the one great sorrow," said Thomas, seeming to prefer this account of things. "I could not save you that. But we will face it together, and it will draw us closer. It will bind you to your father."

"But it isn't a good thing it has happened, is it?" said Julius.

"And freedom to walk alone is one of the best things in life," said Dora.

Thomas again pushed back her hair, as if her felt that it threw some cloud over her mind.

"Suppose we stop quoting other people, and say the things that come into our own little head."

"Quoting is saying things from books in the same words," said Julius. "She wasn't doing that."

"I mean that my little girl's own little thoughts are what I like to hear. I have plenty of those from books and other people."

There was a silence, while Julius and Dora exchanged a glance, and with it a resolution to submit to fate.

"I suppose that losing the same person, and having to live without her, does make people feel like each other," said Dora, leaning against her father. "It would, if you think. Because they would so often have the same thoughts."

Thomas stroked her hair with a surer touch, conveying his appreciation of these natural and childlike words.

"They would, my little one. They do indeed. You and Julius and I will find it so. You shall indeed find it."

"And I suppose they would get to feel more and more the same?" said Dora, with wider eyes.

"You shall find that too," said her father.

"And I don't suppose that even a lot of time going by would make any difference?" said Julius.

"No, my little son, it shall not make any. I give you my word. I can take that weight off your minds," said Thomas, in gladness that his children should have been burdened in this way.

"So everything is planned, and we can settle down in peace and safety," said Dora in a comfortable tone, establishing herself between her father's knees.

"Quaint, little maiden!" said Thomas, now able to stroke her hair in simple tenderness.

"And the future has no danger for us?" said Julius, with a faint question in his tone, as if requiring one more reassurance before following his sister's example.

"None, my little son. You may put away all fear. You are safe while you have your father," said Thomas, looking as if he wished he had a larger supply of knees.

"And you won't—nothing will happen to you?" said Dora, in a sudden, apprehensive manner.

"No, my little one. Humanly speaking, I shall be with you through your helpless days," said Thomas, rising as some instinct told him that this was the point to end the scene. "You may cast off fear and care. Run out into the air in the careless freedom that is the due of your age."

Julius and Dora obeyed him, giving some little jumps to indicate this state, and rewarded by feeling their father's smile upon them. As they moved out of sight of the house, Julius slackened his pace.

"I don't see how we can appeal to the god to guide us, when our life is to be one long course of hypocrisy," he said in a gloomy manner.

"The god will understand the trials of our lot," said Dora. "And it is our duty to fulfil the needs of our father, in so far as it is in us. Chung would not have us fail there."

"It seems that it would be better to have no parents at all, than only one."

"We could not very well pray for that. It would prejudice the god against us, to feel that we would sacrifice a life to our own ends, and that life our father's."

"I suppose we had better take some sort of sacrifice," said Julius, glancing about for a substitute for the one forbidden.

"These flowers for the graves will do. We should choose to put them in the schoolroom, so it is a proper sacrifice."

They approached the rock, but drew back as it came in sight; for kneeling before it, surrendered to personal and audible supplication was their cousin, Reuben Donne.

"And protect me, O god, in my life alone with thy handmaids and my father. For the eyes of the latter rest in hostility upon me. Grant that Jenney may order my days, and that Terence, thy servant, may conduct my higher life, and that there may come no change in my father's thoughts of me as a child. For I have not strength to sustain his equal companionship, being but a weak and halting servant in the walks of thy temple."

Reuben broke off and rose as steps approached, but

stood almost without discomfiture, and with the expression unchanged upon his face. His own feelings loomed too large for the encroachment of others.

Julius and Dora joined him; a look passed between the three; and they began to advance with a rhythmic movement, their limbs keeping time with each other's, and their eyes fixed upon the rock. They knelt in formation, with their heads and hands swaying in unison, and as Dora's tones rose, those of the others seconded it.

"Guard us, O god, in the dangers that loom before us."

"We beseech thee to hear us, O god."

"Grant that the similar trials that beset our paths, may be softened unto us."

"We beseech thee to hear us, O god."

"So dispose the hearts of our fathers, that their claims may not go beyond our powers. For great are their demands, and easy is the path and broad is the way that they have chosen."

"We beseech thee to hear us, O god."

"Turn thine eyes in mercy on the widow and the fatherless."

"We beseech thee to hear us, O god."

"The widower and the motherless are the same thing," said Dora in rapid parenthesis, glancing round.

Julius raised his head and nodded, and bent it again to await the further petitions.

"Grant that our filial duty may not hinder the daily happiness, that is the due of the young, and that we have done nothing to forfeit."

"We beseech thee to hear us, O god."

"As we have not yet put away childish things, grant that real childhood may content our father, and that he may not require of us the strange—strange pretence of it—"

"Travesty," supplied Reuben, in a rapid undertone.

"Strange travesty of it that his heart desires."

"We beseech thee to hear us, O god."

"Grant him a change of heart in this matter, and grant

that Tullia, our sister and thy handmaid, may not deny him her companionship, so that the brunt of his needs may not fall on shoulders too young for the burden, sacred burden though it be."

"We beseech thee to hear us, O god."

Dora repeated the refrain with the others, in indication of the end of the prayer, and rose from her knees.

"Well, that covers the ground," said Julius, as he followed her example. "There is no loophole anywhere. We can do no more."

"Suppose we go and see if the rain has swelled the spring," said Reuben, his embarrassment suddenly gathering and overwhelming him.

"I think that Dora and I had better be alone to-day," said Julius, in a polite, firm tone. "It was well enough for our hearts to rise in accord on this one occasion. But it must not be repeated. And she and I have matters to discuss that do not admit of an outside ear."

Reuben turned away.

"Well, that has disposed of him," said Julius, in an emphatic and complacent manner.

Dora looked after the slighty dejected and slightly limping figure, and a picture took form on her mind, that was to remain to her dying day.

"Shall we make an exception this once?" she said.

"One moment of weakness, and a precedent is created. We must be strong enough to say, 'No.' "

There was a pause.

"We do not grudge him the consolations of religion," said Dora, in a tone that supported her brother. "And he is young enough for a separate faith. But things must go no further. He must know where to stop."

"The hardest thing in the world to teach people," said Julius, stamping his foot. "But I flatter myself that he has learned the lesson. The precincts of our temple cannot be polluted by his presence. Our temple is not his temple, nor our god his god."